MORGAN

By Joy Winkler

First Impressions

ISBN 9798683726478

Copyright © Joy Winkler 2020
Publisher: Sharp Pencils Press, Cheshire UK

Cover design Anna and Jez de Silva

Previous publications

Poetry:

Morag's Garden
Built to Last
On the Edge
Stolen Rowan Berries
Wings, Planes and Weather Vanes

Verse Drama:

TOWN

Script:

Lightning under their Skirts

www.joywinkler.co.uk

Fern is symbolic of sincerity, humility;
also, magic and bonds of love

Part 1

One

In these streets no-one looks twice at a girl with red hair, not even when both she and her hair refuse to be tamed. Here everything is movement, noise, the clockwork motion of feet, hats that don't fit. In these streets no-one looks up at all. The trick is to keep your eyes on the ground just in case you find treasure wedged in the mortar between the paving stones. This is why the people in this town grow old and stooped before their time and why they seldom notice when stars fall from the sky. This is why the svelte stars' acrobatics go unnoticed; their twists and turns, their skilful soft landings on the hoods of streetlights; their cascades of multiple reflections that topple through shop windows.

Morgan stacked the boxes, jars and cans in her allotted space in the communal kitchen.

She was glad to be back after the Christmas break, back with her growing assortment of friends. College life was suiting her just fine. Uncle John hadn't wanted to come in anyway; out of his league all this.

They had spent an uneasy journey, talking about the weather and the farm, and when that conversation ran out of steam, she'd jabbed her finger onto the cassette play button, immersed herself in loud, uncompromising music. She knew he'd be glad to be on his way home. Glad that she was out of the house for a few more months.

'Poor guy, drives you all this way and you don't even offer him a cup of tea.' Ally hoisted the kettle to the tap - the ritual filling signalling sitting, chatting, listening.

As far as Morgan could see, Uncle John had no part to play in that. 'The venerable uncle? I just got him to leave the stuff at the door.'

Her friend looked disapprovingly at her.

'She'll have made him a flask. He'll be needed back at the farm anyway.'

Ally poured boiling water into the large, cracked teapot.

Morgan mustered up mugs and the de-briefing began.

'It's good to be back. Here, have one of Aunty M's butterflies.'

'Christ, how many boxes of goodies have you brought with you?'

'Oh, cooking's a religion for the old bat.' Morgan piled up the tins of cakes and pastries. 'Help yourself.'

Ally was a tiny soul from Glasgow. She reminded Morgan of a dragonfly darting about, hovering near each box and then dipping under the lid to see what was inside. She had met Ally in her first year at college and they had stuck together ever since.

Like pieces of glass in a kaleidoscope, the students moved around the table, sat in the large armchairs, warmed their hands on the stove, piled their cups and plates into the sink, patterned the room. The old felting on the table, the worn embroidered cushions, listened and sighed.

Six of them were sharing the rambling old house that term. As the winter afternoon wore on their voices meshed and counterpointed and their laughter, snorts of disbelief, cheers and groans, all made for a generous accompaniment to each student's holiday story.

Ally went on about her factory job – *push, pull, tweak then onto the next*. She acted it out, making them all laugh with her exaggerated antics.

'Oh, and there was this guy who really fancied me...'

Cat calls, whistles, guffaws of disbelief.

'This one time he cornered me in the stock room…'

More cat calls and the anticipation of what followed hung in the air.

'I gave him something he wouldn't forget – I pushed the pillock into the flour sacks and one burst – heard him telling a real cock and bull story to the manager later on – what a loser!'

The story worked well and led on to more as the afternoon wore on. Morgan held the floor with a story of the Christmas Eve rescue of a fishing boat.

'They all got home eventually, best present their kids could have this year'. She told it lightly, a quick anecdote for the occasion. But she remembered how the news of a lost boat had run through the village, like a charged electricity shock, stopping everyone from their Christmas preparations, making families huddle together as the gales shouted and threatened their security.

The fact that Ally's mother had been beaten up again was mentioned in passing, but not dwelt on. This was a story for night chats. Chats between two people, heart to hearts in the black of midnight and beyond.

Just before she'd returned to college Morgan had received a letter in a brown Post Office package. It was the letter she had sent to her mother returned, unopened.

'I don't know why you bother,' Aunty Molly had said. She had witnessed her distress on other such occasions over the years and could offer no hope.

Morgan lifted the Aga grate and tossed the unopened letter inside. 'They can all go to hell.' She watched as the

11

letter burned then calmly replaced the grate cover.

She didn't tell this story now though. She probably wouldn't tell anyone about this stuff at all. This college life was precious to her, digging about in her past might reveal things that these new friends wouldn't like about her. Maybe it was best to leave well alone.

Caroline's sister had had a baby while she was home for Christmas. 'Puking all over the place it was. Stuff coming out both ends most of the time. Can you believe we were all like that once?'

'Don still is'. They all exploded with laughter, a sure sign that the audience was entertained.

Morgan soaked it all up like a sponge.

Two

In a small village where the sea edges the land and where the waves can be small like cat licks, or tall like angry, spitting giants, there lives a little girl called Morgan. She has been stolen away from her mother, a beautiful princess, who lives in another land, far, far away.

Aunty Molly stands solid as a buttress, hands on hips, as Morgan screams and wails.

'I hate it here. It's dark and cold. I want to go home.'

The little girl thumps her fist on the bed and pulls at her wild, red hair until it sticks up on end, like straw stubble in a sunset.

'I've told you time and time again child, South End Farm is your home for now.' The words come spitting out from Aunty Molly's stern mouth, like tacks to pin the child down.

This is the seventh time that this bedtime ritual has been played out. Aunty Molly is getting impatient.

'I don't want to stay here. I want to go home to my own bed and my mummy'. Morgan is sobbing but subdued. Each time it ends like this. Each time Aunty Molly ends up telling her to be a big girl, to say her prayers and to get into bed. But she is only five years old and she doesn't feel like being a big girl.

It is darker here than at home. It smells different and has more sky. It is so quiet except sometimes you can hear the shushing of the sea. There are no sleepy cars shuffling past on crunching night roads.

Aunty Molly's and Uncle John's bedroom has light in it all night. She says you get used to it and that it comes from the lighthouse. It always comes in great cone-shaped swoops, four swoops then a rest, four swoops then a rest, all night, regular, so Aunty Molly says.

But you don't get the light in Morgan's bedroom, it is at the other side of the house. Aunty Molly says she should think herself lucky. Nothing to disturb *her* night's sleep.

At the child's side of the house you sometimes get the noise from the wind as it whips up and plays with the tides and rocks. 'Straight from Russia, that wind,' Uncle John says, as if it is something to be proud of.

The bad fairies have stolen Morgan and brought her to live in the house of a wicked witch. Each night, as the child sinks into the black well of sleep, she hears the waves crashing against the rocks, which lay at the bottom of the steep, cliff path. And each swell of water pulls and grabs at the crumbling sandstone, sucking it piece by piece away into the ocean.

At home Morgan's mummy used to tell her stories in bed until she fell asleep, dreaming of castles, magic spells, and good fairies with wands of promises. Her mother is a beautiful princess, fragile like gossamer, her pale face framed in wisps of tiny silver curls. Morgan tries to remember the stories, but this damp cold air can't hold on to them.

Aunty Molly isn't beautiful at all. She has big arms and a red face and her dull grey hair is plaited into tight snake coils which wrap around her head, pinned with hair grips, immovable. She knows plenty of stories from when she was a child, tells them without a book, she tells them with her big arms, her red face, with her whole fierce body.

'Bed's for sleeping and the angels will keep you safe until

14

morning,' she says as she stirs milk into their night-time drinks. At South End Farm, Morgan has her night-time drink in the kitchen where everything is as big as the giant's castle at the top of the beanstalk. The cooker is gigantic, and belches flames when it is fed with logs and coke. The large wooden table fills most of the floor and she has to climb up the chairs to reach her drink. Even the grey kettle and pans are twice the size of anything in her mummy's kitchen.

This kitchen is always hot, no matter how cold it is outside. While the child waits for her night-time drink to cool, Aunty Molly tries to brush some order into her effusive red mop of hair. Morgan stares at her drink, willing it to cool faster, as the old woman scrapes and tugs with the brush. 'We should have this cut off,' she says getting redder and redder as she tries to tame the unruly fountain of hair.

'No, no,' Morgan cries. 'I'll try to get it neat, I will, I will.'

The daughter of a beautiful princess needs long hair, her mummy might not recognise her if she has it cut short or plaited into snake coils. Aunty Molly relents for a while longer.

In the darker than dark bedroom, the cold is startling. Morgan tries to say her prayers the way she has been shown, but she is shivering in her Tinkerbell nightie, the one she brought from home. She kneels on the hard, cold floor, presses her small hands together and tries to banish all selfish thoughts.

'Gentle Jesus meek and mild, look upon this little child…'

The cold air makes her cough, and she thinks about the story that Uncle John told her about the hobmen who live in Runswick Bay not far away. She bends closer to the faded moth-balled quilt so that her breath is warm, and the coughing calms a little. 'Gentle Jesus meek and mild...'

Uncle John says that the hobmen are ugly, shaggy little fellows without any clothes, and he draws pictures of them in the air with his dark, hairy arms. Morgan will not show she is frightened, but she is. Uncle John says that the hobmen are hardworking and friendly but not if you make them cross.

She wonders what sort of thing makes them cross. Maybe coughing does if you can't stop doing it.

She wishes she could have the light on to say her prayers, but Aunty Molly says she is a big girl now. She is a big girl and only needs one good-night kiss at the bottom of the stairs and the light from the landing, Aunty Molly says. The light on the landing goes off after a few minutes and she knows it is no good asking for longer. Once Aunty Molly makes her mind up....

Morgan gabbles through the prayers and slides into bed, feeling for the hot water bottle that has been put in there earlier. Even Aunty Molly has a hot water bottle October to April. 'Plays havoc with my chilblains,' she mumbles every night, chanting her spell as she squashes steam out of the pink rubber lozenge shape, hugging it to her chest as she screws in the metal stopper.

Morgan buries her head into the old woollen blankets and curls up like a snail, tries to be deathly still, quiet as a poor church mouse, she swallows and swallows so that she won't cough. She doesn't want the hobmen to be angry.

Uncle John says the hobmen can take away children's

coughs, you just take the child to the hob hole in Runswick Bay and shout into it: *Hob-hole Hob, my bairn's gotten 't kin cough, tak't off, tak't off.*

He says this rhyme over and over, saying the words rougher than he speaks normally, saying them the old way.

Morgan wishes she was at home. When she has a cough there, her mummy takes her to Doctor Aymes and he gives her medicine. She doesn't want to go to the hob hole. She squeezes her eyes tight shut to try to get to sleep. Maybe her mother will fetch her home tomorrow. There won't be any hobs at home.

Under the witch's house there are caves, where the sea monsters live. The caves are hollowed by the tides and have swollen strings of bladderwrack for curtains and cockle shells for jewels. Down here there is no bird song. No chatter of milk bottles rattling onto doorsteps. Down here is only the dull thud of gloom.

Three

In the town voices hunt each other; shout and spit, feral as foxes. Front doors slam one after the other, like toppling dominoes and the heat of the summer that was stored in the myriad bricks and lintels exudes, lets itself out with a rattling sigh.

Morgan loved the late-night noise of the town, especially when the place was otherwise quiet. The soft shush of tyres replaced the ebb and flow of the tide and the distant whine of the trains filled in for the owl that used to screech in the trees that fringed the Dyke. This was the time to tell true stories, time to confide.

'I was so mad when I got his letter. I mean what right had he got? I wanted to visit my own mother. What right had he got to tell me not to bother, that she doesn't want to see me'.

They were sitting in the kitchen. Morgan was making coffee. It was midnight.

'The stuff that's going on at my house makes me feel like I never want to go home again.' Ally looked even smaller curled up in the brown wing-backed chair and she squeezed as close as she could to the radiator. 'I can't handle what he's doing to her. I never could really.'

Morgan sighed. 'It's all manipulation, it has to be. What kind of illness could she possibly have that means she would risk relapse just from seeing her own daughter? What do they think I'm going to do, for God's sake? What sort of monster do they think I am?'

'Well Maxie is certainly manipulating my mother.' Ally drew her finger over the condensation on the window, slow long arches, etching a way through to the black midnight sky. 'I mean, why doesn't she leave him, move away. Our Michael's fifteen anyway, he'll be off soon and looking after himself. Nobody wants to stay in that house, not when things are like they are.'

Morgan stirred the coffee, slowly as she continued her story.

'After I got the letter back, I made a decision. I don't know why I didn't think of it before.'

Her hair was grown long and wild, her red mop had exploded into a mass of wilful curls. She had the look of a witch on the brink of a spell.

'I decided to phone her up. I don't know why I didn't think of it, last term. I mean Barnsley's so close, only a few miles from here, I could get a bus or a train. They couldn't stop me phoning up.'

'And did you?'

'I didn't say who I was, I just asked to speak to Mrs Parish, Mrs Gwen Parish, just like that.'

'And did you speak to her?'

'He said she was out. I never thought about what I'd say if she wasn't in. I just said oh.'

'And you're doing English, that's very articulate - oh.'

'He said she was visiting her mother. When I asked if she'd be long, he said her mother lived nearby, she'd be about an hour and did I want to leave a message.'

'That was a really revealing conversation, I must say.'

Ally was back doodling on the window again, her attention wandering with her fingers.

'But don't you see?' Morgan almost screamed, her face reddening.

'I mean of course I didn't leave a message. I mean where would I start with a message. And anyway, once he knew

19

who I was how would I know he'd pass it on?'

'So, what was so interesting?'

'Well, think about it. She'd gone to visit her mother, and that means *my grandmother*. Obviously, everyone has a mother and that means a grandmother, but it just hadn't struck me before that I had one.'

Ally smiled at her. 'And you're going to teach the cream of England…'

'I know, I know. But it really hadn't struck me before. It means there's another part of my real family who lives nearby. And just maybe this one will be prepared to see me and talk to me and tell me what the hell I have ever done wrong to any of them.'

She gave her friend the mug of coffee and sat facing her.

'So, what *is* it like, at home I mean?'

Ally twirled the coffee mug between her hands, warming her fingers. She looked so tiny, young and vulnerable curled up in the chair.

'It's shite. I can't tell you how bad it is.' Ally looked into her coffee mug, letting the steam dampen her face, warm her. 'It hasn't always been like that. When my real dad was alive it was great. He was a lovely man, my dad was, a real gentleman. He treated Mum like a queen, no less, and then she has to go and get involved with a man like that idiot.'

She sipped at the coffee, her eyes closing from the steam.

'Oh, he's fine when he's not drinking. Mild Maxie they all call him round our way, wouldn't say 'boo' to a goose, you know. But when he's been at the drink…'

Morgan had heard this story before, but she knew that Ally had to tell it again. She knew that in the telling, the hurt let up just a little bit.

'The first time he hit Mum, our Michael was only eight and I was eleven. We didn't understand what was going on. It was late and we'd been asleep, but then we heard him, Maxie, shouting and Mum crying and then screaming.'

Morgan sipped at her coffee. Her hatred for this man, who she didn't even know, grew more and more intense.

'The next day when I saw what he'd done to Mum, I thought about sticking a knife into him while he was asleep. I wanted to. But then she says that she fell, and I didn't know whether to believe her or not.'

'It's not your fault. None of it is your fault.'

Morgan slid the tin of buns over towards Ally.

'You were only a child.'

'Things went back to normal for a while then. They always do after he's had a go. He's as nice as pie, running around after Mum, butter wouldn't melt, good old 'mild Maxie'.'

'But he'd do it again?'

'Oh, yes. We'd relax at first thinking it was a one off, or just another lapse. But you'd soon get to know there'd be another time. And there always was. I can't understand why she puts up with it though. This Christmas was no different, so I told her, I said, 'I'm not coming home again, Mum, not until you throw *him* out.' She didn't say anything. She knows I'll go back. I mean there's Michael. I can't leave him to face it on his own.'

They sat and went over it all again, talking against the backdrop of black skies, drinking the coffee even after it had gone cold. Ally vowing never to go home again and Morgan wishing her family would invite her home even if it was for one visit.

Four

As time goes by, the little girl gets used to living in the house of the wicked witch and the hobman in the village by the sea. No harm has come to her, as they are kind to her in their own way. And anyway, she knows that one day there will be a clash of thunder and a flash of lightning across the wide sky and the bad fairy's spell will be worn away and she will be once more in the castle of the beautiful princess.

Morgan scratches away at her writing book.

I've been staying at Aunty Molly's for a very long time. It is a farm called 'South End Farm' and it is at the seaside. I have my own little bed and my own little room. It is nice.

She knows that Aunty Molly will check her homework before she takes it into school. She knows she needs to keep in Aunty Molly's good books.

I was sent here because my daddy says I was a naughty girl at home, but I am trying to be a good girl now.

Of course, Morgan knows that actually she was stolen away from home by the bad fairies. She told Leanne and Amy at school, but they only laughed at her. What did they know? She shuffles angrily in her seat.

Uncle John has shown her fairy rings out on the flat fields behind the barn. How else would she have got to Flamborough? Her mother would not have given her away. No, she knows she's been stolen away. It happens lots of times in story books. Uncle John knows as well. Why else

22

would he pull faces and wink at her when she cries to go home. Aunty Molly shouts at her and tells her to be a 'big girl', but Uncle John...

He isn't much good at talking, hobmen are creatures of few words. But he can pull really scary faces and he is always winking a lot and he knows where the toadstools grow and where to find fairy rings. Morgan sucks at the end of her pencil. Maybe he's had something to do with the fairies stealing her away.

The little girl spends long, lonely hours imagining the day when she will once again cross the bottomless moat by the solid oak drawbridge and walk up the marble staircase that has been hewn from rocks in a distant land. The princess will be sitting there as pale as milk as she will have neither eaten a crumb, nor drunk a drop of water whilst she has waited all these years for her daughter to be returned. She will raise herself from the golden bed, with its swansdown pillows and its gossamer coverlets, and hold her arms out to welcome the child home.

Morgan draws a picture of herself feeding Uncle John's chickens and she thinks how Amy and Leanne and the others will laugh like anything if she has to read out the 'good girl' bit in her story. But she doesn't care. What matters is keeping in Aunty Molly's good books. This way she can think of a plan to get back home again.

She puts the writing book away and gets out her storybook. She almost knows the story by heart. It's called 'The Gingerbread Boy'.

She can't believe how much Aunty Molly and Uncle John are like the old man and the old woman in this story book. The old man and the old woman don't have any children

23

of their own. Aunty Molly and Uncle John don't have any children of their own, 'hadn't been blessed that way'.

The old woman has baked a gingerbread boy, so she can have someone to look after. Aunty Molly is round and homely and is always stirring and rolling and doing.

Morgan's hair is the colour of gingerbread. She loves her red mop. She doesn't like it to be flat and tame and tied up like Aunty Molly does it. She likes it to be curly, springy and free.

She looks at it in the mirror in her bedroom for a long time. Aunty Molly says that if she looks for too long in the mirror, she will see the devil. Morgan only looks while she counts to fifty. She doesn't think the devil will come until at least one hundred.

One day as she was rolling and shaping a gingerbread boy, tears of regret fell on the dough, right on the heart of the gingerbread boy. Later, when the dough was cooking, there was a knocking on the oven door. 'Let me out, let me out, it's too hot in here.'

'Are you too hot in here?' Aunty Molly is rolling, and baking and the kitchen is getting hotter and hotter. 'You'd better put that book down and get yourself off to school.'

Morgan looks up but says nothing.

'You spend too much time reading those books.' Aunty Molly waves her rolling pin in the air.

'You'll strain your eyes. Fresh air's the best thing for a child your age'.

She rolls and thumps the dough, her face getting redder and redder.

Morgan thinks that Aunty Molly would be better off out in the fresh air, but she says nothing.

24

The little old woman opened the oven door, and to her surprise, out jumped the gingerbread boy, as jolly and lively as any a real boy would. The little old woman and the little old man were so happy they had a child of their own to love and protect.

'Go and find your Uncle John. He'll be feeding the creatures. He likes a bit of company when he's feeding the creatures. There's still time before you have to get off to school.'

However, the gingerbread boy was jolly and lively and wanted to be out and about in the world. He would not do what the little old woman asked, He would not do what the little old man asked. And when they scolded him, he ran away.

'Came to a bad end, the gingerbread boy.'

Aunty Molly gloats as she fashions star-shaped biscuits out of pale sugary dough.

'Wasn't as clever as he thought he was.'

Morgan shuffles her feet under the table, turns the page of her storybook, says nothing.

'That wily old fox - he tricked him and ate him up.' Aunty Molly slams the tray of sugary dough stars on to the oven shelf and clicks the door shut tight. 'I hope my star biscuits don't come alive, eh, Morgan?' Aunty Molly is wiping and clearing bits of leftover dough from the table. Her large red hands are like a machine, moving the dough into little piles with one hand, then sweeping it on to the other hand, which like a mechanical shovel dumps it into the pedal bin. Wiping and cleaning, she is never still.

'Was he dead when the wily fox ate him up?' Morgan

looks up again from her book, feeling sick at the idea of this lovely magical little boy being here one minute, gone the next.

'Dead as a doughnut.' Aunty Molly laughs, wiping bits of dough from under the child's book. 'He should have done as he was told, shouldn't he?' She opens the oven door to turn the star biscuits round to brown on the other side. Morgan looks at them from over the top of her book. There are no signs of life at all.

The little girl watches the skies each day for darkening clouds and she places sticks, in a certain way that she's heard of from the good elves in the valley and lays them by the back door late at night. But although storms come and go in the little village by the sea, so far the bad fairy's spell has held true.

Five

In a time unlike all other times, there lives a handsome Prince. He doesn't have a Palace of Ivory studded with precious jewels. He doesn't have lands that go on as far as the eye can see. He prefers to live simply, tending to the golden wheat that covers his meagre but bountiful fields. His heart is kept pure by the song of the humble garden birds and is made brave by the keening of the fish-ravening seagulls and the cracking call of the gannets.

Ed muttered to himself. He muttered and shrugged his shoulders as he hunched up and walked along the cliff path toward the Dyke. The beer cans he had in his carrier bag were rattling, chattering along with his muttering.

It was late and quite dark apart from the crescent of moon, but he knew the path like the back of his hand. This was his home after all. Not that *she'd* appreciate that. His mother wanted him to be somebody else, to live somewhere else. She hated living here and thought he'd be the same. But he wasn't. He loved Flamborough. He couldn't imagine living anywhere else.

'You need to get yourself an education and move on, lad,' she'd say, 'move away from here. There's nothing here for you only fishing and farming.'

Ed wanted to be a farmer. He always had. It's what his father did and what he'd always known. Why couldn't she see that?

'You don't want to be like your dad,' she'd say. 'He breaks his back every day and for what, I ask you, for what? That bit of land and a few filthy hens?'

Ed's father was a quiet man. He took no offence at her

outbursts. He'd just light up his pipe and pretend he hadn't heard her.

'She's a fiery woman, your mother but she means well, son, she means well. It's just that, well, she's never had the heart for farming, not like you and me.'

The path moved down now towards the beach at the Dyke. The branches of the horse chestnuts were still stark without much foliage and in the scant moonlight they swayed above him like whispering guardians.

But the Prince's mother, who loves him more than words can say, wants him to have a Palace of Ivory studded with precious jewels, and wants him to have lands that go on as far as the eye can see. She shakes the quiet Prince until his bones rattle inside his skin and she says, 'Now is the time for you to go and seek your fortune.'

'I'm your mother,' she'd say. 'I know what's best for you. College. Go away to college and get an education. It's what I should've done, but I never had the chance. I wouldn't be stuck here on this farm if I'd had your opportunities. You get yourself an education and you'll not want to come back then, I know.'

Ed had gone to college. His mother had a way of getting what she wanted. He'd been at college since last September and now he was back.

'And I'm never going there again,' he shouted out loud to the horse chestnut guardians who waved their desolate budded branches back at him as though applauding his boldness.

The fires were lit on the beach. He knew they would be. One big one and a few satellites, set off apart. It was quiet.

28

There were folks around, drinking and talking but it was still quiet. He had never been one for coming down to the Dyke, even when he was at school. He knew some that did, but his mother had always kept him under her thumb.

'You do your homework, lad. Never mind gallivanting down the Dyke with all that riff raff. You'll make something of yourself, mark my words. That lot will do nothing. They'll end up propping up that bar in the Dog, just like your dad does every night, and what kind of a life is that?'

His dad would wink at him and Ed would smile. It was just the way she went on. It was the way she was.

He was a bit unsteady on his feet. He'd been drinking in the Dog with his dad until closing time. They'd had a few pints together, Ed telling his dad about leaving college and his dad smoking his pipe, slowly, slowly and occasionally saying, 'She'll not like it, son. You know that don't you? She'll not like it.'

But Ed had agonised over this for months. He'd been a fish out of water at college. He'd eaten meals on his own, sat on his own, found no-one on the same wavelength at all. They'd all looked at him like he was an out of town hick. And he was. But the thing was, he liked being who he was, so why should they make him feel bad. He'd stewed on it, night after night, like an old tea bag and by the time he got home for the Easter holidays he was bitter all right. Bitter at her for making him go in the first place.

'She doesn't mean to be bossy, son.' His dad brought two more pints over. He'd already had one more than his nightly ration, and he knew she'd be able to tell when he got home.

'It's just her way. She generally knows best, you know.'

'Not this time, Dad.' Ed drank half of his pint off in one angry draft.

'She doesn't know best this time. I'll go mad if I have to go back there, all those weird, scruffy types with blue hair and rings through their noses. I'll not do it.'

His dad sucked air through his teeth. 'She'll not like it.'

'I know, Dad. But once, just once, I'm going to do what I want.'

He looked at his son, blinking, remembering Ed as a little boy, always well behaved, always doing as he was bid. 'You do, son, you do.' He drank his pint to a quarter way down the glass - then looked up, slowly focusing on this angry young man. 'But she'll not like it.'

Ed sat on a rock, surveying the fires and the people milling around, as though they were taking part in some ancient ritual. He loved this place and belonged here but just now he felt like an interloper. He wasn't part of this crowd either. He ripped open his can and drank deeply. The tide was out, and its shushing was a distant echo.

And then somehow, she was there next to him. Her presence warmed him instantly, brought him back from wherever he'd been slipping away to. At a glance he took in her black curls, her tight jeans and her prominent breasts, which seemed to be fighting to escape the baby pink t-shirt emblazoned with the word 'kitten'.

'You'll freeze up here. Come down to the fire with me.' She offered her arm, and he took it unquestioning, like a child. 'I'll soon warm you up'. She laughed and it was like he could suddenly see things how they really were again. She took the beer out of his hand and had a drink of it herself.

30

'Here let me help you over the cobbles. You've had a few, haven't you? Never mind, hold on to me, I'll get you down there'.

He let himself be supported and led down to the big fire in the middle of the white chalky cobbles. There was a smell of old crabs and salt in the air. It was the smell of his childhood. It was the smell of home.

'Caught a big fish there, Leanne.'

Voices he knew but couldn't put a name to.

'Shut up and mind your own business. Me and Ed, well we're keeping each other warm, aren't we?' He looked at this young, pretty girl, in her scant clothing. She'd need to be kept warm on a night like this. He reached out his arms.

Leanne pulled him proprietarily toward her. Lugged him to the ground by the fire and entwined herself around him like an eel.

'She doesn't waste time, does she?' Ed recognised the voice of one of his school mates and tried to get up to talk to him. But Leanne had him fixed to the ground.

The stones on the beach were digging into his back. He wriggled and writhed trying to get comfortable. 'Keep still.' Leanne anchored her lips to his, trying to get a grip. Ed froze, scared that if he wriggled, she would stop kissing him. And he liked it. It was worth the discomfort, he decided, so he lay there, arms dangling somewhere around Leanne's skimpy t-shirt and let her sucker on to him. His eyes were wide open, and the crescent moon smiled down on him like a cartoon face. He thought very briefly about what his mother would think, and then dismissed the thought as though it was just so much jetsam swept away by the outgoing tide.

Leanne came up for air. 'You're not used to this are you, love.' Ed felt his lips swell. Warm and tingling they felt twice their normal size. He tried to speak but couldn't make them go into the right shape. 'Never mind.' Leanne limbered up her arms, took another swig of Ed's beer and spread herself on him again.

He offered himself, willing for her to do what she would.

He stared at the pin prick stars, listened to the driftwood fall and shift on the fire, he was beyond thought, beyond movement. It was the first time Ed had been kissed by anyone other than his mother, that is if you didn't count kid's games like postman's knock and such like.

'Bit of a jellyfish, aren't you?' Leanne didn't sound pleased. She was stretching and limbering again and looking at the embers of the fire regretfully. Ed didn't know what to say, so he said nothing. He wanted her to carry on but couldn't ask her. The others would hear, and he wasn't quite sure how to put it. He was afraid she would go away now and leave him looking foolish and alone. He'd had enough of that at college. Fish out of water. That's how he felt now.

'Don't worry, love.' Leanne was suddenly kneeling beside him again and whispering into his ear. 'I'll soon get you going. Coming down tomorrow, are you?' He nodded. He was a fish swimming now. 'Yes, oh yes.' He found his voice. 'Shall I … shall I pick you up?' She laughed, pulling him onto his feet.

'It's me that does the picking up, wouldn't you say?' He coughed, nervously, not quite sure how to respond. Was she making fun of him?

'Don't look so worried, love'. She was heading back over the cobbles and up to the path. 'I'll meet you here, half ten'.

She was away, running up the path with Ed still collecting himself, trying to get his limbs to do what he wanted them to. He tried to run after her and stumbled, grazing his knee on the gravel path.

'Hey, mate.' A couple of lads were just behind him. The fires were all embers now and everyone was making their way home.

'You want to be careful there, Ed'. He recognised that voice again and this time managed to put a name to it.

'Hiya, it's James, isn't it?'

James slapped him on the back.

'Just watch that Leanne, she's only seventeen but going on twenty-seven. She'll eat you for breakfast if you're not careful.'

Ed thought about it as he walked up with the lads. This was a different place than he went away from. It was as though he had lived his life with strangers and was now meeting them for the first time.

'Get yourself an education,' his mother had said. Well, Leanne was doing wonders for his education now. Ed went down to the Dyke every night. The fires would be burning, and the crowd would be there, drinking, singing, passing the long cold nights. It was all part of the ritual.

And then she'd come and take his hand and lead him to some spot near one of the fires. He'd got into the kissing now. He wasn't half such a jellyfish as that first time. She showed him where to put his hands, where she liked to be touched. He learned each move by heart and the next night they would go over the moves, practice the steps.

'Got a new pupil, has she?' Some voice by the fire commented.

'Leave off, they're made for each other.' Another voice, and then laughter, unkind laughter.

But Ed didn't mind. This was better fun than he'd had in his life before. What did he care if they were laughing at him? They were probably only jealous anyway.

'Are you going out again?'

His mother sounded accusing. One minute she wanted him to go and mix with friends and now she didn't.

'It's riff raff you'll see down at that Dyke.'

She riddled the ashes in the stove fiercely.

'Leave the lad alone. Let him have a bit of fun.' His dad was pulling on his pipe and getting ready to go to the pub.

'You're both the same. Can't see what's good for you.' She threw a hod of coke down into the black hole of the stove, the noise like a rush of chalk cobbles in a rough sea.

'Get your mind on the game, Ed.' Leanne was pulling at him, drawing him closer. The tide was coming in with a rush tonight. They wouldn't be staying long.

'Let's get in the boathouse,' she whispered to him, her mouth right up to his ear.

'We're not allowed.' He sounded horrified.

Leanne put her head back and laughed. She had a harsh mocking laugh and some of the others were looking, wondering what this was all about.

Ed felt angry. She was making fun of him again. He didn't need this.

'Come on then,' he said and dragged her up onto her feet.

'Let's go in the boat house, you got a key or something?'

Leanne laughed again, but softer this time, and pulling his hand she dragged him up the cobbles.

'Don't need no key, you gawk. There's a broken window round the back, everybody knows that.'

It was warm in the boathouse. The lifeboat took up almost all of the space, set on its launcher, ready for action. There were pulleys and iron chains, oil cans and tools. There was a beautiful order about it all, a competence, a readiness.

'Let's do it in the boat.' Leanne was already hitching up her skirt, clambering up the sides of the great hulk.

'Come on,' she hissed, urgently, 'your first time should be somewhere special.'

'We can't.' Ed was horrified. 'What if it gets called out? What if we loosen it from its moorings?'

She laughed, hauling herself over the side into the boat.

'What are you? A man or a tiddler fish?'

Ed stood there, looking around, listening to the wind blowing through the open window, like breath through a hole in a decaying tooth. He thought about her in the boat. Oh, God, he really fancied her. He'd never been the tree climbing kind of boy, never taken risks, always did as he was told.

He looked up the huge side of the boat, saw the name 'ALICE BEASTON' painted under the rim.

'Here's to education,' he thought, and started to climb.

Six

Sometimes the little village by the sea seems to come under a spell. The girl who lives there with the wicked witch and the hobman decides that each time it can only be a good spell, because everything she sees on these days is cloaked in a dazzling, twinkling light. The sky is blue as amethyst and the gulls keen loudly to each other as they wheel and dive in ancient, intricate patterns, telling of their adventures far out to sea and of their journeys to altogether other lands. These enchanted days have nothing to do with earthly seasons, they are truly magical and can happen at any time at all.

Aunty Molly has spent the morning whirling round the house like a fat, red dervish, cleaning, polishing and scouring. She'd been baking the whole of the day before and now the large kitchen table is groaning with melting moments, madeleines and raspberry buns, just waiting for the guest of honour. Gwen is coming to visit.

Morgan is so excited as it has been months since she has seen her mother. She has submitted willingly, for once, while Aunty Molly scraped and pulled at her red mop, assembling it into a neat and tidy ponytail tied with a green bow.

Uncle John has taken time off from the farm to pick Gwen up from the bus station and they come in out of the cold chatting and laughing as though it was an everyday occurrence.

It is on such days that the little girl knows her Princess will come. Knows that somehow, she will find a way through enchanted labyrinths, mole chambers and wormcasts until she finds her way to the little village by the sea. She also knows that her Princess will of necessity have to be in disguise.

Morgan runs to Gwen, instinctively but then waits as she is unsure how to approach her. She has been told her mother is a poorly lady and she doesn't want to hurt her with one of her bear hugs. Gwen puts her arms out as the little girl runs towards her, but then retracts them as she hesitates.

'She's forgotten who I am.' She looks at Molly accusingly.

'Give your mother a hug'. Aunty Molly's voice is sharp, and although Morgan reaches out to her mummy in response, there is only bewilderment in the gesture.

The awkward start is papered over with general talk of the weather and the journey and then a cup of tea is made as a safety net.

Gwen has brought books for Morgan, one is 'The Secret Garden', and the other is 'King Arthur and his Knights of the Round Table'. The little girl can't wait to devour them. She sits in the ingle turning page after page, not reading them, not yet. She tantalises herself by looking to see what is in store for her, glimpsing chapter headings to be read in detail in the quiet of her own room later. She has half an ear on the conversation and is lulled by her mummy's presence and the crackling of the stove.

'Poor soul.' Aunty Molly and Gwen are cooing gossip, like two old pigeons on a warm rooftop. 'Well I heard another story, and I have no reason to think it isn't true.'

'Go on.' Gwen is agog.

There's never time for gossip at home. No time, nor any inclination from Donald. Pat and Dot only visit with stories of their own children and the neighbours seem to stay away.

'Well, it seems that she was well on with the baby; big you know.'

Molly gestures a large protruding stomach. 'Then in the last week before it was born, she was scared by a big black cat.'

'What do you mean scared?'

'Well, she was walking along late at night on her way home, and this cat just leapt out on her. Leapt out from nowhere and jumped on her walking up the road.'

'Oh, how awful. Oh, Molly, that must have been a real shock. What did she do? Did it scratch her or bite her? Did it bring on the baby?'

Morgan's hair is beginning to pull. Just single hairs that Aunty Molly has stretched too tight. She wiggles her fingers around, trying to loosen the offending strands.

'Well, they do say, that just before you give birth, if anything like that happens, a sudden shock you know, well, it could affect the baby.'

Aunty Molly pulls one of those faces, all twisted and suggestive of something horrible. Morgan pulls strand after strand of her red mop loose, and it begins to unravel the whole tidy ponytail.

'Affect the baby? Affect the baby in what way. I've never heard of this before.'

Gwen's face is mirroring Aunty Molly's.

Morgan gets up from the ingle and goes over to sit on Gwen's knee. She is a big girl, really, to be on her mother's knee. She knows Aunty Molly will be thinking that. But it feels right there. Her mother holds her on, safe, warm.

'Well, they say that the baby can 'take on' parts of the creature that has scared the mother, you know.'

38

Aunty Molly squirms as if she had an itch. Gwen holds Morgan tight.

'No! I've never heard that. So, what happened?'

'Well, the baby was born with..' Molly looks over her shoulder, as though she is telling secrets she shouldn't.

'They say the baby was born with a black tail.'

A door bangs in the porch, a sign that the gale is getting up. The fire cowers behind the glass door of the stove, as though it knows a great gasp of wind could soon blow under the vent to burn through its coals and stir up its embers.

Morgan begins to wriggle and itch her back. She stretches her arm over her shoulder, feeling to see if there is anything there that she hadn't noticed before. She is dipping jam, licking, and scratching and nearly falls off Gwen's knee.

'Just look at you.' Aunty Molly's voice is firm. 'Hair all a mess and covered head to foot in jam. What do you think you look like? Go and clean yourself up.'

The little girl looks as though she has just woken up from a dream. She jumps from Gwen's knee, worried she has covered her with jam, and scuttles off to the bathroom to wash and tidy up. She knows not to argue with Aunty Molly. She knows Molly will get her way in the end.

'You were a bit sharp with her.' Gwen is almost in tears.

'You have to be firm. Have you forgotten what a wilful creature she can be? Don't you remember why you sent her here in the first place.'

Gwen takes a hanky out of her bag and wipes her eyes. She is embarrassed at being upset. She wants to seem strong and in control. 'It's hot in here,' she says, loosening her top blouse button and blowing down her chest.

'You go out into the fresh air for a minute.' Molly is refilling the kettle. 'I'll make us another cup of tea. That's what you need, a nice cup of tea.'

'Where's Mummy?' Morgan is back from the bathroom, clean hands and her hair tied up after a fashion.

'She's had to get some fresh air, and no wonder after seeing you in that state.' Aunty Molly gives the teacups a thorough washing and dries them ready for using again. She shuffles the cakes around on the plates, filling the gaps, restoring the symmetry.

Morgan sits back in the ingle and takes out the new felt tips Gwen has brought her. She is drawing a picture for her mummy to take home.

Gwen returns to the kitchen looking tear-stained.

'What's the matter, love?' Molly is upon her, sitting her down, steadying her hand and pouring her a nice cup of tea.

'Oh, I don't know, Molly, it's the least little thing these days. Donald says I should rest, take it easy. But I get fed up of resting. I want to be back to my old self.'

'You've got to accept it, Gwen. You're not a strong person. Your nerves are shot to pieces. You need to get to that doctor and ask him for a tonic. That's what you need, a tonic.'

Morgan is good at drawing. The teacher at school says she is good at drawing. She wants to show her mummy just what a clever girl she is. She sticks out her tongue in concentration.

The chatter moves on. The tea flows and the gaps between the cakes get bigger, even though Molly reorganises them every once in a while. Gwen's bus is at five o'clock and Uncle John will be here soon to take her to the station. She's left Donald his tea, but he likes her to be back before bedtime. He doesn't like her staying out for the night. He likes to be able to keep an eye on her.

'I've got a picture for you to take home.' Morgan holds out the paper, proudly. Molly takes it to pass to Gwen. She holds it out to her, but then retracts it, frowning. 'What is this, what have you drawn here?'

Morgan gets up from the ingle, worried at Aunty Molly's stern voice. 'It's the baby with a cat's tail. A big black cat's tail.' Molly looks again. 'It's disgusting. What does your mother want with such a horrible picture? Why can't you draw her something normal like a house or a horse? There's plenty of nice horses in the fields for you to draw. You are such a strange little girl and no mistake.'

Gwen reaches out for the picture, but Molly has already screwed it up and thrown it on the back of the stove.

Morgan throws the felt tips onto the floor and the drawing book into the coal scuttle.

'Ungrateful child,' Aunty Molly screams. 'Go to your room, I'll shout you down to say goodbye.'

Gwen opens and shuts her mouth, trying to find the words, but she feels like she does at home when Donald is in full flow. She feels like she isn't there.

She watches Morgan go upstairs wiping tears away with her arm. She wants her to come back and sit on her knee again.

She wants to thread her fingers through that red hair, making it grow bigger and bigger.

She knows she mustn't though. Morgan needs firm

41

handling. Molly and Donald both say so. She must be strong for Morgan's sake.

After a measure of hours and minutes, the glister of the Princess begins to dull and tarnish. She must leave, return to the castle with the marble staircase and rest awhile in her golden bed. After all, it has been agreed that she will do so, and the Princess will never sully her word.

Seven

Rain, rain, go away. Come on mother's washing day
Rain, rain, go away. Come on mother's washing day

The children who live in the town are noted for laughing in the face of
a good downpour. They jump two-footed in the gutters, kick sprays of
water into the air drenching shoppers who shout after them, threaten
them with their broken, crooked umbrellas. 'Brats, hooligans! Get off
home and help your mothers.'

Morgan and Ally were on the number 10 into town. The bus was crowded with soaking wet shoppers. It always chucked it down on Saturdays.

'I managed to speak to her today. I just rang up and asked for Mrs Gwen Parish, like before, and it was *her*. She was really taken aback, I could tell.' Morgan shivered, took down her soaking wet hood.

'She didn't hang up then?'

'No, she didn't hang up. I was sort of taken aback myself, now I'd actually got to speak to her. It's been a long time you know.' Morgan shook herself like a dog, the spray from her hair going every which way.

'What did she say, what did you talk about?'

Morgan's eyes were bright as raindrops. She smoothed her coat, pushing the wet onto the bus floor.

'I said, 'It's me, Morgan,' and she said, 'Morgan, yes.' It was almost as though she'd expected me to call. I asked her how she was, and she said, 'Fine thank you'. I asked her if she'd had a good Christmas and she said 'Lovely'. It was hard. I wanted to ask her all sorts. I wanted to ask, why she sent me away, but of course I didn't'.

The number 10 went as far as the market. The bus groaned and trembled as it went round the hills and bends into Sheffield. The view from the window was obscured by the running condensation which Ally rubbed at every now and then with her coat sleeve.

'I phoned my mum today as well.'

She looked absentmindedly at her soaking, dirty sleeve.

'Did you? How was she?' Morgan shifted the weight of the bag of books she was holding on her knee. She would donate these back to the charity shop, then buy some more. She loved to browse amongst such an eclectic choice of books and select randomly, seductively.

Ally sighed and pulled her coat tight across her body.

'We always say that don't we? We always start 'how are you?' and the other person always says, 'fine' even when they're not.'

'So, was she OK?'

'No, I don't think so, but she wouldn't say. I could tell though, she sounded kind of strained.'

'Strained. Yes, that's how Gwen sounded. It was as though she wanted to talk but couldn't and that's how I felt as well. I kept talking about the weather of all things. After all this time and all I could say was, 'It's been a lot warmer today, hasn't it?''

Ally smiled and nudged her friend's arm in unspoken support.

'Well, I told my mum that I wouldn't be coming home anymore.'

'No. How did she take that?'

'Oh, you know, 'do what you think best', it's so easy to walk all over her, she never fights back'.

The bus came to a sharp stop as it pulled in to pick up

more passengers. Two teenagers clumped up the metal steps, pushing at each other, wanting to sit at the front. Morgan stared at them, begrudging their noise and disturbance.

'I asked Gwen about my grandmother and she really freaked out at that. Her voice was dead strange, sort of cold and mechanical. 'She'll be no good to you. She couldn't even look after me. You're best forgetting you've got a grandmother''.

Morgan's eyes lowered into her lap as she re-lived the conversation again.

'Forget you've got a grandmother? What was she on about?'.

Ally's eyes sought hers, pushing her on in the story, knowing that Morgan wouldn't have given in easily.

'Don't worry, it just made me more determined to find her. Make my own mind up. I'm not a child anymore.'

She sat up straight, glaring imperiously at the teenagers who were still quarrelling about the front seat. The bus grumbled on like a great metal dinosaur, swaying from side to side, gushes of rain pouring down its sides in small wayward streams.

'After I'd been talking to Mum, our Michael came on the phone.' Ally turned her head away from Morgan, not wanting to show how upset she was. 'He must have been sitting there when I was talking to her and got the gist of the conversation. He begged me to go home at Easter. Said he'd do something desperate if he had to deal with it on his own.'

'What will you do?'

'God alone knows because I don't.'

45

The driver braked with some finality. They were at the terminus. The passengers were reluctant to leave, they had warmed up in the damp seats and could hear the rain flushing along the streets outside. As they negotiated their way down the twisting staircase, Morgan turned to Ally.

'Strange thing is Gwen stopped talking to me all of a sudden and I couldn't work out why. I kept up my end of the conversation, but she wasn't responding at all. There wasn't even a sign that she was listening. And then *he* came on the phone.'

They clattered off the bus, Ally pushing fiercely at her umbrella in a vain attempt to keep them dry.

'So, what was going on? Did you find out?'

Morgan clutched her bag of books to her chest, lowering her head over them to protect them.

'He just said, 'That's enough now, my wife is ill and cannot speak to you anymore.' 'My wife', I ask you, not 'your mother', just 'my wife'. He said I had better hang up and it would be a good idea not to phone again. For her sake, I was not to phone this number again. Then he hung up. Just like that. Not even hello, how are you after all these years, nothing.'

They moved into the arcade, sensing a temporary reprieve from the elements.

'Cold bastard that one, Morgan. You're not going to get through to him easily, I can tell you. My mum came back on the phone, after I had been speaking to Michael. She said I must do what I want, that they'd manage. At the end of the day, though, the phone's no good. You can't see their faces on the phone, you can't read the body language. It's like trying to have sex without touching.'

They smiled ruefully at each other.

'I phoned Aunty M later and got my grandmother's name out of her. She took a bit of convincing, but I was as nice as pie. In the end, she couldn't resist my pleas.'

Ally laughed and nudged Morgan playfully on the arm. 'She'll be pleased to palm you off onto someone else, I suppose. You're always saying she thinks you're a wild child.'

Morgan tossed her head and with the bright lights of the arcade warming her mood, she said, 'Anyway, I have an address so I'm going to write to her. Grace Williams, she's called. She must be really old. Surely, she'll be pleased to see me, don't you think?'

Red Riding Hood sets off to walk through the wild, wild, wood to visit her grandmother.

Eight

Up on the cliff top was a grand place to think. Ed needed to think. The grass was long and fine up there. It fell to one side where the wind had blown it, like some glorious, blow-dried hairdo. He walked until he came to the old warning post then scrambled down and made himself a nest in the grasses, looking out to sea.

Leanne wouldn't see him anymore. He'd been down to the Dyke and she wasn't there. He'd scoured the village pubs. He'd looked all over but he couldn't find her. The lads kept telling him that Billy was back from fishing and that she wouldn't want to know him now. Billy Myers. Ed remembered him from school. Little lad, he was, blond hair and wily. He was the youngest of six, all boys.

He'd not been a mate or anything, but he remembered one time when Billy had been off school for a couple of weeks. His dad had been drowned at sea and the younger lads in the family were kept off school until finally, the Inspector had to be sent to make them all come back. Now he was a fisherman and most of his brothers were as well.

The seabirds were diving and keening above Ed as he lay in his cover, hiding from the world. 'This place,' he thought, 'sons following dads, Billy following his dad to sea, me wanting to be a farmer. What's it all about? Do I really want this or is it just this place makes it seem right? Maybe Mum's right. I should look at the other side first.'

And what about Leanne? When he thought about it, he wasn't that bothered. He'd fancied her, of course, but then it seemed he wasn't the only one. He wasn't that daft he couldn't see she'd throw herself at anything in trousers. Well, Billy Myers was welcome to her. Plenty more fish in the sea.

The tide was out, far out. It left the rocks prominent, scattered randomly over a seaweed-pocked beach. 'Not picture postcard pretty,' thought Ed, 'but honest. Making a living here is hard. It's dangerous and sometimes hostile, but it's never made out it was anything else.'

Leanne had never made out she loved Ed he knew that. It had been a fling. It had been an initiation. He knew the others would be laughing about him, how easily she had dropped him and gone back to Billy. Somehow though he didn't care that much. He felt like he'd learned something; something about himself, like he'd grown up a bit.

His mother hadn't mentioned college for a few days. She'd gone on and on about it at the beginning of the holiday, but just lately, nothing. Ed had decided he'd go back. Just to the end of term, he might as well, there was nothing to keep him here at the moment. He felt different somehow now anyway, like he'd cope better.

Suddenly the maroon went up, a loud signal that silenced the birds, that silenced everything. Ed knew it was only the lifeboat practice. He got up and started to walk back down to the village. He didn't want to see the ALICE BEASTON launched. He didn't want to be reminded of that part of his education.

The Queen rubs her hands in glee. At last the quiet Prince has gone to seek his fortune.

She rubs her hands round and round, through and through, as she

49

thinks about the spells which were given to her by the wizened three-toed troll who lived under the rock to the left of the thousand-year old bramble.

Leanne called round to the farm to see Ed, but it was his mum who opened the door. The young woman moved a step nearer to the door but didn't cross the threshold. 'Is Ed in?' she mumbled, wary of this alien territory.

'Ed? What do you want with him?' Ed's mother covered the bluntness of the remark with a smile and a gesture for Leanne to enter the kitchen. 'Come and talk in here,' she said, 'I'm just in the middle of scones.'

'Come in, come in,' said the spider to the fly.

Leanne went in, feeling that this was a bad idea after all. There was no sign of Ed, but then she hadn't seen him for a couple of months, hadn't looked for him really.

'Now why do you need our Ed, all of a sudden?' Maggie pressed down on the metal cutter into the soft, thick dough, twisting the sharp edge to give a perfect round slab to toss onto the baking tray.

'Er... well, I just thought I could talk to him, I mean I need to talk to him, you know, about something.' Leanne felt hot and she wished she hadn't come.

'Cup of tea, dear?' Maggie was already filling the kettle, shuffling the baking tray into the oven, setting out the teacups.

'No. I won't stay. Ed isn't here is he?'

'Went back to college ages ago.'

Maggie couldn't hold in her triumph as she spooned two measures of tea into the pot, tapping the lid with the spoon to add emphasis. 'What do you want him for?'

'It's private.' Leanne was flustered now but angry. This woman was a witch. She could do without the bother of all this. 'Can I have his address?'

The kettle on the Aga steamed then whistled. Ed's mother echoed the sound, 'Ooh, no, I don't think so, dear. He'll be far too busy to be writing letters to little bits of girls like you. He's got years of study and then he'll probably not be coming back here anyway. Would you like a scone with your tea, they'll be ready shortly?'

Leanne turned to leave, tripping over the matting in her rush.

'Careful, dear.' Maggie placed the kettle on the edge of the stove to simmer until her visitor had left. 'You need to be careful in your condition.'

'How did...?' Leanne turned her back sharply. Of course, the witch knew, they knew everything, women like that.

'Never mind,' she said, trying to make her exit dignified. 'I'll contact him some other way.'

The next week, Ed received a letter from his mother. Inside it was a newspaper cutting from the local paper.

'The engagement is announced of Leanne Watson to Billy Myers. The engagement will be short as the couple hope to marry in July.'

Nine

Oh, Grandma, what big eyes you've got.

The woman who opened the door was slight in build. Her hair was silver white but neat and she held a white stick tenaciously in her hand.

'Who's there? Is that you, Morgan?' Morgan could not reconcile this frail, blind old lady with the strong, positive tone of the letter she had received. Grace had sounded so independent.

She'd said how much she'd welcomed Morgan's letter, sounded as though she had almost been expecting it. But this little old lady on the doorstep?

'You seem frightened of me, child. No need for that, come in, come in.'

Oh, Grandma what big ears…

The house was dark. The old woman led her along the narrow hallway into a small kitchen, where the table was set for tea.

The brightness and neatness of that table was something she would never forget. Pale blue and white gingham and white crockery rimmed with hoops of darker blue, a tiered cake stand with tiny bread and butter fingers and fairy cakes. Morgan let out a cry of delight.

'How did you manage this?'

'It's only my eyes don't work, not my fingers.' Grace was sharp but there was a twinkle in her voice.

'I can see just a tiny bit now, dear, mostly blurred grey

shapes. I got the postman to read your letter to me.'

She laughed. 'I don't get many letters these days. I was so pleased to hear from you. Then I got Gladys next door to write back for me. Her handwriting but my words. Absolutely my words.' The old woman fingered her neat grey hair.

'My eyesight is getting worse quickly now and by the summer I won't be able to see anything according to Doctor Paterson. But then, what do doctors know?

Morgan sat down without being asked. She felt at home here as she had never felt at home anywhere. She let Grace boil the kettle, watched her brew the tea by feeling her way to the pot with her hands, steady and sure.

They talked together as though they had always known each other, filling in the space of years over brown bread and jam and steaming hot tea, the light in the kitchen getting more and more dim, but neither needing the interruption of electricity.

'I was eleven years old when the Great War started. I was frightened - just mother and me but we had to get on with it. The men went away - we didn't know if they would ever come back.'

Grace sat pencil-straight at the table. Her eyes stared ahead as though she saw the past and could picture what she was talking about.

'How did you live, I mean money. What did you do for money?' Morgan tried to imagine this old woman as a young girl, frightened, not knowing what the future held.

Grace smiled, clasping her hands on her lap as she went on with the story.

'Mother tried to carry on as normal - keeping the shop going, you know. But she soon found out she couldn't. Dad had always seen to everything, you see, she hadn't an idea how it all worked. She hid away from everything then, pretended it wasn't happening. She just couldn't cope with it all. She'd send me out to see to things and I didn't mind. I started to think it was all going to be really exciting, different, you know. I helped Miss Potts at the Post Office. I ran errands all over town for Miss Potts.'

She paused, letting the aura of those times fill the quietness. Morgan looked around the room, dark in the February gloom. She couldn't believe that it was just a couple of days ago since she'd received Grace's letter.

She'd felt so warmed by its welcoming words. After all, no-one else in the family had ever wanted to speak to her, not properly.

She looked at her grandmother, her frail peach skin, white hair and the far away, almost blind eyes and she felt like a child again.

'Then it was all over, and father came home, and they thought it would all go back to how it was before.'

Grace took up the story again, hands clasped, head nodding.

'But it couldn't, could it? I couldn't. What was there for me - going and scivvying in the vicarage - not likely. I'd had a taste for something else now. Seen things I wanted. They tried to lock me up until I saw sense. You can't lock up spirit though, can you?'

Her hands spread over the tablecloth, smoothing and feeling for its neatness.

'I ran away, Morgan. In the end I just packed up my things and caught the coach to London. They were different

54

times, you see, different from what my parents had ever known, and I felt that I wanted to be different as well. I thought I could make my own way. I thought I could be a film star - you saw them on the big movie screen - what a life they seemed to have.'

Grace felt for Morgan's cup and poured more tea for her. She motioned towards the cakes, a little agitated that she wasn't tucking in.

'I got a job in a café near Charing Cross and I met Sean there. Oh, Morgan, we were inseparable. He was just 17 and over from Ireland. He had a special way with him and when he got going, he could pull stories out of thin air like a magic trick and you just wanted to listen to him for hours.'

Grace was far away in her memories and Morgan was trying not to clunk her teacup and break the spell. She loved the way the old woman's face was soft and smiling. What wonderful memories she must have. Grace sighed, went on.

'He wanted to be an actor and so I tagged along while he went for audition after audition. In the end I joined in - why shouldn't I be an actress? Maybe one day I'd be film star. With Sean, I felt that I could do and be anything I wanted.

'Of course, the rosy world didn't last long. We both got bit parts here and there and I still worked shifts in the café, but there wasn't much money coming in. We took a little room and lived there together but we could barely make ends meet. Still we kept hoping for that big chance.

'I sent the odd letter home, just to let them know I was OK – but they didn't write back… I was the outcast now

I suppose, but I didn't care. I had Sean and we were in love. It doesn't sound much in this day and age, Morgan, but it was all we wanted, just to sit in our little room - the fire just about going. I'd be sitting at Sean's feet and he'd be telling me his magical stories of castles, princesses, swans and butterflies. I was so happy.'

There was a sudden slam upstairs and Morgan started. 'What on earth?'

'Oh, it's that bathroom door. The wind must be getting up again. Go and shut it for me will you'. Grace waved in the general direction of upstairs.

Morgan felt her way up the staircase, not thinking to turn on the light. She wanted this place to be just as it was. It was her grandmother's house. *Her* grandmother's.

She settled back down at the kitchen table. Grace was pouring fresh tea. Her face was no longer soft with gentle memories.

'Then, you see, all that hoping for a big chance crumbled. I got in the family way and when he found out about it, Sean was off. I had to come home to have the baby – home to the 'told you so's' to the 'slut and whore' from father – to the constant prayers from mother.' Grace's fingers were twisting at the edge of the tablecloth.

'My baby was born here in this house.' She looked around, only able to see dim shadows.

'She was beautiful. She was the princess from Sean's stories. She was perfect. She was hope.'

Morgan instinctively reached across the table, to still Grace's agitated fingers. She held the thin, old hands for a while, surprised at their warmth.

'The hope part of it didn't last long though. They wanted me to go into service. They said they'd look after little Gwen, but I had to earn my keep, do my duty.

'I tried to do what they wanted, be what they wanted. Things were so hard then and making your way was pretty much mapped out. It was the same map hundreds of other young girls were following. But I didn't want that. I still wanted the magic of the theatre – the make-believe. I still wanted the bright lights and excitement. I still wanted that big chance.'

Morgan knew where this story was going.

She remembered Gwen's voice on the phone. *'She'll be no good to you, she couldn't even look after me, you're best forgetting you've got a grandmother'.*

'It wasn't so hard leaving Gwennie at first. I mean I was going to make my fortune for our future, wasn't I? Then I'd come back and fetch her, and we'd live in a little two up two down in a country village with cows and horses and maybe the odd prince or two. I was so full of dreams, Morgan, it felt like I had everything to look forward to. I visited her, of course I did. I sent money when I could and visited when I could. But they saw to it that I'd never get her back. They poisoned her mind against me. They didn't want her growing up wayward like her mother. I suppose they were right in a way.'

Grace wiped her eyes with the back of her hand and Morgan had a stupid idea that blind eyes shouldn't cry.

'When Gwennie was little I used to tell her some of the stories Sean told me. She liked that. She'd cuddle up on my

57

lap and we'd be in castles and magic lands and she'd be mine again. But London was a long way away, and sometimes it was hard to come home as often as I wanted to. And as she grew older, they must have told her I didn't care about her. Sometimes when I visited, she didn't want to know about the stories. She said she didn't believe in the magic anymore. Then I knew I'd lost her.'

The wolf was shuffling in the shrubs below Grandma's window; the wolf that had come to eat her; the wolf that would swallow her whole.

'I did alright though. I was never what they called a star, but I did all right. I married Andrew in 1935. Oh, he had both feet firmly on the ground. No stories, no magic, just pounds, shillings and pence, a mortgage and a pension. We didn't have children - none that lived, anyway. We asked Gwen to come to us, but they'd got their claws well and truly in by then. She was fifteen, doing well at school, it would be the wrong time to start stirring things up. That's what they said.'

'I was a war widow at 40 and my eyesight was failing fast. I moved back here to look after mother in 1953 after father died - but it was more like we cared for each other in a 'strangers that pass in the night' sort of way. The neighbours never let up on me, though. They remembered what I'd done, and I would always be the scarlet woman in their eyes. I enjoyed that - seeing them twitch their curtains and mutter as I passed them by. Small-minded people, Morgan, and life had certainly passed them by.

'After mother died in 1963, my eyesight seemed to take a

turn for the worse, but I've managed as you can see. Gwennie comes over to see me now and again. She used to come over quite a lot with their Dot and Pat and with David, and we could have got on, given time. But that husband of hers, Donald, well it wasn't good enough for him, nothing ever was. It was as if he took the gossip from the neighbours as gospel. I think he thought I'd taint her. But she always took notice of him and he seemed to have a way of taking away her spirit and her hope. She still comes, not so often now and only on his terms.

'He smothers her, you know. Won't let her do this and that. She lives like an invalid in that house with him in total control. Back then it felt like he'd taken her away from me for a second time but then I didn't deserve better, I suppose. I mean I'd abandoned her in the first place. She owed me nothing.'

Grace started moving the crockery, clearing the table.

'She never once asked me about her father.' Grace's shoulders sunk as she stooped over the sink.

Morgan wondered if she'd done something wrong, but all she'd done was listen.

'They brought you to see me when you were a baby.' Grace sat down again her face soft, her hands reaching for Morgan's.

'My eyes were really bad by then, but I could feel you - a real little fiery bundle of energy and spirit - and I could see your hair - just like Sean's - a bright and beautiful red.'

The wolf slunk off into the undergrowth, he knew he would have to bide his time.

59

Ten

And it is well known that in this glorious stretch of sun-blessed days, goblins live in the harmins of the cliffs that edge the little village by the sea. They slide and slither in the wind-fingered grasses, laughing gleefully in their good humour. They are happy fellows, who don't care to waste their magic on the bobbing sea craft that crimp the horizon. But when darkness foreshortens summer days, the goblins grow cold and seek out tree hollows, empty rabbit holes, and dark corners in cowsheds for shelter.

They are drawn to the slightest light or lantern, and their eyes grow large and their ears prickle with delight at the crackle and roar of a bonfire. Their faces glow with mischief and their pockets bulge with magic.

It's Morgan's birthday. She is eight. She wonders if she will see her mother today.

'Your mummy is one of the poorly people.' Aunty Molly is brushing the girl's hair, scraping it back into order.

'Sometimes poorly people can't be like you and me, so we have to take them as we find them.'

'I'll be really good if she comes.' Morgan feels tears on her cheek, she wipes them away defiantly.

'You've a long way to go yet my girl.' The old woman brushes and scrapes at her hair, faster and faster.

'You're hurting.' She pulls away and shakes her head. Her almost tidy mop cascades like dandelion seeds in a wind. Aunty Molly grasps the red hair firmly. 'Now we'll have to start all over again!' She brushes and scrapes, deliberately, heavily, trying to brush order into both the hair and the child at the same time.

Later, from her bedroom, Morgan hears the front door

squeak open. They only use the front door for visitors, but she'd seen Aunty Molly giving it a good wipe down earlier in the day. 'Get rid of the spiders and flies,' she'd said, scrubbing and puffing to get the door recesses clean as a new pin.

Morgan peeps out of her bedroom curtains. 'Amy. That'll be Amy,' she thinks. There is no mistaking Amy in her 'whiter than white' fairy outfit and a little silver wand with a glittering star at the end of it. With her is Leanne. She feels her face redden as she realises that Leanne is dressed up as a witch as well. Trust her! She'd wheedled out of Morgan what she was going to be dressed as then done the same, just to spite her. Aunty Molly thinks these two are her special friends, but actually they are the only ones at school who bother with her at all. Leanne loves to taunt Morgan and always manages to get away without getting into trouble. They are always together, Amy and Leanne. And now here they are, Amy in white and Leanne in black. Morgan sighs. Still she'll get her own back.

'Your little friends are here,' Aunty Molly shouts, no hint of any recrimination as she knows others are listening. She's been chivvying and coaxing Morgan for an hour to get ready. She's taken her warm honeyed milk, fairy cakes and even a taste of the toffee for the toffee apples. Morgan knows that her good humour won't last long, not even with visitors there. Amy and Leanne know how to play this game too, best manners and smiles. They can turn it on like a tap.

She can hear the bump, bump of music as she puts on the black dress and sparkly cloak that Aunty Molly has made for her. She loosens her red mop from its neatness and twirls a few curls around her fingers. Defiantly she clamps the pointy black hat over the curls and says to her reflection,

'I'll show them a witch.' And she runs downstairs with her heaviest, crossest footfall.

'I don't know how she copes!' Amy's mother arrives at 6 o'clock prompt, together with Leanne's willowy mother in her wake. 'She's a martyr to that child.'

The two of them are collecting their tearful, jelly-stained, traumatised angel and witch from the party.

'I don't want to play with her, ever again.' Amy's tearful whine reaches Morgan who is on the old three-legged milking stool awaiting Aunty Molly's wrath.

'She put red jelly down Amy's white fairy dress.' Leanne's hot tears spring from spiteful eyes.

'She's cast spells on us, Mum, we'll wake up as frogs tomorrow.' Amy is beside herself and Aunty Molly is trying to calm everything down.

'Now, now, it wasn't too bad.' She rubs at Amy's sobbing chest to try to remove the red stains. 'Morgan was only pretending to be a witch.'

'She lit the bonfire, she nearly set fire to us.' Leanne looks over her shoulder at Morgan and gives a spiteful smile before turning back to her mother. 'She's evil, Mummy, she's a real witch.'

The day before, Aunty Molly and Morgan had made a pumpkin lantern together. Morgan had seen one in a book and Aunty Molly said they would make one if she promised to be good at the party. They had sliced off a lid, scooped out the middle and made a face in the striped, yellow skin.

'It's like a real head,' said Morgan, glowering at the twisted, garish features they had created.

'It's just a pumpkin.'

Aunty Molly had laughed, wiping and shifting the fleshy pulp into the bin.

'No harm in it - it'll do for the party tomorrow.'

'It's like a real head,' Morgan insisted and that night she dreamt of her party with a dancing, de-capitated visitor cavorting around Aunty Molly's best front room.

'I don't ever want to play with her again.' Leanne's echo floats across the kitchen and Morgan smiles to herself. 'What do they expect? I was dressed up as a witch, so I had to be evil, it says so in the books.'

After the visitors' departure, silence settles for a while and then Aunty Molly comes back into the kitchen, her straight-line lips set like a plaster mask.

'I hope you are satisfied, young lady'.

Morgan is fairly satisfied. Aunty Molly had said she could be a witch.

'You can wipe that smile off your face. All the trouble I went to.'

'I didn't ask you to'.

'Just you be quiet. I have never been so ashamed.'

'You said I could be a witch'.

'A witch. A witch! You were worse than a witch. You were a devil. A demon. That's the last time, Morgan, the last time.'

Out of the corner of her eye, Morgan can see the glow from the bonfire, which is still burning. Uncle John had been getting it ready for Guy Fawkes night. He had built it out of old wood from the barn and branches he'd cut from the old elm tree which had been dead some two years. He'd fetched in all the cows and sheep ready for the dark nights and he'd promised Morgan a fire to remember.

'What made you light the fire?' Aunty Molly is speaking very quietly. The question hangs in the air like the smoke from the bonfire in the night sky. 'Why, Morgan?'

'That's what people do on Halloween.'

She is feeling a bit uneasy now, a bit unsure of her ground.

'We don't have Halloween, that's American'.

'I read about it in one of my books, Aunty Molly, and anyway it wasn't really me it was the pumpkin head.'

She isn't going to tell her the truth. No-one will believe it wasn't her. She'll get Leanne back another time. For now, she can be a demon, a devil. It is what they expect of her.

Aunty Molly sighs. She is red from the kitchen heat. She is red from anger at Morgan's behaviour. She is red because the other women feel sorry for her and that makes her angrier than ever. She can almost hear their tongues clacking now, saying what she should and shouldn't have done with such a wicked child. Of course, they are real mothers, aren't they? Whereas she... Well, it isn't the same. She wants to cry.

She knows that she can't though, because if she ever starts, the tears will never stop. She wants to cry for the child she'll never have. She wants to scream at Morgan about how she is an evil witch child who she wishes had never come to live under her roof. But Aunty Molly isn't that sort of a woman.

Morgan ends up in the cellar. She knew she would. She's been locked in there before. Aunty Molly always gives punishments and quite often they involve the cellar.

You get to the cellar through a little door in the kitchen. You never notice the door until Aunty Molly mouths the word, 'cellar', and then it is as though there is nothing else in the whole of the kitchen except that little door.

'For those in peril on the sea.' Morgan sings quietly. It helps her to get used to the dark. She knows that after a while she'll be able to see shapes of things again. She just has to wait. The cellar has a light, but the switch is in the kitchen, at the other side of the little door. The light is left on until Morgan seats herself on the punishment chair and then it is switched off. Morgan tries to memorise where everything is until the light goes off. That way she can hold the picture of the cellar in her head in the dark. After a while, though, she always hears noises, the shuffling of rats, or of goblins or hobmen. She sings hymns to comfort herself. It is bound to keep out evil spirits anyway - that is what the chapel is all about.

At last she can just see the outline of the staircase leading out of the cellar. She can just about see the old mangle covered over with a dustsheet. She knows the contents of the cellar by heart, and it comforts her to actually be able to see that they are still in place, like old friends. Morgan closes her eyes and strains her ears. There aren't any noises now. She begins to sing again and waits for the greyness of the rest of the old landmarks to return to the cellar.

Eleven

'You really should go to the funeral,' Ally said. 'You'll never forgive yourself if you don't go.'

Morgan re-read the telegram. She couldn't believe that Grace was gone. She'd had such a short time with her.

'It's my fault, Ally. If I'd gone round when I said I would…'

She clutched at the piece of paper, trying to get some sense out of the few words: *Mother died after fall. Funeral Friday crematorium 2 30. Gwen Parish.*

She hadn't been for a few weeks. She'd been working hard on her studies for the final exams. She'd promised her grandmother a picnic after the last exam and she knew Grace had been really looking forward to it.

'It's not your fault, Morgan.'

Ally reached for her friend's hand, but she'd already moved to the window, still folding and unfolding the telegram.

'I can't go to the funeral. They'll all be there.'

'But you want to meet them, don't you? You've always wanted to meet them.'

'No, I can't.' Morgan felt angry that she couldn't cry.

'Wouldn't Grace have wanted you there?'

'I should have been there for her the day she had the fall. I let her down.'

'Morgan, you couldn't have known she would have a fall. It's not your fault.'

'But that's what they'll think. They'll say I'm still that evil, wicked girl. They'll say that Grace was alright before I started going round.'

'No, they won't..'

'You don't know them. All my life they've blamed me and maybe they're right. You should take care, Ally, maybe I'll ruin your life next.'

'But you should go, Morgan. You loved her and you have the right to say goodbye. They've given the date on the telegram. They must be expecting you to go.'

'Then why didn't one of them phone? My number was in Grace's book, right next to this address. They managed the address for the telegram so why couldn't they phone? Sixteen years and they still don't want to know me.' She screwed up the telegram and tossed it into the rubbish bin. *We're letting you know that Grace is dead, you're to blame, so don't darken our doorstep again*' That's what the telegram really says.'

'No, it doesn't. How can you say that?'

Morgan stormed to the bin, pulled out the crumpled telegram, straightened it with her clenched fist. 'Because it's all there in black and white - you just have to read between the lines.'

Tucked into the outskirts are the toytown houses with their neat little chimneys and square-built garden walls. Their borders are full of petunias and each lawn sprouts an apple tree with twenty-one apples whose summer skins are perpetually flushed to rosy pink.

But all is never as it seems. Just around the corner Noddy's car is up on bricks because someone's stolen its wheels. And Big Ears is pretending to help his friend, even though he's making a fortune from selling contraband hub caps.

Donald opened the door and unsmiling, asked her in.

'Hello, Dad,' she said. 'Long time no see.'

Donald sniffed. 'Trust you to be sarcastic. I can see that the years haven't changed you at all. But I don't want to argue. Gwen, your mother, is rather ill and I respect her wish to see you.'

He was grey faced and dressed in grey as well. She thought he looked like a fading shadow and he didn't frighten her anymore. In the past, she had always conjured up a picture of her father as bogeyman - keeping her mother in chains, locked up and unable to see her daughter. Or maybe that was just when she was a child. She had to admit she had rarely thought of him at all for years.

'What is wrong with her?' Morgan asked as she took off her coat and slung it onto the hall chair.

Donald picked up the coat, shook it and hung it carefully on a spare hook with the others.

'She has always been frail. Ever since you were born, she has never quite picked up her old self. Now her nerves are worse, and she seems to be getting weaker by the day. And then her mother's accident and the funeral... The doctors put different names to it, give her pills, tonics, but she just needs to be looked after. And I do the best I can.'

'I bet you do, thought Morgan, following his measured, slipper-shod paces through the hall and into the tidy lounge. 'You probably dust her down her twice weekly and make her sit in the bay window from dawn till dusk.' She was surprised at her own animosity. Why was she taking such an instant dislike to this man, her father?

Aunty Molly had always gone on about what an important part he played in the community, deputy headteacher of the local school until he retired. 'Too important to care about me, that's for sure,' she thought as she stood rigidly in the centre of the room, ignoring Donald's gesture to sit down on the blue moquette settee.

As quiet as a whisper, the door behind her opened and she turned to see a small, nervous woman enter the room, her mother, Gwen. For Morgan, all the years rushed together. It was overwhelming. She wanted to throw her arms around this tiny, frail person, squeeze some happiness back into her. But the knowledge that Donald was watching them, somehow got in the way.

'Sit down, dear.' Gwen gestured feebly, her strength going into sitting herself down on the armchair near the bay window.

'Sit down here, Morgan, next to me. It's so lovely to see you. You have grown.'

Both Donald and Morgan laughed, and Gwen looked bewildered, like a rabbit caught in car headlights.

Donald turned two bars of the electric fire on and left them to it. Morgan thought a cup of tea wouldn't have gone amiss and would have offered to make one, but somehow, she couldn't find it in herself to suggest it. These four walls really were constraining.

She looked at her mother, remembering her small, square face and blue eyes from those earlier visits, but was quite taken aback by the way she had aged since then. I'm as bad as her, she thought to herself. She's shocked by the fact I've grown, and I'm shocked by the fact she's got older.

'How long, Mother?' she muttered almost inaudibly. Gwen looked up.

'Too long, Morgan, too long.'

Gwen became more nervous by the minute. She shuffled in her seat and eventually said, 'I want to tell you how things were for me. I want to clear the air between us.'

Morgan got up from the settee and went over to Gwen's chair. She sat on the chair arm. Holding her daughter's hand, Gwen found the way forward and started to talk in her quiet, edgy voice.

'My own mother, Grace - oh, I know you knew her, she told me about your visits, well, she was more like a big sister really, a naughty big sister at that. She would be away from home for ages - months quite often and then she'd turn up and it was like my black and white life suddenly became coloured. She'd love me, hug me, and talk so quickly about things in her life - things I didn't understand. She'd tell me stories - hundreds of stories, not like Grandma and Grandad's bible stories. She'd bring presents that smelled of her, but Grandma would put them away after she'd gone. 'Not right for a child,' she'd say. Except I kept the music box with the ballerina in it. I could wind it up and remind myself of her whenever I liked. I could watch it going slower and slower and wish that my mother would be like that - slower and slower, coming down to the speed of our lives.'

Morgan smiled, sadly and squeezed Gwen's hand. 'I got to know Grace really well,' she said. 'I visited her often over the last couple of years. She was a brave woman, I... er... I loved her.' Morgan looked at Gwen quickly, wondering if she had offended her.

'I know how much she thought of you. She told me and I'm glad. I visited her now and again since she lived back in Barnsley, but I never really felt I knew her at all. She was so strong I couldn't understand how she could be so strong - not with her eyes and all that. She overwhelmed me, made me feel I'd failed.'

Morgan shifted to sit on the floor by Gwen's feet.

'Grandma and Grandad didn't used to like it when she came home to visit me. It unsettled them. All her modern clothes and brash ways. They said she was influenced by the devil. I heard them talking. 'Poor Grace, the devil has spoken to her and she dances to his tune.' She danced alright, I knew that, but it was in the theatre. People did dance and sing and pretend to be someone else in the theatre, that's what it was all about, surely.

'They never said I shouldn't love her - but I knew it would be bad to get too close. I didn't want the devil talking to me. Of course, I would have closed my ears to his whispering - but he has ways - oh, yes, he has ways.'

Donald came in with a tray of tea and biscuits. 'Right on cue,' thought Morgan.

He set the tray on the little table and motioned to Morgan to help herself. He looked at Gwen.

'Checking, I suppose,' thought Morgan. 'Checking to see I haven't done anything to her, although what he expects me to have done is beyond me.' She moved towards the tea tray and Donald left, satisfied that all was in order, for the time being anyway.

Gwen went on with her story.

'She never got all that far with the career she set herself up for. She got jobs here and there, then things changed and somehow the jobs got fewer. She didn't come home much at all after a while. I don't blame her. Grandma and Grandad made it clear they didn't approve of her.

'There was one time she came, and they all had a big row. I heard some of it, but they kept talking loud and soft so some of it got missed.

'She wanted to take me with her. *My daughter, after all. She's my child.* I could hear her crying, sobbing. I wanted to go and hug her but knew they'd only turn me away. *Pity you didn't think of that when you dumped her here with us.* Grandad's voice was quiet but deep and it carried. *I have a mother's rights*, she cried. *You have nothing,* he said - and then more stuff about me getting a good education and bettering myself and not ending up like her.

'She went off in tears that time - wet me through when she hugged me. But then, as Grandma said, she was an actress and could turn on the waterworks any time. Crying didn't wash with Grandma. I should know, I'd tried it plenty of times.'

Gwen leaned forward to touch Morgan's hair and it reminded her of when she'd been a child and her mother had visited her at Aunty Molly's. Gwen had loved to stroke her red mop and tease it out of its constraining grips and bands. Gwen was also remembering her own mother's visits, which although they were some sixty years ago, were still fresh and sore in her memory.

'Her visits got further apart after that until they stopped altogether. I was going to write to her - got good marks for my writing in school. But Grandma said best not. She said mother wouldn't write back and I'd be doing it for nothing. I did write to her though. Letters about school, about me, things I couldn't tell anyone else. But I never sent them. I didn't even know the address, not without asking Grandma.'

Morgan remembered the pictures she had painstakingly drawn for Gwen. She'd sent them to her, but Donald had returned them, addressed to Aunty Molly, saying that

Gwen would be too upset to be reminded of Morgan in this way. He'd said she wouldn't cope so please don't send any more. Morgan's hands reddened now with anger and she remembered tearing the pictures up and burning them in the stove.

She shook her hair loose from Gwen's hand and got up to walk around the room. She looked out of the window for a while at the neat garden. She remembered Grace's garden, the clumps of foxgloves, lupins and poppies, the birds, the magic. There was no magic in this garden, only control.

Morgan sat down again looking at Gwen, waiting for her to continue to get to the bit about why she, Morgan, was sent away. Gwen sat back her eyes turned to the ceiling.

She talked about how she'd met Donald when he was at the local college, about how they'd decided to marry. The war was coming, and nothing was certain. She gave a litany of her life in the reality of the war years. There was no lilt, no magic in her voice. Just facts; a grey trail of facts.

'It was hard, Morgan, it was like all the light in the world had faded. We just got on with managing day to day; made no plans. We didn't want to think about 'afterwards.' It seemed like tempting fate to make plans.

'We managed though! I'd had Dorothy in 1942 and Patricia in 1944. But by the end of it all I felt like my youth had disappeared. I had skipped over a big chunk of my life and now I was a mother of two little lives. They needed me. I gave up on the idea of training to be a teacher. Donald needed me. No time to dream, to study. Dreams were frivolous things, things that belonged to a past life, things that had no place in my life anymore.

'When the war was over, though, we did begin to climb

back into some kind of normality. It was like getting over the flu. Legs unsteady, you know, but every day a bit more effort and another step to vitality.

'And then, in 1953 I had David. That was it. Your father had a son and life was good. Kids young, free and healthy, war years behind us, prosperity a good experience. Donald was back working hard in school climbing the ladder, and we made a good showcase family for him. We had holidays in Flamborough on Molly and John's farm. They had caravans then - old ones but sound. It was grand to get out there in the fresh air and peace and quiet, away from town life.'

Morgan flinched at Molly's name.

'Molly was a good five years older than me and she'd tried and tried for a baby, but no luck. She doted on ours when we went over, she was so good with them.'

The old man and the old woman couldn't have any children of their own and so one day, the old woman baked a gingerbread boy and put it in the oven.

Morgan reached for a biscuit, offered one but her mother waved the plate away as though it was too much effort. She went on about the family holidays at Molly and John's and Morgan began to wonder if she was ever going to get to the point of why she was sent away. Gwen's eyes were half closed, and a gentle smile softened the tension on her sallow face.

Morgan got up and stretched. The room was warm, and Gwen's voice made her sleepy.

'I'd try to please Donald, you know, he loved those

holidays with his little family, especially since David was born. And at home I'd try to keep this little house clean and tidy, just how he liked it. It was hard work Morgan, really hard work sometimes. And now look at it. Look at my little house, gone to rack and ruin it has.'

Morgan looked around the room. It was immaculate.

'I used to have it like a new pin, every day, spotless, everything in its place, just like Donald liked it. He never got on with housework himself not then. He has to now. I'm poorly and I just can't do it.'

Morgan looked around for signs of medication, anything to show just what Gwen's illness was. There was nothing. She thought that it was almost as though Gwen had just given up, opted out. She looked older than her years, Morgan thought, small and fragile, like a chipped china doll that had to be locked away in case it became more broken.

'Of course, Dot and Pat help out when they can, but they have their own families. And David - well we don't talk about him anymore. Donald doted on him, his son. He had plans for him, couldn't wait for him to grow up. He left home when he was eighteen and never calls or writes. Donald says leave him - it's his funeral. But I miss him, I miss you. I've always missed you.'

Gwen looked at Morgan. Her eyes, now wide open, had filled with tears and she dabbed at them with a small lace-edged handkerchief. Morgan felt that the story was one that re-wound itself in Gwen's mind day on day, never reaching an ending, but always going back to the beginning again in one last attempt to make things come out right.

Silence hung for a while in the small, closeted sitting room. Gwen sat with her head bowed, as though the memories of the past were just too much for her. Morgan paced around the room, like a tiger waiting to pounce. She wanted to tear at the lace antimacassars, throw the clock to the floor and stamp on it and stop its patient ticking. She became breathless in her hatred of the neatness and order. She felt like a child again, out of place, not belonging. She wanted to shake Gwen, re-awaken her. She felt guilty that she had become frustrated so quickly with this rag doll of a woman.

'So why did you send me away?'

Silence again. The question became a solid thing, there in the room, blocking the narrow path that had been opening between them.

Morgan fingered the lace curtains at the window, her back turned to Gwen. She wanted to rip them down, let light in, remove the secrecy of this dark little room.

Then Donald came in, bustling around the teacups and clearing the table. It was almost as if he'd been listening at the door. Couldn't he leave them for a minute? Would he try to sweep her away with the biscuit crumbs?

'I didn't want to give you away.' Gwen was crying. Her shoulders moved up and down in a sad dirge of rhythm. 'I didn't want to. I didn't mean to. It was supposed to be just for a while until I got better.'

Morgan knelt in front of Gwen, holding both the frail woman's hands in hers, trying to stay their trembling.

'I know… I know I was an evil child.' She glanced at Donald, his face was set stern, his eyes judgmental. 'Aunty Molly used to tell me often enough. But later, Gwen.' She couldn't call her mother. 'Later, when I was grown up, you could have contacted me, sent for me.'

'You wouldn't have been welcome in this house.'

Donald's voice boomed and a little colour flushed in his cheeks. Morgan gasped at his animosity. What on earth had she done to deserve this?

Gwen was sobbing uncontrollably by now, sobbing and choking as she wilted into the armchair.

'He didn't think you were his!' She blurted out between sobs.

Morgan felt her throat tighten; she thought she was going to stop breathing. She looked at Gwen whose mouth was hanging open, although no sound now was coming out. Her eyes were wide open and looking at her as though somehow silently pleading with her to understand.

Morgan swallowed, deliberately breathed deeply, and tried to take control of herself. She hadn't come here for this.

'Come on now, I think that is enough, I'll get your coat.'

'He never thought you were his.'

Gwen was getting hysterical, pulling at the lace covers on the chair arm, worrying their threads. 'I'm sorry, I'm sorry, I'm sorry.'

Morgan looked at her and felt sorry for this weak, prematurely frail woman.

She remembered Grace and her strength, which even in her blindness never gave out. Maybe Grace was to blame for the way Gwen was now.

'It's OK.' Morgan backed off. She wanted more than anything to be out of that room. She needed to consider what had been said in the quiet of her room at college. She would talk to Ally. She moved to the door, colliding with Donald who held her coat in his extended arm.

'Thank you,' Morgan said quietly. She wanted to shout at

him, to confront him, but she took the coat and left the house.

On the journey home she could still hear Gwen's tortured voice. *He never thought you were his.* It was as though the words had been torn from her, dredged up from a thousand years ago.

Twelve

There's this little girl called Morgan whose mummy doesn't love her anymore and she has been sent to live with an old, old woman called Aunty Molly. Aunty Molly pretends to be nice and all the other people believe that she's nice. But Morgan is a magical child, and she knows different.

Just lately Morgan has taken to visiting old George. She goes to see him when he is working in his hut at the top of South Landing.

He is a small man, dark, hunched and always dressed in old denims and a fisherman's sweater. He smokes a pipe and reminds her a bit of Popeye on the television. George has been a fisherman and knows a lot about the sea. Sometimes he tells her stories about ships that were wrecked or about smugglers like Robin Lythe, who used to use the North Landing to bring their booty ashore. He tells about donkeys bringing up the fish in baskets hung over their backs. 'Aye, you could 'ear them donkeys trumping as they come up the track.'

George never asks Morgan about herself but sometimes she finds herself telling him all sorts of things. He doesn't give her answers, he just listens.

'Here's the pen, love. I've left the book open for you.'

She shakes herself like a dog. The rain hasn't stopped for two days. She hangs her raincoat next to George's at the back of the hut door, then opens the door again so that he can see out. It's part of the job that he should be able to see out no matter what the weather.

'Rub your hair on that towel, don't want you getting t' kin'

79

cough.' George points to a threadbare striped towel on the back of the chair. Morgan gives her tangled red mop a cursory rub then shakes her head, glad of the wet, glad of the freedom.

The book lies open on the slatted table next to George's mug and the primus and kettle. Morgan has been entering the boat details for him for a few weeks. He saves the information on scraps of paper to let her have the treat of writing them up in the old ledger.

'Only four out today, George?'

Morgan feels so responsible entering the names of fishermen in the big ancient looking ledger. After all, if they don't come back in, if they are out there in difficulties, who else will alert the coastguard?

'Aye, lass, fair weather fishers these off-comers. Only like taking the boats out with the sun on their backs. Don't know the half of it they don't.'

George has told her that when the maroon goes off that means a boat is in distress and the lifeboat crew will be on its way from wherever its members are and from whatever they are doing to take the lifeboat out and try to make a rescue.

'Even up-ended the new vicar once,' George laughs. 'There he was blessing the boat, stood up in all his regalia when the blower went.

'Well, they didn't stand on ceremony, they just up and launched her, vicar, regalia and all'.

When Morgan imagines the harsh, metallic boom, she sees the brave crew, piling into the lifeboat fresh from sawing up logs, from eating sausage and chips or from earthing up potatoes and racing off to the rescue. She sees a boat, lurching in mountainous waves, listing over, tipping the crew into churning, boiling waters. And sometimes she imagines the vicar, laid on his back with his black-robed legs in the air, blessing and blessing for all he is worth until he is on dry land again.

George was a fisherman when he was younger - not for a hobby, but like a lot of the community in this little village, to make his family's living. She asks him about his earring. Just the one he has.

'Why do sailors wear earrings?' She laughs. 'They're men not women.'

'Well, they do say that no matter what the weather, earrings are a whetstone to keen the edge of the eyes, keep them sharp,' he said. 'And you need keen eyes if you're a sailor. The fog is the worst. Silent and evil it is. Creeps up on you and before you know it, you're that lost, even though you knew where you was ten minutes a-fore. That mist creeps into your bones and before you know it, you're as cold as a boggle-eyed corpse.'

Morgan sits back to admire her neat, big handwriting marking four people 'OUT' on Saturday 4th December 1975. She writes 'heavy rain' under WEATHER CONDITIONS and 'poor' under VISABILITY.

George lights the primus and busies himself about his mug and milk.

'Betty's sent some butterflies.' He opens a square tin box and offers it to Morgan. She thinks Betty's buns are the best she's ever tasted but she won't admit it even to George. She knows she should be loyal to Aunty Molly no matter what. That's how things are done around here.

She turns back to the pages in the old ledger. She likes the neatness of it, the completeness of 'OUT' times and 'IN' times - the regular spidery writing that is George's and the large, neat blocks of her own entries that stand out proudly because they are different from the rest of the book.

'Tells a story that book does.' George is lighting up his pipe and Morgan knows he'll have a story of his own to tell once he has got it going to his satisfaction. She turns the pages back and back, noticing every now and then, the 'IN' column has scribbled notes instead of the usual logging time.

'No brains some of these Wessies.' George puffs sharply a few times on his pipe; tries to get air into his tobacco; tries to get it burning just right. 'I have 'em in the book when they go out and I tell 'em to register when they come back again, and then they change their minds and go off to some other landing place. They haven't the brains they were born with half the time.'

Morgan sees an entry that justifies George's ire.

'Called coastguard as two parties failed to log in at the end of the day. After all night search by lifeboat, parties returned unharmed following day. Explanation vague and given in anger.'

George sits back, facing the open door. His pipe is burning satisfactorily now, and she knows it is talking time. George talking that is. He likes to talk, and she thinks that once his pipe is lit, he will talk whether anyone is there to listen or not.

George turns to her and taps the stem of his pipe against the plate of butterflies, winking his approval as she helps herself to another.

'Did I ever tell you about the great gale of 1871...?'

Thirteen

There are trolls in the town who don't have to wait for the cover of night to make their mischief but move brazenly about the streets in the daytime. The little girl thinks she's found her princess, but the trolls mock her folly, bite her ears and pull at the fiery strands in her ebullient hair.

Round and round, three times four,
Keep on knocking at the little blue door.
Old dreams, new dreams, fine as dust,
Keep on knocking for you must, must, must.

On Morgan's second visit to her mother, she felt even more constrained in the dark, cheerless little room with its oh, so white nets that blocked out the daylight. Gwen had seemed even smaller in the blue, moquette armchair, and when Donald brought in the tea tray, she looked startled like some wild animal frightened for its life.

'I'm so glad you've come to see me again.'

Gwen fretted at the buttons on her cardigan, pulling and twisting them nervously.

'I'll come whenever you want me to.' Morgan put her hand on Gwen's, trying to calm her agitation.

They talked about trivia, about the weather and some inane programme they had both seen on TV. Morgan found herself searching her mother's face for something, she didn't know what. Something of the Gwen she remembered visiting her at Aunty Molly's, maybe, something to identify with. But all she could find was an old lady, old before her time no doubt, but old all the same.

She looked at the white, soft face, surrounded by harsh, wiry, grey streaked hair and she wanted to hug her so tightly, to try to squeeze some of that pink-cheeked young woman that had been her mother back into her.

Then Morgan made the mistake of asking about David. She'd half-remembered a boy being in the house all those years ago, and she remembered Gwen talking about him on that first visit a couple of weeks ago.

'So why did David leave?' The question hung in the air, an affront to the genteel surroundings.

'Oh.' Gwen looked haunted and stared at the door as if she expected David to come in and speak up for himself.

'Well, he just went off, you know.' She was twisting at her cardigan buttons again. 'Young boys do that don't they? He was keen to get on with his life. He… he...' Gwen put her head back against a bank of cushions placed behind her. She closed her eyes. Morgan wondered if she had suddenly fallen asleep. She wondered what she should do.

She found Donald in the kitchen, peeling potatoes. She almost laughed out loud at this dour and formally dressed man kitted out in a frilly, nylon apron.

'It's Gwen.' She had barely got the words out of her mouth when he tore off the apron, dried his hands and rushed into the sitting room.

'What did you say to her?' His voice was accusing as he smoothed at Gwen's hair, coaxed her to sit up. She steadfastly kept her eyes closed. She was shutting herself off.

'We were just talking about David...' Morgan was worried. She didn't understand what was happening.

Donald sat back on his heels, his back against Gwen's armchair.

'You just couldn't leave it alone, could you?' He glared at Morgan, his dislike for her apparent.

'But I don't understand.' She felt a lump in her throat in spite of herself. She felt this was her fault and didn't know why.

'David left home not long after you moved to Molly's. He needed his mother's attention, he needed my attention, but he couldn't have it because even when you weren't here everything was still about you.'

Donald stood up, smoothed down his trousers, his face was like thunder.

'But that's…'

'David thought I was a slut.' Gwen's voice was low and harsh, she did not open her eyes.

'We've been through this a million times, dear, he did not think you were a slut, he left because of the child.'

Even now Morgan realised her father could not utter her name. But what had she ever done to David?

'But that's such a long time ago. Haven't you made it up with him?' Morgan looked first at Donald then at Gwen, who still had her eyes glued shut.

She couldn't believe this. She almost wanted to laugh out loud at these two Plasticine figures looking for anything like something out of an old - fashioned melodrama.

'We had the odd postcard at first but then nothing.' Donald's voice stuck then moved on and Morgan wondered if he was going to cry. 'Nothing in all these years. He is my only son. You drove him away from this house and he's never been back.' Donald glared at her, his lips curling in disdain.

'I drove him away?' Morgan gave a wry laugh. 'I was only a child for God's sake. How could I have driven him away?'

She picked up her handbag, making to leave the room.

'It was me. It was me.'

Gwen was making small animal noises, crying and mewing. 'Donald thought I was a slut and so did my son. It's all my fault.'

She started to rock backwards and forwards crying noisily.

'I think you'd better go.'

Donald held the door open for Morgan to leave.

'I'm going, don't worry. I wonder what you've done to her all these years, Donald. What has she done to deserve ending up like this?'

Donald banged his fist on the door. Two pink circles appeared on his cheeks.

'I don't think you had better come to this house again.'

Morgan pecked Gwen on her wet cheek.

'Don't worry, I wouldn't come back to this mad house if you begged me.'

She felt her own tears welling up and rushed from the house before he had the satisfaction of seeing her cry.

And then there he was calling to her down the street. She wiped her tears on her sleeve and stopped and turned towards him. Her face, angry, was nearly in line with his own, grey and tired face. His hand tightened on her arm and she found herself surprised at how strong he was. Maybe his grey, ethereal figure belied his real substance.

'I said I would apologise, and she is looking out of the window for you to wave, to reassure her.' His voice was hard but desperate.

'And are you apologising?' Morgan was not ready to calm down, to play his game.

'I was a teacher for more years than I care to remember, and one thing I noticed was that each couple of school years, a familiar face would appear.'

Morgan tried to shake off his hand, which was still holding her in a vice-like grip.

'And I'd know, which family that child was from. It's as straight forward as that. It may not just be physical likeness, but there was always something to show - a mannerism, a colour of hair. The cuckoos always stood out.'

'And I'm the cuckoo?'

'Our Pat and Dot, they're mine, they are so like me I know what they are thinking. Our David, well... he's my son in so many ways, but he's also got so much of your mother in him.'

'He did well to run away from this mad house, though, smart boy'. Morgan was getting angrier by the minute. How dare he hold her arm so tight it was beginning to hurt. How dare he call her a cuckoo to her face?

Donald went on, not seeming to hear her. 'But you. You are not like any of us. She says you're mine but how could you be. You are not like her so you must be like your father whoever he is. Don't you see? Don't you see?'

Morgan looked back at the window. Gwen was peering out, her thin, pale face sad and anxious.

'But she's my mother. You can't deny that. Why don't you ask her who my father is? Why are you taking it out on me?'

'She's a sick woman. The time for questions passed a long time ago. She has always said you are my child. But look at you. Just look at you.'

Morgan was aware of her tall, strong appearance, her red mop. Her arm was throbbing where Donald still held it tight. She was beginning to think she couldn't care less about all this. She was beginning to wonder what she had let herself into.

'Well Grace said that I take after Gwen's father, he had red hair and a bit of spirit'.

Donald dropped her arm. 'Grace had no right talking to you about family matters,' he said pompously. 'What did she know anyway, she abandoned her child, never gave her a thought. How dare she interfere?'

Morgan laughed, shook her arm loose and flexed it up and down. She turned to the ghostly face at the window again and laughed as she waved extravagantly to Gwen.

'It's alright, *father*.' She was sure in her own mind now. 'I'll play your game of happy families - but you should know this. Grace and I spent a long time together and became very good friends. She never doubted for one minute that I am your genuine issue. She welcomed me into the family long before my father ever did. And what's more, she has left me her house as a legacy. She knew me the minute we met, but then she relied on much more than her own eyes, much more. Why can't you see the truth - it's right in front of you.'

And with another extravagant wave, Morgan left. She walked quickly down the road, vowing never to see him again.

Donald stood staring after her, his mouth opening and closing like a grey cod fish floundering on the pavement.

Fourteen

Morgan has a new friend at school called Charley Lovack. Charlotte, really, but she'd rather have Charley. Charley hasn't lived in Flamborough for very long. The girls are going to help the toads across the road come February. Charley's family has moved into Flamborough because her parents think it's healthier for children to be brought up here rather than in a rough city or a dirty town. Charley's mother thinks that *saving toads is a good idea, and that it shows initiative and a social conscience in this day and age of consumerism*. Aunty Molly thinks it is daft and will end up in mess and dirt. 'Toads have managed on their own without help so far, I can't see why they need yours or anyone else's now!'

Morgan told Charley about all the frogs and toads that are flattened on the road at South Landing every year. 'When it's the spawning season there are corpses every day. Every day! Come February, there will be more little dead frogs flat as pancakes. There will be all these dried frog-shaped leaves, on the road every day.'

'That's really sad.' Charley was near to tears after Morgan graphically set the scene. The girls decided to plan a campaign to save the frogs and toads when that year's spawning season comes around. In the dark winter evenings, they spend time drawing pictures, marking out maps and drawing up a timetable of who will watch and when. 'They'll cross that road anyway.' Morgan has read up on frog and toad behaviour and she's asked George about it. She is keen to show her expertise.

'They have gone that way to the pond year after year for as long as the pond has been there, so they aren't going to change now.'

'So, we have to throw them into the pond?'

Charley sounds dubious.

No, we have to make sure it's safe for them to cross the road.'

'Like lollipop ladies.' Charley giggles at the scene she is imagining which is like something from a TV cartoon.

'No not like lollipop ladies.' Morgan is scornful, this is serious after all. 'More like... well more like... Oh, I don't know, that's what we have to plan.'

Aunty Molly comes in with Chorley cake slices, the white icing glistening like snow.

'Maybe you should kiss them all, the toads I mean. After all, one of them might be a prince.' She laughs and laughs, her face wobbling and red, as she sets down the cakes and milk for the girls. 'Maybe they've been coming up that road all these years just waiting for someone to kiss them and break that spell - maybe I'll come and kiss a few, I could do with a rich prince to take me away from all this.' She goes off in shrieks of laughter.

Morgan puts the books away and sighs. 'Maybe we could work on this at your house next time'.

She likes having Charley as her friend. She is so different from the other children at school. She and Morgan seem to see the school, the village, life even, through the same pair of eyes. It isn't as though the children in the village don't welcome newcomers in. They are so interested in new people they can't leave them alone. It is as though they have to assess you, label you and then initiate you into the laws of their territory. They don't want any of the baggage you come with, you leave that at the village boundary. You either clone in or you stay forever out in the cold.

Morgan and Charley have joined the sword dancing

classes and hope that they might be chosen for the display on Boxing Day. Of course, there isn't a lot of chance, when year after year the dance team is made up of the same families. But still, as Charley says, 'nothing will change if we don't make it.' Morgan is doubtful, though. She's lived here longer than her friend and she knows how clannish they all are. Still, she loves the stories that go with the dancing and she loves the patterns the dancers make over the crossed swords.

Charley's mum is also teaching the pair of them to knit. Aunty Molly can knit of course, but Morgan doesn't fancy that brown kind of knitting that is such an effort you have to stick out your tongue and bite it the whole time. That's Aunty Molly's style and all that comes out of it are rough socks for Uncle John to wear around the farm.

Charley's mum, though, she knows the sort of knitting that flows from one needle to the other, elegantly, swiftly like some beautiful machine. And the colours change all the time. Oranges, pinks, pillar-box red and duck's-beak yellow. They have competitions to name the colours and Morgan always does well.

'You've got a real creative streak, Morgan.'

Charley's mum smiles, and Morgan basks under the warmth of her praise. She teaches the girls to knit squares and they plan to make up blankets to send to Africa. Morgan doesn't tell Aunty Molly, though. She'll make her do some rough brown squares and Morgan doesn't think that little African children would like those at all.

Morgan and Charley walk around the village, arm in arm, sit on the swings on the Green side by side, share a talking extravaganza, which seems to be never ending. Aunty Molly likes this new friend and hopes that some of her good manners will rub off on Morgan. Charley whispers, 'Miserable old gannet' and the pair of them giggle through supper, the sound of it unsettling the shadows in the dark corners of the room.

*

After the Michaelmas half-term at Flamborough School, it is always time to start making Christmas things.

The smaller children are involved in cutting out and making decorations and for the older children it is the nativity play. After so many enactments, you would think some originality would be welcomed, but no. In Flamborough School it is always done by the letter of some unwritten law, down to the last tea-towelled shepherd and blue-cloaked Mary.

Morgan is bored with the preparations. She has seen them year after year. Always exactly the same. She has been given the job of helping to paint the scenery for the play. But it is just a matter of painting over last year's fading colours. Morgan thinks she will add a little originality of her own and starts to paint little rabbits and squirrels on the bottom of the backdrop and then a spaceman and then a creditable Yogi Bear. Miss Appleby takes her off that job and asks her to re-paint the manger brown. 'What, over last year's brown?' she asks wearily. Miss Appleby doesn't bother to reply but sighs as she has been doing with Morgan for half a term now.

Morgan paints with a will though and sings carols at the top of her voice just to give something to the job. Aunty Molly has been singing carols at the top of her voice for weeks now and Morgan tries to copy her trilling soprano. Miss Appleby smiles to herself but wonders how long before Mr Huxstable comes in to complain.

'Morgan.' She calls her over and gently removes the brown paint laden brush from her hand. 'Morgan, why don't you like the Christmas story?'

Morgan considers the question. She takes it absolutely as a genuine question and seeks a truthful answer.

'I don't 'not like' the story, miss, but it is just a story.' She wipes her hands down her green school skirt, immediately regretting it.

'But, Morgan, don't you know it is a true story?'

'Most stories are true, miss, but we don't go on and on about them year after year without a bit of a change. I mean I know it's a perfectly good story but so are lots of others. Why this one over and over until it makes you never want to hear it again?'

'But what do you think the story is telling us? Most stories are telling us something aren't they?'

Morgan thinks of the hundreds of stories she has read in the books that her mother keeps sending her. She has read them over and over and loves some and hates some. But she has never before thought that they are telling her something other than a story.

'I don't know'. Her face is troubled as though she has suddenly found out a vast flaw in her universe.

'The story of Jesus is telling us how to love our fellows, no matter what they do to us, and to forgive them for anything that they do, no matter how hard that is.' Miss Appleby feels quite proud of her precis of the whole of the Christian philosophy.

'Now,' she smiles, 'take this cardboard and foil and sit over there and make me some stars. And think, Morgan, think about what I have just said.'

Morgan sits down and wonders for a while about whether to make a five-pointed star or a six pointed one. She doesn't suppose it matters as she knows stars aren't that shape anyway. She thinks it will be different to make a seven pointed one and that keeps her busy for a while. She smooths the kitchen foil to a silver sheen. She wonders if Aunty Molly knows what the story of Jesus means. She spends all that time going to chapel and singing the hymns. And yet, when Morgan is naughty, Aunty Molly still puts her in the cellar, in the smelly, black and scary cellar to think about the error of her ways. Not that it happens much these days, the cellar that is. Morgan has learned over the years what Aunty Molly will and won't put up with.

Morgan doesn't argue back anymore, she sets her mouth in a straight line just like Aunty Molly and they stare at each other, each one keeping their own peace.

Fifteen

Dear Donald

I can't call you 'father', not because I don't believe you are my father, more because you've never been a father to me. So, I will call you 'Donald' and my mother, 'Gwen'. I think it is best to make that clear. As I write this letter, I'm not sure I'll be sending it. I probably will, though, in the hope that you will read it - unlike the ones I wrote at Aunty Molly's when I was a child. They always came back unopened. I always thought that whatever I had done to make you send me away must have been really terrible and evil. I could never understand why you would not read my letters, but I kept on sending them, didn't I? Did Gwen ever know about them, or did you just send them back without telling her? But this is not meant to be about recrimination.

I am writing this letter to set out in my opinion, why I truly believe that you are my father. I am not doing this for gain, either emotional or material. I can stand on my own two feet. I want nothing from you. But speaking to Gwen, oh, that has touched something in me.

I know you think of me as being hard and defiant, but you can't know all of me. Anyway, for the record, I think of you as being pig-headed and stubborn, so maybe we have something in common after all.

It is strange, isn't it, that your own child should be the outsider looking in, but from where I am standing all I see is Gwen hurting, wanting to be absolved from some false sin you have saddled her with, wanting to get to know her own daughter and to see her son again. I mean, why would she go on all these years if it wasn't the truth. She could have admitted the affair, if there was one, been forgiven and moved on. You are my father, she never had a lover, and I think deep down you know it.

95

Something I remember from the time before I was sent to Aunty Molly's, was how we, you and I, would spend time in the garden together.

I have never lost the love of the soil - watching seeds sprout and grow. Sometimes I thought this was because I grew up on a farm, but no. It goes back much further to some moments between us, which I hope you can reach back to.

I remember you telling me the story of Airmid's mantle, as we planted our herb garden in the spring the last year I was at home. Airmid picked each of 365 herbs which grew on her dead brother's grave and which would cure the ailments for each of the 365 organs of the human body and she arranged them on her cloak according to their properties. Her father, jealous of his son's healing legacy, shook the cloak and lost the pattern.

I know you will remember telling me this. I certainly have never forgotten that special feeling of hearing a story, gently told.

Donald, maybe whatever animosity is between us now can never be undone. I am not appealing to you in this letter to own me or to love me. I am appealing to you to put Gwen at rest about all this. You are right, she is a sick woman, I could see that. I will not interfere in your lives to make things worse between you, but I only do this for her sake.

Morgan

*

Donald had grudgingly made it clear that she could visit Gwen whenever she wished, as long as she telephoned him first as sometimes her mother was not herself and would see no-one.

Morgan had just finished her course at college and was on her way to Flamborough to take a holiday before looking for a first teaching job if she had passed, of course.

'How did your exams go?' Donald held the door open stiffly.

'Fine, I think.' She smiled. 'I intend to keep the teaching thing in the family.' And she nudged him playfully.

'Hmm.'

Donald obviously did not want to continue the conversation and showed her into the living room without another word.

Gwen was sitting in the same blue moquette chair in which she always sat. The antimacassars were pristine, the smell of polish was almost overpowering. Morgan bent to kiss her and to hand her the clutch of roses she had brought.

'They are lovely, Morgan. You must take something back with you from the garden. We have lots of flowers at the moment.'

Morgan could feel the walls of the neat living room moving in, the air was heavy with the scent of the roses, the atmosphere was tense. She could hear Donald bringing tea, the cups rattling to his measured tread along the hallway outside.

He delivered the tea and digestive biscuits to the walnut coffee table and then left, announcing his plans to tidy up the borders in the garden.

'He spends all day out there at this time of year.' Gwen's voice had a whine to it. 'I don't know what he finds to do, the garden never has a leaf out of place.'

Morgan laughed. 'Oh, that's men, like to be little boys, digging and delving.'

Gwen smiled. 'How are you, dear, you look very well.'

Whenever Morgan visited Gwen, she could never get over the feeling that she was dealing with a small child.

The conversation had to follow safe routes, familiar patterns, so as not to unsettle this frail woman, framed in the weak sunlight that passed through the heavily brocaded and laced windows.

'I was so sad when Grace died.' At last, she'd found what felt like a safe moment to mention her grandmother.

'Ah, well, she was 83 and she didn't have such a bad life you know.' Gwen sipped at the milky tea.

'She left her house to me in her will, I expect you know about that.' Morgan felt flustered, guilty, as though she had stolen something.

'Oh, yes. That was really nice of her wasn't it, dear?' Gwen picked at the lace, inserting her finger into the filigree work. 'Well, we don't need anything, do we. I had thought she might have left it to Dot or Pat, but then they didn't visit her that often, not these days. And you were very much in her mind, she told me.'

Morgan thought about her visits to Grace. She hadn't expected the generosity of being left the house. She had visited it only once since Grace's will was announced and had felt she could never go back there again, that somehow, she didn't deserve it.

Gwen seemed to be falling asleep in the warmth of the room. Morgan took her cup and put it back on the tray.

'Would you like me to open a window?'

'Oh, no.' Her mother seemed to be alarmed. 'Donald doesn't open the window in here, not ever.'

Morgan sat down. How could Gwen put up with this place, these constraints.

She felt like racing around the room flinging open every

window, letting some glorious air in.

'I was supposed to visit her the day she died.'

Morgan could keep it in no longer.

'Visit who, dear?' Gwen seemed vague, sleepy again.

'Grace. My grandmother. I was supposed to visit her on the day she died.'

Morgan was almost shouting but checked herself. She didn't want Donald rushing in. She needed to get this off her chest.

'Just as well you didn't.' Gwen screwed up her face, picturing a memory. 'It was days before anyone found her. She'd had a fall. Not a pretty sight by all accounts. One of the neighbours phoned us and Donald went straight away to sort it out. It seemed she'd been on a chair looking for something and had fallen.'

Grace had promised Morgan a photograph of Sean. She said she had a spare one somewhere. Suddenly she knew this was what she had been on the chair looking for. Why hadn't she waited for her to help?

'If I had gone to visit when I was supposed to, maybe I could have got help. Maybe she would have lived. I can't bear to think of her lying there, no-one to help her, no-one.'

Suddenly she was crying. She let the tears flow without check. Gwen watched her. The clock struck four.

'Donald will be coming in soon.'

She made it sound like a warning and Morgan wiped her eyes, blew her nose, composed herself.

'Morgan,' Gwen's voice was strangely urgent. 'Morgan, it wasn't your fault. I could say that I should have visited that day or that Pat or Dot should have visited. We are none of us to blame. Grace died, and God rest her soul.'

Donald came in as he always did, almost as though he had been listening at the door. 'You are looking tired, my dear.' He was fussing around Gwen, placed her feet on a small pouffe, straightened the antimacassars.

'I had better be going.' Morgan felt weary herself all of a sudden and moved to kiss Gwen goodbye.

'You'll come again?' Gwen held her hand tightly and wouldn't let go.

'Of course, I will. I'll come and see you again after my holiday in Flamborough.'

Later at the garden gate, she asked Donald, 'What is she taking, Gwen? She's half asleep most of the time. What on earth are you giving her?'

'Only what the doctor prescribed. They are to calm her down. She was in such a state when her mother died. I hope you didn't mention…'

'Oh, no.' Morgan was angry with herself for giving in to him.

'Here is some lilac for you to take home, Gwen insisted I cut some for you.'

Morgan took the large bunch of heavy blossoms, which were well past their best. Grace had loved lilac. She had loved the perfume, the softness of the large cone-shaped flowers. Was this Gwen's way of telling her she was forgiven?

Sixteen

Welcome, Moon of the Fiery God! The Sun at full strength bathes the long days and short nights in heat. We draw the fullness of the light into ourselves.
(Celtic ritual)

Ed was off to the Dog. As if it hadn't been hot enough today out on the tractor, his mum had to add her two pennyworth, nagging him about getting another job - making the most of his education. It was hard work on the farm, he'd grant her that, but he loved it.

As he'd told her, he could put his education to use making the farm a more viable business. It made perfect sense to him, and to his dad, so why was she being such an old moaning Minnie.

The Dog had some tables out under a wooden awning. It would be cooler out there. James was there and Ed joined him, sinking into his seat with a crash. 'You getting them in me old mate?'

James smiled, 'Certainly my good friend.' He winked at Ed.

'They've got two new barmaids just started, and one of them is a real looker. I could be up and down to that bar all night, I reckon.'

It was busy in the courtyard. There were quite a few visitors in the village this time of year and they liked to bring their kids down to the Dog. Ed relaxed. His dad would be down later, no doubt, and he would talk to him about the farm. He'd be on his side he knew. His dad was looking tired these days. Ed knew he welcomed all the help he could get. And fair enough, he didn't earn a lot more than board and lodgings, but he had ideas, he had plans. The front of the awning looked out onto the quiet village road. Not much traffic passed. It wouldn't, not until July and August when the visitors would make the place feel like it was bursting at the seams. But in this early promise of summer, Ed felt that everything and anything was possible.

James came back with the beers.

'Well, did you get anywhere?' He'd noticed a smirk on his friend's face.

'Her name's Alexandra. Just finished college. Going to be a teacher. I'll tell you what, Ed, she can rap my knuckles any time.'

'And the other one?'

'Oh, you'll know the other one. She used to live here. Go and have a look'.

He didn't need to. Suddenly she was there; tall, imposing, her hair wild and red like the burning bush in the bible. She looked a bit familiar, but he couldn't really place her as being from round Flamborough.

James knew it all. 'You know, she used to live with Molly and John Flowerdew. Bit of a wild girl, always in trouble at school. Morgan Parish.'

He went on but Ed didn't hear him, not properly. He was watching Morgan collecting glasses, emptying ashtrays. He couldn't take his eyes off her. She came over.

'Hm, been working up a sweat, have we?' Morgan nodded towards Ed's vest, playfully.

'I was hot, didn't have time to get changed.' Ed was flustered, wishing he'd put on a proper t-shirt, not left on his scruffy working vest.

'I know, you're just showing off your muscles, aren't you?'

Morgan laughed, picked up the ashtray and emptied it into a bucket.

'No.' He was getting hotter. 'It's just what I work in, honestly.'

'Calm down, Ed, mate, she's just winding you up.'

'You look very handsome in it anyway,' Morgan moved away to another table. Ed put his head in his hands, she'd been making fun of him. Why hadn't he got changed? She was lovely.

James went off for another pint. He'd drunk the other one in record time. It was Ed's round, but he grabbed the money from him and went to the bar.

'They've been at college together, Alexandra and Morgan. They're friends.' James had been at the bar for about half an hour.

'A man could die of thirst while you're on the pull.' Ed was disgruntled.

'I should steer clear of that Morgan, though, mate. She was trouble back then and I don't suppose she's changed that much.'

'Trouble? Now I can do trouble. I get trouble every day, what with Mum going on about me bettering myself, and the old tractor breaking down half the time. That sort of trouble I can do without. But if she's trouble, well that's the sort I'd welcome with open arms.'

'You go and get them in then, ask her out.'

'I can't, James, mate. Not dressed like this. You get them in, your round anyway. Tomorrow I'll be in dressed properly.'

'Can't your mate walk at all then?' Morgan pulled at the beer pump steadily, like she'd been doing it all her life.

'You've embarrassed him, talking about his vest and that.'

'Oh, poor lamb, he doesn't look the sensitive type.'

'He's not, normally, but he fancies you.'

Morgan put her head back and laughed. 'Fancies me? Doesn't he know I'm trouble?' And she pulled a face, to indicate her horrible potential.

'I told him, but he still fancies you.' James liked her directness. He began to wonder whether all the stories about her were true after all. This village could be vindictive to people who didn't fit in.

Morgan held her hand out for the money. 'Hey, Ally,' she called to her friend, without turning from James, 'when's our next night off?'

Morgan and Ally were staying for the summer on the Thornwick Bay Caravan Park. It was a large site and yet so corralled onto the headland that you wouldn't see it until you were just about there. It was like an oasis in a desert for the off-comer visitors who peopled it. The stately arms at its entrance belied the brashness of its bars, cafes, Treasure Island and Bingo. The swimming pool in high season became a wall of screams and laughter. There was constant noise and yet none of it was heard from the village.

This was late June, and the visitor population was only just a trickle. However, the girls were still privy to hot dog and bacon smells, which hung out on the sea breeze. The track-suited youths went around in clutches, one notch more cheerful than the ones they'd seen hanging around on night's out in Sheffield. This lot teemed into Treasure Island and dallied for the day among the spewing fruit machines and the plock of pool balls.

Yet even though the villagers relied on the income from these visitors, they preferred this kind of townie enjoyment to be kept apart up on the cliff waste. The odd few would stray down to the village where the bars, fish and chip shop and souvenir shop relied on their trade. But they were eyed suspiciously, welcome only on the villagers' terms. Morgan had lived in the village for thirteen years but had never been accepted as one of them. She had been glad to leave to go to college but now she was surprised to find how much she had missed it. She took Ally round all the coves, special places, secret hidden places and acted like she was a guide. She took her up Lighthouse Road, a long walk on a narrow footpath, which seemed like a grey ribbon leading them to the sky.

'I thought you said it was always cold and windy here.'

Ally was striding out, loving the open space and the golden sunshine.

'I'm sure it always was, then.'

Morgan took off her cardigan and tied it round her waist. 'I can't remember when there was ever a day like this. There must have been, I suppose, I just can't remember it that's all.'

A light breeze sprang up as they got nearer to the sea. They sat a while facing the old lighthouse, which stood on the land belonging to the golf club.

It was a white, fat tower, four storeys high built of chalk. It had been built so that a coal or brushwood fire could be lit on the top, but Morgan had never found anyone who could tell her it had ever been used like that.

'The present lighthouse was built in 1806,' Morgan read

from a tourist leaflet, 'following the loss of 174 ships off the Head in the late 18th Century.'

They sat there thinking about the horrors of sea disasters and all around them there wasn't a sound, apart from the odd car passing and the trill of birdsong.

'Aren't there any people living up here?' Ally was quite taken with the unusual peace of the place.

'People playing golf.' Morgan pointed towards the back of them to the manicured fairways and greens. They could see the odd tiny form, like metal caste models a child might have set out there in a game.

'There's something surreal about this.' Ally got up, shaking herself. 'It's like a place suspended in time.'

They carried on walking up to the new lighthouse.

'Just look at those bungalows,' said Morgan, pointing to an arc of buildings behind the lighthouse. 'One car each, garage containing full complement of gardening tools. No villagers up here. This is the domain of the NR.'

'The NR?'

'Nouveau Retired.'

'No chance of us having a house up here then. Not yet a while, anyway.'

The girls laughed, moved on.

'I really love this place.' Morgan was sitting with Ally, Ed and James outside the Viking. It had been another idyllic sunny day and they'd spent the afternoon walking. 'I mean, there's just something about its wide empty roads, its peacefulness, it just draws me.'

'And its handsome young men.' James clinked his glass on Ed's.

'I know what you mean.'

106

Ed leaned back in his chair, stretched lazily.

He sat up suddenly. 'I mean about loving the place, not about the handsome young men.' He blushed and accepted their laughter in good humour. He'd taken the afternoon off and it felt good.

'It's strange though.' Morgan scanned the view; started by looking out to sea, then went around 180 degrees and finished by looking down to the village. 'The place itself seems so big and so perfect, and yet when you think of the people that live here, their lives seem shut in somehow, do you know what I mean?'

'Haven't a clue,' said James rocking himself on his chair.

'Would anyone like another drink?'

'I know what you mean.' Ed hung on Morgan's every word. James kept pulling his leg, said he looked like a little puppy with his tongue hanging out. 'They're friendly enough here but they only want to know about themselves. They don't want anything to do with what's outside this village. Not really.'

Morgan nodded in agreement.

'Who cares?' said Ally, bored with the serious line of the conversation. 'We're on holiday! Let's act like it. I'll get them in, James, what are you having?'

'I'll come and help you carry them.' James got up, flung his arm around Ally, drawing her into the pub.

'Are you cold?' Ed felt the breeze spring up with the tide change. It whipped down the long open road and Morgan had shivered.

'No, not really.'

She held his gaze, wondering about this man, this farmer, this person born and bred in the village and yet still able to see it from the outside.

He held his hands out. 'Here, let me feel'. He rubbed her cold hands in his, searching for a spark.

Now that his armour was clean, his helmet made into a complete head piece, a name found for his horse, and he confirmed in his new title, it struck him that there was only one more thing to do: to find a lady to be enamoured of. For a knight errant without a lady is like a tree without leaves of fruit and a body without a soul.
Cervantes, Don Quixote (1605)

Ed Bainton loved Morgan Parish. It was official. At least to Ed it was official, in his head. Of course, his mother was onto him.

'People have seen you with that Morgan Parish, you know. They keep telling me. Your Ed with that red head who works in the pub. You want to steer clear, lad, mark my words. She's no good that girl. Everybody says so.'

Ed remembered the walk they'd had on the cliffs. Morgan had told him he was her Knight on shining Tractor, rescuing her from the locals' gossip.

'You're too gullible, Ed.' His mother just wouldn't leave it alone. 'You'll believe anything she says but she's up to no good, I'm sure of it.'

He got up from the breakfast table, leaving his food half eaten.

'What do you know about her, anyway?' He pulled on his boots at the kitchen door.

'I know plenty, believe me. Didn't she used to live with Molly Flowerdew? Well, Molly has told me things about that girl that would make your hair curl. She's wild, Ed. Got the devil in her. I mean, her own family gave her up, you know, they couldn't deal with her shenanigans.'

He laughed. His mother liked to get her own way, but she was dabbling in the ridiculous as far as he could see. 'Got the devil in her? Well, I don't mind a bit of that. Could make life interesting.'

'I'm not joking, Ed. Poor Molly spent hours on her knees in that chapel when the girl lived with her. She prayed for the demons to leave her body, she prayed until her knees were sore. But it never made a difference. The girl went her own way, the devil's way.'

Ed was down the path, moving as fast as he could from her ranting. He'd seen other people looking sideways at Morgan in the street. What did they think she was going to do?

'This village,' he muttered to himself, 'it's a wonder some of them can see over the mountains they've made out of molehills.'

He'd been working hard. They had to have a good harvest this year. His father's health was not good. They didn't talk about it, but he knew.

They'd had their son late in life, Maggie and Peter, and Ed realised that they'd have to be bowing out of the farm soon. He had to work especially hard this year and build up the business. It was all falling onto his shoulders.

There were no fortunes to be made round here but with a bit of planning and a lot of luck they'd be alright.

The sun forced sweat onto his head as he sat in the cab of his tractor. He had to squint to see where he was going. It was going to be a hot one today.

Morgan, told him stories about the courtly knights and she stroked his hair as they lay on the soft dry sand of the North Landing beach.

She told him stories of dragons and castles and damsels in distress. It was like hearing echoes of childhood.

Clouds overshadowed them as the afternoon wore on. She kissed him, told him what a gentleman he was, called him 'Sir Knight,' pulled close to his body for warmth and protection.

He told her he wanted to catch her in his arms and carry her off to a dark cave where they could live together forever, away from the world, away from everyone. She laughed and flung herself on top of him.

'You're not carrying me off anywhere, Ed Bainton.' She lay all her weight on him, while he tried to push her off.

'You're heavy, Morgan.' He gasped and spluttered, taken by surprise at her strength.

'Beware, I am the Morrigan.'

She deepened her voice, put her face close to his. 'I will take you in my power.'

They laughed and rolled in the sand until both fell exhausted side by side, fingers gently entwined.

'Morgan, I truly love you.' There was silence until the sharp cry of a gull stabbed the lull. She sat up so that she could see his face, his eyes. No-one in her life had ever said that before.

'You don't know me, not really.'

'Yes, I do.'

He was earnest, sat up to face her. Took both her hands in his. 'I know what I need to know. You are beautiful, magical and you make me feel alive.'

He looked so boyish, so vulnerable. Morgan felt like a sorceress who'd charmed the young prince into loving her. She was uncomfortable and didn't know how to respond.

'Let's go and get something to eat,' she said at last, trying to break the spell that held them there in limbo. She released her hands from his and got up.

'No.' He stood facing her, smiling. 'I'm not hungry. Don't worry, Morgan, I won't 'plight my troth' any longer this afternoon. Not that I didn't mean what I said but I can see you are uncomfortable with it.'

'It's not that...' She felt she had hurt his feelings.

'It's OK,' he whispered gently. 'Let me get shells for you and we'll spend the rest of the afternoon building castles.'

'In the sand?' she asked.

'In the sand.'

And ever the more Sir Gareth beheld that lady, the more he loved her; and so, he burned in love that he was past himself in his reason; and forth toward night they yede into supper.

And Sir Gareth might not eat, for his love was so hot that he wist not where he was. Sir Thomas Malory, Le Morte d'Arthur (c. 1470)

'The horizon isn't straight,' said Morgan. 'You'd expect it to be, but it isn't.'

The girls sat side by side on the beach at the Dyke. It was early evening. The great curve of land hooked around the bay protectively.

'It makes you wonder what is beyond the horizon.' Ally squinted through half open eyes, trying to see.

'Deep-sea divers? Seals? Oh, I know, catfish, cod, lugworms and rotting sailors.'

'Ugh.'

'I used to believe some things were out there because it said so in books, like Neptune and his trusty trident and crown of seashells. When I was a child, I thought he was a

111

bit like a Jesus of the sea, blessing the fishes.'

'I thought Davy Jones's locker was real. I used to think that if all the pirates had ghostly lockers, then how did Hans and Lotte Hass find space to explore.'

Morgan laughed at the picture Ally conjured up.

'Well, maybe Atlantis was a city of highrise lockers - that might solve the problem.'

They had brought sticks from the woods, and paper and barbecue coals to light a fire. The flames licked reluctantly at first, as though sensing the tide. But the tide was out as far as it could be and the fire, encouraged by the sea breeze, soon caught on.

'The sea is so relentless.' Morgan passed Ally a can of beer.

'Tide upon tide making the subtlest of changes, pushing time up and down the beach.'

'Someone in the pub said there was nothing between us here and Russia.'

'Under the sea. Just think, Ally, there might be gold and jewels leaking from uncharted wrecks.'

'Ooh, yes, or a whitewashed sailor's skull with sapphire eyes and a ruby in place of a mouth.'

'Or Captain Cat looking for his dead soulmates.'

They each sat a while, drinking their beer and wallowing in imagination.

Ally broke the silence. 'I wish we could stay in this day forever.'

'This is the longest day, Midsummer's Eve, it would certainly be the day to keep forever if that was possible.' Morgan poked a few more sticks into the fire.

It had been a warm day and the fire was not really needed.

But no doubt it would be cool later.

'I've enjoyed being here, Morgan, I'm glad you fixed it up for us. I don't want it to end. I don't like to think about the future.'

'Why not, you've got a job lined up, your future is all mapped out.'

Morgan hadn't started looking for a job herself yet, she didn't know where she wanted to be. She had thought this break would give her space to think, but somehow the place was grabbing at her, pulling her back into its clutches. She couldn't decide if that was a good thing or not.

'I know, I know.' Ally hugged at her knees, stared out to sea. 'But I'm nervous, you know, first job and all that. It would be a lot easier to just stay here.'

'What and be a barmaid all your life,' Morgan laughed. 'It's not like this in winter you know, it's dark and cold and you don't see anyone for hours on end. Except for the ghost of the White Lady, of course, who may pass through your room in the chill of a winter's evening.' She stood up, arms wide, with a ghoulish expression on her face.

'What's going on?' James scrambled down onto the beach, mimicking Morgan's antics.

'We were talking about the White Lady,' Ally explained as he came to sit next to her. Ed wasn't far behind, his soft approach going almost unnoticed.

'The White Lady,' he echoed. 'What are you doing filling her head with that nonsense, Morgan Parish?' He took her hands and kissed her gently.

Ally could see how things were going between the pair of them. She and James, well they were having fun, they were having a good time. But the other two, well, it was beginning to look serious. Ally was anxious for her friend.

113

She knew she'd had precious little love in her life, and she didn't want her grabbing at this and getting hurt.

'We were just talking about the future, about moving on.' Ally passed the boys a beer each out of the basket.

'No, we weren't.' Morgan stirred the embers of the fire. 'We were talking about how lovely it would be to keep this day forever.' She leaned back, her head on Ed's chest.

'Well, we couldn't do that, it's impossible.' Ally was sharp. 'I was just daydreaming. The reality of it is we have to make plans. We have to move on.'

More fires were starting up now and quite a cluster of young people were gathering on the beach. Someone had brought a guitar and the sounds of gentle strumming shimmered in the heavy June air.

'The idea on Midsummer's Eve is to make sure that we preserved and stored as much of the sun's energy as we can. It's important to show the sun god that we appreciate her so that the harvest will be a good one.'

Morgan had been reading about Celtic mythology.

'Oh, we've moved from ghosts to pagan gods now, have we?'

James was thinking it would be nice to take Ally for a walk on the cliff top, just for a bit of time to themselves. His finger was tracing the line of exposed skin on the nape of her neck. He was planning his next move.

'Go on Morgan,' urged Ally, shaking James's away, sitting up expectantly. 'Tell us some more about preserving and storing. You know, all that you were saying. Maybe we can keep this day forever.'

'Well, bonfires were a big thing, they would be circular and built in a ritually significant place.'

James laughed. 'Folks round here have been building fires on this beach, like forever. We like a bit of hot stuff.'

He made a grab for Ally, but she jumped up to hand round more drinks.

'They would be lit precisely at sunset and their powers would consecrate the growing crops; protect them.'

'We could do with protection on our crops.' Ed knew the farm needed a good harvest, it could be do or die this year.

Morgan went on, 'Well, then the young people of the community would plan boisterous and reckless games with the fire far into the night.'

'Boisterous and reckless sounds good.' James had caught up with Ally and they were larking about around the fire in mock dances, flinging their arms and legs around as though they were mad things.

Morgan and Ed were laughing so much at their antics they decided to join in, it looked like fun.

'I don't think the gods would be impressed,' James said, pulling a ridiculous face and setting them all off laughing again.

'And then the embers of the fire would be thrown onto the corn,' Morgan added eventually, collapsing onto the sand.

'No'. Ed was horrified, 'Didn't it set the corn alight. It's a wonder they had any crops left.'

'Or the fire would be taken symbolically through the fields, like in a procession of torches, you know. Not battery torches - fire torches.'

'We could do that,' said Ally. 'We could take fire through Ed's corn.'

James started rummaging about in the fire for a lighted stick. Ally found one and waved it about, recklessly.

'No, no.' Ed stood up, serious. 'No, you can't, you wouldn't!'

'Don't be a softy, Ed.' Ally said, finding a lighted wand for herself. 'We won't do any harm.'

And the two of them careered about waving their torches, which without the mother fire, faded and sputtered and went out.

Ed sat down, relieved. Morgan circled him with her arms. 'It's alright,' she cooed, 'they were only having you on.'

The day cooled and the tide brought in a comforting freshness. The people on the beach moved and shifted, pausing now and again as though in tableaux.

Morgan and Ed walked hand in hand to the water's edge looking for shells in the dying light. They chattered like old friends, nuzzled like doves, and Ally watched them with a weather eye.

Seventeen

Ed's mum had been furious when she'd heard that Morgan was getting married from the caravan. 'What will people think? She could have gone from here. She could have gone from Molly's. This girl is headstrong, mark my words, Ed, she'll be trouble if you don't handle her properly.'

She'd pulled a pie out of the oven, like a magician pulling a rabbit out of a hat. She'd clattered the dish onto the trivet and started to dig out a portion for Ed and his dad. Ed was used to her nagging. He'd been seeing Morgan for a year and his mother had been moaning on to him about her unsuitability for all that time.

He'd laughed. 'She's not a horse Mum. You handle horses. And anyway, things are different these days, not formal like in your day. Neighbours won't think there's anything amiss at all.' Then he'd tucked into his meat and potato pie with gusto. It had been hard working on the farm. Him and his dad had tried to get jobs done in advance, allowing a bit of leeway for the wedding.

'She'll be alright.' Ed's dad had salted and peppered slowly. He didn't like to rush his food.

'Oh, that's the line you take with everything, Peter Bainton.' Maggie had turned red-cheeked with exertion and the heat of the kitchen. 'As far as you're concerned everything will always be alright.'

'Well, things have a way of sorting themselves out.' Peter stuck his fork in a piece of kidney. He'd always eat his kidney first, then the steak and then the pastry. Maggie couldn't watch him, and she couldn't watch Ed either. She'd eat separately after the men, after she'd cleared up their mess. She'd satisfy herself by banging and clattering the pans in the sink.

'Mum, couldn't you leave the washing up until after we've actually eaten our food.'

'I suppose that's what your new wife will do. Leave things until later. Or leave you to wash up and do everything else, come to that, that she can't be bothered to do. She's a right lazy madam, according to Molly Flowerdew, and she should know. I say again, Ed, she'll need firm handling, I don't care what you say.'

*

In the daytime, the sticks and twigs of trees in the Dyke thrust their buds into greenery. The preparation for summer is well underway and the tender sun smiles as she holds her head on one side, surveying the progress. At night though, the White Lady roams, picking at the bursting buds, snapping barren twigs and letting them fall into dry ditches. She scratches at the faces of villagers who scuttle home late, and ruffles visitors' hair as they shuffle up dark, unfamiliar paths from the pub. She sings loudly, sometimes riding on the rough winds that come with the changing tides. She sings about how she has kept the Morrigan trapped for a year and a day until she promised to be wed. The Morrigan has always hated this place, but the White Lady's sticky ectoplasm binds her, and she cannot get away.

There had been dew on the grass earlier that morning, but now the sky was ocean blue, and the sun was drying off the wetness. Morgan was sitting on the caravan steps watching Ally parade up and down in her bridesmaid dress. The slight girl moved gracefully in the emerald satin, the faintest swishing sound emanating from her dips and swerves.

'Another pose, please,' laughed Morgan, and her friend

118

complied by dropping a large and gracious curtsey.

'Oh, no,' Morgan was suddenly alarmed.

'What's wrong?' Ally turned to look at the back of her dress, wondering if she had caught in on the wet grass.

'It's Aunty Molly, she's just arrived on the bus. That means she'll be here ages. The next one isn't for at least an hour.'

Ally turned to follow Morgan's gaze and saw Aunty Molly in full sail making her way across the caravan park towards them.

'I might have known.' She was still twenty yards away, but her voice carried very well.

'Day before your wedding and here you are in this filthy caravan, where's your dress, Morgan? What's happening with the flowers? Are you organised at all?'

Ally pushed past Morgan on the caravan steps and went to change. Morgan got Aunty Molly a chair and snapped it open, setting it on the grass facing her. Might as well let her get it all out of her system.

'I suppose you'll be having your hair done, won't you? You could have stayed with us you know. You didn't have to hide yourself up here like a gypsy. You have got a home to come to after all. What will everyone think, getting married from a caravan.'

She sat down heavily in the canvas chair, almost tipping it up on the uneven ground. She set her bags down either side of her and flapped at her red face with her hand. She was still a robust woman even in her seventies. Morgan noticed the overly brown tinting to her hair, wiry in its short manly style.

'She'll have had that done in the village,' she thought to herself, 'especially for the wedding, I suppose.'

'Can I get you a drink of water?' Morgan made to go inside.

'No, no I'm alright. You can get me a cup of tea in a minute when I've cooled down.'

Morgan sat down again, thinking how much older she looked. Older and fatter and her fierceness somehow a parody of itself.

'Now, Morgan.' Aunty Molly had her conciliatory tone in sway now, as she let her glance wander over the caravan windows. She smoothed her dress down and settled into the canvas chair.

'Uncle John and me, think you should come home tonight and go to the chapel from our house tomorrow. It would be a lot nicer wouldn't it, dear. You can have your hair done in the morning and we can get the taxi to come to us instead of right up here for you. What do you think?'

Morgan could just imagine it. Her wedding day and her red mop scraped back and tied back underneath some white flowing veil. And her dress would suddenly be larger than any known to the western world. Talk about looking like a blancmange, Aunty Molly would make her wear a dress that was actually made from blancmange and it would be so big she wouldn't be able to get out of the farm kitchen door. She smiled to herself at the thought of it.

'So, you'll do that?' Molly saw the smile as Morgan's acceptance.

Ally appeared at the top of the caravan steps.

'Anyone want a cuppa?' She waved the camping kettle in the air invitingly.

'Lovely, dear.'

The old woman rummaged in her bags and Morgan heard the unmistakable noise of cake boxes bumping together.

'Oh, here we go,' she thought, 'bribery by butterfly buns.'

The sun was getting warmer, but Aunty Molly kept her coat on, showing she didn't belong here or approve of the place. Morgan and Ally drank their tea and clucked over the buns as they were meant to, but Morgan knew that sooner or later she would have to burst the bubble of Aunty Molly's hopes.

'Now just look at that young woman.' Molly nodded her head over to the path which led to the swimming pool.

'Poor lass, her husband died at sea last month and her with that child.'

Morgan recognised Leanne Hall from school. Her pinched face and peevish eyes hadn't changed over the years. It was always Leanne who had pretended friendship in those early days. She had egged Morgan on in her mischief and defiance and yet she'd never stood by her when it really came to it. She was a sly one, that Leanne. But Morgan had heard how she'd been married to Billy Myers and had a daughter a few years ago. And she'd heard about the cobble sinking from the locals in the pub, about the tragic drowning of local fishermen. The bad news had bounced around the village like beads bumping against one another on a string. The families involved had held their grief close, but Morgan had felt it and felt sorry for this young woman, robbed of her husband so early.

Leanne and the child were obviously heading for the swimming baths on the caravan site, each with a bright bag and towel. Leanne saw the group by the caravan though and changed direction to come over to speak to them.

'Now I know you and she didn't always get on.' Aunty

Molly was smiling towards Leanne, but hissing to Morgan, 'but you should be nice to her after what's happened.'

'Of course, I will, what sort of monster do you think I am?' Morgan had become unused to being told what to do and how to behave.

'Even though she should have known better that to go off having a baby at seventeen, we have to feel sorry for her now.' Leanne was in earshot and Morgan was worried she'd heard Aunty Molly's comments.

'Hiya, Morgan, nice to see you. I hear you're getting married tomorrow.' Leanne smiled, and the child echoed, 'Hiya, Morgan.'

Morgan reached her hand to the child and smiled warmly at her.

'You are just like your mum aren't you.' Jessica reached forward and allowed Morgan to haul her up onto her knee.

'I am so sorry to hear about Billy.' Morgan didn't know how to go on. She hadn't known Billy that well and had no comfort to offer in any case.

'We're managing.' Leanne's eyes hardened. It had been so difficult over these past weeks. People talked and offered condolences, but they didn't know how she really felt. How could they?

Morgan reached for daisies on the grass and started to thread them into a chain for Jessica.

The child was impatient and jumped off Morgan's knee to find more flowers for her.

'If you need any help.' Again, Morgan trotted out the cliché, not really meaning it, not thinking it was relevant to her.

'Help? Well, it would help if Jessica's real father stumped up some cash. Now that would be a help.'

Leanne's eyes narrowed and Aunty Molly looked at her sharply, her mouth in a straight line.

'Real father?' said Morgan.

'Do you mean Billy wasn't Jessica's father?'

She didn't really keep up with village gossip, even though she'd heard plenty of it in the pub over the past year. She had always felt on the outside and it had suited her not to be involved. They had never been interested in her, not even when she was a child. And now she was about to become a schoolteacher in town, well, she'd have to be seen to be above all that wouldn't she?

'No, he wasn't.' Leanne was getting ready for her triumph. Her eyes narrowed and the pupils shrunk to pinpricks.

'Ed's her real father, didn't you know? I would have thought he would have told you seeing as you're getting married and all that.'

Morgan's hands stopped working on the daisy chain, and the child whimpered a little, eager for her to finish it.

'You always were a spiteful cow, Leanne Hall, you'd say anything to get at me, even after all this time.'

Leanne shrugged her shoulders and dragged Jessica away from Morgan. The child let out an angry howl and tried to free herself from her mother's grasp.

'Ask him,' she crowed, 'see if he denies it. We had a bit of a thing, me and him, but he wasn't my type. You're welcome to him, love. But just ask him about Jessica. You ought to know what you're getting yourself into.'

She tossed her head and pulled the screaming child toward the path and the swimming baths.

Morgan looked at the half-finished daisy chain, tears pricking her eyes.

'You shouldn't believe a word that girl says.' Molly was

123

uncomfortable in the canvas chair. She tried to wriggle but there wasn't much space for manoeuvre.

'I'll put the kettle on again.' Ally tried to break the tension.

'No, I'll do it.' Morgan dropped the daisy chain and stretched her legs. She smiled, keeping her doubts hidden. 'I need a drink to get rid of the taste of her lies. You stay here and talk to Aunty Molly. I won't be long.'

The afternoon wore on. Molly told Ally lots of stories about Morgan as a little girl, her head always in books, her hair always unruly and untamed. Morgan was only half listening to the stories. Her real thoughts were elsewhere. She needed to talk to Ed.

'So, Morgan.' Aunty Molly was ready to go now. The bus was due, and she was stiff from sitting in that chair. 'Are you coming home to us tonight - it would make sense, dear, wouldn't it? Nice hot bath and I've got casserole on the go in the Aga. Your friend can come too, or course. We can soon make a bed up, that's no trouble at all.'

Ally was sending out warning signals, they had the evening planned. She knew it meant a lot to Morgan to go with what they had decided. She knew as well that Leanne's visit and bombshell had to be dealt with. Aunty Molly's wasn't the place for that.

'It isn't that I'm ungrateful, it is really kind of you and Uncle John to offer…'

Molly waved her hand dismissively.

'But I've made plans to go from here to the chapel. Ally is going to do my hair and the flowers are being delivered here in the morning. I'm happy here and it feels right to be married from here, so don't worry about it.'

Molly fastened the top buttons of her coat. She knew Morgan's stubborn streak. Well, she'd made the offer and she'd had it thrown back in her face. John had said it was a waste of time. No-one could say she hadn't tried to give the girl a decent send off.

Morgan and Ally helped Molly as she struggled to get her large backside out of the chair. They were both close to laughter, but Morgan steadied herself enough to pull the chair off Molly's bottom and help her to stand.

'I'll leave these bags here for you.' Molly gruffly maintained her dignity. 'There's sausage rolls and cakes. I dare say you girls never eat a thing half the time.'

And she waddled off over the grass towards the bus stop.

'I'll see you tomorrow in the chapel, I expect.'

She tossed these words over her shoulder without looking round. Morgan felt a bit guilty. She knew that it would have been hard for her to come to see her after all this time and that she had hurt her feelings badly.

'Yes, see you in the chapel, Aunty Molly,' Morgan called after her, wondering wryly if the wedding would be going ahead now. Her words trailed off, evaporating in the dryness of the June sunshine.

*

Ed was in the pub with some of his mates and his dad. The Dog was always busy on a Friday night and Ed let the noise and bustle wash over him. His mates were trying their best to get him tipsy and in the spirit of a stag night, but with each pint Ed just got more and more relaxed and sat there with a smile spreading uncontrollably across his face.

'Oh, he's no fun at all.' James, his best man, threw his

hands in the air. 'Come on, let's have a game of darts.' They moved off, Ed's dad along with them, leaving Ed to his grinning and mooning about.

A shout went up in the pub. Ed looked up and saw the lads crowding round his dad and patting him on the back. James came over with another pint. 'Great at darts, your dad,' he said admiringly. Ed looked at his dad, shy but beaming at all the attention.

'Oh, he hides his light under the proverbial bushel, my dad.'

'I'm not surprised with your mum being like she is, he probably hides the bushel as well.' James laughed and Ed laughed along with him.

'He's hustled us alright, anyway. Are you coming for a game?'

Ed declined, smiling, supped off half his pint in one go, and slipped further down into his chair.

'Aye, well, you look comfy enough there, so we'll just get on.' James moved back to the darts players, telling them Ed was well away and best left at the moment.

Ed was thinking about Morgan. He pictured her as a red-haired Amazon, capable of anything, strong and fearless. She was actually smaller than him, physically. He was a typical farmer's son, big built, muscular and fit. But somehow, Morgan seemed so much stronger than he was. She was the one who let snide remarks and insults bounce off her. His mum's hardly subtle comments to her about needing to smarten up for the wedding had been like gnats' bites on an elephant. She seemed not to notice at all. Ed tried to remember her as a little girl. After all, they'd grown up in the same village. They'd been to the same school, albeit he was a bit older. He remembered stories about her

126

alright. People, his mum for one, were always going on about that little monster that Molly Flowerdew was bringing up. They made her sound like she had horns and a tail the way they went on. About how she'd lit the bonfire before it was bonfire night and nearly roasted all her friends. About how she was wild and would never behave herself and Molly had to lock her up in the cellar. But he couldn't remember her really. Not in the flesh as it were. It was all just stories.

He wondered what she would look like in the chapel tomorrow. He felt nervous just thinking about all the pomp and ceremony, but it would be worth it. His glass was empty, and the lads and his dad were still jostling turns round the dartboard. Ed thought he might get up to join them, but his legs didn't seem to want to carry him. Then James seemed to appear out of nowhere. 'Ed, mate, there's been a call for you.'

'A call? What sort of a call?'

'A phone call, you fool, at the bar.'

'A phone call at the bar? What sort of a phone call at the bar?'

'Oh, god, this is going to be difficult.' James sat down across from Ed and tried to engage his eyes which seemed to be rolling about in his head.

'It was Morgan.'

'What do you mean it was Morgan? What does she want?'

'It was Morgan, and she wants to talk to you - now.'

Ed sat up, trying to take in the information and make some sort of sense of it.

'Is something wrong?' He was registering worried now.

'Well, she was crying, but she might just have had too much to drink.'

Ed leapt up, nearly knocking the table over. 'I've got to speak to her, get me to her, James, mate, I need you to help me to get to her.'

James looked round and all the rest of the lads were still happy at the darts. He thought it best if they slipped out. No good making a song and a dance about something that might just be sparked by too much drink. However, she had sounded upset, genuinely upset. And from what he knew of Morgan Parish, she wasn't given to getting upset easily. He led Ed out of the pub and walked him down the road towards the North Landing.

Morgan met them as they were halfway up the road. She hadn't been able to settle to any of the things she and Ally had planned. They had drunk plenty of wine to try and relax and eaten Aunty Molly's sausage rolls and cakes in some false attempt to celebrate. But it had ended up that Ally had fallen asleep and Morgan, feeling sober as a judge, had started fretting about what Leanne had said about Ed being the father of her child. She had circled the caravan time and time again, thinking it over.

Ed wasn't the sort of bloke to lie to anyone. At least she didn't think so. And Leanne, well Morgan could remember her trickeries and deceptions of old. But still. She remembered the child on her knee as she had made the daisy chain. It would be wrong to turn away and deny that child of a father. If anyone knew about being denied parents, it was Morgan. She had to speak to Ed before it was too late.

James delivered him up to her with a worried look.

'What's all this about?' he asked.

128

'I just need me and Ed to talk, James. I'm sorry to spoil your evening but it's important.'

James knew she wasn't about to give anything else away.

'I'll take a walk up to the headland. It will probably do me good anyway. Sober me up for my best man duties and all that.' He laughed but the sound disappeared into the thickening foliage of the hedgerow.

'Just give us an hour, and please, James...' He noticed she'd been crying. 'Come back for him, won't you?'

The moon lit the night sky, drawing attention to the damp on the ground, but Morgan sat Ed down on the verge anyway, remembering Aunty Molly's frequent warnings of getting King-cough from damp grass. She sat beside him, her hands rummaging in the long grasses for the silky, closed heads of buttercups.

'I knew you'd find out,' Ed said, becoming accustomed to the darkness and able to see Morgan's face clearly.

'What do you mean?' Morgan was alarmed.

'About me being a frog, dressed up as a prince.' Ed laughed feebly at his own joke.

Morgan pulled a fat blade of grass, split it and blew a harsh, bitter call through it into the silent night air.

'Ed, I need to ask you something and I need you to answer me truthfully.' She felt like the schoolteacher she was.

'I wouldn't lie to you, Morgan, you know I wouldn't ever lie to you. Don't you?'

'This is important. I need to be sure about something.' She sat up straight and turned him to face her, close up, urgently.

'Are you the father to Leanne Hall's... I mean to Leanne Myers' baby. She says you are.'

'Father? Me? I'm not anyone's father. Not yet.' Ed laughed, tried to catch her hands which had let his head go.

'This is serious, Ed. She came here today and said that Billy wasn't Jessica's father but that you were. What is going on?'

Ed stood up and walked across the road from Morgan. He was trying to get his beer befuddled head to get this to make sense.

He made his way back to where Morgan was still sitting on the damp grass verge. He wasn't laughing, he wasn't even smiling.

'Morgan.' He offered his arm to pull her up from the ground. 'Morgan, I had a fling with Leanne for a few weeks in my first holiday from University. I was unhappy with life at the time, and she was around, more than ready to pick up the pieces.'

Morgan plunged her hands back into the cold, long grasses, desperately feeling for something to hold on to.

'And?'

'And, well, she was the first woman... The first time... Oh, you know what I'm trying to say. She threw herself at me and I didn't refuse.'

'So, you are the father…?'

'I'm no-one's father!' Ed broke off a piece of twig from the hawthorn, not even feeling its thorns dig deep into his hand. He threw it into the field as far as he could.

'She was going out with Billy before she met me, and she dropped me the minute he got back from fishing. That baby was Billy's, it had to be. She's never said anything to me about it being any other way.'

Morgan remembered Leanne at eight years old, urging her to light the bonfire, egging her on and finding her the

130

match. Afterwards to Aunty Molly she'd said, 'It wasn't anything to do with me, Mrs Flowerdew, I tried to stop her, honestly I did.'

She remembered the look of triumph she had given her earlier in the day, delivering her news, issuing her threats.

Ed stood as though cast in stone. He wanted to say so much to reassure her, he wanted to sweep her off her feet with passionate words of love and assurance. But the words were lost somewhere up in the midnight blue of the sky and would not come to earth.

Morgan pulled herself to her feet. She cupped his face in her hands and drew him to her. 'I believe you, Ed Bainton, thousands wouldn't.'

She kissed him, meaning it, but somewhere in each of them lay a seed of malice, planted deftly and waiting for something to nurture it.

The next morning was shrouded in a sea fret. 'Do you believe in sympathetic weather?' Morgan peered out of the caravan window and could see no further than the next van.

Ally roused herself and as she stretched the sleep out of her limbs, the anxiety of the previous evening came back to her.

'What are you going on about, Morgan? Sympathetic weather?'

Morgan laughed.

'It's OK, Ally, me and Ed are alright. I saw him last night and we sorted it out. The weather will clear too. Trust me, it will be glorious in time for the wedding.'

Ally leapt out of bed and checked the time. It was 8

o'clock which meant six hours to the wedding.

'We've loads to do, Morgan. Stuff we didn't do last night, you know. We've got to get going, come on.'

And she rampaged around the small caravan like a trapped animal.

Morgan was in fits of laughing. 'Stop, Ally. Stop. We won't get anywhere if you just panic. We need a plan.'

They had saved a sausage roll and a madeleine each from Aunty Molly's bounty for breakfast and together with mugs of milky coffee this set them into the right frame of mind.

Morgan was adamant that she wouldn't wash her hair until the sea fret had lifted. 'The fog will flatten my red mop - I want it to be as big and wide as ever it can be.'

'But what if the fog doesn't lift? What if it waits until this afternoon to clear?'

'Don't fret.' They laughed, and Morgan was sure of herself.

*

On one of her visits to see Grace, Morgan had taken her red roses. Grace had cried. They had reminded her of Sean, and Morgan was surprised that something could hurt after so long a time.

'He used to come into the café where I worked on Charing Cross Road, and he'd bring me a single red rose and he'd stand there in front of all those people and sing, *Oh, my love is like a red, red rose*. Of course, the boss didn't like it at first, but he had a lovely voice, did Sean. And after a couple of times, the customers used to ask if the young man who sang, was coming in. And the boss slipped him a couple of bob for doing it.'

Grace had run her fingers over the blossoms and held them close to her face, searching for those memories.

'Of course, I thought it was so romantic at first, but then I realised he was just trying to get someone to notice him. Me being there was incidental. I could have been anyone. I was only young though, and I took it all in. What with my soppy face and his singing, we gave them a right floorshow.'

Morgan had reached over to hold Grace's hands. 'Shall I put these in water?' She slipped the flowers from the old woman's grasp.

'How long did you work in that café?'

'Oh, on and off for a good few years. They even took me back after I'd had our Gwennie. I mean they weren't as fussy in the city as they were in the towns about that sort of thing.

'And they were good about letting me off when I got a part now and again. Not that it was very often, really. Sean was a lot more successful than I was. He had the voice you see. They liked a good voice for those soppy songs in the Music Hall.'

Morgan had put the flowers in a vase she'd found under the sink. She'd stood the vase on the kitchen table where Grace could just about see the colour.

'So why didn't he look after you and Gwennie? He must have been earning enough.'

'It wasn't like that in those days, nobody earned enough really, not even if you were quite famous. And Sean wasn't anywhere near that. Being on the stage meant everything to him. He would have done anything to get that next job, anything. He didn't want to know me when I took for our Gwen. He just left me and went off in search of his next job. I'd thought he would stand by me, but I was wrong. Well, I wasn't on my own, was I? Still happens these days I daresay.'

Grace had stood up and moved towards the kettle. 'I'll make the tea.' Morgan was up and filling the kettle in a flash.

'No, dear,' Grace had felt for her hand and taken charge, 'I have to keep myself going. It does me good to keep going.'

And she'd moved about the kitchen in her sure, steady way. Feeling for the familiar teapot, the sugar bowl and neatly stacked cups and saucers.

'I went home to have Gwennie. Mum and Dad were beside themselves that I was in the family way, but they took me in. Of course, they told the neighbours some cock and bull story about me being married in London and the sad death of my new husband. But they never believed it, I'm sure. I didn't care. I didn't care what happened to me after Sean left. I went home, had our Gwen and just curled up inside myself like a startled caterpillar.'

*

Ally and Morgan had not ordered cars or taxis to get them to the chapel for the wedding. The sea fret had lifted and given way to a cornflower-blue sky. There was a cool wind but that didn't worry the girls who had been rushing about washing hair and preening and who now welcomed the freshness of the sea breeze.

They walked arm in arm down the North Landing Road, past hawthorn clumps, which used to be hedges but which

134

had been left to ramble. They passed old, paint peeling railway carriages, holiday retreats with overgrown gardens.

The helicopter was busy droning somewhere out over the sea or the cliffs and the sound of it was answered by the raucous calls of huge gulls, hungry for fish.

There was hardly a soul about, it was too early in the season for all but a handful of visitors. A car passed them and tooted its horn and the girls waved back merrily. They passed the bungalow where Charley used to live, Morgan's friend from schooldays. Outside the house were lupins, once an orderly arrangement but now a straggly line of tall and small blooms.

'Charley and her mother were just like those lupins,' Morgan told Ally as she stopped for a while, remembering.

'Her mother tall and stately and Charley... Well, Charley was like me. Ragged and didn't give a monkey's.'

They laughed and moved on. It was almost time for the ceremony.

Ed was waiting anxiously in the chapel. James was trying to talk about everything and anything to keep him calm. Ed kept looking back. It was almost time. She would turn up, wouldn't she?

His mother had picked up on his anxiety.

'He's worried to death you know.' She prodded Peter in the ribs.

'It'll be alright,' he said and earned another prod.

'And her mother's not here.' She looked sideways to the seats alongside them at the bride's side of the chapel. 'You'd think they could have made the effort.'

'Shh,' hissed Peter, 'she's here.'

And all eyes in the small chapel turned toward the door.

There stood Morgan and Ally, faces flushed from their walk, Morgan's hair wide and glorious framed in the doorway.

Uncle John was giving her away. She hadn't asked her father. They had been invited, of course, but the only person sitting on the front seat on her side of the chapel was Aunty Molly, alone and splendidly imposing in her heavily fruited hat.

'She couldn't come,' she mouthed to Morgan as she approached the front of the church, 'too poorly.'

And Morgan nodded her understanding and turned to smile at Ed.

Her dress was ivory silk. It had belonged to Grace. 'Well,' thought Morgan, 'at least if my mother couldn't be here, I know that wherever she is, Grace will be able to see me.' The minister held out both his hands and the ceremony began.

Part 2

One

Gwen's story

I seem to spend my life on buses, one way or another. Are you the same? I remember I always caught the stopping bus back after college. Why not, I wasn't in a hurry. It wasn't as though I had to get back for the children anymore, not then. Dot and Pat, my two eldest, well they had homes of their own. There was only David at home then and he was more than capable of looking after himself.

Of course, Donald didn't like me catching the later bus. He wanted me home for tea-time, just like I'd always been. Men can be like that, can't they? But I always left his tea in the refrigerator, he only had to warm it up. It wasn't as though he had to cook it or anything like that. He wouldn't have liked all that.

Second time around it was. College I mean. Well at my age! Donald thought I was mad. 'You have a nice home, and you want for nothing. Why go through all that again?' But I hadn't gone through it properly the first time, first the war and then the children had seen to that. Now it was my chance.

I liked to be on the top deck of the stopping bus, especially late in the year. I could look out onto the dark as it passed lit up shops, then later the open fields lit by stars. I could listen to my thoughts and dreams without Donald forever saying, 'penny for them' and putting paid to the flow.

But being on that bus reminded me of when I was a little 'un. I loved being on my own. It gave me time to think. And that's why I'd go home by the hilly fields.

I loved those hilly fields, I did! In Barnsley right enough. Do you know where I mean? They were just off Park Road at the top, you know, and you could slide down, right down to Doncaster Road. It was steep and dangerous, and I weren't supposed to do it, but I did. I got my legs slapped many a time for wearing holes in my knickers.

But when I was sliding down the hilly fields it was the nearest thing to flying.

I had to be home in time for tea though and Grandma and Grandad always had tea at the same time, day in day out. They got Mrs Jubb in to mind the shop for an hour and we always sat down to a proper tea. I could have got home on time going the long way round, but the hilly fields was an adventure. You could run and run down the first part and then slide. In the early dark of December, it was even better. Dark nights and it felt mysterious, exciting. I would slide down the last steep slope and feel truly myself. Until I got back to the shop that is. Grandma would be waiting in the dark brown little kitchen round the back where we sat down to our proper tea. And there it was, always the same food on the same day of the week. Even the boiled ham would be the same shape week after week with the same number of portions of tomato and lettuce and the same number of pieces of thickly buttered brown bread.

'You've been coming home by those hilly fields again. I can see by the grass stains on your knickers. I'll have a devil of a job getting them clean now. How many times, Gwen? You are not allowed to come that way, not on your own, not in the dark.'

Hark at me going on. Here, have a sandwich, or a Madeleine. Lovely, aren't they? I've been visiting Molly Flowerdew. And she never sends me home empty-handed. I'm not making this public knowledge or anything, but I can tell you. My little girl, Morgan, well she's been very difficult lately, and Donald doesn't like disruption in the house. So, Molly has taken her for me, just for a while, until my nerves get a bit better, and I can cope with her again. I just need a bit of peace for a while, I feel so tired with it all. And I mean Morgan will enjoy all the attention and the space of being at the seaside. She'll love it.

Of course, Grandma and Grandad had a hard job bringing me up and I'm grateful. Really, I am. They said I was too much like her.

140

They never called my mother by her Christian name, Grace. She was always, your mother or her. And yet she was their only child. And when I did anything wrong, they always said, 'I suppose you've taken that from your mother.' I heard them call her a slut more than once but only when they didn't know I could hear.

Donald called me a slut, when I told him I was expecting again. Can you believe it? I mean all of a sudden, I was a slut at 45 years old, I ask you. When I told him that we were having another child, well, he didn't seem to take it in at first. Then, as the penny dropped, he started walking around the room faster and faster, huffing and puffing like some great pantomime giant.

He's a big man, Donald is, balding a bit but he still cuts a dash in a crowd, you know? I wanted to laugh, really, even though I knew it was all serious, but he looked so comical. Strutting about in that theatrical way, like he had an audience. I was just another actor on the stage, like he didn't know me anymore.

'Donald,' I said, 'calm down, you'll have a heart attack.'

'Calm down,' he says, 'calm down, Gwen. How can I calm down? What have you done?'

'Well, I mean, pardon me, but it wasn't just me you know.'

'And who else was it then?'

It all came out then. All the things he'd been storing up since I was at college. Why did I call the lecturers by their first names? Why was I always out until late when college finished at four o'clock? Why was I always seeing those young women and going off with them to goodness knows where? Young women? I mean they were just students like me - only younger. I enjoyed their company. Where's the harm? And there's Donald still going on, huffing and puffing in his tantrum. Did I have to wear those short skirts at my age, and drinking beer, well women of my age shouldn't be cavorting in bars drinking beer - that was just asking for trouble.

141

I went to bed, cried myself to sleep. Donald and me were having a child when I had thought I was past all that sort of thing and instead of support all I was getting from him was suspicion and verbal abuse. In all my life I'd never known him so angry. What was wrong with the man? What exactly did he want from me?

Oh, I am tired. I'll just have a bit of a rest if you don't mind. Give you a rest too, from me going on. There's a flask of tea in the basket. Molly packed it, bless her. Just help yourself.

Two

The trees know everything: which leaves will brown and fall, and which will hold their colour through the storms and the spray thrown by the sea. They sough and sigh at the wind's turn. They snag the gossip, hide it in the crux of their branches until inevitably it turns to canker and gall.

Morgan knew they were short-handed on the farm, but this was ridiculous. Maggie, Ed's mother, had started dropping larger than subtle hints about Morgan having a baby. What had it got to do with that old biddy anyway? They were young, Morgan and Ed. People didn't have babies early like they used to. Nor did they have them in dozens to make sure there were enough left to man the farm.

Morgan strode up and down the tiny kitchen. She loved this little cottage, looking out over the cliffs onto the sea and sky horizon. 'Nothing between us and Russia.' Ed's eyes had twinkled as he mimicked his father.

But it gave him the excuse to hold her tight in the cold of the winter's gales. They had stoked up the stove and huddled around it with hot mugs of tea. These had been happy cosy days. But now! She looked again at the test result, not wanting to believe it.

Morgan felt sure Ed didn't want to have babies yet, either. They hadn't exactly discussed it properly, but when she'd told him about his mother nagging about it, he'd just said, 'Huh, you know what she's like.' And left it at that.

He was never one to tackle a problem wasn't Ed though. Sidestepped trouble like a world class rugby fly-half.

What would he think now? Maybe she wouldn't tell him. I mean he knew she took precautions, and he wouldn't expect her to be pregnant in a million years. Not if she didn't tell him. She could deal with this herself.

But Maggie knew. Morgan didn't know how she knew, but she knew. She had started fussing and clucking round Morgan like some mother hen. They had never really got on, not from the beginning, but now…

Somehow Ed's mum had got wind of a grandchild. Sixth sense? Guess work? More likely to be the way she'd caught Morgan with her head down the toilet one morning and put two and two together pretty damn quickly.

'Better tell Ed then', Maggie had said with an expression that meant 'if you don't, I will'.

Morgan couldn't believe how pleased Ed was when she told him about the pregnancy. She thought she knew him. She tried to explain to him how she felt. She didn't want to give up teaching. 'You don't have to, not altogether.' He stroked her hair, always soothing was Ed. She told him she was too young, that they were too young, they wouldn't be able to do stuff together, not in the same way. 'Of course, we will. Mum will look after the little one.' He sat her down, made her put her legs up on the settee. She struggled but he was strong, insistent. She felt like she had felt as a child at Aunty Molly's. She was being pushed a way she didn't want to go.

'Just think, though,' she'd said to Ed. 'Grace, my grandmother gave away her child. Gwen, my mother, gave me away to Aunty Molly. Don't you think there's a chance that I'll be cursed as a mother too?'

'Don't be so daft.' Ed was already stirring the cup of hot

milk in the mug that he knew was her favourite. 'You spend too much time with your head in books, Morgan, you're a real fanciful creature, you really are.'

Morgan sank her head against the old cushions, smelling their mustiness, feeling their comforting scratchiness. She knew she had to give in. She couldn't fight against Ed's mum, against Ed. Least of all could she deny this child a mother, something she'd never really had.

The little girl who lives by the sea packs her dreams into a box covered over with shells and white stones which she'd gathered at midnight from the shore. She locks the box with a silver key which will never tarnish and never warp. This she hides in the fork of a sweet chestnut tree, covering it with moss softened by the dew.

Morgan carried her pregnancy from one season to the next, stoically, like a cross she had to bear.

Maggie was uncharacteristically nice to her, but Morgan knew it was just a temporary cessation of hostilities. Maggie coped with her bucks and dips of temperament like a cowboy breaking in a wild foal. She knew there'd be an end to it and was sure of a tamed creature in due course.

William was born to the sound of March gales. No time to get Morgan to the hospital, there was a tree down in the farm drive and the midwife had to be fetched from the main road by Ed in his tractor. Morgan had been at the farmhouse when the pains began, and Ed's mother had assured her that she had hours of time left before they needed to get to the hospital.

'I think she thought I was one of Uncle John's ewes,' Morgan said to Ed later. 'For two pins she'd have had me down in the straw on all fours delivering as nature intended.'

'Don't be silly,' Ed was doing the soothing thing again.

'You just had a faster labour than could have been expected.'

'Yes, I wanted it over so I could get on with my life.'

Morgan had grown sick of the imposed tranquillity that had pervaded her pregnancy. She looked at the little bundle in the cot. She could not see how this tiny being could be a part of her. It could just as well have been an alien in there under the white cellular blanket. Morgan could not feel anything but cheated. She had been cheated out of making her own decisions. Cheated into motherhood before she was ready for it.

'You'll be fine.' Ed was bright eyed, glowing. He could easily recognise his son. Nothing seemed more natural to him.

The wind rattled at the windows. It seemed eager to unsettle this domestic scene. Morgan felt like she was being blown about by the gales, somewhere, anywhere. Maybe these turbulent feelings would settle like the March winds would settle. She hoped so. She felt she had been buffeted around enough already. She looked again at the bundle in the cot. Maybe she would settle into motherhood. She wondered how that was supposed to feel.

*

'It'll be alright.' Ed was always assuring her, settling her down.

'It'll be alright,' Morgan said, mimicking him sarcastically.

146

'They'll come round, put everything in order, she'll cook the splendid Christmas lunch and I'll feel totally useless in what's supposed to be my own home.'

Ed sighed. He knew Morgan was right, but he was trying to be peacemaker, for William's sake. The baby's first Christmas - welcome to the war zone.

'She'll be… I mean Maggie will be…' Morgan had started by calling them Mum and Dad at their request - but she found it difficult. After all, no-one she had known had ever earned those titles so why should she give them away gratuitously now. She had explained, tactfully she hoped, and Ed's mum said, rather too brightly, 'Oh it doesn't matter what you call us dear, 'a rose by any other name,' don't they say. Just call us Maggie and Peter, that will be fine, no need to feel awkward about it'.

Of course, there was 'Granny' and 'Gramps' to add to the mix now.

'Maggie will be in her element, back in her house, cooking on her Aga, I wish we'd never taken over this damn farmhouse in the first place.'

'They wanted us to have it - it is a family house and now we have a family.'

And to prove it, the dulcet tones of William drifted down the stairs. At the same time the doorbell rang announcing the entrance of Maggie and Peter.

'Is that child not up yet?' Maggie strode through the hall in full sail.

'I'd have thought you would have had him up and dressed by now, on Christmas morning.'

'Here beginneth the umpteenth lesson,' thought Morgan and she helped Peter with the bowls and bags he had been saddled with.

At first it had been easy to give William over to Maggie's ministrations when she went back to school to teach. She had even allowed her to organise the christening that she didn't believe in and the bunfight she was too tired for. But gradually there was a bond growing between Morgan and her child which she hadn't expected and which she was warming to. She found herself resenting Maggie more and more. She was taken aback at how sometimes she felt sick at the thought of Maggie touching William, kissing him and holding him.

Maggie was halfway up the stairs. 'I'll sort him out for you.'

'No, no, Maggie it's alright.' Morgan managed a bright, bustling tone to rival her mother in law's. 'You come down here this minute and let Ed get you a drink. I'll sort out our little rascal, you do far too much for us.'

'Fifteen all,' thought Ed as he put his arm round his mother's shoulders and steered her into the sitting room.

Morgan had discovered that William liked the sound of her voice. She told him stories while she dressed him and fed him and played with him.

She sang rhymes from somewhere deep in her memory. She talked incessantly to him, never minding whether he understood or not.

'When I was very little, my mummy used to tell me stories.' She was dressing William, stroking his hair, full of wonder at her own adeptness and the warmth she felt for him.

'I remember the sound of her voice, quiet but clear. I remember her telling me the stories, but I don't remember the stories. I wish I did. I wish I could remember.'

She sang a little to him as she took in his Ed-blue eyes, and the smile that had a radiance that was only ever a kiss or a hug away.

'They were part of me and her being together, those stories, but I can't remember them. I seem to have spent my whole life reading and reading to find those stories again, but would I recognise them, would I know them? Or were they just her stories and no-one else's?'

'What are you going on about?' Ed was at the bedroom door looking amused. 'Talking to yourself, first sign of madness, you know.'

'I'm not talking to myself. I'm talking to William.' Morgan was fierce, defensive.

'Keep your hair on, the white van's not coming to take you away yet.'

'It might be if your mum stays here all day.' Morgan hoisted William up onto her hip.

'Come on little rascal, let's go and find the wicked witch of the north.'

Ed smiled, happy to see Morgan and William together.

'You be careful what you're saying, little children pick things up quickly you know'.

Morgan grinned, 'Diplomacy will be my middle name from now on, trust me - the child will never know his grandmother's true identity from me'.

Maggie was at home in what was once her own beloved kitchen. She performed her cooking magic as only a true farmer's wife could.

'Born to it,' thought Morgan, remembering Aunty Molly and her incessant baking and cooking.

It felt good as she dandled and twirled little William, and

she felt herself enjoying the domesticity of the moment.

'He likes this little piggy,' Maggie said over her shoulder as she basted the turkey.

'He likes lots of things.'

Morgan was cross at the interruption.

'Yes, but he particularly likes this little piggy.'

Maggie wasn't going to give up on this one.

'OK, Willums, let's do this little piggy'.

Ed and Peter had gone to the pub for their ritual man to man pint before Christmas dinner. Morgan sat in the old easy chair, the one in which she knew Maggie liked to sit with him and took hold of little William's big toe.

This little piggie went to market,
This little piggie stayed at home,
This little piggie got slaughtered,
This little piggie made ham bones,
And this little piggie…

Maggie crashed about with the pans in disgust. That girl… that girl…. They had put up with plenty, her and Peter, they wanted to see Ed happy. But really, she was an evil little minx.

Morgan was pleased to have sparked Maggie off. And once she had started, she couldn't stop.

'Maggie you sound as if things are out of control in there, can I help?' Her false cheeriness was blatant in her voice. 'I could easily put William into his chair and peel something or chop something. You only have to say.'

'I'm fine, dear, just getting into the spirit of it all.' Maggie gritted her teeth, at least they had their lovely grandson,

150

best not to let things get too heated.

'I know, William and I will set the table.' Morgan danced around the room with the baby.

'Mummy and Willums set the table, Mummy and Willums help Granny do the dinner...' She wheeled faster and faster, knowing Maggie was getting more and more agitated.

'Take care, Morgan, you'll drop him.'

'He's my baby, Maggie, I'll drop him if I like,' Morgan said lightly, and made grand gestures of pretending to drop the baby.

Maggie was beside herself.

'You really are a cruel, vindictive girl, aren't you?'

Morgan stopped and looked hurt. 'I was only playing, Maggie.' She smiled to herself, but then felt a bit guilty. William was looking bewildered and in fact had been a bit sick. Maggie had gone silent and all she could hear was the bubbling of pots and the spitting of the roast turkey.

'I'm sorry, Maggie.' Morgan was back down to earth. 'I didn't mean to upset you, really. Maybe you could sit with William and I could do some of the cooking.'

'It doesn't matter.' Maggie stiffened. 'I can manage. Make the most of your time with William. You will be back working before you know it. A child needs some time with its mother.'

Morgan bristled again. She knew she was supposed to fit in as the farmer's wife. She knew Maggie disapproved of her going back to work teaching. It had been one of those unspoken grievances ever since she and Ed had been married.

'You can't deny though, Maggie, the farm also needs another income.'

Maggie couldn't deny it and until the men returned from the pub the two women settled down uneasily to the background of bubbling and spitting and their own thoughts.

Three

Welcome, Moon of the Tide! Darkness has reached its peak and sweeps away the vestiges of the past year. We sweep away memories of past failures and prepare ourselves for new beginnings. (Celtic ritual)

First day of a new term, a new job and a new school. And the first day that William had really screamed and protested at being left with Maggie. 'Poor little mite,' Morgan thought as she raced down the hill into the village. It was still dark, dark and cold, and she felt like screaming herself. She wished she could have stayed in the warm, bright farmhouse. Wished the first day of term could have been another Monday.

She kept thinking back to William's tear-stained face and his kicking, fighting body as she passed him over to Maggie and fled. The trees that surrounded the cricket ground were bare branched and overbearing in the winter darkness. They seemed to be pointing to Morgan's hurrying form, pointing her out as the unfeeling mother.

She allowed herself a bit of a smile, though, in spite of William's anguish, which she realised would soon be smoothed over by Maggie's asinine crooning. It felt good to be missed. She'd thought William wouldn't mind being passed about like a Christmas parcel. That he would coo and smile at anyone who took him and played with him, especially Maggie. But she and William had developed a bond that she hadn't expected, and she was glad he didn't want her to go. Did that make her a bad mother after all?

The gush of heat in the small staff room was overpowering, yet even in such a confined space they managed to avoid each other - each still clinging to the holidays and not wanting to break the spell of that all too brief freedom. Pleasantries were observed, Morgan was welcomed half-heartedly, and then silence until the first bell.

Morgan stood behind her desk as the patchwork of children filed in. It felt strange to be here, in the school she herself had attended not such a long time ago. She even remembered how it felt when you had a teacher who was new to the school. She felt the children's eyes on her as they pretended to be absorbed in settling down at their desks. She hid a smile in spite of herself.

Jessica was in Mrs Bainton's class for the first time. She knew she would be of course. These things were decided the term before and she had taken her mum a letter to say that Mr Gorton had left, moved on and Mrs Bainton would be her teacher for the next few terms. Her mum's reaction had been amazing.

'Morgan Bainton? Oh, well, that's it isn't it? I mean I know it's hard to get teachers in this bloody backwater, but did they have to bring in a slut like her.'

Jessica was used to her mother's foul mouth. It was because she was unhappy. She'd told Jessica many times. That's why she drank maybe a drop too much of the old vino. But anybody would resort to a drop of drink if they'd had a life like hers. And so on and so on.

'Are you listening, Jessica?'

Leanne was flapping the letter from school around, trying to get her daughter's attention.

'I went to school with this *Morgan Bainton*, only it was Morgan Parish then. She was a little witch. I could tell you some stories about here and no mistake.'

Jessica looked at her. Her mother used to be at school with her new teacher. Was this the truth?

Leanne knew she had her attention now, and she slyly put the letter down and pretended to be resting, her eyes closed, her head against the back of the chair. Oh, she knew a thing or two about Morgan Bainton alright, only now that Jessica wanted to know, she could bide her time in the telling.

A few days later Leanne was packing up the Christmas tree decorations, winding the tinsel round her arm to pack away for next year.

'Jessica, get that dog out of the chocolates,' she sighed. No joy in this end of Christmas, just a load of extra work and dark nights to come now.

Jessica picked up the white Westie and threw him into the kitchen.

'Go on, Mum, tell me about the naughty girl and the bonfire.'

Jessica was taken with this tale that her mother had been unravelling recently. It wasn't as if Leanne was in the habit of telling stories. True, grim facts were more her style.

Leanne had always spoken to Jessica as if she was another adult, someone to listen to the gossip and trials of the village. There was just the two of them, always had been with Billy gone. They had to look after themselves and there wasn't time for fairy stories.

'It's not just a story, Jessica, it's the truth.'

Leanne was halfway up the loft ladder with the weary tree over her shoulder.

'It's the truth alright,' she muttered to herself, 'and if that Morgan Parish thinks she can just swan in here all holier than thou, miss smarty-pants schoolteacher, and forget about what an evil little bitch she was, well she's got another think coming.'

*

'Are you going to stand there all day?' Morgan's voice hit Jessica between the eyes. She glanced around and realised that the rest of the class had already sat down and were sniggering at her doziness.

She crashed noisily into her chair, sparking off a round of class giggles.

'Well, no need to break up the furniture.' Morgan was cold, in charge, a little nervous and still wondering if William would be alright.

'I'll get you, you evil witch,' Jessica muttered to herself. She picked away at the desk with her hair grip. By lunch she had worked out 'W' in the wood and a growing grievance was heavy in the pit of her stomach.

'I don't know what you're going on about.' Jimmy Huntley was waving his ruler about in the playground - it was covered in soil from the mole hill.

'She's a witch, I'm telling you, my mum told me, and she should know'. Jessica stuck her hands deep into her pockets, shredding up her paper hanky as she tried to remember the stories Leanne had told her.

'She keeps bats and eats frogs and can do spells and fly around.' These weren't exactly the stories, but they would do for now.

'They don't let witches be teachers.' Jimmy stuck his ruler back into the molehill and started to gallop around it on his imaginary horse.

'How do you know, you're not in the government or anything. There are teachers who are witches and she's one of them.'

Jimmy got off his horse with a flourish and bent to pull the ruler out of the molehill.

'I am King Arthur, and this is Excalibur'. He got on his horse to gallop away again, shouting to Jessica, 'You're just cross because she made you look silly. A witch? Huh, it's you who's the witch.'

Jessica kicked at the molehill until it was flat to the grass. She knew what she knew. She would ask her mum to tell her the stories again and then she'd tell Jimmy and the rest of them just what Mrs Bainton got up to when she was a girl in this same village, going to this same school.

Jessica felt Morgan's eyes on her all afternoon, and she began to regret her outburst in the playground. If she was a witch, she might be able to read minds and know that Jessica had been slagging her off.

In the afternoon, Morgan read more from the story of King Arthur and his Knights of the Round Table. She remembered reading it herself when she was a child and wondering why her mother had called her the same name as Arthur's wicked half-sister. Did she know right from the start what an evil little girl she was?

Ruefully she remembered how she'd thought that maybe

157

that was why the goblins had stolen her away and taken her to Aunty Molly's.

She smiled to herself and tried to put some of the magic of that legend into her telling of the story. The children in the class fell silent, spellbound.

Four

Gwen's story

It was early June 1966 when I realised I was expecting again. You could have knocked me down with a feather. I'd thought I was in the change - you know, no show for months, moody, and I thought putting on weight was all part of it. I mean I was working hard at college, I had to keep up… Anyway, the doctor said it happens, although that didn't stop him looking down his nose disapproving. You'd think men had nothing to do with making babies - the way they get disapproving and holier than thou when it suits them. Well, it was too late to do anything about it. Baby was due in October. Maybe Donald was right, and my place was as a homemaker and mother.

This bus takes a long time, doesn't it? I don't know why it has to go this way round. They never pick up at any of the towns. It's amazing how tired you get travelling, isn't it? I hope Morgan settles at Molly's. She's probably forgotten about me already.

You can still have men friends these days, though, can't you? mean friends who are men. Nothing amiss, nothing untoward. Just friends. There was this English lecturer at college, I mean me and him, well we were just good friends. I was comfortable with him, if you know what I mean, he was like the brother I never had, he was a good bloke. We'd talk about books mainly and I learned so much from him - outside the course I mean. But Donald, well he didn't understand at all. Made such a lot of it when I was out late after college. I told him that Tom was just a friend, a colleague, if you like, almost, except he was qualified, and I wasn't. But Donald wouldn't have it - made me feel dirty somehow - and I'd done nothing wrong.

Then things settled down a bit. I mean, I didn't talk about being pregnant and I just carried on as if everything was as it was before. And Donald? Well, it was as if nothing had happened. He seemed to have forgotten all about it. We were never talkers, Donald and me. He always did the talking for both of us - well for all of us really, I suppose, and we let him. King of the Castle! I remember when he got us all bikes - before David was born. He made us go everywhere on those bikes with him, me and the girls. We'd ride along in this long crocodile following the master, arms going out signalling left and right turns like a dance troupe in a routine.

'We'll just ride to Locke Park,' he'd say, and we'd have to go. I would have rather finished the ironing or whatever but that would have to wait until later. Dot and Pat sulked and created, and I'd have to have a word with them. He never knew we all hated it. I suppose we should have said.

Then when David was born it was as if he had what he wanted. His boy! The bikes rusted in the shed then. He was prepared to wait for his boy to grow up in his own image. He planned to groom him, tutor him, his son. Still does - wants David to get back to his studies now the house is quiet again. I dare say it'll all work out in the end.

Are we nearly there? I haven't done so much talking in a long time. I'm sorry if I've worn you out.

All soul's day when I had the baby. Halloween they've started to call it these days. It was a really cold day. I'd seen a robin that morning sitting on the fence looking quite perky in his red and brown. I watched him for ages, kept meaning to get on with Donald's tea. Then I started with the pains and that was that.

The baby was born at six in the evening. Donald couldn't be at the hospital as he was working late. Can't blame him. Oh, but she was beautiful. I know everyone says that about their own baby, but, oh, I don't know. Maybe it was because of all the to do about the pregnancy, maybe I was glad to see her so - well perfect, unspoilt. And I know that this sounds fanciful, but as she lay there so 'knowing', she seemed sort of magical.

160

I'd been reading about King Arthur and his courtly knights and all that. Chivalry! Now that was something. Men knew their place in those days - all protection and politeness for the lady. I was tempted to show the books to Donald, but he would have taken it the wrong way. Anyway, the baby was so beautiful and sort of mysterious, that I decided to call her Morgan after King Arthur's half-sister Morgan Le Faye. I knew that in some of the stories Morgan Le Faye was a witch, but she was a powerful lady - knew her own mind. I hoped that this little one would know her own mind in time.

Donald came in with Dot and Pat to see baby Morgan. He was very quiet. Wouldn't hardly say a word, except 'was I alright?' and 'were they looking after me properly?' You know, just smallest of small talk. I was quite upset when he didn't want to hold the baby, but he wouldn't come anywhere near. He went after half an hour and I was so upset I burst into tears. Dot said, 'Mum, don't you see. He still won't accept it's his'. I didn't see. I didn't see how the man who has fathered three children already could possibly not cope with another birth, late in life and unexpected as it was. I'd have to cope after all. I had no choice in the matter.

The next morning the sun was shining through the ward window. It didn't stay out for long though and except for its occasional fleeting appearances, the ward seemed dark and cold and contained no hope. I could hear the drying leaves dancing against the window. The wind was blowing them, they had dried in the sun, they had no choice but to be part of the swirling, crackling dance that sounded like a death rattle. Morgan had a mop of red hair even as a new-born. No-one in our family as far as I knew had red hair. I knew Donald wasn't into leaps of faith and I remember wondering, how would he ever take her to be his.

Five

Welcome, Moon of the Stag! The Stag of the Gods leaps out of the cold forest, a spark of sunlight shining between his antlers. We set our minds to follow the light as it grows and guides us through the dark time.
(Celtic ritual)

Morgan's class filed in, noisy, ragamuffin and relaxed. They had got used to her being their teacher over the past few years and looked forward to each new term with its stories and projects. They were always eager for what she had in store. Morgan waited until the coughing, chatting, scraping of chairs had settled down. They looked at her expectantly and she smiled. 'Right, children, last term, as you know, we studied the Romans. Now I suppose we should really go on and look at the Roman invasion of Britain.'

She turned to the blackboard and wrote THE ROMAN INVASION OF BRITAIN in large white letters.

'Does that mean we can be soldiers fighting, miss?' Jimmy Huntley was already waving an imaginary sword about and glowering menacingly.

'However,' Morgan went on, 'it occurs to me that we may have overlooked something. I mean, who were the Romans fighting, Jimmy?'

'Er, the Britons, miss, I suppose.' Jimmy made a few more parries and thrust finally at his imaginary foe.

'But who were the Britons, Jimmy? That's what I was thinking. I wondered if we could have a look at who these people were that the Romans were coming to invade.'

The children settled like autumn leaves in their chairs.

162

They knew a story was about to start. They loved Morgan's stories, she made everything come alive, seem real.

Jessica's mother still went on at Jessica about how unsuitable Morgan was to be a teacher, but Jessica didn't listen anymore. She would nod and make the odd remark as Leanne expected her to, but her heart wasn't in it. Morgan was no more a witch than she was. Jessica loved to listen to her stories, she would do anything for Mrs Bainton.

'So, I thought we would have a look at the Celtic People, first. These were the people who were in Britain when the Roman's invaded.'

'I thought the Celtic People were all witches and wizards, miss,' Jessica shouted out, her arm waving for attention.

'You and your witches, Jessica Myers.'

Morgan laughed and the whole class joined in, even Jessica.

Morgan rubbed out the large white letters, THE ROMAN INVASION OF BRITAIN, and replaced it with THE CELTIC PEOPLE.

'The Celtic People worshipped the sun as it was the sun that ruled whether or not their crops grew. They believed that they had to perform certain rituals and sacrifices so that the sun god would be kind to them over the part of the year when their crops grew. They very much believed in the land, the tribe and something they called the Otherworld.'

'What's the Otherworld, miss?'

Jessica was first with the question they all wanted to ask.

'It is a magical place where the Celts believed you went to when you died. In fact, they didn't believe people died altogether but that they went to the Otherworld and that at certain times of the year you could contact the departed by conducting certain ceremonies.'

'Does that mean I could talk to my dad?' Jessica was eager, twisting her pencil around in her excitement.

'Does that mean we could talk to our dogs and cats what'd died, miss?' Jimmy Huntley was bouncing up and down in his seat.

'And our goldfish and our grannies?'

'But wouldn't they be all rotting?'

'Yes, and their eyes popping out, and their skin dropping off.'

The hubbub was increasing, the idea of the Otherworld certainly setting up a wild picture of half de-composed rabbits and pets and zombie-style beings.

'Please settle down, class.' Morgan had to shout to make herself heard over the product of their imaginations. She dreaded to think about the graphic pictures, which would accompany this lesson.

'I wanted us to think about how important the sun was to these people and why they would think they had to worship it.'

'My mum worships the sun,' Jessica said. 'She sits in the garden all the time when the sun is out, moves around when she goes into the shade, she ends up sitting right at the bottom of the garden by the dustbins.'

'Yes, you're right, Jessica, we do call people sun worshipers these days when they are the sort of people who like to sit in the sun and get a tan. But for these Celts, the worship of the sun was a very serious thing to them.

164

They believed as much in the sun as a god as we believe in our God now.' And as if on cue, the clouds suddenly parted and the classroom was filled with a bright light, pinning Morgan to the blackboard in a pool of weak April glow.

The children shrieked and ran to the window. 'It heard us, miss, talking about it.'

Morgan sighed. This lesson was becoming a circus. She had noticed a shadow pass the door and knew that she would be hauled out of the staff room at lunchtime to be brought before Mr Huxstable, once again, to be counselled on how to maintain order in her classroom.

It was such a lovely day, with that blue sky and sunshine. She wondered if she would get away with a nature ramble that afternoon. Did she need parental consent forms for a nature ramble?

She sighed again, then bellowed. 'OK you've had a look at Leuh, the sun god, now sit down, please, before he gets angry, and Mr Huxstable as well.'

The little village by the sea is inhabited by the strangest creatures called Truths and Lies. Some of them live on the beach, covered by boulders and white, chalk stones. These are the old Truths and Lies that have been quite forgotten about by the villagers and their children. Others (the more recent of them), live in the village and are to be found in the most unusual places. The Truths are smiling creatures who live in the sunshine or on the sweet breath of children. The Lies are mostly ugly things who live in decomposing cardboard boxes or under the shadow of Time itself.

The cackle at the school gate consisted of many layers. Not orchestrated counterpoint like some fine Bach opus, but more natural and earthily arranged, the music of young mothers.

Leanne addressed the gathering generally, her head tilted back to catch the last few weak rays of the setting sun.

'You all knew her at school, didn't you? She was a witch then and she's still a witch now. But a witch teaching her evil to our children.'

Someone snorted, repressing a laugh. 'Not this again. Don't you think that's a bit over the top, Leanne?'

'No, I don't. You've heard what they're doing now, haven't you?'

'Our Jimmy is full of it. Never have any trouble getting him to go to school. I don't know what you're making such a fuss about.'

'You don't? Well look at it this way. I was brought up to be a Christian, as I expect all you were. This village has a lovely church and chapel…'

'… neither of which I've ever seen you at, Leanne Myers.'

'Well that's got nothing to do with it. Just because I don't have the time to go to church, even though I would if I could, it doesn't mean my child should be instructed in the ways of witchcraft.'

'They're just a few stories about things from history, from the past. She's not running about with headless chickens and casting spells and curses everywhere.'

'Huh, just give her time, that's what I say. I can remember when she chased after me with a frog, waving it about and shouting all sorts of rubbish I couldn't understand.'

'That was years ago, we were kids. She was just trying to frighten you. There was never any love lost between you two.'

'I thought most people here hated her like I did. She never

166

had any friends. She was wild and strange.'

'Well, it's all water under the bridge now. She's teaching our kids whether we like it or not and there's not a lot we can do about it.'

'We'll see about that. I'm going in to see Mr Huxstable about it. He ought to know what's going on.'

'But we don't want our kids without a teacher, not in their last term.'

'They won't be without a teacher. He'll just tell her what's what and she'll have to stop telling them all this rubbish.'

But one day, Old Lady Gossip goes around with her large wicker basket and collects lots of Truths and Lies and mixes them up in her black cooking pot seasoned with the holes from cobwebs and the poison from stinging nettles. When they are stewed and laid out on the table, no-one can tell the one from the other so each caller to Old Lady Gossip's house must decide for themselves whether to eat or fast.

Down towards the Dyke, while you were still in the woods, there was a clearing, which had a raised area forming a natural platform. At the beginning Morgan told them more stories about King Arthur's Court and his Knights of the Round Table. Someone had brought an old car seat down which they called Arthur's Seat and they set it among the primroses. She told them that the famous Arthur's Seat was way up north in Edinburgh, but they didn't care. This was *their* Arthur's Seat. After Morgan had collected William from nursery, she would take him home, change him and then make her way down to Arthur's Seat where they would be waiting for her. The thickening foliage on the horse chestnut canopy kept off most light showers but if it really poured down, they moved to the old rock overhang down on the beach if the tide was out or reluctantly abandoned the session if not.

Jessica loved to hold William so that Morgan could give all her attention to the stories. The children were hungry for them, they loved the tales of monsters, dragons, romance and magic.

In the classroom, they were back to the syllabus with the ROMAN INVASION OF BRITAIN, but here… here were other stories, stories they didn't hear in class.

Morgan told them about Etain, the most beautiful girl in Ireland whose wicked stepmother used magic to change her first of all into a pool of water, then into a worm and then into a beautiful butterfly. Later she conjured up a wind to blow Etain to a rocky shore where she lay helpless for seven years. The children sat open mouthed as Morgan told them how the wicked stepmother conjured up another wind, which blew Etain into a glass of mead, which was then swallowed by a woman. Etain was eventually reborn as a human girl, one thousand and twelve years after she was first born.

She told them the story of The Salmon of Knowledge, Fintan, who was eaten by Finn MacCool who could then see into the future. She told them of giants and more about the Otherworld and of the Morrigan, the supreme Celtic goddess of war who would stalk the battlefield filling warriors with fury and picking over the corpses of the fallen.

'She was a shape shifter,' Morgan told them, watching their eyes go round with wonder. 'She could see into the future and could change her shape into a crow or a raven.'

As they got used to the stories, they would act them out,

changing them sometimes by mixing the characters and creating new stories of their own. They started to bring down old dressing up clothes to Arthur's Seat and kept them dry in a bin sack under a big rock.

Someone in the village commented that it was as though the Pied Piper had paid them a visit and stolen the children away but only on a temporary basis.

Jessica and William became great companions, soul mates. Morgan looked at them playing together and noticed how alike they were. She tried to keep this thought buried in her mind. Life was good at the moment.

She told them about the Hawthorn Giant who was big, strong and spiky. He had a beautiful daughter called Olwen, whose name meant 'white track' because everywhere she walked, four white clovers would spring up.

The Hawthorn Giant guarded his daughter with his wickedly long and sharp thorns and would not let her move about in the world.

A young hero called Culhwch, whose name means 'pig run', came to rescue Olwen but first he had to complete thirty nine tasks set for him by the Hawthorne Giant.

The last task was to chase the Boar, Trwyth, who was really the son of a prince who had been magically transformed into a boar. Between his ears was a comb and shears which were stronger than any others in the world and the Hawthorn Giant wanted them to cut his own strong beard. Culhwch, with the help of King Arthur and his men, chased the boar, Trwyth, across the sea to Wales, and then drove him into the River Severn.

As he struggled against the current in the river, two of

Arthur's men snatched the comb and shears from between his ears.

Culhwch returned to present these prizes to the Hawthorn Giant but instead of letting him have them to shave his beard, the hero chopped off the giant's head and claimed the beautiful flower maiden, Olwen, for his bride.

Morgan explained how the story was really about one season making way for another. About how the cold of winter held back the flowers until the sun came to shine on the flower seeds and release the growing time again.

She told them about how the Celtic People would celebrate on May Day, welcoming the sun, welcoming the death of the Hawthorn Giant who was really winter.

In these parts everyone knows that the tide can be cruel or kind. Some days the white lips of the waves chatter and spout in the most amiable way. But some days they bicker and spar, roused to anger by absolutely nothing at all as far as any sensible creature can see.

Barely three years she'd had with Billy. Leanne walked down into the village, her arms overflowing with purple lilac from the tree at the bottom of her garden.

He had always gone on about the lilac had Billy. He wasn't a gardener, never even tended any of it, he was a fisherman and that was that. But there was something that always touched him about the lilac and its heady scent. 'Reminds me of my gran,' he'd say and then that would be it.

He was a man of few words. 'A man. Little more than a boy,' Leanne thought as she nodded to people standing outside the library, waiting for it to open. 'Why had he been taken?'

She knew there was no-one to tell her. She moved on, letting the tiny, purple bells brush her face, the strong perfume remind her of death.

Now it was six years to the day since Billy had left the warmth of their bed; softly so as not to disturb her. He'd gone off out on a cobble, local, just for a bit of a change. As if he didn't see enough of that ocean, he was on it most of his working life. But he couldn't stay away, and it was such a lovely day. Leanne reached the memorial in the Village Square. There were flowers there already, there was more than her in the village that had need to remember. She lay the lilac gently by the white lilies and the roses, and she nodded in satisfaction at the correctness of it all.

Six years ago, the sun had been shining and the sky was the bluest it could have been. There had even been a few visitors in the village getting the season off to an early start. She remembered walking with Jessica to the Post Office to get some sweets, she'd walked in and they were all staring at her. She'd known straight away it was Billy.

She had wanted Jessica to come with her to put flowers on the memorial as usual but this year she was too busy. Oh, yes, too busy galivanting around with that Mrs Bainton from school. How could that be?

Jessica had always liked to carry the lilac. It had been a small ceremony they had always performed together. Until this year. Leanne walked home, knowing she was walking back to an empty house. No-one else had thought it was weird, all this meeting the schoolteacher out of school, all the stuff she was filling their heads with. The others had been glad the kids were out and not under their feet at

171

home. But one or two were starting to listen to Leanne, now. One or two were having doubts and it was these one or two she intended to phone up this morning. Something had to be done.

Six

Welcome, Moon of the Flowers! Summer is come, the earth blooms, the world is green, birds build their nests, we become free in the pleasure of being. (Celtic ritual)

The flower maiden was covered from head to foot in white clover. Jessica had been up early. She knew she should have gone with her mother to the memorial, but this was important as well.

She'd wondered about using lilac on her dress, but the flowers were too big and heavy, and the perfume smelled of death.

Today was the opposite of death. It was to celebrate the birth of summer.

Mrs Bainton said that as this was their last term at junior school, the celebration of summer was also celebration of them all moving forward on to the next stage of their new challenges. She was great Mrs Bainton, she made Jessica feel important. She made her feel there was something to look forward to.

Jessica had spent a lot of time on the dress. She'd stapled the clover on to an old white bridesmaid dress she'd begged off Mrs Malloy at the post office. She was a great hoarder Mrs Malloy. She was always good for costumes for fancy dress or plays and things.

She had also made a long daisy chain and hung that around her neck. It wasn't perfect, but Jessica thought it looked beautiful. Olwen, 'white track', the flower maiden. She wished her mother could see her. She might even think she was beautiful for once.

173

Her lips are red as rubies and her hair shines like fine spun gold. Her eyes are the colour of blue hyacinths and each footstep leaves behind it four pure-white clover.

The children arrived at Arthur's Seat at 10 o'clock. Jimmy Huntley had brought water in a bucket his mother usually used for lugging.

'It's a good way to carry water though,' he said, justifying the old sandy bucket to his laughing classmates.

Morgan had been up at dawn much to her mother-in-law's disgust. 'It's the first day that poor little boy has to sleep in and not be dragged up to go to nursery, and you have him up at dawn, out collecting goodness knows what rubbish out in the woods. And for what, I might ask. For what?'

Morgan and William took their early morning walk down to South Landing. All along the side of the path on the way down were nettles and thick forests of dock leaves. William helped her gather the dew from the dense greenery and they pretended to be sorcerers gathering up magical potions into a jar. Later in the morning they ceremoniously poured the dew into Jimmy's lug-worm bucket ready for the May Day procession.

Morgan had told them how they would be, in a way, acting out the hunting of the boar Trwyth so that they could present the comb and shears to the Hawthorn Giant, to cut his thick, wild beard. This was the May Day celebration the Celtic People would have had. They would have wanted to kill off the Hawthorne Giant who was winter, by marrying his daughter the Flower Maiden to Culwych, her prince. The Hawthorne Giant had a curse

174

over him that when his daughter was married, he would die. 'This, was their way,' said Mrs Bainton, 'of getting rid of the old, undesirable but necessary winter and making way for the summer.'

She took out three plant pots and in each was a different flower. One had the flower from the oak tree, barely a flower really, more like a loose catkin. Another pot held the bright golden broom, and the third, meadowsweet, its flower heads ripped from the plentiful supply down in the gully of the Dyke.

'My mum says it's called mother-die,' said Jessica. 'She says, you pick it, and your mother will die.'

'Well, it was me who picked it, Jessica, so don't worry,' Morgan said, smiling. 'I'm sure your mother will be fine'.

On her way back from the memorial, Leanne called in as usual at the bungalow on Croft's Hill. Harold did brisk business on May Day.

He set up a trestle table at the entrance to his drive to catch the locals and visitors alike.

'How are you doing, Leanne, lass?' He had his pipe aglow and was at peace with the world. 'On your own, where's the little one?'

'Not so little, anymore, Harold.' Leanne set down her basket and started looking at the display of plants on the trestle table. 'She's got a mind of her own. She's gone off with that schoolteacher, Morgan Parish as was, you know, used to live with Molly and John Flowerdew up at the farm.'

'Oh, aye. I do remember. She's schoolteacher, now, is she?'

'Mm, at Flamborough School, you wouldn't believe

they'd take her on, would you? Not after the life she led them when she was a girl. They seem to be able to forgive and forget though. But she'll always be that little witch Morgan Parish as far as I'm concerned.'

'So, what's your Jessica up to going off with her? It's not school today, that I do know. Our little Chloe's not at school, she's in my house with her mum.'

'She's taken a load of them off, Harold. Practising all sorts of witchery with them, I reckon. But no-one round here seems to mind that, not one bit. They all want their kids out of the way, and they don't seem to care what they're doing.'

Harold pulled hard on his pipe, thinking. 'Aye, well, there's strange things can happen even in this day and age. They think they know everything. But what about you, love? This isn't a good day to be remembering things, is it?'

'I've just been to the memorial, Harold, but it did seem lonely without Jessica. I still can't believe what happened, you know. It was a day just like this. I mean, blue sky, hardly a cloud and yet just out there it was storm and mayhem. You just don't know what's round the corner, do you?'

'You're right, lass, you're right. Best get on with things, because you just don't know.'

Leanne found what she was looking for on the table, three pots of herbs, chives, sage and thyme. It wouldn't be May Day without the start of her herb garden. Her dad had always sown his herbs on May Day morning, and she had followed on. Except she wasn't that green fingered, so she bought them from Harold, knowing they'd had a good start.

She set off back into the village. She'd done what needed

176

to be done so she could get on now with the rest.

She'd call in at Mary Miller's. She wasn't happy about the schoolteacher either. Maybe they could get their heads together and come up with something to see her off for good.

At Arthur's Seat they assembled the pots of flowers and the bucket of water, North, West, East and South. Each child came up to take a pinch of flowers and sprinkle them into the water. 'Come to us, flower maiden'. Jenny Miller had hay fever and there was a difficult moment when she sneezed and nearly scattered the whole proceedings.

Jessica had brought in the doll, Babog, a strange, ancient name that no-one liked to say as it seemed alien to their tongue. This was actually one of Morgan's old dolls that Aunty Molly once bought her to encourage her away from her books. Morgan had loved the doll but only as an ornament.

She couldn't love and cuddle it like she'd seen other children do. Now it was a grand ornament as Babog, all decked with flowers of the season, with buttercups, vetch, coltsfoot and white clover. Morgan sprinkled some of the water from the lug bucket over it to 'enliven it with the spirit of the flower maiden'. Babog was then carried by Jessica to be at the head of the procession.

They had talked about the procession for many hours in the weeks leading up to May Day. How it should look, who should do what, where it should go. Jimmy Huntley, as self-proclaimed best fighter in the class was to carry the hawthorn branch, which represented the felling of the Hawthorn Giant's power. Morgan helped him to cut off a suitable piece and he was under strict instructions not to wave it in anyone's face.

When he was telling his mum about it, she somehow got the idea that he was to be some sort of soldier, so she let him wear her grandad's medals from the Great War 'as long as you look after them, lad.' Jimmy knew this wasn't quite right for the part, but he wore them anyway as he was proud of his great grandad from the stories he'd heard. No-one seemed to mind.

The rest of the costumes had been made over the weeks and kept in the Dyke in black bin sacks. They'd been very inventive and had a lot of laughs over them.

They had somehow come up with a hobby horse costume based on Peter Wilcox riding on his own old hobby horse bought from a craft fair and him, dressed up in a flowing kind of frock which covered the wooden horse over and made him look large and comical.

It was decided that Graham should play the fool, because, as Mrs Bainton pointed out, that's what he did best in class anyway. He got some old curtains from his mum and they made a big tube with one of them, which he got inside. Then he let them tie string round his waist and ankles and made bits to cover his arms.

'You look like a clown on Tuby's circus', laughed Jessica.

'Well, a clown's like a fool, so I must be right.' Graham careered about the woods, popping out from behind trees and shouting 'boo' and making everyone shriek with surprise, then laughter.

Some of the girls in the class had been in the Judy Johnson dancing show the previous July. They had all sorts of costumes from that, so the rest of the procession consisted of tin soldiers, fairies, country wenches and dutch dolls. Not quite traditional, Mrs Bainton had said, but in the spirit of things so that was all right.

However, one of the sticking points had always been what they should sing. Morgan said she didn't know any of the songs the Celtic People would have sung and neither did anyone else.

In the end they decided to sing songs they all knew but with the words 'tweaked' a bit to make them appropriate to the occasion.

The characters assembled, the rituals had been observed, the procession began. They marched from the Dyke to the cliff top to All Things Bright and Beautiful, and from the cliff top down to South Landing to sundry lyrics from Ghostbusters.

The blue sky had hardly a cloud and the sea birds keened and cried in counterpoint to the children's songs.

Jimmy marched proudly, his great grandfather's medals bouncing on his chest and the hawthorn branch borne so high it was a wonder his arms didn't drop off with the strain.

Jessica glided behind; and in her imagination, she left four pure white clover flowers for each step she delicately took. The rest of the motley crew leapt and danced in great delight. They took great gulps of the fresh, salt air and drew into themselves the warmth of the day.

In the little village by the sea, the Truths and Lies long for warm weather. They are sick of the hard slap of gales, the vicious sting from the icy rain. The Truths, who tend to be dreamers, love to lie about all day on the barmins, mooning over signs of a turn in the season.

But the Lies. Oh, the Lies! They gang up, brazen as the edges of a storm, make themselves into a wall of bullies and rage at the reluctant sun.

Leanne was sitting in Mary Miller's garden with a cup of tea. They had been chatting a while and she was feeling a bit chilly.

'I don't know why you've got such a skimpy t-shirt on,' Mary said to her, shivering in sympathy.

'Oh, I always have my sleeveless ones on from the first of May.' Leanne flapped her arms about and moved her chair a little to follow the pool of sunlight on the grass.

'Well, I must be nesh or something, because I could no more go without a cardigan in this place than fly.'

Mary huffed off to the kitchen to make another pot of tea. It was making her cold just looking at Leanne. Still, she'd been interested to hear what she had been saying about that schoolteacher. That Mrs Bainton said their Jenny needed some help outside of school to catch up with her reading. What a cheek. What right had she, to poke her nose in saying Jenny was slow?

Her husband, Jeff was furious. 'We were all slow readers in our family,' he'd said, 'but we've not come to any harm.' And Jenny was so upset. She said the others called her names. Mary Miller was going to go and give that woman a piece of her mind, teacher or not.

'There's one or two don't like her you know,' she said as she came out with the fresh pot of tea. 'They don't say much to your face, but you can tell they don't like her.'

Leanne took the cup and wrapped her hands around its warmth.

'Well, I think we should go and look what she's up to

180

down there today and then see if we can report her to Mr Huxstable again. At least he stopped her doing all that witchery stuff in the classroom last time, didn't he? I bet he doesn't know the half of what she's doing with his pupils when she isn't in school. It's not right. It's not her place.' She drank the tea, glad of it, and tilted her head back to catch the midday rays of the late spring sun.

The procession had reached South Landing and there resplendent in the middle of the beach was the maypole. Morgan knew Ed wouldn't let her down.

His mother had objected as only she could when she heard Morgan ask him to fix it up. ''They've never done that before round here, you know, Ed.' She'd rattled the pots in the sink, speaking to Ed with her back to him.

'You want to be careful, son. There's some that won't like it and when they know you've set it up, well…'

'It's only a maypole,' laughed Morgan, taking up a cloth to wipe the dishes just washed.

'But we've not had them before, not here. Not that I can remember anyway. We have the sword dance on Boxing Day and that's it. Never a maypole.'

She snatched the cup Morgan was about to dry, and re-washed it, putting it back on the draining board with a clatter.

'And it's a pagan ritual, Morgan, we're all Christians in this village.'

'Oh, Maggie.' Morgan held back from outright laughter. 'They've been holding maypole ceremonies in England for centuries, even within Christian schools. There's nothing new, it's not as if we're slaughtering lambs or sacrificing

181

children or anything like that.' And then she did laugh outright, unable to stop herself. Really it never ceased to amaze her how this little village was so locked into itself. Sometimes it felt like the bounds were so tight you would never, ever break free of it.

'Great maypole, miss,' said Jimmy, admiringly. 'Were they always made of driftwood?'

'No, Jimmy, people had to improvise, make the best of what they'd got. Driftwood is fitting for a fishing village though, don't you think? But what do you think of the Cailleach?'

She pointed to the right of the makeshift maypole. There lay a scarecrow-like doll, spread-eagled on the warm rocks like a hessian sun-worshiper.

'Wow, miss, that's seriously weird.' The hobbyhorse stopped in his tracks and the rest of the May Day circus fell silent.

'Remember, the Cailleach is supposed to represent the Goddess of Winter and we have to make her give way to the flower maiden, Olwyn, and let summer in.'

Morgan had spent the previous few evenings making the doll. She had filled it with flowers, rice and sweets. She took it up now and hung it out on the end of a stick.

'Right, Jimmy, you have first whack'.

Aunty Molly had always said that. 'You have first whack, Gwen.' Except Gwen wasn't even there when she thrashed Morgan. But Morgan knew that the first whack of any beating was from her mother, who according to Aunty Molly was a poor woman, who hadn't the strength to beat some sense into the girl herself.

Jimmy came forward, his medals thumping on his chest,

and he gave the doll the biggest bash with his hawthorn stick. Everyone cheered.

'Now, come on, everyone can have a go.'

Morgan beckoned the children forward and they all came and took turns to beat the Goddess of Winter, until the flowers, rice and sweets burst forth and spilled onto the sand.

After they had found and consumed the sweets, Morgan re-convened her raggle-taggle procession back into shape for the remainder of the ritual.

She led Jimmy to the maypole, which Ed had sunk into the sand as best he could, wedging it with large white boulders. She helped him tie the hawthorn branch to the pole with farmer's twine.

She helped Jessica tie the Babog doll to the top of the pole, sitting her in the cleft part of the whitened driftwood, looking out to sea. And then they danced around the maypole, weaving and plaiting the ribbons, singing and generally having the celebration of their young lives.

Ed came down later with a couple of baskets of sandwiches and cakes. The children sat and ate their picnic. Then to mark the very end of the ceremony Morgan got out two large candles and sank them into the sand.

'Now,' she said, 'we all have to pass between the lighted candles to cleanse ourselves of the winter and make ourselves fit for the summer to come.'

In the end there were only the three of them prepared to go down to South Landing to see what was going on. Really, Leanne couldn't believe how little some people cared about their own children. Mary Miller, Amy from the garage, who really would have done anything to get away from that husband of hers and his oily hands, and Leanne all walked with a purpose down the landing road.

The light was fading by now and as they neared the beach, they could hear the children singing and laughing but could not at first see exactly what they were doing.

They saw the flames from the candles and then saw the children and Morgan and her husband as well, dancing in and out of the flames, laughing and singing like mad people.

'Barely a stitch on them,' gasped Leanne, moving on quickly to get to the scene.

The costumes lay in a pile near the remains of the picnic.

Morgan thought it would be risky to dance near fire with all that on.

The singing stopped when Leanne arrived. The children started to wander away, picking up their costumes and getting ready to go home. They knew a storm was brewing. Leanne stood hands on hips, not realising the remains of the hessian Cailleach was dangling above her head.

'I've seen it all now,' she started, 'the local schoolteacher defiling the beach with satanic rituals.'

'Absolutely,' echoed, Mary, noticing the weird doll's remains and hoping it would not fall down and grab them both.

'Oh, come on Leanne, it's only a bit of fun.'

'A bit of fun! You entice children down here and make them dance naked in the fire of candles and you call it fun! You always were a witch Morgan Parish and you're a witch still.'

Ed stepped forward. 'Now then Leanne, you have no

right to go calling people names like that.'

'No right?' Leanne was beside herself.

She flung her arms in the air and bashed the sacking dolly bringing it down on her head. Mary screamed and the children laughed.

Leanne threw the sacking away and stepped nearer to Ed, glowering. 'Your wife,' she spat, 'she brings children down here on the anniversary of the death of my husband, in a place where his body was washed ashore, and she has them cavorting around like devils and you call it fun.'

'Your Billy was not washed ashore here.' Morgan was also angry now and the children had stopped packing up to go and were agog listening to the argument between the two women.

'I'm sorry you had this loss in your life, but you can't go around expecting people to stop everything they are doing for evermore because of it. It's your tragedy and you have to deal with it'.

Jessica ran to her mother. 'I'm sorry, Mum, I should have come with you today. I miss my dad as well.'

'Your dad! Your dad!' Leanne was marching around, not able to find an outlet for her anger.

She kicked over the candles, spat at the maypole. She marched up to Ed, waving her arms about and pointing at him. 'Billy wasn't your dad. This is your dad.' And she thrust her finger into Ed's face.

The silence around them was only broken by the crash of the incoming tide.

Seven

The skeletons in the cupboard are beginning to dance. They are proud of the mischievous rattling noise they can make, heel, toe, heel toe, rattle of clavicle, clatter of vertebrae. They peep through the crack in the door, squint through the keyhole, wanting to show off the knowing hollows of their eye sockets, to let out secrets held in their ever-open sneering gapes. But the cupboard is in an attic and the attic is in a castle, a castle on top of a mountain, a mountain too high in the clouds to be seen by the eyes of mortals. And although their rattling and cavorting is loud, no-one is listening.

Morgan went on the bus to see Gwen. Donald had phoned her on the Friday morning, saying she was ill, very ill and had been asking for her. He was subdued on the phone, resigned somehow and Morgan had felt sorry for him. 'I'll be there tomorrow,' she'd said, already planning what to pack and whether or not to take William with her.

She had taken him to see his grandmother several times in the past years and although Gwen loved to fuss over the little boy, the strictures of the closed room often made him fractious and naughty. Once or twice, Donald had taken him into the garden. After a couple of hours, they'd come back in, flush cheeked, the pair of them, and William chattering ten to the dozen. Morgan caught Donald's eye on these occasions, wanting to thank him, but her father looked away, scurried into the kitchen to make the tea.

It was hot on the bus. Morgan was glad she had decided to go on her own. William would have been fidgety and bored.

He would be far better off with Peter and Maggie. After

all they'd promised him, a day out including a picnic and a ride on the train in Sewerby Park.

She sat slumped in her seat. It had been hard work, the last few weeks. So many people seemed to want a piece of her. After Leanne's melodramatic announcement Jessica had constantly been at their house asking about Ed, was he her father? Was William her brother then? Poor kid. And then Leanne would be up there dragging her back home, telling her she shouldn't visit Mr and Mrs Bainton, they were far too busy for the likes of her. Leanne always reeked of drink when she came. She'd got a job now at the Dog and it seemed was taking a little too much comfort from it.

The bus dragged its way across the Wolds. There were only a handful of travellers, but it was airless stuck in the faded, dusty seats, the sound of the engine chugging and dragging in between heavy gear changes. The fields looked dry; although the furrows upheaved in some of them had greenery showing. She tried to read for a while, but the words shrivelled on the page as her eyes grew heavy, wanting sleep.

Sleep evaded her though. She was haunted by the events of the past few weeks, the weeks which followed the celebration of May Day. At first, Morgan had been hauled in front of Mr Huxstable. Just a friendly chat, was how he put it, but in effect he'd said she shouldn't be fraternising with children on her own doorstep, not the children she taught. Unwritten rule, bad practice. Apparently, she should keep a professional distance.

Leanne and Mary Miller had obviously bent his ear about the May Day procession. They'd bent almost everyone's ear about it, so Morgan had heard.

She hadn't been able to go in a shop, the library, anywhere in the village without someone mentioning it. Oh, they'd been complimentary for the most part, but Morgan knew to be wary of flattery. And then there were the comments when she wasn't there. Mike the village policeman, gave a very amusing rendition of the proceedings. Ed had heard him telling the story in the pub.

'That Leanne, you know, the barmaid at the Dog, she comes in to make a report. She says that these kids were dancing in and out of fires, not a stitch on, some of them. That's what she says.' Mike had gathered a crowd. They all wanted to know.

'Children naked, she says, and my mind's racing on, thinking who on earth am I going report this to. So, I quiz her a bit, and I asks her if she's sure they were naked. Almost, she says, and looks at this friend of hers, you know Jeff Miller's missus, but she's saying nothing. So, I quiz her a bit more and I say what do you mean, exactly? And I try to look stern, even though I'm thinking about my pie in the oven, probably burning to a cinder.

'Then this Leanne says they'd been dressed up in fancy dress and they'd taken off most of their clothes to dance about in the fires. And my mind is running on a bit. If what she is saying is true...

'So, I say, and how big were these fires, love? And she turns away to her friend, kind of embarrassed like. And this friend she colours up like and says, candles. Aye, I'm not kidding. Candles, she squeaks they were candles really.'

The crowd had laughed, Ed said, at Leanne's expense. But Morgan had been quick to see the sadness behind the usual twinkle in his eyes.

And then there was the accusation from Leanne about

188

Jessica. It was meant to hurt, of course, but was it true.

Morgan and Ed hadn't talked about it at all. The farm was busy and there was always a distraction. But it hung between them like a dirty net curtain waiting to be washed and aired.

The bus was picking up speed now on the motorway. There was a bit of breeze coming in through the window. Morgan felt sleepy. How many times her mother must have made this journey when she was a child and living at Aunty Molly's.

She tried to imagine that first time, did she remember any of it? She drifted into sleep dreaming she was a child being lifted from her bed at home and carried by fairies to that house by the sea where she could hear waves crash against the cold, grey, perilous rocks.

Gwen was frail. She was in the chair in the front room with the antimacassars as clean and neat as ever. But her face was grey and hollowed. Morgan didn't remember her looking so ill last time she saw her. She had scarcely noticed Donald as he took her through. He left them alone. He did not offer her tea.

'Morgan, is it you?' Morgan went to her and kissed her. She held Gwen's agitated hands and smoothed them over and over between her own.

'I'm so sorry I let you go.' Gwen began to weep. The tears cascaded down her cheeks unchecked.

She wiped Gwen's eyes as she did William's when he cried. Gwen seemed not to notice, allowed herself to be tended as a child.

'I let you go, Morgan. I let so many things go. My dreams and plans, they all slipped away somehow, somewhere.'

'Don't blame Donald.' Gwen looked at her intently. She needed reassurance on this. 'He did what he thought was best. I let him take me over. I never fought back.'

Gwen slumped into her chair, her eyes closed, and Morgan was alarmed. Should she send for someone? There was no air in the room. No windows open even in the stifling June heat.

Gwen once said that Donald didn't like the windows open. Morgan felt her mother's cheeks. They were cool and damp and soft as feathers.

Gwen opened her eyes and smiled. 'I love you Morgan, will you forgive me?' She took her hands out of Morgan's clasp and cupped her face tenderly. Morgan felt her own eyes prick with tears. This was all too much. She stood up, pretending that her legs were cramped up from kneeling.

'Can I get you anything, a drink?'

Gwen smiled. 'Nothing at all. Just remember though, Morgan. Life is so short. I know older people say that and the young choose not to care. But believe me, it passes like when you're watching a slow cloud go over the sky. You know? It seems to be taking forever but when you take your eyes off it for a moment and then look back, well, it's gone. That's how quickly my life has passed.'

'It's not over yet.' Morgan knew the lie hung heavy in the swelter of the room. She would have given anything at that moment to hear Donald with the tinkling teacups. But all there was, was silence. And in that silence, she remembered the years she had hoped for her mother to fetch her home, the years she had hoped for even a letter, a card, something to say, 'with love'. She stood up.

'Of course, I forgive you, nothing to forgive.'

Her words hung there hot, sticky and uncomfortable.

'I think I'd better go. You need your rest.'

And still denying her own tears she left the room. Donald met her in the hall.

'I hope you haven't upset her.'

'How long has she got?' Morgan was blunt.

'A while yet, we hope.' He was defensive, wouldn't let Morgan in even now.

'Well, I'll come again, then.'

She moved to the door, opening it herself, eager to be away.

*

Leanne had been round to the Bainton farm to pick Jessica up. Of course, as Jessica had pointed out that she was old enough to come home on her own. But she spent more time there these days, playing with William, messing about in the barn, than ever she did at home.

'I don't know what they have that I haven't got.' Leanne was dragging her by the hand down the road back home.

'Well, it was you told me Mr Bainton was my dad, and that makes William my brother, and why shouldn't I go and play with him. And anyway, its nicer round there than at home. There's more to do.'

Leanne clipped her around her head and ignoring the yells, continued to drag her down the road.

'Never mind what I said. Your place is at home with me. You are an ungrateful little bitch. After all I've done for you.' Jessica stopped yelling. She could see the curtains twitch in the house on the corner. She hated being the middle of a scene.

'OK, Mum, I'm sorry. I won't go round again for a while. I want to go home. Let's go home. Come on Mum, let's go.'

Leanne let go of her daughter's hand. 'Right then, come on. It's about time you realised what side your bread's buttered on.'

She walked quickly down the road with Jessica running to keep up. She could see her mother was still angry.

'Let's do something together when we get in, Mum.' Her voice was breathless, fearful of this angry mood.

Leanne didn't reply, but gradually her pace slackened and then she turned to her daughter.

'Let's make gingerbread men,' she said. 'It's ages since we did that.'

The house was dark. Leanne hadn't opened the curtains in days. Jessica sighed. She saw the chair in the garden, and the bottle of wine balanced precariously on the grass. Leanne must have been in the garden soaking up the sun all day. The dishes were still in the sink and the beds unmade. Jessica set to, made a cup of tea for Leanne, which she took into the garden and then washed the dishes and cleaned up. She opened the curtains and let in what was left of the daylight.

'Looks like chips again for tea,' she muttered to herself and she rummaged in her mother's purse for some change.

'Just going for some chips, Mum,' she called.

'What about the gingerbread men?' Leanne shouted back.

*

Morgan wasn't exactly invited to the funeral this time

either, there was simply a message on the farm phone from Donald, giving the time and the place.

She went on her own, Ed couldn't be spared from the farm and William was too young. She stayed at Grace's house, which was now really hers. She hadn't sold it or rented it out. She had intended to, they could do with the money, but somehow it was as if Grace was still there, and she just kept putting off the decision.

They hadn't contacted her to join them in church, so she just turned up. She sat on her own at the back, not able to even recognise her sisters, although she knew Donald of course. He acknowledged her with a brief tilt of his head, but he did not beckon her forward.

Another lone mourner sat alongside her at the other side of the church. He had a child with him, a boy. The child was noisy, and the man had to keep shushing him.

'Gwen was a good woman...' The vicar was addressing the congregation. He who knew nothing about her departed telling those who knew her very well. 'And we will sing, 'All things bright and beautiful,' which may to some seem like a child's hymn, but which was a favourite of the dearly departed.'

'He makes her sound like an idiot,' thought Morgan, remembering, though, the last time she had heard this sung. At the May Day procession, when the year was ready to burst into blossom and had held promise.

Gwen had been right. Life was short. She ought to have known her mother for longer, much longer, and now she felt as though she hadn't known her at all. Or Grace. She had been a short chapter, but one that Morgan often re-read and one that she kept close to her heart.

The noisy little boy from the adjacent pew came to sit next to Morgan. She held out her hand to him. He took it and they sat in silence for the remainder of the ceremony.

Outside the light was vivid, burning their eyes as they filed out of the church. Morgan thought she would pay her respects to Donald and then leave. There was nothing for her here.

She felt someone touch her arm and turning came face to face with the other lone mourner. 'Thank you for looking after Jake.' He smiled but his face remained sad. 'You're Morgan, aren't you.' She nodded. I'm your brother, David.'

She looked at him. There was a slight family resemblance, a shadow of her mother, the finest of threads of something to hang on to.

'Pleased to meet you,' said Morgan, immediately regretting her own formality. She saw that his face was drawn and tearstained and she softened. 'This is your son?'

The boy looked up at her, the father's sadness was echoed in the child's face.

'It's my weekend for access,' David explained. 'Not much fun to be dragged to a funeral when you're expecting the zoo and McDonalds. Still, I knew I should come.'

'I didn't think you still kept in touch.' Morgan hesitated. She didn't want to sound critical. Heaven knows she wasn't in a particularly good position herself.

'I don't. I mean I didn't. I heard about Mum through a friend, a fluke remark. I haven't seen any of them for twenty-five years.'

People were moving. The coffin was in the hearse ready to be taken to the cemetery. Donald was bearing down on them, his face seeming to catch fire as he saw and then recognised his son.

194

Eight

It was shady in the Dyke. Arthur's Seat was cool, regal with its carpet of ferns licking at the mouldering, frayed car seat. Morgan looked up at the tall canopy provided by the many large green hands of the horse chestnuts. Somewhere high up the late July sun bore relentlessly down.

'I wonder if anyone's coming,' William whined. He had his sports kit on including new trainers bought only that morning. He was desperate to show them off. 'I thought we were practising for The Games.'

Ed hadn't wanted her to go down to the Dyke, of course, not after what Mr Huxstable said. It was as though he thought Mr Huxstable was God.

Anyway, as Morgan pointed out to him, she was a mother as well as a teacher. She could take her child and his friends where she liked in her own time, talk to them about what she liked in her own time. She'd been angry, especially when she'd caught a glance of Maggie in the kitchen, looking smug.

The children that had been with her all those years in Flamborough School had finished their last term now and had moved on. They would be at secondary school in September and most of them had other interests for the holidays. A few of the group were still keen to hear the stories though, but she had to be careful, she realised that. She had come up with the idea of 'The Games', a bit like sports day at school, but in the woods. A bit of fun, good for physical health, who could object to that?

They could have all sorts of events in the woods, feats of strength and endurance, feats of cunning and invention. This had caught the imagination of quite a few of the old crowd when she had suggested it - but now, where were they all?

'You get going then.' Morgan was tired. She wanted to lie down in this cool, shady spot and sleep and sleep. 'You run up and down the banking, that should get you fit.'

She had a job to sound enthusiastic and William sat down in a sulky heap. 'I don't want to, not on my own. You run with me Mummy'.

Morgan sighed. 'You're a big boy now, William, you don't need your mummy to hold your hand when you run up and down, surely.'

William was silent for a while. It wasn't fun down here anymore. The other kids had stopped coming, they were busy doing other stuff. Jessica would be coming, she always did, but not many of the others. 'I wish I'd stayed with Daddy.'

Morgan sat up and looked at his sulky little face.

'Well, you should have. I'm not just here to provide entertainment for you, you know.' She lay down again, shutting her eyes tight, against the daylight, against his disapproval.

William pulled up clumps of fern, tearing them into shreds, tossing them back onto the earth. 'I could have helped Daddy on the farm.'

His voice was quiet but persistent. 'He needs a lot of help, he said so.'

'Oh, and I suppose you think I should help out, do you? You think I'm not pulling my weight?'

Morgan sat up again, rest was obviously not an option this morning.

'I could have helped Daddy.' William went on with his litany. 'He says I'm a good little helper. And Uncle David

196

might be coming today. He'll help out as well. I like Uncle David.'

'Oh, so he's one of the good guys, is he?' Morgan bit her lip. Ever since the funeral, David had been visiting them occasionally. He and Ed got on and obviously he had made an impression on William as well.

The jury was still out on 'Uncle David' as far as Morgan was concerned. She couldn't get out of her head the way that Donald had looked at him at the funeral. She was surprised at the strength of her own jealousy. Why couldn't Donald feel that way about her, his daughter. As far as she could see, David had chosen to stay away from his family, whereas she'd had no choice. What did that say about him? How could he have let all those years go by and not go back just once to see Gwen? And then the minute he chooses to turn up again, Donald has forgiveness, love, adoration almost, held in that one look at his son.

'Come on then, William, I'll race you up the banking.' She got up and stretched.

'Don't want to, now.' William flung himself on the car seat in her place, buried his head in his arms, and pretended to be asleep.

Morgan sighed. She looked around her at the overgrown verdant Dyke. There was almost a jungle feel to it, much cooler of course, but the ferns seemed taller than she had remembered from other years and the smell was a thick, green vegetation smell, overpowering and powerful.

The daylight seemed so very far away, blotted out by tree foliage, the sun high and throwing in a spear of light just now and again through the movement in the leaves.

Her thoughts went again to David. What was he after? He

197

fitted in easily with Ed, with Maggie even. He helped out doing whatever was needed. He was no expert, but he seemed to pick it up easily. Ed couldn't afford to pay him much but that didn't seem to bother David. Morgan was uneasy. As far as she could see, he had lost his own family, his own child and now he was moving in on hers.

Maybe he blamed her for all those years away from home. But he chose to go away. That's how Morgan saw it.

'Hiya.' Jessica was framed at the top of the banking, smiling and eager to see them.

'Not many here,' she said, looking around, half expecting some of her friends to surprise her from behind the trees.

William sat up, rubbing his eyes. 'It's boring.' And he threw himself back onto the seat, sulking.

It was unusual, even in July, to be so near to the sea and yet have no breeze, no let-up whatsoever in the oppression of heat. When Jimmy Huntley and Jenny Miller turned up, they all made a valiant attempt in performing feats of athletic endurance. Jimmy and William ran up and down the banking twenty times before William fell in a pile of nettles. The girls decided to make a flower chain to decorate the winning hero but got talking about this and that and never quite finished it off.

The day was slipping away, the heat sucking it into lethargy. The sides of the Dyke seemed to rise above them, enclosing them. Morgan was drowsy, slipping in and out of sleep and the gentle chatter of the children floated around her. She felt like she was in some kind of vortex, being pulled down into giant vegetation, into the earth. It was a dream maybe or it was…

'Hah! So, this is where the great witch of the North

gathers her children together.' Leanne appeared suddenly, teetering on the banking. She was dishevelled in her scanty shorts and top, her hair rumpled as if she'd just got out of bed. Her face was red and blotchy.

'Mum!' Jessica was horrified. She knew straight away that Leanne had been drinking. She ran up to take her arm and guide her down the banking.

'Don't worry, I won't interrupt the coven.'

Leanne shook Jessica's hand away and stood precariously on the top of the ridge, looking down on them all.

'Just came to have a look at you all, see what you're getting up to.'

She pulled a bottle of wine from behind her back like she was pulling a rabbit out of a hat. She waved it around grandly.

'Tada!! Your friend Mrs Bainton isn't the only one who can do tricks. You could all have a sip of this, might liven you up a bit. I must say you look like a set of dead ducks.'

Jessica tried to grab the bottle, but Leanne held on tightly.

'Not for you my little one, but old Witchy might fancy a taste of my brew'. And she waved the bottle at Morgan who was shaking herself from the drowsy lethargy she'd sunk into. Her heart sank as she made her way up the banking to help Jessica with Leanne who was really unsteady on her feet.

Leanne hooted in delight. 'Ah, here she comes, can't resist the old potion, eh?' She waved the bottle in the air, slipped and then regained her footing. Jessica was in tears. 'Mum, sit down, you're going to fall.'

'Me fall? No way, I'm as steady as a rock, look.' Leanne hopped about first on one leg, then on the other, like a child taunting its elders.

199

Morgan reached her and managed to take the bottle away. She tried to take Leanne's arm and guide her down the banking, but Leanne shook her away violently. 'Child snatcher!' She hissed. 'Don't think you fool me for one minute, Morgan Parish, I've always known you for a witch.'

Morgan tried again but Leanne pushed her, and she nearly lost her balance.

Jessica was really sobbing now, and the other children were sitting watching from the seat.

'Leanne this isn't the place, you're upsetting Jessica, come on you need to get home.'

'Get home! To what? It's all right for you with your nice little family and your farmhouse and your money. What have I got?'

She started to swing and reach with her arms, trying to grasp the bottle but Morgan gave it to Jessica and signalled her to go down the banking with it.

Leanne was getting hysterical now, and Morgan wondered how many bottles she'd had already. Her shrieking hung in the sweltering air, trapped between the trees, unable to escape. The rooks echoed back with a raucous, mocking harshness. Morgan tried again to reach Leanne's arm.

'Oh, no, you won't catch me. But you could cast a spell if you like.'

Leanne was crouched on the edge of the jutting rock, which led to the higher part of the Dyke. She looked like an ancient bird, desperately trying to take flight.

'Leanne, Leanne.' Morgan was beside herself, she had to get her off that rock, it was all getting far too dangerous.

'Here we go, she's working one up.' Leanne stood up,

stretched herself wide, arms above her head. 'Go on, say some of your mumbo jumbo, get me a nice little home and family too.'

She started to flail her arms about, mimicking the movement of trees. Morgan tried to reach her, but it was too late. The Dyke echoed with Leanne's cries, three of them and then an eerie silence.

Trees know everything. Proud as swans they hold their regal heads high as they pattern the landscape, while unbeknown to sojourners their roots cavort through subterranean detritus to spit on worms and rudely poke their noses into rabbit holes. Season upon season they fill the soil with the kind of gutter language that is not fit to be heard above ground.

Nine

Morgan decided to take William and Jessica to Grace's house for a couple of weeks. Leanne had broken her leg in the fall and was being looked after by her mother in Whitby. She was still adamant that Morgan had bewitched her into falling, but the story was wearing thin, and no-one listened to it anymore.

This was the first time Morgan had been to the house since Gwen's funeral. She made the excuse that she needed to clear it out to be able to rent it out, but she knew she wouldn't be able to. Grace was still there. It was still her house. Morgan didn't feel she had the right to invite strangers to live there. Goodness knows they could do with the money though. Ed would never press her exactly, but he dropped enough hints. The farm was doing OK but even with Morgan's salary there was barely enough to keep it afloat.

Ed had no time for her just now anyway. He had no time for anyone, not even himself. Morgan couldn't understand.

'I never see you these days.' She had got up early to make sure he had breakfast. He was up before daybreak and back at dusk. He'd collapse into bed exhausted. It was like living with an automaton.

'I'm sorry, love,' Ed said from somewhere inside his weariness. 'It's just until after the harvest, you know.'

'Can't your dad help? I haven't seen him on the farm for months.'

'No.' Ed shovelled his breakfast in quickly, moving for his boots before he'd chewed the last bit. 'Dad's got a bit of a bug.'

'First I've heard of it.' Morgan realised she hadn't seen

Peter for ages. She'd seen Maggie in the post office where she'd been helping out since her and Peter had handed over the farm. She was as uppity as ever to Morgan, but Morgan still took William in to see her, she wouldn't deny her that.

'Anyway, as I said, it's just until after the harvest. I'll be around more then, I promise.'

And he was off, striding down the path with purpose. Morgan envied him that purpose. The holidays were already lying heavily on her. She would have liked to help Ed on the farm, but she would have been a liability. She was brought up with creatures and this was corn. William tried to help, and Ed let him now and again, but he was just a little boy and Morgan could see it slowed Ed up, even though he would never turn the boy away. No wonder David was made so welcome. By Ed at least.

Here in the town the hot spell was unbroken. and it was even more sultry. Jessica and William played in the garden most of the day. Grace had such a beautiful garden. It had hidden parts, sheltered spots and such a variety of plants it really appealed to the children.

They got into a routine. Picnic in the garden at lunchtime and fish and chips or a burger at night. Not healthy at all, Morgan knew, but this was the holidays.

She had found an old book at the back of a cupboard. She had not seen books in Grace's house before. Each night as it got dark, she'd read to the children from the book by the light of a candle. The stories became part of the fabric of the holiday.

There is a dub or pool, on Ballacoon stream, which the children of

Laxey call Nikkesen's. It is the home of Nyker, the Water Goblin. It has no bottom; and brambles and ferns are growing round it, and fir trees and hazels are hiding it from sight. No child, no grown-up person even, will go near it after dark.

The place in Grace's garden for story telling was by the shed. They'd throw a rug on the small patch of mossy grass, which was held by foxgloves, lupins and invading brambles from the back of the shed.

Jessica would put her arm protectively around William as Morgan told the stories. His eyes were never still. He looked around as the darkness fell, imagining the story, living it.

A great many years ago, a beautiful girl living at Ballaquine was sent to look after the calves which had gone astray. She had got as far as Nikkesen's when she took a notion that she heard the calves over the river in John Baldoon's nuts. At once she began to call them: 'Kebeg! Kebeg! Kebeg!

'Kebeg'! Echoed Jessica, hugging William closer. He wriggled a bit, not wanting to be held so tight. She relented and they listened on.

So loud that you could hear her at Chibber Pherick, Parick's Well. The people could hear her calling quite plainly, but behold, a great mist came and rolled down the valley, and shut it from sight. The people on one side of the valley could hear her voice still calling through the mist: 'Kebeg! Kebeg! Kebeg."

And even in the sultry warmth of the late July evening, they

204

all shivered and shifted about to get the mist out of their bones. William disentangled himself from Jessica's hold and ran about, looking behind bushes, in the shed, shouting 'Kebeg! Kebeg! Kebeg!' until Jessica and Morgan laughed so much at his antics, they had to hold their sides from pain.

When the two children settled again, it was almost dark. Morgan continued with the story.

There came a little sweet voice through the mist and the trees in answer: 'Kebeg's here! Kebeg's here.' And she cried: 'I'm coming! I'm coming!'

And that was all. The Fairies who live in Nikkesen's had pulled her in and carried her to their own home. She was never heard of again.

And although as the days wore on, and the children began to know the story by heart, the ending was always held in reverent silence as they imagined the beautiful girl with the water goblin, deep, deep in some bottomless stream.

Morgan looked in on the children as they slept. She had put them in the spare bedroom, which Grace had never used for years. They shared the bed in there in their sleeping bags - like 'Babes in the Wood'.

She smiled to herself. Looking at them asleep, side by side, the likeness between them was unmistakable. She took in the thought, let it drift like the lines of a story to which she didn't yet know the ending.

She went back downstairs. She couldn't bring herself to use Grace's room with its dark, heavy furniture, its wooden floors and the small bottles of medication still arrayed like soldiers on the bedside cabinet. She didn't want to banish Grace from the house. She still felt that she was very much there.

Morgan got out her sleeping bag and tried to settle on the settee in the front room. She fell asleep easily as she was so tired these days. But after a couple of hours, she was suddenly awake again with thoughts and concerns flicking about in her brain, flooding her consciousness like a blinding light.

Why was Ed shutting her out? He wouldn't talk about the farm, about their financial difficulties. He wouldn't even begin to consider that Jessica was possibly his child. He seemed to regard Morgan like a china doll, fragile and not able to deal with real problems. She rolled off the settee with a crash, wriggling out of the sleeping bag and making for the kettle.

'China doll I am not.' She smiled ruefully to herself.

Nor did she have the emptiness of a china doll's brain. Two in the morning and all the old questions returned as they had done many nights before, and as they would for many nights to come. What was David, her long lost brother up to? He was at the farm more and more these days, ingratiating himself, as far as she could see, into their family. Maybe it was the prospect of a job? Well, there'd be no money to pay him long term for his work that was for sure.

Or maybe, she filled the kettle slowly, so as not to make so much noise, maybe he was hoping to steal the affections of her son.

She was beginning to recognise the irrationalities of the early hours but still the buzzing of doubts unsettled her, kept her from the comfort of sleep.

Morgan paced around the kitchen waiting for the kettle to boil. She stood in each of the squares of the quarry tiles, like a child playing hopscotch. Up and down, faster and faster as she tormented herself with memories of Gwen's funeral, of the love shining in Donald's eyes at the return of his prodigal son.

The kettle boiled, but she set it aside. Tea wasn't what she wanted. She needed to sleep but her mind was too awake. A couple of days ago she'd had a visit from Pat and Dot, her sisters. Morgan and the children were just on their way out to the shops, when the two sisters waddled down the path, bold as brass and their faces full of sour determination. They looked for all the world like the two ugly sisters from the pantomime. She's had to stop herself from laughing out loud.

'Oh, is this not a convenient time?' Pat thrust out her ample bosom.

'No, we're going out.' Morgan would not give them the satisfaction of opening the door now it was locked.

The two sisters sniffed, in unison, and Dot shoved Pat to one side. 'We want to talk to you. We are family you know.'

'Well, I know that.' Morgan was incensed. 'But I wonder that you acknowledge it after all this time.'

'Now then, we only want to talk to you.' Pat tugged at Dot's sleeve. 'Maybe we could come back another day.'

William and Jessica were looking from one to the other of the speakers with open mouths. Who were these women? What had they got to do with Morgan?

'Come again on Friday,' said Morgan, stiffly. 'Say what you need to then and that's that.'

And she turned to grab the children's hands and swept

207

out into the road, never turning to look at her sisters, not caring if she ever laid eyes on them again.

With this on her mind, she paced faster and faster around the kitchen. This was madness. She should be asleep. Her body and her mind were exhausted, yet neither would slow down, neither would rest.

The house was silent. She moved around its darkness, careful not to waken the children. Occasionally a car would shush past even in these early morning hours, and she wondered where they were going at such a time.

She moved back towards the settee thinking about Grace, of how she had moved around the house with such elegance, such confidence even though she could hardly see at all. Morgan half closed her eyes, walked slowly down the hallway using her fingers to guide her, feeling for a sense of her grandmother.

She stumbled against the narrow staircase, taking each step slowly, as Grace would have done.

Her fingers grazed Grace's bedroom door, it was closed, she wasn't ready to deal with it yet. Then another staircase and she was in a room she didn't recognise. It had no electric light, only the moonlight through a round roof window.

Even with her eyes fully opened now, she could only make out shapes in the darkness, two large wardrobes, a settee.

She felt her way around and touched clothing, boxes, things which seemed to have fallen out of the wardrobes or been left spilled onto the floor and not cleared away. Grace must not have come up here once her eyesight had deteriorated to almost total blindness.

'Things take on a whole new meaning when you can't see.' Grace would sit feeling each tiny part of a flower, before putting it into the old green vase.

Every time Morgan had visited her there had been fresh flowers in that vase. Their smell welcomed her, drew her in to Grace's world.

She sat in the dark, feeling at fabric she'd found on the floor. She closed her eyes to make the darkness more intense and ran her fingers through a piece of rough, stiff material.

'Let your fingers be your eyes, let your nose help out. It's only one sense gone you know.'

Grace would draw each stem to her face, smell the blossom then feel it with the tips of her fingers. Her calm would reach Morgan as she sat and watched the ritual. She knew not to offer to help. Grace was in perfect control.

The garment Morgan was holding was small. She could feel buttons, small buttons. It was a child's garment. She wondered if washing it would soften up the fibres. It seemed so harsh for a child. Maybe it was old. It probably was. She suspected no-one had been up here for years. Maybe it had belonged to Grace. Maybe it was something of Gwen's she had held on to for years. Morgan felt the ribbed border of the little cardigan, neat and even stitches. She smelled it but got no clues from that.

Once when Grace was arranging roses, she was eager to smell the flowers close to and grabbed at the stem, catching her finger on a thorn. The blood the thorn drew was as crimson as the bloom. 'You see what happens when you want something too much.' Grace had sucked at the blood, ruefully. 'It brings pain.'

Morgan thought of Grace as a young woman, travelling around, away from home, away from her child, knowing that her child was being turned against her, growing up to hate her maybe. She clutched the little cardigan and rubbed her face in its harsh fabric, and she wept for Grace and her loss, and she wept for herself and the loss of her mother.

She would get the children up here tomorrow and they would clear out this room, put everything in order.

The next day was hotter than ever. Morgan was drowsy from lack of sleep and she told the children to go out into the garden to play. She had made them eggs and bacon for breakfast but could eat none of it herself. She looked around the kitchen, Grace's kitchen, knowing she should be putting the house up for sale, but not able to make the arrangements.

Jessica was making a daisy chain. Morgan watched her methodically pick flowers and pile them in small heaps. Then as she sat cross-legged and with her face displaying total concentration, she nipped a hole into each of the stalks and threaded the daisies. Occasionally she held out the chain to see how long it had grown.

Morgan remembered the unfinished chain she had made for Jessica all that time ago. William had made himself a game throwing stones into an empty flowerpot. Every once in a while, he would throw his arms in the air, shouting, 'Yes!' as a stone landed home in the pot.

Morgan reached out to them to try to feel some of their

peace, but she could find none for herself. The heat was in her clothes, her skin was anxious with sweat. She sat for a while with a cool drink, but couldn't settle and prowled the house again, conscious of something she had meant to do but couldn't recall.

She was looking at the photographs on the wall in Grace's bedroom when Jessica shouted up to her, 'Morgan, there's a man in the garden and he wants to speak to you.'

Donald looked ill at ease throwing stones into William's pot. He found it difficult to bend and his smile was equally as stiff.

'Good morning, Donald, to what do we owe this pleasure?'

She moved towards him, hand outstretched, observing the protocol.

He stood up straight, passing the boy a handful of stones, which he hadn't got around to throwing. He ruffled his hair and William smiled a hesitating acknowledgement.

Donald was overdressed for the heat of the day, and as he rubbed the dust from his hands, Morgan saw that they were shaking slightly. She moved forward quickly and took his hand in welcome.

'I... er... I came to see you, Morgan, because I wondered if we could have a talk.'

She wondered what an earth had disquieted him. She took him into Grace's kitchen, telling the children over her shoulder that lunch would be ready in an hour and they should play out until then.

Morgan filled the kettle, remembering Grace's careful hands doing just the same thing on her first visit.

211

She made tea in the brown teapot and set out the white and blue teacups and saucers just as her grandmother would have done. This was all done in silence.

At last, as the sound of the tea pouring into the cups soothed the tension, Donald said, 'I know that things haven't gone well between us, Morgan. I know that I have been to blame over the years for keeping you out of our family and from your mother until more recently…'

'Oh, you know that do you?' Morgan was getting even hotter now she was in the kitchen and her anger was rising.

'But when I saw David at the funeral…'

David again. Was Donald only ever going to take notice of him?

'…and when I saw his son, Jake. He looked so much like you, Morgan. I suddenly saw a connection. I don't know why I never saw one before.'

He drank deeply from his cup, covering over the awkwardness.

Morgan waited until he had finished drinking and politely poured more tea, offering milk and sugar, feeling like a geisha girl.

'Why now,' she thought. 'Why now should he have this revelation?'

She drew in her breath, her heart was pounding, and the heat was crawling up her back, threatening to engulf her.

'Donald,' she said, trying to sound calm, reasonable, 'I have absolutely no idea why the scales have been lifted from your eyes at this moment in time.

'I don't even care that you have suddenly realised I am your daughter. After all, I've known it all along. And Gwen never doubted it. Congratulations! Is that what you want

212

me to say? Congratulations, you have a bouncing, twenty-seven-year-old daughter.'

Donald looked down into his teacup. She noticed he had grown stooped since Gwen died, stooped and old.

'But the thing is, I needed my father and my mother when I was a child, not now. I needed parents to love me, a family to belong to then. Where were you when I needed you?'

She got up to hide her hot tears, looked out of the window to make sure the children were alright.

Jessica was decorating the bushes with her daisy chains. They looked like tiny white strands of bunting celebrating something. William was following her, holding up the lengths of chain, dutifully admiring her work.

'I'm sorry.' His voice was shaking. It had taken him a lot, Morgan knew, to come and say these things.

'Morgan, I can only say, I was wrong, and I'm sorry.'

She emptied the teapot ready for the new brew and brushed agitatedly at imaginary crumbs on the tablecloth.

'I did what I thought was best at the time.'

He tried to sit straight, pushing his hands firmly on the table and his back into the chair.

'After all, we made sure you were with a family. Molly and John were desperate for a family. Surely that meant you had plenty of attention?'

A silence hung in the swelter of air. Morgan's anger rose and then collapsed suddenly. She had no energy for this.

The kettle whistled, breaking the tension and she filled the teapot slowly, clinging to the action, hoping it would keep her going. Molly had given her plenty of attention, of course she had. And even Morgan had to admit that whatever the rights and wrongs of Molly Flowerdew's

213

treatment of her, she had done it in all good faith, the best she could. But she could never have been her mother. Not when her own mother was still alive.

'If you need salve for your conscience, then take it. I was brought up by a god-fearing, diligent woman. Maybe I fulfilled her and John's needs for a family, but I doubt it. I don't think I was ever the child they wanted. They made do, though. They never gave up on me. And look at me now. I have a family and I have not come to any harm. That's the best, the only reassurance I can give you.'

Donald had sunk into a slouch again. He was fiddling with the fringing on the tablecloth. She could see the perspiration thickening on his hair, his neck.

'I've had so much time since Gwen... since your mother… I've had time to think things through. I just wanted to ask you to forgive me, Morgan, before it's too late.'

'Don't throw that at me. You will have to make peace with yourself. I don't believe in platitudes, and I can't forgive you. You denied me my family for whatever reasons. You denied my mother her child. I can't forgive you that.'

He nodded and got up from the table. They left the newly brewed tea untouched and moved out into the unrelenting sunshine.

Donald looked around Grace's garden, so different from the scrupulous tidiness of his own, and yet so perfect.

'You know, Morgan, sometimes you look at what you have achieved over years and years of work and the beauty is always somewhere else and you realise you've missed it.' He touched the daisy bunting gently and looked at her and suddenly he seemed so old and lonely.

214

Morgan felt herself wanting for all the world to hold him and comfort him, but she could only shake his hand formally as they said goodbye.

Ten

It is said there is a wizard called Lexicon. He has a way with words that is unparalleled in the entire world. He can make them stand in ranks like an army or turn and tumble on the floor like acrobats. Some days he has them fight with swords, sharp as razors, and other days he dresses them up in silk, crimson, aquamarine and emerald. But on the seventh day of each month Wizard Lexicon takes the day off to visit his ailing aunt. On these days the words sit around dressed in sackcloth grumbling and weeping into their bowls of Alphabetti Spaghetti.

Morgan received a letter from Ed asking her to go home. He had things he wanted to talk over with her. The letter was short and written on paper you would wrap bread in, just a scrap. There was no phone at Grace's house, and she had promised to phone home now and then, but she hadn't got around to it. The heat was getting her down. It was even getting the children down. Maybe this was a good time to go home.

The sea breeze was a tonic as soon as they got off the bus. Morgan shepherded the children and the luggage to the point where Ed would pick them up.

'Here he is,' shouted William, jumping up and down. 'Here's Daddy.'

The Land Rover pulled in and before she knew what was happening, Morgan heard the shrill tones of a woman's voice.

'Hiya, Jessica, it's Mummy.'

There was Leanne sitting up next to Ed, she couldn't believe it.

'Nice homecoming, eh?' she muttered.

Leanne's leg was still in plaster, so she had to sit up front all the way home. Morgan sat with the children and the cases in the back, bouncing along, her anger fanned by the foetid air.

Ed lifted Leanne down from the cab of the Land Rover. She made a big point of encircling his neck with her arms and shrieking, 'Oh, Ed, you are strong. Be careful, don't hurt me.' He carried Jessica's things into the house for her and it was a while before he returned.

Morgan didn't understand why this was bothering her so much. Ed had welcomed her home with a big hug, hadn't he? She thought back to their meeting at the bus station. His eyes had been empty, his touch impersonal. She tried to put it down to tiredness.

William kept up a non-stop litany of what they had done, what the house and garden were like, the games, the stories. Morgan could see Ed was getting irritated at the sound of his son's chatter. His face was set hard, and his eyes were shadowed, set in.

'So how often has she been coming round to see you?' She couldn't help herself.

'Who?' Ed didn't take his eyes from the road.

'Who? Leanne, the trollop, of course. You and she seem to be very friendly.'

'Oh, Morgan.' He spoke to her as though she was a tiresome child.

'Never mind, 'oh, Morgan', I asked you how often. I can see it now, *I need you to help me, Ed, poor little me with my broken leg.*' Morgan mimicked Leanne's voice, knowing all the time she should just let this go.

'She's certainly taken a new tack to get you.'

217

'Don't you think I've got more than enough to do?' Ed was driving erratically round the sharp bend leading up to the farm.

'Steady on, then.' Morgan felt ashamed of taunting him. After all this was probably all in her imagination.

They screeched to a halt outside the house. Ed jumped out and stalked off leaving Morgan and William to get the bags and cases out themselves. She had never known him like this. Maybe it was a guilty conscience.

She put the bags in the hall and went into the kitchen. The dishes and pans were piled high in the sink and plates and empty food packaging adorned the table. It looked as though no-one had cleaned up for a month. Ed was slumped in the armchair. Morgan didn't speak but went around slowly picking up the debris and tossing it into a rubbish sack. William went upstairs. He could sense a storm brewing.

She thought she was doing well, under the circumstances. Maybe she was rattling the pots and pans a little harder than necessary, but still, she kept her temper, got on with the job.

'Do you have to make such a song and dance about it?' Ed held his hand to his head, as though the noise from the washing up was causing him physical pain.

'It's a pity no-one else made a song and dance - I know you've been busy Ed, but really...'

'You don't know anything.' He got up and stormed out of the room.

Morgan sighed and tears sprang hot in her eyes. What was going on? She seemed to have returned home to a stranger. She finished sorting out the mess in the kitchen, working automatically, soothing herself. She got some cheese and bread for William, which was all she could find and took it up to him on a tray.

'Is Daddy alright?' The boy looked small, alone.

'He's just tired, we need to help him out.'

She went back downstairs, noting how run down everything looked. Surely, she hadn't left the house looking like this.

The day was getting hotter. The usual sea breeze seemed to have deserted them. She slumped into Ed's chair, trying to get a feel of him, trying to connect somehow. Maybe he was cross that she had left him on his own to cope.

He'd said it was OK. He'd said it would be for the best, get William out from under his feet on the farm. And anyway, Peter would have been there to help.

Or maybe her gut reaction about Leanne was accurate. Maybe she'd been generous with her affections, she wouldn't put it past her. It was obvious she still carried a torch for Ed, or for his property and lifestyle more like.

Morgan spread herself out, trying to get some cool air to her limbs. She heard a footfall behind her and sprang up. 'I wasn't being lazy, Ed.' She was amazed at her own defensive reaction.

'I'm sorry, Morgan.' He put his arms around her. His clothes were stiff with sweat, he smelled of defeat.

She ran a bath for him, took him by the hand and guided him to the bedroom to get undressed. It was as if all his strength was used up. He was like a child.

Later, having got food from the village shop, she cooked him eggs and bacon and watched as he devoured it as though it was the first meal he'd had in a week. They didn't speak.

As the afternoon turned dark and thunder rumbled in the distance, Ed told her about how hard it had been while she had been away.

'It's always busy getting ready for the harvest. David's helped when he could, but he's not used to farm work and he has his own job. Still, he tried. I was scared I couldn't get the crop in before the storms.'

The rumble of thunder was getting nearer.

'And have you?'

'Just about. I've done what I can.'

'What about your dad? Surely he's been helping you.' There was a shrill scream from William's bedroom, and he came running down the stairs.

'Did you see the lightning, Mummy?'

Ed held out his arms and William jumped into them, snuggling down, glad things were back to normal.

The rain plopped in large drops on the lean-to roof. Slow and steady to start with and then each drop falling over the next as the speed of the shower increased.

They sat together in silence, listening to the storm, glad of the let up in the heat.

The evening edged on and when William was settled in bed, Ed and Morgan sat looking out at the slowing rain. They could see the steady pulse of the beacon in the lighthouse, and behind it, the sky navy blue and streaked with grey cloud.

'I'd have thought your mum would at least have been round to clean up for you. She'd know you and your dad were busy with the harvest.' Morgan sat with her head backed onto Ed's chest. She felt him shiver and looked round at him.

'Dad's sick.' The words leapt out of him like he was getting rid of something that tasted nasty.

'It's serious?' Morgan suddenly knew it was.

'I've known for ages, but he didn't want anyone else to know, not even Mum. Especially not Mum.'

'But now?'

'That's why I wrote to you. I really needed you back home, Morgan. The work's one thing but this.'

She put her head back on his chest. They sat in silence for a while as though the silence would halt time.

'Mum guessed a while back and she's given up work to look after him. They say he could have gone into hospital and had an op, but he wouldn't. Says its best to let nature take its course.' Morgan felt Ed convulse and knew he was crying. She tightened her grip on his hand.

'How long?'

'Six months, maybe not so long.'

*

'Mummy says they were the ugly sisters, Daddy. They looked just like the ugly sisters.'

William was enjoying making Ed laugh. He'd seemed so tired after they got back from Grace's house. The child was becoming quite the little showman.

'Pat had this enormous dress on, with big black squares on it, and a really floppy hat. The other one, well she was all yellow.'

'What did they want?' Ed looked at Morgan.

'I don't know really, to have a moan about the house

221

coming to me I expect. They seemed to think Grace should have left it to one of them, not to the black sheep. They never visited her, well, not often anyway. She told me she'd hide under the stairs if she knew they were coming.'

'But they were her family...'

'I was her family. Everyone seems to forget that.'

'I know, I know. I didn't mean...'

'They seemed to think I should let Dot's son have the house, him being out of work and still living at home. I mean why should I?'

'No, you shouldn't. We should sell it, Morgan.' Ed was serious again. 'We need the money, really we do.'

'I know. I will sort it out, Ed, it's just hard. I still don't even think of it as mine. For me Grace is still there. I would feel as if I was letting her down somehow.'

Ed sighed. Morgan just didn't seem to get it. This was about economics.

William appeared in the doorway. He was dressed in an old dress of Morgan's and had a broken straw hat on.

'This was how they looked, Daddy.' He paraded around, strutting like a pantomime dame. Morgan and Ed admired and fussed him, happy to let their problems dissolve into their laughter, for the moment at any rate.

Eleven

Welcome, Moon of the Salmon! Nuts ripen on the trees; symbols of wisdom and the harvest is ready in the fields. We reflect on our achievements, letting them ripen in our hearts.
(Celtic ritual)

'I hear that you had some hassle from our lovely sisters?' David was helping out on the farm almost every weekend now that Peter's illness was common knowledge. Morgan still couldn't relax with him. She still felt he was a stranger trying to get something out of them.

'You should ask our William about that. You should see the way he can take them off.' She feigned friendly banter, making an effort to ease the way between them.

'It's the way they are, you know.' David stared at her, smiling.

He was a quiet man, but not quiet, like Ed; his was a complicated brooding hidden by a smile.

'Well, they can keep the way they are.' Morgan poured him a coffee out of the flask. 'They only seem to turn up when they want something. I mean they've never wanted to know me before. But I got the house, and they don't think that's right.'

She passed David the coffee angrily, the coffee spilling out over the packed corn bales.

'Steady.' He smiled at her, taking the coffee mug in his two safe hands. 'When I said, it's the way they are, I didn't mean it was right.'

'She could have left it to you.'

'What, the prodigal grandson? I don't think so. I visited her even less than them.

223

I was always scared of her as a child. Scared of her staring eyes.'

David sat on the ground, his back against the barn. Everything had dried quickly after the storms of the previous week. Morgan stood watching him, aware that here they were brother and sister, yet strangers all the same.

'I know my running away wasn't right either,' he continued, 'especially for Mum, but going back was just too hard.'

Ed would be along soon, and she would wait to pour his coffee too. She stood straight, flask in hand, waiting in the uneasy silence.

'You could sit down here, next to me, I don't bite you know.' David looked at her, laughter never far from his mouth. She felt his eyes mocking her, as she stood there, formal, uneasy.

Side by side they looked out beyond the path, beyond the fields, to the cliff edge. The clouds were billowing, chugging along in the wind, occasionally skimming then quickly moving on to release the gushing heat again.

'This is such a beautiful place.' David tilted his head back against the barn wall, smiling into the sunshine.

'It's not like this all the time, you know.' Morgan set the flask down, sat with her body erect, unable to relax. 'It's like the little girl with the little curl, sometimes it is good, but sometimes it's horrid.'

'I remember when we used to have our holidays here, when you were really little, you know.' David turned his face to look at her, lazily opening one eye.

'I don't remember.' She refused to look at him.

'No, I'm sorry.' David shifted, sat up and turned to look at Morgan properly.

'When I was really little, me and Dot and Pat used to have holidays on Aunty Molly's farm, in the caravans there. Mum and Dad as well, of course. Doesn't sound that exciting, I know, not by today's standards, but it wasn't that long after the war and for us it was like paradise.'

Morgan wished Ed would hurry up, she didn't particularly want to listen to this idyll. She wondered why David was rubbing her face in it.

'They had everything they wanted, you see, Mum and Dad, back then. They had their three children, one a boy, the war was well past, and life was on the up.'

He tried to take her hand, to comfort the truth of his story, but Morgan clasped the flask with both hands and wouldn't look at him.

'That must have been very nice for you all.' She could not keep the bitterness out of her voice.

'It was, I suppose.' David sat back to stare out at the landscape again. 'I can't say it wasn't really nice, but that was before you were born, Morgan. I can't undo the fact that I had a life before you were born and that those holidays were … are among my best memories.'

Morgan stood up. She would not listen to this.

'I'll go and find Ed with his coffee. I'll leave you to your 'best memories'.'

David stood up, grasping awkwardly for her arm.

'No, stay, Morgan, I have other memories too, some good but some amongst my worst. I thought it might help for you to know how it was.'

Morgan pulled her arm away and suddenly there was Ed.

'Your coffee, Ed, I thought you were never coming.'

She tossed him the flask and flounced away, across the stubble of the shorn wheat, towards the house.

225

'What's all that about?' Ed was tired, there was still a lot of work to do.

'Nothing much.' David turned to go into the barn, to get on with his work. 'We were just reminiscing, you know, like brothers and sisters do.'

Ed poured his coffee, drank it quickly and left the flask on the ground. He didn't have time to worry about all this, not now. He strode into the barn, letting the burden of his work fill the spaces where more sinister worries might so easily slip in.

The Prince is rich beyond his expectations. He has grown wise, and his hair is as golden as his fields of wheat and as plentiful. He is a kind and modest prince who cares not for jewels and trinkets and who indeed wears a cardboard crown that will not tarnish in the brine-soaked air.

Yet sadly there are days when he walks around his realm in high dudgeon. Days when the trill of the skylark goes unheard, and the rising sun goes unacknowledged even though he tips his hat in such a brotherly way.

Twelve

Morgan had been looking forward to Ally's visit for weeks. She hadn't seen her since William was a toddler and the telephone conversations had dwindled to pleasantries over the intervening years. Ally had always been off looking for the perfect job, working hard at 'progressing' as she called it. She'd been down in Cornwall for a while and up as far as John O'Groats, but she hadn't settled yet.

'Oh, Morgan.' Ally's eyes brimmed with tears. 'It's so good to see you. It's been - how long...?'

Morgan searched her friend's face for the shared secrets and intimacies of former years.

'Too long,' she responded, hugging Ally. 'And you haven't changed one little bit,' she added lamely, not wanting to admit even to herself that both of them had changed quite a lot.

William was bounding around, so pleased with his 'auntie' that he fetched all his toys from the bedroom down to show her. They sat in the garden, among the long grass and the weeds.

'Maggie's beautiful garden has gone to wrack and ruin,' Morgan said apologetically, nodding towards the unkempt borders and straggling hedgerow, 'especially with Peter being so ill, you know?'

'Oh, well, life's too short.'

Ally looked around her, wondering at the shabbiness of it all. She hadn't remembered that the farmhouse and garden was like this when she'd visited the last time. She looked at her friend, bubbling and laughing rather too energetically with William and his endless cars, soldiers and farm animals.

227

Maggie and Peter had organised a bit of a party when she was here last - a big picnic buffet in the garden with chairs and cushions set out strategically near the swathes of flowers.

Ally had noticed a tension in Morgan then, but had put it down to tiredness from her working and having a young child to care for.

'You have it all, don't you?' Ally looked searchingly at Morgan who was pouring them another glass of wine.

'Mm,' Morgan was tight lipped, non-committal, not ready for a heart to heart just yet.

'You're doing OK yourself, aren't you?'

She held out her glass to wish Ally good luck.

'Cheers.'

Ally clinked glasses, hoping the wine would work its magic, get them back to where they used to be.

'Where's David gone?' Ally and Morgan were clearing the dishes in the farmhouse kitchen. The mealtime had been raucous, noisy, with all of them chattering ten to the dozen and Morgan was glad of the peace and quiet.

'Oh, he'll have gone to Aunty Molly's for the night.' Morgan noticed Ally's surprised look. 'He stays there with her,' she explained. 'Not at their farm, they sold that when Uncle John got too old to cope with it. They live in one of those old people's bungalows and David sleeps on the settee'.

Ally looked hard at her. 'He's your brother, Morgan. Why doesn't he sleep here? Surely, you've got at least a settee going spare here. Or is it because I'm here. Oh dear, am I taking his bed up? I feel really bad if I am.'

Ally got up, walked anxiously around the kitchen, pulling

the curtains straight, rubbing over the draining board with her hand.

'What are you fussing about, Ally? He never sleeps here. He always sleeps at Aunty Molly's. Likes to gossip about me behind my back, I suppose, you know, about what an evil child I was and how I drove Mum to a nervous breakdown. Then when he goes back to his own job, doing whatever it is he does, he sleeps in his own house. I don't know why you care anyway.'

Morgan slumped deeper into the armchair. David was the last person she wanted to talk about. He was in and out of their lives at the moment as though he had always been there, and she resented it.

'Chippy,' said Ally

'What?'

'Chippy, a carpenter, that's what your David does, for a living I mean.'

'How do you know?' Morgan craned her neck round to see Ally perched up on the draining board, looking out over the farm, towards the sea.

'He said so. We were talking about it over the meal. You were nodding at him, going along with the conversation.'

Ally looked like a sea nymph. She only needed a trident to go along with her imperious tone.

'Sorry. It's been a long summer - a long year. I drift off sometimes, you know?' She got up and went over to Ally.

'Let's start again, Ally, let's talk like we used to.'

Ally jumped down from her perch and flung her arms round Morgan's neck.

'Open another bottle then, it's going to be a late night after all.'

There was just one armchair in the farmhouse kitchen. It

229

used to be Peter's chair and now it was where Ed collapsed every evening after work. It was a shabby, green leather wing back, with broken springs, but Morgan loved to curl up in it when Ed was out working or in bed. It was a fortress against the world, a safe place to be. She sat in it now while Ally, no longer in imperious sea nymph pose, perched on a kitchen chair, her legs crossed so that now she looked more like a Buddha.

'How do you get your legs to do that?' Morgan felt her own legs ache at the prospect.

'Oh, I do yoga, keep fit, all that stuff.' Ally was proud of her figure, she smoothed her hands down her trunk and waist, emphasising its neatness.

They chattered on, stretching themselves into the long evening.

Ally talked about her jobs and the people she worked with and the gym she went to. And Morgan talked about William and the funny things he did and said.

It was as if they were licking at the icing on top of the cake. Neither one of them wanting to take that first, testing bite.

'How's your mum?' Morgan had licked all her icing.

Ally dropped her legs out straight and let her shoulders slump.

'She's OK, I suppose.' She held her hands outstretched over her face, as though clearing the picture for herself.

'She got rid of Maxie you know. At last, she'd had enough of being beaten black and blue and she got rid of him. It was the bravest thing she'd ever done, and I was proud of her.'

'But?' prompted Morgan, anchoring her friend's eyes, forcing her on.

'But after that, well she just seemed to lose all her spirit, do you know what I mean? I mean, she could do what she wanted now and go out when she wanted, but she just sat in the house and did nothing.'

'And Michael?'

'Aye, well, he left home anyway, I mean he would, should, he's a grown man now. But there she sat lonely and pathetic.

'She'd call me up, you know, every few hours she'd be on the phone. I mean what could I do. I was living miles away from her, working, in class. I could well do without it I can tell you. I wouldn't take the calls in the end, just phoned her when it was OK for me.'

Ally got off the chair and sat on the floor.

Morgan said, 'Gwen never had any confidence…'

'Sorry, Morgan, but Gwen was somebody different altogether. My mother was OK before 'him', and you'd think she'd be OK again after he left, instead of giving in like that. No, I'm sorry, but I don't understand her at all.'

The night spiralled on. The summer darkness wrapped around them, listening to the cadences of their stories, the whispers of their regrets.

Morgan refilled their glasses. 'Do you visit her?'

'I used to. But it was like trying to coax a mouse out of its hole. She wouldn't come out into town with me, she just gave me a list and sent me off, watching me from behind the curtain.'

'Sounds like she needs help - won't she see a doctor?'

'Morgan, she's beyond help. I had her come to stay with me once last year. It was awful. She just sat watching the telly and picking at her food. Anyway, I don't worry anymore. I've given up on her.'

'But Ally, she's your mother.'

'What? And you saved your mother from Donald's dominance I suppose!'

Morgan was shocked. Ally had never been so hard before. She wasn't the same person that she'd shared her life's secrets with through those long, anguished nights as students.

'Well, no, but I visited when I could…'

'There's no point. You can't change people. They'll just be who they decide they're going to be. It's not worth the energy. Best get on with your own life, I say. The only person you can change is yourself.'

'Does Michael visit her then?' Morgan wouldn't give up.

'Oh, he does, every Sunday, like a good little boy.'

Ally screwed up her face, the harshness of her words keeping away the tears. 'And he's not the only visitor. Maxie has started going round again. And she doesn't turn him away.'

'Oh, Ally!'

'Aye, well. There's no fool like an old fool, don't they say. I've only got to hear about that first beating he'll give her, and he will, and then that's it. I'm done with her.'

She walked to the window, looking out on the darkness that seemed to stretch for miles. She drew her hand briefly across her face and Morgan looked away, not sure how to react to these hot, unbidden tears or to her friend whose sorrow was obviously not up for discussion.

Thirteen

The mist that is fretted from the sea gets through to your bones eventually. Chills the heart if you're not careful. It's best to keep moving if you can, or else make your way home to that fire, kindled by the man of the house, stoked high to keep his family warm.

'Does your mother know you are here?'

Morgan asked Jessica this question every time she came round for help with her homework.

There had been something of a truce since she had taken William and Jessica to Grace's house in Barnsley. Leanne seemed happy for Jessica to visit and Morgan didn't want that to change.

'Yes, you said I had to tell her, and I have.' The girl was tired. It was hard work at her new school, but she could cope with that. Life wasn't so easy at home, though.

'She couldn't care less, you know,' she went on. 'As long as I turn up and cook her supper and clean up, she doesn't care where I am.' She knew she sounded bitter and smiled brightly to make it seem like a joke.

'I'm sure that's not true.' Morgan tried to take the girl's hand in comfort, but Jessica withdrew it. She didn't want anyone to feel sorry for her.

She liked it in the farm kitchen. It was warm, cosy and she felt safe. She'd do her homework here even though she didn't need much help, and then she'd go and play with William for a while, before trudging home, hoping against hope that her mother hadn't been drinking again.

Leanne was getting worse, and Jessica knew it. She didn't bother cleaning or cooking any more, she just hung around the house after her shift at the caravan park, painting her nails, soaking in the bath and soaking up the bottles of wine. She'd stopped the evening bar work. She wasn't needed out of season, apparently, or maybe they were just fed up with her volatile behaviour. That, and the suspicion that she was drinking more than her fair share of the profits.

Jessica would have loved to talk to Morgan about it all, but she was afraid of what might happen. She knew that children got taken away from their parents and for all that was wrong with her life she didn't want that. She decided that she wasn't going to blab about it, she just had to make the best of it.

'You can have something to eat with us if you like.'

Morgan had noticed how the girl looked wistfully at the table being set, the pans rattling on the stove. But Jessica knew that Ed would be in from the fields when the meal was ready. She knew it was nearly time to go.

'No, Mum will be expecting me,' she said. 'I'd better be going.'

Ed came in, blank faced and tired as usual. He made his way to wash his hands, ruffling first William's hair and then Jessica's, absentmindedly, affectionately.

'David's been working today. He'll be in as well soon.'

Morgan sighed quietly. He'd been staying more and more frequently these days. You wouldn't think he had a job of his own. He never brought Jake anymore though and he never seemed to want to talk about that.

'Can't he go to Aunty Molly's for his?'

She knew she sounded petulant. 'You know she loves to cook for him.'

'Morgan, she's an old lady, and he's been working here.'

Ed was annoyed at her suggestion. David was a good hardworking bloke, and she should be more welcoming.

'OK, OK.' Morgan held up her hands in submission. 'You can stay you know Jessica,' she added, softly, looking again at the girl's woebegone face.

Before she could answer, the door flapped open, and Leanne staggered into the kitchen.

'Now this is cosy, isn't it?'

She moved over to Jessica and clutched the girl round her shoulders, just a bit too tightly judging from the wince on her face. 'Playing happy families, are we?'

It was obvious she'd been drinking, and Jessica's mind was racing, trying to plan how to get her out of there without her making a scene. She needed to get them both away from the inquisitive stares of Ed and Morgan.

'I was just on my way home, Mum.' Jessica edged towards the door, but Leanne didn't move with her. She sat down at the table, fingering the knives and forks that Morgan had just set out.

'You are very welcome to stay and eat with us, both of you.'

Morgan tried to take the sting out of the situation, for Jessica's sake.

'Oh, we're welcome, are we? First I've bloody well heard of it.' Leanne pushed back from the table and went to the stove, lifting first one pan lid, then another. 'And what sort of witches brew are you concocting tonight?'

'That's enough.' Ed moved toward Leanne angrily.

'Enough? You never used that word when we were together down on the beach.' Her laugh was harsh, rasping. 'Couldn't get enough then, could you.'

She turned to her daughter, putting her arm around her.

'That's men for you, Jessica, they take what they want and then move on. They don't worry about who they leave behind.'

Ed snorted, angry now.

'It's you who always took what you wanted, Leanne, and as much of it as you wanted and when you wanted. Everything was always for your convenience. You were nothing but a slag, ask anyone around here. And look at you now, can't even hold your drink, that's a fine example to be setting your daughter.'

'Our daughter.' Leanne was laughing at him now, taunting him. 'Don't forget, I told you, Jessica is your daughter as well as mine.'

Jessica was crying. She had seen William sneak in during the row and he was looking from one person to another, bewildered, stopping his ears at the shouting.

Ed moved toward Leanne and for a minute Morgan thought he was going to hit her. She moved to intervene and then David came in and she felt so ashamed, ashamed that he was staring into the dark corners of her family.

She took Leanne's arm firmly, and nodding at Jessica to take the other arm, she steered the woman out of the kitchen, out of the house. 'You get the dinner out, Ed,' she shouted over her shoulder. 'I'll be back in a minute.'

By the end of the path, Leanne had shaken herself free, and was smoothing down her dress, patting her dishevelled hair.

'So much for being welcome to eat with your family.' Her voice was low. She was almost spitting her words out.

'You think you have everything, Morgan Parrish, but

you'll see. I could twist that man of yours round my little finger if I wanted to, and I might, I just might.'

She pulled herself up straight and grabbed Jessica's arm. 'Come on love, let's rustle up our own dinner. We don't need the likes of this woman to do anything for us.'

Morgan turned to go back into the house, but then suddenly she changed her mind.

'Look, Leanne, I think we need to talk.' She took her arm again. 'Jessica, you go on ahead and get your mum a cup of tea ready.'

The girl released her mother's arm, and with a grateful look at Morgan, she sprinted down the road, letting the sea breeze rid her of the tight caul of embarrassment. The two women followed in the girl's wake, silently.

Morgan and Leanne sat side by side on the seat outside the cricket ground, each lost for a while in her own thoughts. Some of the late September days were quite warm and sunny, but as always by this time in the evening, the mist seeped in, cooling the air, dampening down the foliage.

'I can remember when I first came to live here, at South End Farm, you and Amy were the only friends I had then. I've always wondered why you let me go around with you. Neither of you liked me, did you?' The question was almost one to herself, but Leanne took it up.

'You were different from kids round here. You looked different with all that red hair, and you were big for your age and, well... you stood out because you had that impressive temper.'

Morgan laughed, ruefully. 'The temper comes with the hair, or so I'm told.'

'Well, it wasn't hard to spark you off. Amy and me, we'd

just wind you up and watch you go. There wasn't much else to do - everything round here always seemed boring.'

A car moved slowly along the road, hesitated at the junction, and then moved off again along the landing road. There were times of day in this village when hardly anything moved and now the smoke from the chimneys was signalling the closing down of the day's work, almost everyone was home.

'I never really fitted in.' Morgan stretched her legs out over the path, looking up at the sky as it clouded over. The cool air was a big contrast to the warm farm kitchen.

'You did alright though, didn't you? Nice home, husband who's potty about you, child. And you laud it over the schoolchildren, don't tell me you don't enjoy that. You've got it all, Morgan Parish.'

Leanne was hunched over, hugging her knees, digging at the dry soil with her shoes.

'Is that how it looks to you? I still don't belong here you know. I don't suppose I ever will. It seems that no matter what I do, I'll never be accepted.'

'Accepted? I don't know what you're worried about. You should try being me for a change. You'd have something to moan about then, I can tell you.'

Leanne stabbed fiercely at a clump of grass. 'It's this place, it gets you and won't let you go. At least you got away for a while, and you chose to come back. I know I'll be here forever, doing the same dogend jobs, saying the same things to the same people, day in, day out.'

'You don't have to...' started Morgan.

'Oh, yes I do,' hissed Leanne. 'You said it yourself. You don't belong here, so how would you know. Well I do and I know that this place will hold on to me until its ready to

238

spit me into my grave.'

She stood up to face Morgan, her face contorted into dislike. 'And if you don't like what life's doled out to you then let me have it. I'll take your man, your home, your child even. You just walk away.'

Some people from the village were starting to move around again. The ones who were out with their dogs, pushing into the evening, driven by their routine.

Morgan stared at Leanne, she could see the spite of that child that she had been, the envy of the adult she was now. Nothing had changed.

'You must stop drinking, Leanne, you can't go on like you have been doing.'

'And you can't tell me what to do, Morgan Parish, you never could.'

'But what about Jessica, she needs her mother, she needs you to be there for her.'

'Yes, that's as maybe, but she needs a father too, and where is he then? Doesn't want to know, does he? So, don't you come to me with all your fancy advice. Maybe some of what you've got is mine after all, by rights. Yes, by rights.'

Some days the skeletons come down the mountain to roam. They tap dance joyously on the concrete paths, delighting in the sound they make. They can be quite nifty for bags of old bones. Until the mist drifts in, cloaks their shoulders, hangs heavy in sodden flounces around their clanking bony knees. The sea fret is voracious, swallows everything in its path; flattens itself, muffles sound. Then it wends away, leaving the skeletons shivering and bare.

The newspaper sat on the kitchen table like an accusation.

The headline: WHAT ARE WE TEACHING OUR CHILDREN THESE DAYS? A photograph of Morgan stared out, her hair in unkempt disarray, and her face, frozen in the instant of the camera's click, with a look of wild-eyed madness.

The story that went with the picture bore no resemblance to the one Morgan had explained to the reporter who had visited her at Arthur's Seat. The young woman had been so interested in her storytelling. This was a story of debauched feasting, of burning pagan fertility symbols, of teaching young children the ways of dark magic.

'They've twisted everything I said.' Morgan turned her cup round and round in her hands. 'It was nothing like this, I was just…'

'They're out to sell papers.' Ed was shovelling in his breakfast.

'I know, but this makes it sound like I was teaching young children some kind of black arts.'

'You must have said something to her, where did she get these ideas from?' Ed stabbed a finger at the print on the open page.

'I told her some of the background, some of the mythology behind corn dollies and the end of the harvest rituals, she seemed interested, I thought she was just interested, for herself.'

'Oh, Morgan.' Ed smiled, his eyes sad and tired. 'You'll tell anyone a story, won't you? Just wait till Mum sees this, you'd best keep out of her way for a while.'

'Wait till Mr Huxstable sees this. I can't keep out of his way, can I?'

'What possessed you to contact the papers anyway?' Ed was making his way to the door.

'I didn't. She just turned up when I was in the middle of telling them a story. The first thing I knew was the flash of a camera and this young woman, full of enthusiasm, coming down the bank to ask us about what we were doing.'

'Someone's set you up then.' Ed came back, put his hands onto Morgan's shoulders. 'And you don't have to be a genius to guess who.'

'Leanne.'

'Bingo! Now you'll have to lay low for a while, Morgan. You'll have to stop going down to the Dyke, stop having Jessica round here every two minutes. You've just got to think what other people are saying.'

He squeezed her shoulders firmly and planted a brief kiss on her cheek.

'But…'

'No 'buts'. You know what people are like in this village. You should do by now. You have a position of trust in the community, you've got to be seen to be whiter than white. You can't afford to lose your job, Morgan, the farm can't afford it.'

Ed raked his fingers through his hair, he wanted to shake her. 'Can't you see it? This sort of thing could get you sacked. It could mean the end of your career. There's no doubt about it - Leanne Myers is doing her damnedest to paint you black, but here you are handing her the pot of paint and the paintbrush.'

He stormed out, leaving Morgan smarting at his words. She moved around the kitchen, washing the breakfast pots, setting things straight. She was angry. Angry at Leanne and her vindictive little games. Angry at Ed who seemed to have nothing but criticism for her lately. She was even

241

angry at Maggie who hadn't spoken to her about the article yet, but she would. And Morgan was already angry at what she knew Maggie would say.

She tipped coal down the open mouth of the Aga and her face reddened as the fire wrapped itself hungrily around the fuel. She let herself stare into the flames, looking for answers. Her face burned as tears started to fall. She wept for the little girl who never went home to the beautiful princess in the castle, and she wept for the gingerbread boy who would always be running away from the little old man and the little old woman. Her tears welled but dried quickly before they fell. She slid the steel plate back into position and closed the stove lid, wiped her face and allowed her temper to cool.

She'd have to go into school soon and face Mr Huxstable. She could hear herself, 'wrong end of the stick', 'totally misrepresented me'. But she knew it wasn't going to wash with him. And just as he'd agreed she could work on a Halloween project that she'd been planning for the children in her class. Maybe that wasn't such a wise choice now. Maybe she should back off, think of another subject.

Morgan stood up, put on her coat and shook out her fiery hair. Or maybe Mr Huxstable would understand after all, maybe she should just delay the project, start it in a couple of weeks. People would have forgotten all this newspaper nonsense by then.

Fourteen

The fallen leaves lie as dry as tinder, waiting to be piled onto the bonfire. They rustle in the wind, ask each other what it will be like. They don't know Fire and they are afraid. Then some Lies come along who tell them not to be afraid, that Fire is clever, that Fire is a king. He will take them in his scarlet ship over the sea to new lands where they will adorn his palace.

But along come some Truths who tell them to be very afraid. That Fire will destroy them and that not even a speck of dust will be left of them when he has finished his wicked work.

So, half the leaves believe the Truths and they allow the tickling wind to blow them into the hedgerow, and half the leaves believe the Lies and they wait eagerly for Fire to come along in his scarlet ship.

Of course, Mr Huxstable reported the criminal damage. The classroom was in a real state and the Halloween display was ruined. But the pure hatred displayed in the graffiti was something else. And how anyone got hold of photographs of the defaced work was never found out. For the local newspaper it had made a great follow-up article with its hints at dark arts and innocent children. Morgan was surprised at the support she had from some of the parents, but even with that she knew her position in the school was clearly untenable.

Her resignation letter was on Mr Huxstable's desk shortly after the newspaper report hit the doormats of the Flamborough villagers.

Ed said it wasn't her fault, but he was tight lipped when he said it. And Maggie stayed away, fiercely trying to protect

Peter from the rumours and unpleasantness. David kept William occupied but Morgan fancied she saw a look of smugness on his face. And Leanne? She was over in Whitby visiting her mother, apparently, at the time of the incident.

'How convenient,' thought Morgan furiously, as she raked up the autumn leaves in the farm garden. She was trying to work off her anger.

She paused as more fell on the grass, sent to their death by the sharp gust of wind from the sea. *Nothing between us and Russia.* Morgan smiled to herself, as she remembered Uncle John. She remembered helping him build bonfires at the farm when she was a child.

'There's a right way and a wrong way to everything, Morgan,' he'd said as he showed her how to build the bonfire up.

'I always seem to find the wrong way,' she'd said to him, remembering Aunty Molly's fierce, straight-line mouth of disapproval.

'You'll learn, lass,' he'd replied, ruffling her red mop of hair and laughing quietly.

She smiled to herself as she remembered how she'd thought Uncle John was a bogey man, a Fynoderee, from one of Aunty Molly's stories. But he was a gentle man, a quiet man, and Morgan realised that he'd loved her in his own quiet way.

She ought to go and visit them both, but maybe now wasn't a good time, not with the swell of the press against her. Aunty Molly would only say, I told you so.

She raked the leaves into a pile. It looked almost like a fire on its own with the red hands of horse chestnut leaves, the

244

yellowing flicker of sycamore.

She looked around for William, her anger cooling a little.

Aunty Molly always said that her temper would be the undoing of her.

Once Morgan overheard her talking to Leanne's mother.

'She's really got the devil in her. I don't know what to do with her sometimes. She stands there, defiant, and just will not do what I say.'

Leanne's mother made sympathetic comments.

'That hair,' Aunty Molly fired off again. 'I'd cut it off if I had a chance, but you've only got to get near her with the scissors and she's screeching like a demented owl. The best I can do is brush it and tie it back. It grows like Topsy.'

More sympathetic mewling from Leanne's mother and hidden in the shadows Morgan touched her hair, smoothing it into submission.

'I don't know where all this defiance comes from. The others aren't like that.' This was the nearest Morgan ever heard Aunty Molly get to tears. 'Pat and Dot were sweet little things when they visited. I'd give them one of my cakes and they'd sit there, quiet as little mice. And David? Oh, he was a lovely little boy. He had the manners of a gentleman.'

Tears pricked at Morgan's eyes as she remembered the overheard conversation. Maybe Aunty Molly had been right. She fingered her hair. It was still unruly. She tried to smooth it, knowing it was a waste of time.

William came running up, his eyes sparkling. Morgan tried to shrug away her thoughts.

'Want to come sticking with me William?' She smiled at him. He seemed to bounce with vigour and happiness.

'No thanks.' His words tumbled out quickly, so that he had to pause to draw breath. 'I'm going to help Uncle David mend the fence, I just came to tell you.'

And he turned in his tracks and skittered off again without waiting for her to reply.

Morgan kicked at the pile of leaves. Manners of a gentleman? He'd come into her life again without being invited, made himself at home on the farm, taken over her son's affection. She kicked again and again at the pile of leaves, the dust from them flying into the air like smoke from a real bonfire.

'Now look, Morgan.' Ed was steaming towards her, his eyes glaring like they always seemed to do these days, 'I know you're upset but there's no need to take it out on us.'

'What have I done to you now?' Morgan took up the rake, made out she was tidying the debris.

'You just seem to be in a temper all the time. I saw you just now, kicking hell out of the leaves. Don't do the job if you can't be bothered to do it properly. I'll make a bonfire later when I've finished my other work.' Ed was angry. He was worried and upset about his father. He was tired and worried about the farm. It was even worse now that Morgan had resigned from her job. She knew how he felt, but she wouldn't excuse him.

'You do it, then,' she said throwing down the rake, 'or better still, get the sainted David to do it. He's the blue-eyed boy round here now, isn't he?' She stalked off, grabbing a sack and shouting over her shoulder, 'I'm going sticking in the Dyke, on my own, where I can't offend any of you. You lot can carry on playing happy families and you are welcome to each other.'

Ed sighed and rubbed his unshaven face ruefully. The

wind was getting up. It rattled the pile of dead leaves that Morgan had left dishevelled and wild. Ed gave them a kick and made his way back to the farm.

The leaves belong to the fire's flames,
The fire belongs to the wind,
The wind belongs the white-capped waves,
The waves will sink or swim.
The thighbone's connected to the knee bone,
The landscape's connected to the eye,
The heart is connected to sad things,
And the truth is connected to a lie.

You could get lost in the Dyke if you really wanted to. Morgan was walking around the top path, picking up sticks for the bonfire.

People went 'sticking' round here for their house fires. She remembered Aunty Molly sending her when she was a child. She had been afraid of the Dyke then with its dense woodland, its sharp shrubbery and the threat of the ghost of the White Lady or the spooky flying hand.

Now she found it a refuge, a place to hide. From her vantage point on the top path, she looked down on the autumn colours of the woods that she had once feared. Mostly the trees were horse chestnuts, bronze and crackling gold. She had a love for this place, a tug of belonging, which she'd not felt anywhere else in her life. She felt tears pricking at the natural beauty which was spread out before her. She picked up some debris from the recent high winds. 'Maybe I should just camp out here in the woods and eat nuts and berries like the squirrels.' She smiled to herself as she thought about what Maggie might say about that.

As she descended into the Dyke, Morgan became quite dizzy looking up at the piercing blue sky, her head craning backwards, looking up through the intertwining branches. It was so quiet. Down on the beach she knew she would be able to hear the shrill keening of gulls, the clash of the sea, but here, if there was any sound at all it was just a brief rustle in the undergrowth, which hinted at wildlife.

'And here we are at good old Arthur's seat,' she mumbled to herself, throwing down the bag of sticks and collapsing onto the old tyre, disgruntled. After the first newspaper article, Ed had insisted that she moved all the costumes and bin bags that had been stashed there for story telling sessions.

'People don't understand this,' he'd said, heaving the sacks onto his broad back. 'You need to be more... well, normal, Morgan.' He did not meet her eyes, knowing he was forcing her to abandon something she cared about.

Her fingers explored the undergrowth, the soil was dry, friable. She found a conker case, empty. She wondered how they'd all be getting on without her, back on the farm, in the kitchen. They won't have missed me at all, she thought. They all seem to fit in and get on with things. When I try to be part of it, it doesn't work.

She remembered another time, another bonfire, and telling Uncle John about how she didn't fit in, didn't belong. 'You've not been here two minutes,' he'd said, as he helped her haul a large branch over the rough ridges of dried ploughed earth.

'You have to be born here or live here at least a hundred

years before they'll accept you, you know.' And he'd laughed as he tossed the branch onto the bonfire.

'So, I'll never fit in then?' She'd rubbed her eyes fiercely, trying not to cry.

'It's all in the mind, love.' Uncle John had put his great arms around her, he smelled of soil, of the farm. 'You just need to do what your Aunty Molly tells you to and stop losing that temper of yours. It'll all be alright then.'

And she'd promised herself she would. There and then, she'd promised herself that whatever Aunty Molly told her to do, she would. And that she'd never lose her temper again, not ever in her whole life.

They'd finished building the fire in good humour, but as Morgan remembered now, all these years later, you can't hide your true nature.

*

'You need to get away, Morgan.' Ally sounded calm, in control at the other end of the phone. Morgan pictured her, elfin, neat.

'Professionally speaking, you need to get another job in another town. Make a distance from what's happened. A bigger town, they'll not ask so many questions there. Different mentality from where you are.'

'But what about Ed and William?' Morgan recognised the sense of what her friend was saying.

'Ed can look after himself, and William? Well, you either take him with you or leave him on the farm. It's hard Morgan, but I can't see another way. Anyway, it's not forever.'

Morgan's fingers twisted in and out of the phone wire.

249

Maybe she could take William with her. He could go to school in another town.

She'd be able to send money to Ed and everything would start to get better again.

'I could live in Grace's house,' she volunteered.

'Now you're thinking,' said Ally. 'Live there, new job, new start.'

Ed wasn't so sure. 'You don't have to be living in the house to sell it, Morgan. There are people who will do that for you. It's only a house, it doesn't need a nursemaid.'

They were walking back from visiting Peter. He'd looked so very frail, and Morgan realised Ed really wanted her to be at home.

'You could get a job not too far from here and travel. We'd get you a little car with some of the money from the house. They'll soon realise you're a great teacher, once you leave all that funny stuff out.'

William came running down the path. 'Uncle David and me have fixed the trailer and he says to tell you he's got the kettle on.'

'Taken over my kitchen, now,' Morgan thought.

'And this little lad.' Ed hauled William onto his shoulder. 'He's going to make a grand farmer one day.'

Morgan looked at them both. Ed's face relaxed for once and William high enough up to be able to see the farm that would one day be his.

The chapel organ wheezed and pumped, and the congregation's good hearts sang for dear life.

One voice wavered, though, not up to her usual full throttle. Aunty Molly sat in the front pew shrouded in voluminous black. The hymn ended and the congregation sought comfort on the hard, wooden seats.

Uncle John was to have a plot in the village churchyard. Morgan hoped he wouldn't be in an eternal draught from the cold north wind. She thought of the bonfires they'd built together, his rough attempts at comfort and she wept.

Afterwards at The Hollies, she went to offer condolences to Aunty Molly. She was surprised at how old she looked, how defeated.

'I'm sorry I haven't visited you for a while.'
She took the old woman's hand and was surprised at how rigid and unfriendly it felt.

'Well, no need, Morgan, we heard all about you from the gossips and there was plenty in the papers.'

She had lost none of her sharpness.

'I thought that Ed and that lovely little boy of yours would be the making of you,' she went on, holding tight to Morgan's hand, 'but you went your own way, didn't you? Just like you always did.'

Morgan tried to free her hand, but the old woman held on and pulled her nearer.

'You'll never belong here, not with your temper and your fanciful ideas. Go away, Morgan, they're quiet folk here, your Ed as well. Leave them be.'

Later when Ed asked her what Molly had been saying so fervently, Morgan laughed. 'Oh, just some tips on cleaning up in the house. Strange thing to talk about after a funeral but you know what she's like.'

She made some excuse to go outside into the cold yard. Her whole body was burning.

'God Bless you, Uncle John,' she muttered, looking up at the stars. 'Every time I light kindling or read about the Fynoderee, I'll think of you.'

As the night air began to cool her down, Morgan began to think that maybe Aunty Molly had a point.

She'd never taken any notice of what she'd said in the past. Maybe it was time to start.

'I came to check that you were alright.' Suddenly David was there. He tried to put his arm around her, stop her shivering.

'I don't need you to.' Morgan shook him free.

'I don't mean now. I mean after you were sent here from home. When you were a little girl. I couldn't stand what they did, and I came to check on you.'

Morgan turned to look at him and knew straight away he was telling the truth.

'I would have seen you.'

David took off his coat and put it around her shoulders. She let it stay there.

'It was hell at home. Dad trying to make me go to college when I didn't want to and Mum sobbing in her room all the time. I put up with it for a few months then I ran off without telling them but the only place I could come was here.'

'I would have seen you.'

They sat together for a while in silence, each deep within their own thoughts.

'Uncle John set me up in a barn. It was like camping when we were little. I made them promise to tell no-one where I was. I said I would just run off again if they did. Aunty Molly said you were settling nicely.'

'I went in all the barns. I would have seen you.'

'I saw you running about and playing. You looked so happy. I knew what a great place this was. I'd always been happy here.'

'Why didn't she say? Aunty Molly. She knew how miserable I was. Why didn't she tell me you were here? It would have made all the difference.'

'After I knew you were alright, I took odd jobs all over the place. Became a bit of a wanderer.'

David turned her towards him. 'Don't blame Aunty Molly. I made her swear on the bible.'

Morgan shook off his jacket and threw it back at him. She was angry and hot tears raced down her face. 'It would have made all the difference, David.'

'I needed to make my own way. I needed space.'

'I was a child. I needed my family.'

Fifteen

Morgan takes the suitcase down from the top of the wardrobe and fills it with her things. This place has held her twice in her lifetime now. Held her but not embraced her. She knows that she has to pull away or she will destroy everything she loves here.

She is dry-eyed and methodical. She brings the suitcase downstairs and slips two separate notes under the kettle. Ed and William will be bound to want hot chocolate when they come in. She goes back once more into William's bedroom. There is the usual stuff scattered around. Toys, books, clothes abandoned in disorder. Only his miniature farm is neat and orderly. His prize possession set out in pride of place on the shelf that Ed has made for him. Morgan breathes in deeply to catch the essence of her son.

The taxi is in the back lane where she has asked to be collected. In the back of the cab it is dark, but Morgan knows all about the dark, knows that when her eyes adjust to the light, she will be able to see around her. She hums under her breath out of habit. 'For those in peril on the sea'.

'New moon, Miss.' The driver's conversation is sparse.

'Dark on these lanes, I'll drive a bit slow if you don't mind.' The car edges along the back road like a hearse. There is no moon and there are no stars in all that enormity of sky as far as Morgan can see.

Part 3

One

Even though the house is hers and she is living here, Morgan moves nothing. She makes Grace's bed with clean sheets and lies there every night listening for something familiar. But without Grace there is nothing familiar, nothing of comfort at all. All that Morgan can find in Grace's house are absences.

Last year she'd watched William playing in the garden chasing butterflies and making daisy chains with Jessica. They had lived a few glorious weeks in that house feeling Grace's blessing around them. But now there is the absence of William along with all the other absences, and the house is dark and cold.

Morgan looks out onto the long, overgrown garden that her grandmother had loved. Since late October the Miscanthus has turned from green, to green and yellow, and now it is almost straw. Grace had loved these grasses so much. *I can feel the life in them, the rush of their green, and then in winter, I hear them rasping in the wind and I can imagine the beautiful golden blades dancing in frosty moonlight.*

Morgan stares at the miscanthus, wishing that Grace was here now watching as its tapering fingers beckon the advancing dark of the afternoon.

The house is deathly cold. The only heating is a gas fire in the front room and the gas oven in the kitchen. She leaves the fire on day and night, but it doesn't seem to make any difference. She feels as though she is the only person left alive in a house of ghosts.

'God knows how I'll pay the gas bill'. She turns the switch

guiltily to the low setting, but after a few minutes she turns it back up again to full power. She sends most of her salary home now, conscience money for William and Ed. No, the farm needs it really. The farm needs her money. She'll manage. She needs very little.

The days are at their shortest, but she doesn't care. She sleeps when it is dark. Long, dreamless, black sleep. The daylight brings pain.

Beauty falls asleep for one hundred years. The briars and thistles grow tall and knotted and surround the castle, creeping along its old stones, tightening itself around her enchanted slumber.

Grace's garden is really overgrown. It had been beautiful and wild when she was alive, but now it needs attention. Not much I can do at this time of year, Morgan thinks as she kicks at the blackened, wet leaves and leans against the old sycamore. One defiant leaf is clinging to the place it knows, the place it had leached to as a spring bud and the place where it had waited for the promises of a strengthening sun.

The garden here has no sea breeze, no wakening gust of north wind like on the farm. Here everything is defeated and damp after days of rainfall or gritty after a spell of dry weather. Nothing seems fresh at all.

Gwen and Donald had a neat garden. Morgan thinks back to her few visits there and remembers the perfectly edged lawn and weed-free borders with their tidy clutches of summer bedding. Gwen and Donald lived in that house for over fifty years and every year it had become neater, more ordered.

That isn't counting the years after Morgan was born, the few early years she had spent there as a child, the years of which she has little recall. Apparently, Gwen had told Grace that Donald's house had lost its orderliness for a few years then. The disorder in the house had so annoyed Donald and then had spread to his garden where plastic toys and dolls dresses were to be found in great abandon.

Apparently, his complaints were drowned by Morgan's tantrums and by Gwen's hysterical sobbing. It was like living in a jigsaw picture, Gwen told Grace, where the pieces kept leaping out no matter how often you put them back and smoothed them down.

Morgan can't remember it that way, but she can picture it, nevertheless. She can imagine Donald painstakingly clearing the toys away while scoring another notch against the disruption caused by this 'cuckoo in the nest'. Donald, the father who couldn't own his child until it was too late.

There are masses of photographs in the house, Grace's house. Morgan has spent her exile looking at everything but changing nothing. She makes the bed, sits on the kitchen chair, touches only what she needs to touch and apart from that she is an observer looking at someone else's life. At school in her new job, she manages to be more normal. At school she is Mrs Bainton reading the roll call, saying prayers, wiping noses, but at night, at weekends, she is a living ghost in a house of memories.

The photographs are of another time, of other people. There is Grace, head and shoulders on a postcard, a beautiful young woman with coquettish eyes and a demure smile. And there is Grace's mother and father. Morgan recognises them because Gwen had the same photograph on her wall. They stare out from another age, from somewhere strangely far away and look disapprovingly into this dark, silent house.

And there is a small, creased photograph, obviously lovingly smoothed and mounted, of Sean, Gwen's father. It shows a boy, little more than a boy at any rate. He has a pretty face, curly hair and misty eyes that look out from another place altogether.

Morgan wonders if he is still alive, wonders where he is, what he has made of his life. He is her grandfather after all. You would think he would want to know her. Still, what have blood ties to do with their family? Grace and Gwen both gave children away. And hasn't she just left William, her baby, her son? Maybe there's a curse on her family. No, that's just in stories, isn't it?

There are photographs of Grace in some of her acting roles, framed posters with her name emblazoned on them, small snippets of reviews and mentions from the press. Why had she plastered all this onto the walls of her house? She wouldn't have been able to see them, certainly not for some years anyway.

Morgan knows she should eat. Weekdays she eats school dinners, but at the weekends it is all she can do to buy bread and milk. She's finding decisions hard to make, existing on some kind of animal instinct to survive. She sits in the dark kitchen, forcing dry bread into her mouth, gagging as it sticks to her throat, grimly washing it down with scalding hot tea. A letter has arrived and having read through it once, she sits with it on her lap.

Ed's writing stares into Grace's kitchen. She doesn't have to re-read it. She knows it by heart already.

The letter is short but then Ed isn't into long explanations. You get what you see with Ed. That is the attraction for her. Ed is uncomplicated, straight. The few lines say it all.

It had come after her visit. The one where she'd arrived home on Christmas Eve, phoning from the station for a lift, bearing gifts, offering no explanations or hope. William had been delighted. He had taken what she had to offer without question. He had his mummy for Christmas and that was all there was. Ed found it hard to look at her, there were so many questions that he could not even begin to articulate. And anyway, questions came way behind forgiveness and forgiveness was not even on the horizon. He played happy families for William's sake, knowing Morgan would not be staying, knowing he would have to cope with his son's distress all over again, fresh as it was when she'd left them in the first place.

'Why do you put up with her?' Maggie had been beside herself when she heard Morgan was home for a couple of days. 'I won't be civil to her, you know, I won't mince my words. That evil little baggage has no right to stir it all up again. I'll be telling her straight, just you wait.'

Ed smiled wryly to himself. He knew that his mother's 'telling her straight' would be down to black looks and slamming doors. Still, it would mean he could do a couple of days work on the farm, Christmas or no Christmas and the money Morgan sent was useful. He couldn't think it through beyond that.

What she'd said was plausible. She would sell Grace's house when she could and meanwhile, she'd send money from her new job. On paper, on the surface, it was a business-like suggestion.

But under the surface was a maelstrom, a pot of emotion that simmered but that he couldn't tend to. When Morgan had left, she had taken something from him that he couldn't identify or own up to. She had ruthlessly stolen something from him, and he wouldn't let her back in to take any more.

They had all played along into Boxing Day, gilding the holiday just like many other families were doing. Morgan had borne the brunt of Maggie's tantrums without a word, knowing it was the price she had to pay to be with her son. And no-one wanted to upset Peter, Ed's father, who was so ill now that they knew it wouldn't be much longer.

Morgan had sat with him for many of her precious hours, talking to him even when he had no strength to speak back. She'd talked about the old ways of farming that she'd read about in books, about husbandry, cultivation, rituals and folklore. The words came easily but from somewhere she didn't know.

And he'd listened, calm and comforted. Morgan could see her husband in this man, and she loved him because of it.

The week after Boxing Day she'd tried to explain to William why she couldn't stay, not just now, anyway. William had stopped up her mouth with his fists and clung to her, venting words of hate on her like spitting, gale-driven rain.

Ed had pulled him from her, holding down the pumping arms, and said, 'If you are going, it would be best to go now. Things will settle down when you have gone. And anyway, Mum and Dad are moving in until Dad... well until things are sorted out.'

She'd looked at him, wanting to say something that would take away the hurt. Her words hung in the festive air, like the chipped and tarnished baubles on the old family Christmas tree. She could say nothing. She'd left for the second time and it had been so much harder than the first.

The letter says that Peter died two days ago. The funeral is arranged but it will be better if she doesn't come. No point in upsetting William all over again.

The money is useful, and can she manage a bit more. He does not send his love. He does not send William's love. Maggie's love has never been hers in the first place. And Peter's love, if it was ever there, has gone with him.

The rain lashes down on the garden, hacking at plants, whipping the last straggling roses, stripping off the last tenacious old, dead leaves.

In Grace's house Morgan goes up the second staircase to the room with a small round window. Grace had never spoken to Morgan about this room, and she wonders if the things in it had belonged to Grace or to some earlier occupant.

There are two large wardrobes in the room which have their doors open and the contents spill over onto the floor. There is a large settee which has a faded green quilt thrown onto it as though someone is using it as a bed.

Morgan wonders how the old wardrobes and settee were ever got up the narrow staircase and why she has never noticed the small round window from outside the house. She will check tomorrow if she remembers.

William doesn't need Maggie to tell him stories - he's a big boy now and he can read for himself. And anyway, Maggie always put on this posh, sing-song voice when she reads stories as though the stories are strangers to her. When he reads stories, he reads them silently, in his head. He reads them in his mummy's voice.

'That boy's just too serious, Ed.' Maggie is washing up after supper. He's told her over and over she doesn't have to, but Maggie knows he needs the company. Especially now that little madam has left him and the child. And anyway, she needs the company herself, now with Peter passed on. She's gone back to work in the Post Office but there are so many empty hours to fill these days.

'He should be outside, playing, not shut in his room with books for company.'

'That's how he's dealing with what's happened.'

'Well, that's as maybe, but you should make him go out - take him out of himself, invite some friends round.'

Maggie dries her hands and begins sweeping fiercely at the kitchen floor, banging the cupboards and the table and chair legs with the brush.

'There's not many that'll come. They're all saying his mother is a witch who flew away on a broomstick.'

Maggie pauses, 'Well, that's just plain daft. Their parents should have more sense than to encourage them.'

She whisks the day's debris onto a dustpan and throws it into the stove's furnace.

'Aye, well, you know what they're like round here. They like a good story to get their teeth into.'

Maggie puts away her brushes, takes off her apron and smooths down her dress. She looks in the mirror, her mirror that she placed there years ago. She has missed this

264

house so much it hurts. Ed says that she should move back in properly now, but that's not really what she wants. She wants the years back, the years with Peter in this great farmhouse. The years she didn't appreciate at the time. She pats her hair and sniffs.

'Well, I still think you should make him go out more, Ed. You could go with him, a good walk round the dyke would do you both good.'

Ed shows her to the door, her door, and holds it open for her to leave.

In the silent house, Ed goes over it all again. No matter how many times he reads the note that Morgan left, or the letters she's sent, no matter that he reads them twenty or thirty times a day, he can't understand why she's left him. And because he can't understand why, he can't forgive her. He thinks back to Christmas and the charade that was played out. Why didn't he talk to her properly then?

William is reading on his bed. He's sitting in the dark with his curtains open and each time the lighthouse beam comes around it floods the room with a brief burst of light. But he doesn't need to see the words. He knows them by heart.

*

When Truths and Lies die of old age they are laid to rest by being scattered over leaf mould in the lea of shadows; composted, raked over and ignored. And Time is a worm that turns the matter over and over, slouches its way through decay. Leaves slime in the runnels until one day by the miracle of osmosis it all smells of sweetness and light.

Morgan has decided she will tackle the garden. It's January, it's cold enough for snow, but somehow, it feels right.

There are tools in the shed. Ancient tools, rusty with remnants of old seasons still clinging to them. It's nothing like the neat shed of Gwen and Donald, tools hanging in rows, clean as a whistle, not a dead leaf in sight.

Grace's tool shed is like everything else in the house, it is bursting to tell a story.

Morgan hesitates. She feels like an observer again, she can't bring herself to touch the twisty tined fork or the rake with the rotting wooden handle. She just stands and looks at them, waiting for them to tell her what it's all about.

A cold gust of wind blows more fallen leaves into the open shed door and she shakes herself, physically and mentally. She grabs the hoe, strides off and starts by rattling about in the wilderness beneath the beech hedge.

The next morning, when she draws back the bedroom curtains, she gasps out loud at the transformation. The previous day's gardening had been completed in darkness. She'd been like a machine, working, digging, bagging up old debris. She'd been so tired when she got into the house that she'd not eaten anything at all but gone straight to bed. The temperature had plummeted in the night and her good labour is now revealed in the morning light, a frosted wonderland.

She can't wait to get dressed and go out to look and to touch this miracle of nature. Where she's cut back dead stems, there are frosted new shoots, red and brown shoots, nestling the earth. There are the sharp green succulent shoots of bulbs and a robin surveying the red berries on the holly tree.

Morgan walks and wonders, sometimes frowning. She

266

doesn't deserve to feel this amount of pleasure.

*

William sits in Grace's chair, sulking. Morgan moves from seat to seat, unable to settle. Her mind is whirling, working, but getting nowhere.

'Sit down for goodness sake.' Ed's voice is harsh, he looks haggard. She aches to hold him, to comfort him, but she doesn't feel she has the right.

'I'm bored.' William kicks at the table leg, his angry feet reaching further and further from Grace's chair to find deliberate mischief.

'Don't do that.' Morgan moves to stop his feet from damaging Grace's furniture but William kicks at her, shouts, 'Don't touch me. I'll kick you to pieces.'

She turns her back on him to hide her tears and Ed says gently, 'Go and play in the garden, son, you can kick about all you want out there.'

The latch sucks and clicks, open and shut, as William makes his escape.

Ed sits with his hands cupping his head. He looks out of place with his large, strong frame in this dark, old lady's kitchen.

'Would you like a cup of tea?' Her hand searches eagerly for the comfort of something to do.

'We've had gallons of tea.' His voice is muffled, defeated. 'I brought William to see you because he's nagged that much. I didn't know he'd be like this or I wouldn't have bothered.'

'It's alright.'

'No, it's not alright.' Ed stands and starts to pace the small

267

room, not able to look her in the eye. 'None of this is alright.'

His fist thumps down on the draining board, making the pots rattle. He stares out into the garden but sees nothing.

Morgan stands in one place, frozen by Ed's fierce reaction. She's not fidgety anymore, but only wants to melt into the background, not have to deal with any of this.

'I'm so sorry,' she whispers, the tears flowing unchecked. She makes no effort to wipe them away. The silence grows into a wall between them, and neither have the strength to break it down.

At last, the latch cracks, and William runs in smelling of fresh air, of frost. 'You've got to come and see this.' He directs them both into the garden.

'Look.' His face turns to Ed and to Morgan in turn. 'They look like monsters.' He mimics a monster. He's found a patch of ferns where the leaf balls are so tight that they look like a cluster of green snails.

'Now it's Spring they're getting ready to grow.' Morgan strokes his hair. 'Isn't that brilliant?'

They scour the garden for a while, all three together, looking for signs of new growth. For a while they feel a sense of each other. With one hand Morgan circles William's shoulder and with the other she reaches for Ed's hand.

William pulls free and rattles the locked shed door. 'Let's have a picnic like we did last summer with Jessica.'

'We can't, William, not now, it's too cold out here.' Morgan hears herself laughing and it sounds like someone else.

'Well, come home with us then.' William kicks at the shed door. 'You'll be warm back home with us.'

Ed releases Morgan's hand, picks William up as though he were no more than a feather and swirls him round and round in the twilit garden.

'Nice try, son, but your mother's staying put, I think.'

Morgan aches to be the one in Ed's strong arms, being swirled around as though she were little more than air. She aches to be a child, loved and free, seeing the wonder of spring almost for the first time.

Ed sets William back on his feet.

'We'd better get going. School tomorrow.'

Morgan sees them to the car, her promises of selling Grace's house soon, of coming home soon, are no more than pretty frost crystals fitting neatly into the wintry landscape.

After William and Ed have left, she puts everything back in its place. This is still Grace's house, and she is only a custodian.

Two

Morgan is clearing out the room with the small round window. The wardrobes are overflowing with random items of clothing, books, faded jewellery but Morgan can't seem to find anything that would have belonged to Grace. There is nothing of Grace here at all. She finds she can clear out this room in a way she can't move anything else in the house. Everything else in the house reminds her of Grace and must remain as she left it.

She stares at the dark, polished wardrobes, seeing pictures in the grain like she had seen pictures in the fire flames in Aunty Molly's front room. When Morgan had been sick and couldn't go to school, Aunty Molly made her sit by the fire with a wool blanket wrapped around her knees.

'Don't you move from there while I go and fetch the eggs.'

She pulls an old wool blanket from the wardrobe. It's crocheted in a loose neat stitch and in colours that change, making wide circles that sweep round and round. It smells of mothballs just like Aunty Molly's had.

'When I've done the hens and picked up the eggs, I need to go into the village for flour and sugar. It's my baking day today whether you're sick or not young lady.'

Morgan had been told not to let anyone in while Aunty Molly was in the village. Uncle John was busy with the creatures and wouldn't be back until dinner time. 'Don't let anyone else in,' said Aunty Molly. 'You'll know it's me. You can let me in.'

And there was once a grey goat who was going one Good Friday to the shore to gather shellfish. She left the three small grey kids and the

270

little he-goat at home. And she said to them that they were not to open the door to anyone especially to the fox who would eat them up and spread their bones to the four winds.

'And,' says she, 'when I come home you will know it is myself as soon as you see my foot under the edge of the door, for there will be a red thread and a blue thread about my foot.'

As Morgan hauls out the contents of the wardrobe, the smell of camphor fills the room. It is as though she is stirring up tens of years of memories, which have been left undisturbed and quiet in this strange little room.

There is a bag of knitting needles of all shapes and sizes. There are plastic ones, metal ones and great thick wooden ones with round bead stoppers on them. Morgan hunts deeper into the wardrobe hoping there will be some wool.

There were lots of times that she chose not to do what she was told but Morgan never opened the door until she was sure it was Aunty Molly on the other side.

In the back of the wardrobe, Morgan can feel the cold striking through from the wall behind. Everything at the back of the wardrobe is cold, smelling not of camphor but of air, of outside. There are books at the back and Morgan grabs for them eagerly. The books are old library books, never returned for goodness knows how long. Morgan starts to look up the dates in the front but is side-tracked by the stories. 'Romance' it says on the spine and a red rose logo confirms this. *Sister Sadie Falls in Love* and *Doctors in Love*, and the rest. These were the sort of books Aunty Molly hid under the cushions on the sitting room settee. On the table would be the 'good book,' the Bible. Now that has what you call decent stories in it, she'd say, not the sort of rubbish Morgan always had her head in.

'Put that book down for a minute, Morgan, and go and clean your bedroom.' Morgan wasn't an untidy child. She had never been allowed the luxury of mess. She knew that 'cleaning your bedroom' was just a way of getting her away from what she enjoyed doing. She also knew better than to refuse to do what Aunty Molly said. Although she had got used to the cellar and was not as scared of its noises and the dark as she used to be, it wasn't a place to go if it could be avoided.

Sometimes Aunty Molly would tell her about the Bugganes, far uglier creatures than the Fynoderee. They were horrible, cruel creatures who could appear in any shape they pleased. They could be ogres with huge heads and great fiery eyes, or they could appear with no heads at all; or as small dogs who grew larger and larger as you watched them until they were larger than elephants. Then maybe they would change into the shape of men or disappear into nothing as horned monsters or as anything they chose. Each Buggane had its own dwelling place, which might be a sea cave, a lonely hill or a ruined church.

Morgan feels the cold covers on the books, books Aunty Molly would have loved. She remembers the fear that she once had that the Bugganes or the Fynoderee might find their way into that childhood punishment cellar. She remembers that child's voice, her own voice, trembling out the hymns she had heard Aunty Molly singing, hoping this would keep these monsters away.

Abide with me fast falls the eventide, the darkness deepens, Lord with me abide.

She finds herself weeping for that child, for herself. She had been so defiant, so strong, that child had. She had battled with Aunty Molly, with her motherless childhood, she had put up a tremendous fight, put on a haughty, insolent front. Yet now Morgan can still feel the loneliness, the fear, the great sadness she'd had and still has in spite of the intervening years. She starts to sing, up there in that strange little room.

Abide with me....

As Morgan sits singing amidst the debris of the turned-out wardrobe, she hears and feels the wind stirring. It becomes even colder in the strange room and the draught is rattling at the door.

'It is me, Morgan, open the door.' But Morgan thinks it is the fox, pretending to be Aunty Molly. The fox will eat her up and spread her bones to the four winds. 'Morgan, open the door, my arms are full of bags with flour and sugar.' But Morgan knows the fox can put on Aunty Molly's voice. 'Morgan, if you don't open the door, we'll have no cakes for tea, we'll have nothing to eat.' Morgan is hungry, so much so that her stomach hurts. She will open the door a bit, look to see if there is a piece of red thread. Then she will know that it is Aunty Molly at the other side.

Morgan is hungry. So much so that her stomach hurts. She decides that she will clear out this room another day. Today she must eat.

In the little village by the sea everything is decked out for Eastertide. The Bugganes are wearing jackets and ties (albeit it makes them look like spivs) and the Trolls, (having made an effort,) are sporting Easter bonnets covered with a profusion of ribbons and trims. It has to be said that there's nothing so comical as a Troll in a hat. So much so that some of the Fairies are tittering behind their hands and the Elves (being less polite) are lying on their backs with their legs in the air laughing until their fat stomachs ache.

Morgan hasn't asked for anyone to meet her from the station this time. She catches the bus from the town to the village shops and then walks up slowly towards the farm. It's four o'clock and she can smell the fires just getting going. She walks past the small village library and onto the Landing Road and is struck by the quietness of it all. There is an occasional car, a handful of children, and a vastness of blue sky. Barnsley had been overcast and rainy when she set off. But then this place was always contrary.

She sits on the seat just outside the cricket ground. She isn't in a hurry to get home. They don't know she's coming, and she is expecting all sorts of recriminations from Maggie, if from nobody else.

She is amazed that she can sit here, only a stone's throw from the farm, and yet feel so alien to it. She's lived here in this village for the biggest part of her life so far, and yet she still feels like a stranger. She can admire its clear air, blue skies and wild beauty but she knows it is a closed in place which welcomes visitors but never accepts them as its own.

After a while Morgan feels cold and knows that she must move on. She stands up and flexes her shoulders, which have stiffened in the stirring sea breeze. She lifts her head, tucks in her chin and prepares to take on Maggie, Ed and the farm.

'It's Mummy.' William shrieks with delight and hurls himself at Morgan as she comes into the kitchen. But Morgan barely notices him, as all she can see is Leanne stirring at some cooking pots on the Aga, looking as if she owns the place.

'Leanne.' William is so excited at her return, he is pulling at her coat, pushing her into a chair. 'Can we make Mummy a cup of tea?'

Leanne turns to face Morgan, her face in a feline smirk, her hands running down the silver Aga rail, suggestively, brazenly.

'Of course, Wills, go and get the biscuits out, you know where they are don't you, honey?'

The women stare at each other, not speaking. Morgan has an urge to get up and scratch at Leanne's mocking eyes, tear her hair out at the roots. But she forces herself to smile.

'Thanks. A cup of tea would be great.' She chokes down her anger, thinking, thinking.

Jessica moves to Morgan's chair and puts her arm around her shoulders. 'Lovely to see you again, Mrs Bainton.' There is something in the girl's touch that yearns for a response.

Morgan shakes her arm away and stands up. Her anger is bubbling inside her like the contents of the pots on the stove.

'This is so cosy.' She can feel her throat tighten and her voice sounds high pitched, strained. 'I didn't know that Ed had to get domestics in.'

'You don't know anything about Ed at all.' Leanne tosses her head and turns her back on Morgan to stir at the cooking pots.

She moves the pots around, banging them unnecessarily.

'If you took the trouble to be here…'

Morgan leaps forward, catching herself on the kitchen table, the dishes rattle and shake and a glass falls over, smashing onto the floor.

'Mummy!' William shrieks in alarm, and suddenly Morgan feels that the heat in the kitchen is just too much for her. She gathers the boy up in her arms and runs upstairs with him.

'What shall we read, William?' Morgan is determined she won't cry.

William runs his hands across the top of the row of books on the shelf. Which shall it be? His hand hesitates, moves on. He wants to make this a good story. Mummy might decide to stay if he chooses a good story.

By the time Ed comes in, Leanne and Jessica have gone home, and Maggie is in charge of supper.

'She's back.' Maggie nods towards the small bag in the hall.

Ed knows already, he's seen her coat hung up in the porch, buried his head in it to find the scent of her.

He sighs. He wants Morgan home, of course he does. But every time she comes home it means trouble one way or another.

They can't seem to connect with each other anymore. She's distant. It's almost as if she's living in a different world to him.

He can hear them laughing upstairs, her and William. He stands at the bottom of the staircase for a while, pretending it's 'before'. They had all laughed a lot then. Ed runs his hands through his hair, trying to scratch at the memories of the good times.

When William sees Ed at the bedroom door, he hurls himself at him. 'Mummy's home.' His voice is a squeak, he is so excited. 'Mummy's home, Daddy, do you think she'll stay?'

Ed looks at Morgan across the room, he wants to run at her the way William ran at him. He wants to throw his arms around her and cling to her and beg her to stay.

'Hi.' His voice is unsteady, uncertain.

'Hello, love.' Morgan stands up, moves towards him. 'Busy day?'

'They're all busy days.' Ed's face is tense, and the words sound harsher than he intends them to.

'They must be.' Morgan turns from him and looks out of the window, over the farm and towards the sea.

'They must be really busy if you have to get Leanne Myers in to cook for you. Scraping the bottom of the barrel there aren't you?'

Tears spring to her eyes but she keeps her head turned from him so that he can't see.

'You turn up out of the blue and there you go, straight away, criticising.' Ed is angry. He doesn't need this.

'Oh, so I should have phoned ahead so you could get rid of the floozy!'

William starts to run his hands over the row of books again, maybe there's a better one they could read. He sings to himself to drown out his parents' conversation.

'Supper's ready,' Maggie shouts from downstairs.

'You have got them running around after you, haven't you? Poor Ed, needs some female company, needs to be looked after. And then I come home, the old witch, and spoil your fun.'

Morgan wants this to be different. She wants Ed to hold her and tell her everything is alright, the way he used to. It's all going wrong.

Ed stamps out of the room, the muscle in his cheekbone is twitching and Morgan knows he is holding on to his temper but only just. She's sorry for her outburst. She doesn't know how to make it better.

At supper Maggie tries to paper over the cracks. She asks Morgan about the school she's teaching in, and about how the sale of the house is going.

'Oh, should be finalised soon,' Morgan lies. The truth is she hasn't even put the house up for sale yet.

When it's William's bedtime, he asks both his mummy and daddy to read him a story together. Ed laughs but his face is serious.

'Better have your mother read it, son. Get her while you can.'

He stamps out of the house, muttering something about going for a pint.

Catching Maggie's eye, Morgan sees sadness instead of the disapproval she had expected.

'This isn't good.' She reaches over the table to put her hand briefly on Morgan's.

'I know,' says Morgan. 'I know.'

Easter Sunday and Morgan decides to go for a walk. The others are all at chapel, but she can't face that. There is nothing like a chapel congregation for gossip. She knows what will be first on the agenda.

On the cliff top she can see forever. It's so quiet up there.

She's forgotten how this silence can get into your bones, like the sea mist, like fine rain. The gulls are swooping and keening as if in some preordained ritual. The sky is clear blue and tucks into the horizon in a neatly drawn line.

She realises how much she loves this place. She loves how the gardens spill onto the pavements, and no-one bothers to trim them back. She loves how a ten-year-old rambling rose can invade a nearly new privet and no-one puts it straight.

But she doesn't belong. Since she has been home, Leanne has been around every day, cleaning, doing. Ed says he's hired her, but Morgan doesn't believe him. How can he have, he's broke?

She watches a ship, far out on the horizon. It makes its way across the skyline like a target on one of those arcade machines. She wonders briefly where it is going.

And Maggie has been so subdued. Maggie, the harridan who always has an opinion, sits looking at her family as though they are strangers.

Morgan supposes it's the shock of Peter's death. She wants to comfort her, but she can't. She wants to love Ed, but she can't.

She's a fish out of water, a plant without roots. She lays back on the cold, windswept barmins and wishes she could just sink into the earth, become part of the landscape.

Three

Around about the 8th of February 1871 there arose a violent storm blowing straight into Bridlington Bay, trapping many anchoring ships. Some ships masters made to run their ships ashore in the hope of reaching safety. Others who were trying to ride out the storm were driven ashore by the mountainous seas and rolling surf. In a short period of time some seventeen ships ran aground and were quickly broken up by the pounding waves.

Morgan loves being at Charley's house. Her friend's bedroom is an attic room and through the skylight window you can look out towards the North Landing Beach.

The girls are spreading out their collection over Charley's bedroom floor. They have been gathering stories for a school project. They can collect anything, but these two have decided to collect stories. Morgan has just brought a new one. George has been telling her about the Great Gale of 1871 and she can't wait to show it to Charley.

'I've written down what George told me, and I've done pictures as well, look, look.' She can't wait to get the papers out of her bag. She hasn't noticed that her friend has hardly said a word since she arrived.

'Just imagine, people were just watching from the shore, knowing it was going to happen and they couldn't do anything about it. All those ships and the sea bubbling like a witch's cauldron. It's a true story you know.'

Charley looks at the pictures of boats tossing on a stormy sea, of sailors in the water, of the black unrelenting sky.

'And the brave lifeboat men. What must it have been like? They had to row the boats, no motors then. Rowing out to

280

save the sailors and maybe drowning themselves. You just can't imagine it.'

She notices that her friend isn't really listening, and that her face is tight.

'We're moving again.'

Morgan holds the pages of George's story tight in her hand. She knows in that moment that she is going to lose something precious, something it has taken her such a long time to find.

She doesn't really listen to Charley's explanation of why the family is moving away, she just stares at the stories, neatly stacked in rows over the carpet in her friend's attic bedroom. And then she starts to tear each sheet of her new addition into tiny flakes of paper as though she is ripping up a part of herself.

The following morning, piles of debris littered the beach for several miles, and in some places the timber was piled eight or nine feet high. The death toll could not be accurately ascertained even at the time, but the most widely quoted figure was no less than seventy lives lost. Many of the victims were buried in a mass grave at Bridlington where a service has been held every year since that time. Even today, more than a hundred years later, Bridlington seafaring men remember stories of that awful storm, and the part their forbears played in the rescue.

Four

In the room with a small round window all is quiet. Morgan sits amongst the debris on the floor. She comes here to this room quite often now but each time it seems a little different. Today she notices the old handbags, which are spread onto the carpet, each in turn spilling its contents like waves lapping the beach.

Morgan picks at the strings of old beads, the neatly folded lace-edged hankies, the small rubber-stopped scent bottles and the creased faded photographs. She feels like a beachcomber sifting through beach litter.

A letter has arrived from Donald. She has placed it amongst the clutter on the carpet. She has been sitting there for a long time, quite how long she can't remember.

The letter is white and neat amongst the splay of jumble, like a raft on the sea, like hope. She knows she should open the letter.

Donald's writing is small and perfectly uniform. She would have expected no less from a former deputy headteacher. She smiles to herself ruefully. She would have expected no less from the man who was always in control.

She hasn't seen or heard from Donald since the previous summer. He'd visited her at Grace's house when she was there with William and Jessica. She feels a little ashamed as she remembers how he'd held out an olive branch, which she had refused.

Morgan peers at the old photographs in the dimming light. There's a young woman on a beach in a long, spotted skirt, a man looking jaunty in plus fours and a flat cap, a baby, mouth smeared with ice cream, looking seriously at the camera. She doesn't recognise any of them. They are from another time, a link with someone else's family.

The letter opens easily, no messy slitting of paper. The envelope flap shows no resistance.

The room is dark now and yet Morgan can't remember time passing. She feels tears running down her cheeks and yet can't remember starting to cry. Why should she cry? She picks up the letter, deciding she needs to eat. She'll read the letter later.

*

Morgan has been late for school three times this week.

'Three days Mrs Bainton.' Mr Pickering, the head, isn't at all pleased.

'I've been up since dawn, Mr Pickering.' Morgan tries to explain. 'I've been collecting dew for year seven.'

Mr Pickering has heard some excuses over the years, but this is a new one.

Morgan continues. 'We're studying the May rituals of the Celts, you don't mind, do you?'

She has met little interest so far in what she is teaching in class in this school. It seems that anything is OK as long as peace and quiet reign.

'I've no problem at all with that, Mrs Bainton,' Mr Pickering says. 'It's better than half the class absconding and putting paid to my statistics. But I don't see why you can't just put a spot of tap water in a stone bowl and be done with it.'

'Well, I had to get the marsh marigolds and rowan as well.' Morgan opens her carrier bag for him to see.

Mr Pickering scratches his un-shaven chin, wondering what on earth she is up to.

'Not for ingesting in any way, Mrs Bainton?' He wiggles his eyebrows in a worried, suggestive way.

Morgan looks puzzled, then realises what he means.

'Oh, no. Oh, no Mr Pickering. They're for pinning to the windows and throwing over the floor.'

'Oh, I see.' Mr Pickering decides to be relieved. Teachers pushing unwanted substances could not, of course, be tolerated, but if Mrs Bainton's slightly eccentric ways only meant trouble with the cleaner, well, that would be the lesser of two evils really. He'd have the devil's own chance of replacing a member of staff at this time of the year.

'Well, carry on then, Mrs Bainton, but you'll have to make sure you're on time in future.'

*

Dear Morgan

I know you like stories, like your mother did. I thought you might be interested in this one. It's mine.

My father had his own business - if you could call it that. He was more of an odd job man really. He'd do building, gardening, anything he could get his hands on. And he had a good reputation. People trusted him and word got around. I used to go with him when I was ten or so, when there was no school. I'd go and 'earn my crust'.

I enjoyed the gardening work. I was a big lad and I could do my bit, weeding, fetching and carrying with the wheelbarrow. I found the building work hard, but I loved the gardening. I liked to see how neat and orderly it all looked after a couple of days' hard work. It gave me a real thrill that did. And father would be proud of me. Our Lol and

284

Pete were too little to be much use, but father said I was his 'right hand man' and that was grand.

But my mother, well I reckon she always thought she was a cut above all that. When they got married, father had said he was building up his own business, and as far as he was concerned, he was. He took on labourers when he could, and he made enough money to get by. But 'getting by' wasn't enough for Mother. She was always ahead of herself. She'd spend on decorating the house, dressing us boys like little toffs. She'd spend money before he'd even earned it and then there'd be nothing left to pay the bills.

I can remember seeing him come home, tired and dirty from a day's hard grafting, and she'd wait until supper was in front of us all and then say, 'Oh, Joshua. The rent man came today, and I could not pay him.' And then she'd go on and on about having to buy us boys this and that, about trying to make the money stretch, to make ends meet and we three boys sat there, her silent witnesses. All the time she'd be dabbing at her eyes with a hanky.

He would sit there eating his food, as if it tasted of dust and ashes. He never shouted at her, he just got quieter and quieter, worked harder and got old before his time.

There was this way she looked at him, when he was sitting there, 'in his muck' as she used to call it. It was as though she was a queen, and he was, well, less than nothing really. It wasn't that she didn't love him. She just despised the lowliness of his job, the fact that he got his hands dirty. I wonder that she'd ever let him touch her.

Then there was the other side to her. She was pretty and clever and really cared for us when we were sick. She taught us lads the three R's before we went to school and that was unusual in those days, you know. She'd read to us all the time, she was great at making things seem real, making the stories come alive. Our favourites were the adventure stories. I can see her now, legs tucked under her body, sitting on that dusty, old settee. We'd be at the table, building domino towers

285

or sticking bits of newspaper cuttings into a scrapbook, and our eyes would be popping out of our heads as she read to us. That room became a magical place full of spies, dragons or spacemen. She gave us our love of books and nothing could take that away.

Uncle Graham wasn't a real uncle. He had the corner shop and a military moustache. You could tell mother liked him, she'd send us out of the shop to wait on the street, while she 'finished her order'. She was always going on to father about how well Graham was doing for himself, how smart he looked, clean fingernails, nicely groomed.

I was eleven when she left home to live with Uncle Graham. She took Lol and Pete with her but said I had to look after father as I was the eldest. It wasn't as if I never saw her again, or my brothers. I mean, they only lived above the corner shop.

But the stories stopped. At least the stories she told us stopped. The other kind, the gossips' kind, they were whispered wherever we went. You could hear them, 'poor little lads, mother a slut' and all that. I always held my head high and walked by as if I hadn't heard, although I wanted to shout at them and tell them to shut up.

I had to get father his supper and clean up after school. It wasn't difficult really. It was just that I missed her even after what she'd done. And our Lol and Pete: I missed them being in the house and I knew Dad missed them worse than me. He wasn't a man of many words normally, but now he hardly spoke at all.

It was books that kept me going, I suppose. School work and books. I worked so hard that the teachers were starting to treat me like a wonder boy. That helped I suppose, considering how things were at home.

Then a few months later she came back. Father had been taken ill and she said she'd come back to nurse him and that they should let bygones be bygones. But she'd become terribly thin and one of her eyes was black.

286

Lol and Pete said that her and Uncle Graham were always screaming at each other and that sometimes they couldn't sleep for the rowing going on.

Father got better, and everything went back to the old routine. He was still working all the hours God sends and he was still eating his supper 'in his muck'.

By then there was another brother, Gregory, to feed. No-one said anything, but we knew it was Uncle Graham's.

The corner shop thrived, and Dad carried on getting old before his time. Mum never did get back into telling us the stories, though. I never heard her telling Gregory any either.

On the day of the accident, they'd just had a row about Gregory. We'd never heard our father lose his temper like that before. He called her all the names under the sun and slammed the door so hard it nearly sprang off its hinges.

And that was it. He never came back. He was doing a roofing job, no scaffolding, no labourer, and the usually careful and patient man lost his footing and fell. Death was instant, mother was told.

The insurance premium was one thing she had kept up and some years later there was still enough left to help me through college, along with odd jobs, something that thanks to my father, I was more than capable of.

Lol and Pete weren't that keen on studying so they both left school at 15 to become colliers. They earned good money down the pit. Gregory went off the rails a bit, I think, but then I never kept in touch really, never felt the need.

When I met Gwen, she was a little elfin thing. I was in my first teaching job and she was waitressing in the café down the road from the school. She said she was trying to earn enough money to go to college to be a teacher, so we had a lot in common. I could tell her all about college and I think she looked up to me for that.

She'd been brought up very respectable by her grandma and grandad.

She said her mother worked away down south. Her face used to cloud over when she talked about her mother, so I didn't pry. Maybe I should have, maybe I should have found out earlier that there might be a flighty side to her family.

Anyway, with the war looming, we decided to get married even though we'd only known each other for a few months. The war didn't touch us really, not directly. I got called up but failed the medical. After a couple of years our Lol got me a desk job at the colliery. Only temporary until I got a job teaching. Apart from rationing and other deprivations, we managed alright.

Gwen seemed happy with our growing family. She mothered our Pat and Dot like they were two little angels. She never had a moment's trouble with them. And then when our David was born, well, she bloomed like she was going to burst.

So, you can imagine how surprised I was when she suddenly said she wanted to go to college, catch up on what she'd missed. I just never understood it. She had a lovely house, three wonderful children and a good husband. What she wanted by going to college I really do not know. She went though. And that was when it all came back. It was mother all over again. She'd be going on about so and so and such and such a body, how interesting they were, how amusing they were. It made me feel as though I was nothing to her. There was me trying to be the model teacher and father and all the time she was off flirting and galivanting with that young crowd from college. And then when she told me she was pregnant!

Father never talked about Gregory not being his, but I wasn't going to make the same mistake. It wasn't as though we'd been doing a lot on that front anyway. She came up with some lame excuse about some flimsy nightie, a night of passion I seemed to have forgotten, but I wasn't going to be fooled. I made sure I was back in charge, though, there'd be no more flirting and going on after this.

Mother died the night you were born. I didn't tell Gwen at the time,

288

she had enough on her plate. I took it as a sign though. You looked nothing like the others had when they were born. I thought you weren't mine. I will never forgive myself for that.

We buried mother while Gwen was in hospital. I swore our Pat, Dot and David to secrecy. I told them their mother would be ill with any more upheaval to contend with. Dot and Pat thought I was wrong, I know, but they kept the secret anyway.

Of course, I told her eventually but when the time was right. And things were done my way from then on. It was for the best.

I know it will sound conceited when I say that I haven't made a lot of mistakes in my life. What I know now though, is the one mistake I did make was to give you away. I hope you will forgive me.

Donald

*

Maggie is sitting in Grace's garden. Morgan can see her out of the kitchen window, and she gets a tray ready to take out some tea and cakes. Maggie is rubbing her fingers on the makeshift table, testing for dirt.

William is pulling at Morgan's skirt. 'Please may I have a drink of squash.'

She wonders briefly about 'please may I have.' It isn't from her vocabulary and sounds vaguely old fashioned.

She finds him the glass with the stars on it, the one she knows he likes.

'I'll carry it out on the tray for you.'

She looks at him all neatly done up in clean shorts and t-shirt. She suddenly has an urge to ruffle his hair, streak his clothes with dirt from the garden. He looks too constrained, too tied up by someone else's standards.

'Here we are.' She sets the tray on the table, hoping that Maggie hasn't noticed how her hands are shaking. They seem to shake all the time these days.

Maggie looks at her, searchingly.

'You are far too thin, Morgan.' The older woman hands William his drink, holds on to the glass until he responds with a soft 'thank-you'.

'Oh, I'm cutting down on snacks and things, you know, trying to be healthy.' Morgan feels like a girl again, making excuses.

'It looks to me like you're cutting down on everything.' Maggie's face is stern, but her voice is soft, concerned.

'Well, I try to send as much money home as I can.' Morgan waves her hand towards the house. 'Once I sell this place I can come home.'

'And are you trying to 'sell this place'?' Maggie's voice is harsh again, back to normal. 'I didn't see a notice in the front garden.'

'They're bringing it next week. The other deal fell through.'

She feels the lie sink guiltily into her stomach. William is driving his toy tractor up and down the shed steps. The bees are droning lazily around the clump of chive flowers and Morgan pours the tea into the silence left by her blatant invention.

Maggie shuffles in her chair, adjusts her skirt, takes one of the offered cakes.

'Oh, Morgan, butterfly buns. Now I haven't had one of these for years. They always remind me of Molly Flowerdew. She did her best by you didn't she? I'm sure she'd like to see you next time you come home. She's a lonely old lady now, now that John's gone.'

Morgan picks at the butterfly bun, tearing the wrapper into shreds.

'It was Aunty Molly who told me to move away. She said you'd all be better if I wasn't there. She's probably right, she was always right. I've never belonged there after all.'

In the summer air the skeletons stretch themselves over the damp shingle and whiten in the sun. They crack open their stiff mandibles and yawn noisily. Butterflies and bees alight on them but find no sustenance. Small breezes try out love songs, but skeletons aren't renowned for their commitment. They know that they'll have to return to that dark, damp cupboard eventually. They hope the summer will stay hot and long.

Maggie looks keenly at her but says nothing. They talk on into the afternoon. Mostly it's Maggie talking, telling stories about different people in Flamborough, what they are doing now or tales of past events which still live on in village legendry.

'Garden looks a bit of a mess.' Maggie gets up to walk around and picks at the messy brown daffodil stumps and kicks gently at the proliferation of buttercups to draw attention to them.

'It's how Grace liked it. She didn't like it uniform.' Morgan is on the defensive.

'It doesn't matter what Grace liked, now, does it?' Maggie sighs wearily.

'It's about what it looks like to a buyer, Morgan, that's what you've got to think about. You *are* selling it aren't you?'

'Yes, yes, of course.' Morgan begins to stack the cups and plates, ready to take the tray indoors.

'Well, how about I stay on a couple of days and help you sort this garden out?'

Maggie is striding about the garden now, seeing its potential in her imagination.

'Oh, no.' The cups on the tray are rattling as Morgan's hands start shaking again. 'Honestly, Maggie.' She forces herself to smile. 'You don't need to do that. I'll get onto it straight away. You're quite right of course.'

Maggie isn't fooled. Morgan carries the tray indoors, washes the cups and plates and puts them back on the shelves, just the way Grace liked them.

The older woman is determined to make the property more inviting and nothing Morgan can say will stop her. She has been working for an hour or so, and Morgan keeps anxiously coming out into the garden to check what Maggie is doing, following her around, not wanting anything changed, not wanting anything spoiled.

'Come and sit down now, Maggie,' she begs, helping to put the weeds into the sack and trying to tie the bag off.

'Come and tell me how you are getting on, you know, after Peter… you know.'

Maggie stands up, stretching her back, easing the stiffness.

'I get by, Morgan. I can't pretend that life's wonderful, but I get by.'

'I expect you miss him a lot.' She gently takes the tools from Maggie's hands, and leads her towards the house. They stand together in the kitchen looking out into the garden.

'You've made a lovely job of that.' Morgan is honestly surprised. Nothing much seems to have changed. It is still

Grace's garden, but everything is tidier, in order.

'I love gardening, but it gets me in the back these days.' Maggie rubs ruefully at the small of her back, her fist kneading round and round.

'But you've never liked the farm.' Morgan remembers how she'd complain loud and long when Peter was alive.

'Well, that's different.'

Maggie sits down, stuffing a cushion into a ball behind her.

'The farm was only supposed to be temporary. Peter said he'd make his money then we could retire and do what we wanted, go where we wanted. I don't know if I would have stuck around all those years if I'd known it was only a pipe dream.'

Morgan walks around the kitchen, not able to settle.

'But you're still there?'

'I've no choice, have I?' Maggie almost spits the words out at her. 'And for goodness sake, sit down, you are making me dizzy.'

Morgan sits on a chair arm, uneasy, guilty.

'But a garden, well it's different from the farm.' Maggie relaxes back into the chair. 'I love to see it neat and tidy after a day's work.'

'That's what Donald says, you know my father.' Morgan is surprised at herself bringing him into the conversation.

'Well, he's right. You can control the garden, make it what you want it to be. It takes hard work of course, but you're always guaranteed to come out on top. No garden has ever got the better of me, I can tell you.'

'I believe you,' Morgan gets up again and starts pacing the floor.

'How is Ed?' The words slide out of her mouth,

293

unbidden. She hadn't meant to ask. She is angry that he hasn't brought William himself.

'How do you expect? He's working himself into an early grave. I try to help but what can I do on the farm. I'm not getting any younger you know.'

'And Leanne? Is she still hanging around?'

'She comes and goes. You know how she is. She's always been after him when it suited her. And Jessica and William, well… they get on so well, Morgan. It would be a shame to stop them playing together.'

Grace's hall clock begins to strike, and Maggie eases herself out of the chair. She gets her coat from the hall and shouts William to tell him it's time to go home.

William comes downstairs, his face screwed up, puzzled. 'Mummy, why have you put bits of paper on my bedroom wall?'

Morgan is surprised. She doesn't know what he means. Then she remembers. 'It's the stories,' she says, putting on his coat, giving him a hug. 'I'm worried I'll forget them, so I write them down and pin them to the wall. It doesn't matter in that room. Grace didn't use that room.'

William wriggles from her clutch, she is holding him too tight, she is hurting him.

Maggie moves to hug her, but Morgan backs away. All of a sudden, she's distant, thinking about the stories, wondering if any of them have been moved, lost.

'Come on, Morgan.' Maggie moves again to hug her and holds the girl tight in spite of herself.

'Come home soon,' she whispers, not demanding, just sad. 'Come home soon, Morgan, everyone misses you.

There are many corridors in the castle and the little girl goes down one after the other, trying to find her way to the Princess. She spends a year and a day walking along the corridors leading to the east and a year and a day walking along the corridors leading to the west. She has a magic sack with her in which she carries all the stories of the world. She wants to give them to the Princess to show how much she has missed her.

When at last she finds the Princess, she tips the contents of the sack onto the golden table and weeps with joy. 'Here are all the stories of the world, my lovely Princess. They are the best treasure I could think of to bring you. Take them and be happy.'

Sheets of white paper flutter down onto the golden table like a flock of a thousand doves. They are as white as snow, as white as the down on a magpie's breast, for no ink has spoiled them. The stories have all disappeared.

Five

As the long summer holidays stretch before her, Morgan puts off the idea of going home. She has the feeling that here is where she needs to be to find a sense of Grace, a sense of herself. The trees along the avenue of Intake Lane are heavy with blown leaves and blossom. The grass verge hasn't been mowed for a while and Morgan finds daisies and clover there. She stoops to feel the clover patch, then sits cross legged smoothing her hands over the patch, separating the leaves, searching for the elusive four leafed clover.

Winnie Thompson watches her from the bedroom window. Strange young woman, she thinks as she dusts the many ornaments she has on display on the ledge. She's seen her sitting there many a time this summer. She knows that the children will come in a minute and that this young woman will be talking to them for hours. She flicks at the net curtains to dislodge any dust.

'She's here again, Arthur.' Winnie talks to her dead husband's photograph; the one where he was being presented with a snooker trophy, the one that had been in the local newspaper. Nice pictures are all she has left of him now.

'The children will come in a minute.' Winnie looks down the lane and sure enough, a couple of youngsters from round in the new estate are making a beeline for Morgan.

'Do you think she's alright in the head, Arthur?' Winnie sits on the bed now, watching. 'I mean, she couldn't do those children harm, could she, not in broad daylight. You hear of such funny things these days.'

Winnie wants to go outside and join Morgan and the children, just to hear what is going on. But it's eleven o'clock and she and Arthur always have their tea and digestive at eleven.

She sighs, wipes the face of Arthur's photograph and goes downstairs.

'The harvest was always really important,' Morgan says, warming up her audience. Beth and Rick are two children from the estate, and Gary is a large, slow speaking boy from Lark Crescent. Gary is a regular. The others change day to day.

'If people didn't get the corn in, they would starve and die.' The children gasp and following her lead, they also feel amongst the clover patch, not really knowing what they are feeling for.

There once was a greedy, cruel Archbishop of Mayence, who one year, when the harvest had been bad, still insisted on being paid lots of money for his corn. The poor people couldn't afford to pay and some of them were dying.

Morgan wishes she'd had something to eat, now. Her stomach is empty and sick. She can't remember the last time she ate. She must get something on the way home.

One day a ragged mob of men, women and children with their hollow cheeks and pale faces threw themselves at the Archbishop's feet, crying for bread. He decided to play a trick on them, a very cruel trick.

A van goes by and toots its horn at the strange little

gathering, but the children are wrapped up in the story and no-one waves back.

He led them into the barn where there was some of his corn, and he told them to take what they needed. Then he locked the doors on them and set the barn alight. You could hear the screams of the poor wretches even back in the Archbishop's palace. 'Listen how the mice are squeaking among the corn,' he joked. 'Now maybe they will stop begging me to let them have corn. May the mice bite me if it isn't true.'

'Why would they want corn?' Rick screws up his face.

'Corn makes bread and cakes and fills up your tummy.'

Morgan can hear her own stomach rumble and she shifts her position on the grass.

'But it wasn't the mice squeaking, was it?' Beth is nearly in tears. 'It was the poor people.'

Morgan wonders if perhaps she has chosen the wrong story. Gary comes and sits close to her, his arm linked in hers. 'Go on, miss,' he says.

The Archbishop had been so cruel that Heaven sent down a punishment and the punishment was terrible.

'You're a teacher at our school, aren't you?' Rick's question is direct as he stares at Morgan.

'Yes, which class are you in?'

Not yours,' he laughs and there is something unpleasant in his laughter.

'Tell us about the punishment then, miss.' Beth is staring at her as well. She feels that somehow, they are mocking her or testing her. Never mind, she has their attention again.

298

Thousands of mice came out of the burning barn, made their way to the palace, filled every chamber and corner and at last attacked the Archbishop himself. His servants killed them by the hundred, but their numbers seemed only to increase. The Bishop fled on a boat, but the mice swam after him, and when he reached his tower on the island, thinking at least he would be safe there, the mice followed him, gnawing the tower and tearing an entrance for themselves with their sharp teeth. The cruel man was eaten by the mice, who attacked him by the score.

'Yuk that's a horrible story.' Beth is disgusted and stands up, shakes her skirt as though shaking away memories of the mice and the corn with it.

'I think it was great.' Rick is scrambling about the grass on all fours, squeaking, pretending to be a mouse, nipping Beth's arms and legs. She runs off and he follows, the pair of them screaming and laughing up the road. Rick turns and sticks out his tongue.

'Come back.' Morgan needs them to listen to the stories, to remember them. If they don't, they will be lost forever.

'I'm going home for my dinner, miss.' Gary disentangles himself from Morgan, leaving her sitting alone on the clover patch.

'Want a cup of tea, dear?' Winnie is at the gate. Her curiosity has got the better of her.

Morgan would love a cup of tea. She stands up eagerly but then she suddenly finds she can't reply to this motherly woman standing at her garden gate. She shakes her head as tears suddenly well up in her eyes. What is happening to her? She has an overwhelming desire to speak to her mother, to Gwen, but that is impossible. She wants Grace back, or even Aunty Molly would do. She feels like a child

299

again, wanting her mummy. Winnie goes in, her friendly gesture spurned.

'Strange girl,' she mutters, 'not right in the head, if you ask me.'

Later in Grace's house, the storm wakes Morgan. She must have cried herself to sleep. Her eyes are sticky, she struggles to open them. Her head is heavy as though from some illness. She sits, head in hands, for a long time before she can move at all.

She makes her way around the house in the darkness, the lightning occasionally darting into the rooms, as though punctuation to her movements. She moves from room to room frenetically, unable to stop or pause, not knowing what she is looking for.

She is in the room with the round window, everything is all over the floor as usual. At the back of her mind, Morgan makes a note to come and sort it out once and for all. Why does she keep forgetting?

In the corner, behind the settee, she finds another pile of books, not the ones Aunty Molly would have liked. These are different.

Grace didn't have many books as her eyesight couldn't deal with them. Her stories were in her head, given to her by Sean and kept safe over all the years. Maybe these were Gwen's books. How could they be Gwen's books? The storm is quietening now, moving away.

'Always got your head in a book.' Aunty Molly always makes it sound like a crime. 'I don't know why your mother sends them. You'd be far better off out in the fresh air. No wonder you get strange ideas, my lady.' And she thumps away at a mountain of dough, face red in the kitchen heat, the stove lit even in the August swelter.

Morgan tries to see what is in the books but in the darkness, all the pages are empty of words. The storm has passed but the wind is still rattling the window.

One, two, three, four, five, six, seven
All good children go to heaven,
When they die, put 'em in a pie,
One, two, three, four, five, six, seven

Aunty Molly knows some stories and rhymes, of course she does. And her pies sizzle in the oven, apple pies, meat pies.

Aunty Molly is as huge as a house from the pies she eats. She tastes them, glazes them, sniffs and admires them.

Morgan sometimes wishes she was a pie.

The stepmother pretended not to be angry with the girl, and she began to comb the girl's hair. The hair hung right over her knees and down to the ground.

'Morgan, just go and get a brush so I can tidy up that red mop of yours. If you spent more time brushing your hair, and less time with your head in those books…'

And Aunty Molly chop, chop, chops at the carrots, the noise regular and harsh, until Morgan fetches the brush.

Then she lays the knife aside, sits the girl in the chair by the stove and brushes and scrapes at Morgan's hair until it is straight-jacketed into a tight ponytail.

And all the while Aunty Molly tells her stories the way she brushes hair, firm, no nonsense.

The stepmother said she could not comb the girl's hair with an ordinary comb, so she sent her to fetch first a billet of wood, and then an axe. With these she cut off the girl's head. She cut out her heart and liver and stewed them for her husband's supper.

With the storm gone and the wind calmed, Morgan begins to feel chilly. She finds a big, knitted cardigan in the pile of clothes that are tipping out from one of the large wardrobes. She snuggles into it. It smells of roses. She goes back to the books, the covers are hard, the pages smell of mildew, she still can't see any printing on them.

There are stories she remembers that Gwen must have told her, stories of fairies and enchantment. Like the books she holds now, she knows the stories, but just can't find the words.

Sometimes when Gwen visits the farm, she sits on her knee and listens to the stories again. The words aren't important. What is important is being held by her mother, her voice protecting her like the covering of moss that protected Hansel and Gretel in the enchanted forest.

Red Campions are known as fairy flowers. They must never be brought into the house, though, never at any time. If, by chance, they are, that night the fairies will come for them, and then woe betide the person who picked and brought them in. Their bed clothes will be pulled off them on to the floor and bad dreams and pinching black and blue will be their punishment.

Morgan giggles as Gwen pretends to pinch her black and blue but really is tickling her.

'You'll spoil her with all that attention.' Aunty Molly comes in with an armful of logs for the stove. 'You've no idea the trouble I'll have when you go home.'

Gwen drops her arms as though she is holding hot coals.

*

The grass is long from the August heat and dusty from passing cars. Morgan sits fingering the verge's straggly shards, searching for something, coolness perhaps. She is on her own today as the children haven't come. Winnie is watching her from the window.

'I told you she'd be back,' Winnie says, her head tilted slightly towards her dead husband's photograph. 'There's something wrong there, Arthur,' she says. 'I've said it all along. She's not right in the head, you know.' And Winnie carries on polishing the window ledge, slowly. Her hand makes small circles with the duster, while her eyes take in all there is to see of Morgan. Morgan is telling her story even though there is no-one there to hear it.

'There was this father and he had three daughters,' she says, as her hand smooths the clover patch, settling her shaking voice.

And all the time Winnie is watching and moving the duster in small circles, wondering at the young woman talking to herself out on the grass verge outside her house.

The weather is heavy, the sky full of rain. The first large thunder spot hits Morgan on the head, but she doesn't look up, she doesn't move from the ground. She must finish the story even though there is no-one there to listen to it. If she doesn't finish it, it will be lost.

The father, who was rich and had a fine house filled with silver and gold, asked the three daughters to tell him how much they loved him. The first daughter told him she loved him as she loved her own life, and he was very happy. The second daughter said she loved him better than all the world, and he was very happy. The third daughter thought a long time about her answer and finally said that she loved him as fresh meat loves salt. The father was not at all happy at this reply, in fact he was very angry. 'So, you don't love me at all,' he thundered, and he drove her out of his house and shut the door in her face.

So, the third daughter was out in the wild fenlands without shelter. She gathered a lot of rushes and made them into a cloak to hide her fine clothes. Then she walked on until she came to a fine house. There she offered herself as a maid and lived there for many a day, cleaning the pans and doing all manner of dirty jobs in the house. And because she gave no name, they called her 'Cap o' Rushes'.

Winnie is pulling her arm. 'We're just having a cup of tea.' She pulls the young woman to her feet. 'Come and have a cup of tea with me and Arthur, out of this rain.'

Morgan hasn't noticed the rain but feels at her dress, which is soaking wet.

'It's alright, dear.' Winnie guides her into the porch and hands her a towel. 'Just give yourself a rub down and you'll soon dry off in the kitchen. We don't want you catching your death out there in that storm, now do we. It's nice and warm in my kitchen.'

Morgan looks around Winnie's kitchen. It is nothing like the kitchen at Grace's house.

The light floods in from the large windows onto the blue units and white walls. The large double doors lead out onto a small, glass porch and then a neat garden, which has a clutch of bird tables in it, nesting boxes and water troughs.

'I see you're taken with my garden,' smiles Winnie. 'I like to watch the birds. I talk to them, you know. Oh, yes. Some people think that's funny, but I like talking to my birds and they're grand to look at, don't you think?'

Without waiting for a reply, she moves round the kitchen, making two cups of tea in china mugs. Even the mugs are covered with pictures of birds.

'Yes, I like my birds,' she goes on. 'Arthur didn't like them much, but he didn't stop me putting out my boxes in the garden. Good man was my Arthur, a real gentleman.' She indicates 'her Arthur' by inclining her head towards his photograph.

Morgan's eyes flicker briefly towards the photograph but then return to the garden where she can see a robin and a couple of blue tits splashing in the stone bath, turn on turn.

Winnie notices Morgan's every move and smiles when she sees her watching the birds' antics.

'Yes, there's a great deal of comfort to be had in watching birds,' she says quietly, almost to herself.

As if coming out of a dream, Morgan turns to the table and clasps the mug of tea. She feels damp and cold and can't remember how she came to be sitting at this kitchen table.

'I was telling them the story of 'Cap o' Rushes',' she says, more to herself than to Winnie. 'I didn't notice it was raining. I have to get to the end or…'

Winnie turns to the photograph of Arthur.

'Didn't notice it was raining.' She cocks her head at the photograph. 'It had been coming down in buckets for ages before I fetched her in.'

Winnie notices her puzzled face. 'It's alright, dear, I talk to Arthur all the time, but I do know he's not really here.'

Morgan's eyes flicker in recognition of what Winnie is saying.

'It was about the daughter whose father thought she didn't love him and if I don't finish it, he will never know...'

'But there was no-one there, dear.'

Winnie sits down with her, trying to get her to look at her, to come out of this daydreaming. 'Those children didn't come today.'

Morgan suddenly feels hungry, almost to the point of sickness. What is she doing here? What was she doing, telling stories to the empty air?

Winnie is up on her feet again, opening and shutting the cupboard doors, buttering bread, making cheese and pickle sandwiches.

'We'll break a rule, today,' she says, her hands working quickly, used to the actions. 'Me and Arthur don't usually have our lunch until half past one, but you look hungry, my dear, so just for once we'll have it early.'

'Oh, I don't want to trouble you.' Morgan gets up, moves towards the door.

'It's no trouble.' Winnie guides her back to the table, sits her down.

'I like the company. You just sit there. It won't take me a minute. And anyway, it's still chucking it down outside.'

Morgan looks out on the garden again. The expanse of windows in the porch is streaked with rain, like tacking stitches running down new curtains.

She shivers, suddenly feeling the dampness in her clothes.

Winnie seems to have noticed the shiver before it happened and is surrounding Morgan in a large, yellow cardigan.

'May not look that pretty, love, but it will keep you a bit warmer, just until you dry out properly. Don't think one of my dresses will fit you.' She laughs, the flesh on her ample chin wobbling.

Morgan eats, as the hunger of weeks catches up with her. Winnie replenishes the sandwiches, wondering at these young women who half starve themselves these days.

'I know they don't want to end up fat like me,' she thinks, 'but nourishment has to go in somewhere.'

'Grace Williams,' she says, suddenly. 'You live in her house now, don't you? Did you know her?'

Morgan stops eating, the sandwich held mid-air.

'She was my grandmother.' The words are quiet, hushed as a lump comes to her throat.

'I see.' Winnie smooths her apron, allowing a few moments of peace.

'Did you know her?' Morgan searches for the conventional remarks needed to go on.

'Oh, just to say hello to. She was blind wasn't she, but it didn't seem to stop her doing things.' Winnie senses the girl's loneliness. 'You must miss her, then. But you'll have other family?'

'Oh, yes. Yes of course.' Morgan didn't want to go into her own story.

'I'm just here to sell up, you know, it has to be done.'

'Yes, I know. But it's hard, isn't it? Getting rid of things feels like you're saying goodbye all over again.'

Winnie puts a few iced fancy cakes on a plate and offers them to Morgan. 'Only shop ones, I'm afraid dear, no-one to bake for these days.'

Morgan says she feels much better after the food, says it must have been lack of it that made her do all that, out there, earlier. And the pair of them sit looking out at the birds in the rain well into the afternoon. Their conversation remains the surface sort.

...before the wedding, she went to the cook, and says she: 'I want you to dress every dish without a mite o' salt.' 'That'll be rare nasty,' says the cook. 'That doesn't signify,' says she.

'Very well,' says the cook. Well, the wedding day came, and they were married. And after they were married, all the company sat down to the dinner. When they began to eat the meat, it was so tasteless they couldn't eat it. But Cap o' Rushes' father tried first one dish and then another, and then he burst out crying.

'What is the matter?' said the master's son to him. 'Oh!' says he, 'I had a daughter. And I asked her how much she loved me. And she said, "As much as fresh meat loves salt." And I turned her from my door, for I thought she didn't love me. And now I see she loved me best of all. And she may be dead for aught I know.'

'No, father, here she is!' said Cap o' Rushes. And she goes up to him and puts her arms round him. And so, they were all happy ever after.

*

When Ally arrives at Grace's house, Morgan is surprised to see her. 'Why didn't you let me know you were coming?'

She glances around the room, conscious of the mess, aware that she hasn't been keeping Grace's house as it should be.

'I wrote to you, several times.' Ally looks closely at her friend, shocked by her unkempt appearance. 'I can't phone you as you haven't got one here. I wanted to see you before...'

'I've been busy.' Morgan is defensive. 'I have had some letters, but I haven't had time to open them.' And she indicates vaguely towards the small coffee table. 'Selling the house and all that, you know,' she adds lamely.

'I didn't see a notice up.'

Ally is sifting through the unopened mail.

'Well they don't always, do they?' Morgan tugs at her mop of hair, tries to smooth it down, senses Ally's disapproval.

'You've lost weight. Have you been eating properly?' Ally is looking at her, her voice accusing.

'Just been exercising, like you said.' Morgan flings her arms about vaguely, trying to make her words ring true.

'There's all these unopened letters here. Why haven't you opened them?' Ally picks up the pile of letters from the coffee table. 'There's ones here from months ago, bills and all sorts.'

'Oh, they'll keep, let's have a cup of tea. I'll just...'

'A cup of tea won't get all this sorted out.' Ally flicks at the letters from the top of the pile, one after the other, like someone looking through playing cards.

'Honestly, you'll have to sort yourself out.'

Morgan fills the kettle, her hands shaking. She knows she isn't coping. She has precious little money left and the bills will be for gas and electricity and she knows she can't pay them. She doesn't open any letters anymore. Letters mean decisions and she can't seem to make those. She hasn't put the house up for sale yet even though she knows she has no other option.

'Maybe you could stay and help me.'

She tries to look at Ally, but her eyes won't stay on her

friend's face, they dart about the kitchen, wild and anxious.

'Morgan.' Ally holds her friend's two hands in hers and tries to get her to look at her properly. 'Morgan, I'm going away. I've got a job in Australia. I've just come to say goodbye.'

'Oh.' Morgan lets her hands go limp, stares Ally in the face. 'Australia? Well, that's nice. Lovely place, all that sunshine. You'll have to look out for the spiders though. You always hated spiders.'

'Morgan. I don't think you're well. I think you should go home to Ed. Let him deal with the house. You don't need to be here.'

Morgan pulls away from her friend and starts to set out the cups ready for the tea. 'Oh, I'll be alright. Can't leave Grace, now, can I? Don't look like that, I am just joking. I'll be getting it all sorted out soon. Someone's coming round tomorrow as a matter of fact. Someone looking at the house before it's even on the market. How about that?'

Ally looks around the room. Apart from being untidy, there is something strange about it, something she can't quite put a finger on.

'So, when are you going?

Morgan's, ultra-cheery voice doesn't fool Ally for a moment.

'Well, I'm actually on the way to the airport now. Plane goes in four hours.'

'Ah, so you must have got a taxi waiting have you - for a quick getaway?'

Her voice is hardening. Obviously, she is last on a long line of goodbyes.

'Not quite.'

'So, you'll have time for this cup of tea?'

Ally looks around the room again and then back to her friend's tired, thin face.

'I think I should cancel the flight and stay and help you out.' She tries to sound matter of fact.

Morgan looks out of the window. How much she wants her friend to stay. How much she wants to curl into a ball and sleep for a hundred years like Sleeping Beauty.

They could take walks together, get the house sold, pack away all of Grace's things. She could do this with Ally to help her.

'I'll be fine,' she says, trying to sound level, trying to sound normal. 'Honestly, I know I've been dragging my feet, but I'll get on with the sale and then I'll be back with Ed and William before the month is out. You get yourself off. Enjoy Australia.'

Ally wants this job more than anything she's wanted before. She wants to get away from her mother's incapability and, if she's honest, away from this mess Morgan has made for herself. She looks at her friend again. Maybe she's just imagining her strange behaviour.

'I'll keep in touch.' She moves to give Morgan a hug.

'Of course, you will.' Morgan offers herself up, stiffly.

'I'll be out to see you before you know it.'

Leaving the empty cups on the table, the teapot full but not needed, the friends make their way out of Grace's house, arm in arm. And yet they walk distantly as though in a dream, each deep within her own thoughts.

'That car is familiar.' She sees David's car waiting for Ally at the gate.

'He's coming with me.'

Morgan stops, falters a little, it is as though everything has fallen apart.

Chicken-Licken says, 'the sky is about to fall in, I am on my way to tell the King.

'You knew we were seeing each other.' Ally is taken aback at Morgan's reaction. 'I told you in the letters.'

Then she remembers all the unopened letters on the coffee table. Surely, they were only recent ones.

'Oh, yes, of course, I remember, you should have both come in. I could have said goodbye to both of you together.'

'Well, he said he thought there'd be floods of tears and all that girlie stuff.' Ally laughs, uncertainly, not sure what to make of the seesaw of her friend's reactions. She knows David wasn't sure he would be welcome.

'Oh, well, better give him a firm handshake, then.'

Morgan's dry mouth says some words that somehow seem to fit the situation, and she hugs, kisses and shakes hands like some automaton flicked into life by a heavy bolt of electricity.

Doctor Foster thinks about going to Gloucester as his wife needs a barrel of fish. But it looks like rain, so he spends the afternoon playing Tiddlywinks with the cat instead.

His wife is angry about the fish, but he tells her that when he got halfway to Gloucester the road was under water. She sniffs and leaves the room. Doctor Foster salutes the Lie and kicks the Truth under the carpet.

Six

Winnie is getting a bit fed up of Morgan's daydreaming. She feels like shaking the girl. She's told Arthur as much.

'Oh, I don't mind her coming round, it's a bit of company for me,' she tells him, 'but when she wanders off on one of her blessed stories, well, I just want to shake her and tell her to get on with her life.' Winnie takes a tray of shortcakes out of the oven. She's started doing a bit of baking again, now that company's coming.

'I've brought you some of Grace's red roses.' Morgan hands over a bedraggled bunch and Winnie wipes her hands down her pinnie, takes the flowers and beckons the girl into the kitchen.

'There'll not be many more this summer.' Morgan smiles, trying to be what Winnie expects of her. 'Hello, Arthur.' She nods towards the photograph, her voice timorous. She wants Winnie to like her.

Winnie stuffs the flowers unceremoniously into her third best vase. 'There'll be greenfly and all sorts over the place,' she thinks to herself. 'That's more mess to clear up when she goes home.'

Morgan makes the tea. She's used to where everything is kept in this airy kitchen. She tries to get Winnie to talk about her and Arthur, about how they met, how they fell in love. She looks forward to seeing the light in the old woman's eyes when she recalls how he proposed on the front at Southport, how they got married the week before war broke out. She listens carefully to the stories and laughs in the right places. She knows Winnie likes to make her laugh.

Today, though, the old woman is on a different tack.

'So, what are you doing about selling this house of yours?' Winnie's face is set stern. She is determined to stop all this dreaming.

'You need to be getting on with it and getting back to that little boy of yours. He'll have forgotten what you look like you know.'

'Someone's coming round tomorrow.' The usual excuse. 'Tell me again about Arthur going swimming in the sea with his pipe still lit.'

'Don't use my Arthur to get out of it, young lady. You're as slippery as an eel when I try to pin you down. Now who's coming round tomorrow and what exactly are they coming round to do?'

Now, Morgan, no more stories, just go and tidy your room and get that red mop of hair brushed and in a ribbon. You've had your head in those stories all morning. It can't be healthy for a girl your age to be doing all that reading.

'Did I ever tell you about Aunty Molly?'

Morgan sits down, tired suddenly, weary like the bedraggled roses in the third best vase.

Winnie is about to try to nag her about the house again, but she notices something urgent in the younger woman's face. She knows Morgan needs to tell someone this story.

'You think I'm a nice person, Winnie, don't you? You must do or you wouldn't let me have tea with you and Arthur. But I'm not nice, not really.'

'What do you mean not nice?'

Winnie flicks the tea towel at the seat of her chair before sitting down.

'You're not a child molester or a mass murderer, are you?'

She laughs a little, glancing nervously at Arthur's photograph.

'No not that.'

Morgan sits stooped over the table, her memories ready to pour over the shortbread, to set the teaspoons rattling.

'I did kill my mother though.' She giggles, even though it's not funny and even though it hurts. She looks at Winnie's shocked face.

'Oh, not directly with a knife or poison, but slowly over the years I drove her mad, Aunty Molly said so. She said my mother was poorly with all my antics and they had to send me away so that she could sort out all my bad ways. It's this hair, you know.'

She starts to pull at the profusion of tangled, red tresses until Winnie moves her own hand to steady her, to calm her.

'It sounds to me like this Aunty Molly was just trying to force you to be the person she wanted you to be. You can't kill someone by having red hair.'

Morgan looks up at Winnie and smiles. 'No, I know.' She sits up and tries to do justice to the older woman's cooking. The birds are whistling in anticipation of the leftovers, the sun is flooding light into the blue and white kitchen. Winnie relaxes, the girl is in a state but chatting about it will probably help.

'You know, there was a time, just after my Arthur, you know, passed on, that I thought I'd killed him.'

Winnie giggles, pulling one of those, 'if you can do it, I can do it better,' faces.

Morgan looks up at her. Those large, flabby arms look as though they could do no more harm than beating up eggs for breakfast. She smiles, waiting for the joke.

315

'No, I mean it.' Winnie sits down, takes the girls hands in hers. 'I nagged him silly all his life. I know I did but I couldn't help it. It's just the way I am. He was always trying to please me, to get me to say something, anything, nice about him. But I just kept on and on, asking him to do this, to do that. I think I wore him out in the end.'

'Oh, I'm sure that's not true.'

'Ah, well, you might say that, but that's the way it feels. I just wish he'd known how much I thought about him. But you never think to say it when they're alive.' Winnie wipes a tear with the corner of her pinnie. She doesn't turn to the photograph, she can't bear Arthur's fixed, celluloid stare, not just now.

'I cried for a week after he died. Every day, for a week. But then I packed all his stuff up, all his clothes and his music from when he used to play the piano down at the pub. He did that at weekends to make up the money for my nice conservatory and the bird troughs. But I'd cried myself out and it wasn't bringing him back, so I packed it all up and got rid of it. And I've just got his photographs now. And I talk to him like I never talked to him when he was alive.

'And sometimes I cry a bit, but you've just got to get on with things. We've all got regrets but you can't do anything about what's gone already.'

Morgan squeezes Winnie's hand. 'I'm sure he must have known you loved him. I mean you'd been together a long time.'

Winnie sniffs. 'Aye, well that's as maybe. But I'm telling you, my dear, you should get yourself back to that little boy of yours, before your regrets become so big you can't do anything about them, never mind all this 'red hair' and 'evil' nonsense.'

316

'But I don't think he wants me to go back.' Morgan is close to tears. 'He hasn't come to see me for weeks, and I think Ed might have found someone else.'

'Well, make him want you to go back, you don't look like someone who gives up easily. Just leave all this nonsense telling these children stories. Who are they to you anyway and what good is it doing? Get that house sold and go home to your family. I don't care what you say, they need you and that's where you should be.'

And to emphasise the point Winnie indicates the door.

Morgan has to stop herself from skipping on the way back to Grace's house. Winnie's advice makes sense and for once the cloud she has been under feels like its lifting. That's what she'll do. She'll go home, sell the house first, pay off all those bills, then surprise Ed and William with the money that is left and with her own homecoming. She blows kisses to the trees, not caring if anyone is watching.

I'm a little teapot short and stout,
Here's my handle, here's my spout.
When I get all steamed up hear me shout,
Tip me up and pour me out.

She can see that Dot and Pat are waiting on the doorstep. William's version of the pair of pantomime dames, flashes through her mind so she is smiling when she gets to where her sisters are standing.

'It must be nice, gallivanting around, taking tea with your neighbours.' Dot is rubbing her ankles, her face red and bloated from standing in the heat.

'Nice not to have to be working and slaving, having your

nice little house given and nothing to pay.' She rubs the back of her neck with a tiny, embroidered hankie.

Pat smiles, but her eyes are wary and cold.

Morgan feels her good mood slip and slither away. What has she done wrong now? What were they talking about?

She ushers them into Grace's kitchen. It's cold, not welcoming like Winnie's.

Dot and Pat look around the room like mice smelling out cheese. Noses up, noses down, sniffing the air, sensing the room's potential.

'You haven't done much to it, have you?' Dot runs her fingers along the draining board. 'It's just like it was when Grace was alive.'

'Oh, you actually visited her, did you?' Morgan wasn't in the mood to be sisterly.

'You cheeky young madam!' Dot starts but her sister takes her arm, shushes her. Morgan knows then that they are after something.

She pours the tea and hands them the mugs, not asking them to sit down. 'So, to what do I owe the honour?'

Pat puts her mug of tea on the table, and comes to lean against the sink, sidling up to Morgan, their elbows nearly touching.

'We just wondered if you were going to sell the house. We'd heard that's what you were down here for, but no sign's gone up yet.'

Morgan moves away a little. 'What has it got to do with you?'

'I told you.' Dot slams her mug down on the table, shuffles herself into the armchair, her feet stretched out as though she is settling in for a long visit.

'It's just that, well… if you were thinking of selling the house, I know someone that is looking to buy. Our Tina, she's just found out she'd expecting, and they're looking for somewhere. They haven't much money, but as I said, you are family and you wouldn't charge them that much, would you?

Dot sits forward, chips in, 'Not the going rate. Not when it's your own family. They're just a young couple, setting out. You know how it is. They should have waited, before starting a family. But you know what they're like these days. Their Tina never did like to wait for what she wanted. Still, now the baby is on the way, there's nothing they can do about it. So, as we said to her, I bet your Aunty Morgan will help you out.'

Pat wobbles her head from side to side, proud that they have at last come to the point. She looks hopefully at Morgan, assuming now that she will be more conciliatory.

The silence that follows wells up and presses the three women to the sides of the room.

The sisters look at Morgan, waiting for her to speak. When she doesn't, they look away, wondering what to do next.

'I know you'll need time to think.' Pat's words float around, almost tangible.

Morgan knows she should respond, but her mouth won't form the words. In the end, Dot loses patience. She hauls herself out of the armchair and grabs her sister's arm.

'Come along, Pat, love, I told you she was a stuck-up little madam. Hard as nails, she is. Hasn't changed a bit. This is just a waste of time.'

As they move towards the door, puffed up with their anger, Morgan manages to find her tongue.

'You talk about 'family'. You come here and talk to me about your 'family'.'

Her words drip out quietly. Each word is like a thunder spot warning of a storm, soft and deliberate.

Pat looks at her, waiting hopefully for her decision but Dot can see the dark clouds on Morgan's face. She knows what is coming, grabs her sister and tries to move her out of the house, away from the tirade she knows is coming.

The teapot just misses the sisters as it explodes against the wall.

'I was your family. Did you ever think about that? All those years and you never visited me. All those years and you never even acknowledged I was alive. I am your sister, but I might as well be a stranger. I cried for you and my mother and my father while I was at Aunty Molly's. I wrote you letters and sent you pictures but you never once wrote back. And you dare to come here and go on about 'family'.'

Dot pushes Pat out of the door and turns to face Morgan.

'No wonder we never wanted you in our family, you're just an evil little witch. Look at you, mad as a hatter, throwing pots, wailing like a banshee. We just came round to try to be civil and look at you.'

Morgan sinks to the floor, her tears falling like summer rain.

'You made our mother ill with your antics. Every time she got a letter, she'd be off crying again, so Dad stopped giving them to her in the end. You're bad through and through, even Aunty Molly said so. And now she's gone...'

Dot sees the surprise in Morgan's face.

'Oh, you didn't know. Ah, well, I don't suppose she'd want to see you at the end anyway. She died a couple of weeks ago. We all went to see her, before the end. I expect she'd had enough of you, though. We've all had enough of you!'

Pat and Dot, the pantomime dames, exit 'stage left'. They go home to re-tell the story, to reinforce the family myth about the red-haired black sheep.

Jessica finds Morgan squatting on the floor in Grace's kitchen. She let herself in as the 'ugly sisters' left the door open. She leaves her holdall in the hall and moves slowly towards Morgan, not knowing what to say or what to do.

Morgan looks at the girl and wonders what she is doing here. She has no energy to form words. Jessica sits with her, their arms are just touching, the afternoon passes and neither of them speaks.

Seven

It's dark. Jessica is asleep in the spare room. Morgan moves around the house like a ghost until eventually she finds herself sitting on the floor of the room with the small round window.

She fixes her eyes on the stars through the skylight. Her face feels swollen, tight.

She wonders if Aunty Molly is watching her from Heaven. She wonders if all the hymns and praying paid off. She wonders if Aunty Molly really had not wanted to see her again in those last weeks of her life.

She realises that a thin wail, which is circling the room is actually coming from her. She clenches her teeth, but the wail comes out anyway. She can't stop it. She wants to see Aunty Molly one last time, she wants to see Grace, Gwen, just one last time.

Her shoulders shake with an emotion which is coming from somewhere dark and deep, somewhere basic and powerful.

The stage has no curtains, it is an expanse of solid blue ocean, wider than any eye could see or any soul could imagine.

Grace is on the stage. She is singing and dancing with row on row of others, millions of performers. The colour of their costumes shades from left to right, red through to violet, a perfect rainbow.

They are singing one of a thousand songs from their repertoire. They are singing all the stanzas and all the refrains, from song number one to song one thousand. And when they have finished song one thousand, there is silence for a while and then a tiny echoing ripple of celestial applause.

The front row of performers takes a bow before tap dancing to the back of the ensemble. The whole performance begins again.

Grace is no longer blind in heaven. Her eyes look out with wonder onto the solid blue ocean and the sea of reachable stars.

*

With her head bowed over a large book, Gwen's eyes move left to right like an automaton. Line after line of print to be read, devoured, as she sits at the wooden desk absorbed in her work.

Next to her sits another and next to her another. To the left and to the right of her, in front and behind her, rows of desks, row upon row of readers. Their eyes sweep the pages, compute the black print into words, into meaning, into story. The cold, thin air of the mountain plateau on which the desks are arranged stings their eyes and makes them cry, but they do not wipe away the tears. The tears freeze on their cheeks and they read on through perpetual haze.

After a required time, they all, as though with one hand, turn the page and in the hush of the reading and under the clearest amethyst sky, swallow-like birds wheel and dive as though in some cosmic dance. In and through each other's flightpath they weave a text of their own against the expanse of Heaven.

By evening, as the sky darkens to ink, a trumpet sounds and, as though with one hand, each one of the million readers closes their book.

After a moment's purest silence, a cymbal crashes and again, as though with one hand, each one of the million readers takes their book and passes it to their neighbour, left to right, in readiness for another eternal day.

*

Molly is baking cakes for the angels together with a million other red-cheeked cooks. The swelter in the kitchen rolls over them, like heat wave after heat wave rolling over a sun-baked desert. There is a symphony of egg whisking, soft flour sifting, flapping of hand-beaten batters and a bass line of bread dough thumping and kneading. The air is thick with steam from thousands of ovens and a sweet, persistent white cloud of airborne icing sugar.

The kitchen is earthbound. The ovens are built inside grey caves now empty of salt sea which once bathed their cracked stone. A wind occasionally fans the flames, reaching the kitchen from distant howls of sinners bound for hell.

Each afternoon a band of angels descends to test the cakes, but most are found wanting. The cooks' cheeks get redder as their food is rejected and their straight-line mouths get sterner as they clash and clean their bowls, spoons and dishes, ready to start cooking again. They are compelled to try and try, as they must, in the search for that perfect angel cake.

*

Morgan has stopped crying. She tips her head back to look out of the skylight and sees the moon, just a part of a moon. She wonders if it is waxing or waning. She is overwhelmed by its comfort.

Eight

There's a ship sails from China with a cargo of tea,
Laden with treasures for you and for me.
It brought me a fan, just imagine my bliss,
When I fan myself daily like this, like this, like this, like this.

There are three knocks at the door that day. Jessica doesn't like answering the door at all. She is worried about who will be at the other side. She isn't used to this house, to this town. Everyone is a stranger, except Morgan, and she is in bed. Jessica had checked first thing when she got up. Morgan is asleep in Grace's old bed and Jessica doesn't want to wake her, not yet.

The first knock is a 'tip tap' sort of a knock. Jessica thinks it sounds like the wind when it blows overhanging tree branches against the window at home. But she isn't at home and it isn't windy. The girl opens the door and steps over the threshold so that she is speaking to a plump woman in the garden. She whispers, indicating with her head that Morgan is asleep, not feeling very well.

'Just as well she's got a little helper, then.' Winnie is trying to see into the kitchen, she would have liked to see Morgan there, see that she was alright.

'I'm Morgan's friend.' She hesitates, waiting for the girl to introduce herself, but Jessica remains silent. 'She didn't seem well yesterday, and someone just mentioned to me that they heard raised voices and breaking crockery.' Again, another pause, but Jessica is staying quiet.

'Maybe I should come in and see if she is alright.' Winnie makes a move towards the door, but Jessica blocks the way.

'She's fine.' The girl forces a smile. 'I've come over to help out because she wasn't feeling well, but she's asleep now and I don't want to wake her up just yet.'

Winnie steps back. She can't very well force her way in after all. She looks at the girl. Can't be more than eleven or twelve, she thinks. Never seen her before and she doesn't sound like she comes from around here.

'So, you're looking after her on your own?'

'Yes. My mum knows I'm here, I told her. That's not a problem.'

Jessica looks at her shoes for a moment but then looks up at Winnie and beams. 'My mum's a good friend of Morgan's and she's happy for me to look after her, just until she's feeling better.'

Winnie shuffles off down the path. She'll go and talk it over with Arthur. There's something not quite right here and she's not quite sure what to do about it.

'Tell her I've been then, won't you? Tell her Winnie came to visit.' But Jessica is already at the back of the door, shutting it, locking her out.

Jessica makes herself busy by tidying the kitchen. She's good around the house. She's had to be since Leanne started to prefer wine to washing up. She has remembered where everything belongs from last year when she was here with William. That had been a good holiday. She smiles to herself remembering the hot summer and the picnics in the garden.

Once she's put all the clean crockery away, she starts to tidy up the paperwork, which seems to overflow every surface. There are scraps of paper everywhere, and each piece has Morgan's handwriting on it. Jessica piles them up, squares the sheets up, tries to get them to look neat. She notices some of the words, recognises the stories that Morgan used to tell them down at Arthur's seat. She puts the pile down on the little table next to a pile of letters, all unopened.

'*All things bright and beautiful…*' She starts to sing to herself, quietly, she still doesn't want Morgan to wake up. '*All creatures great and small.*' Everywhere she looks now she can see more pieces of paper, covered in Morgan's handwriting, covered in words. There's a piece in the sugar basin, several pieces pinned to the wall, some are stuck in a row of cups set out on the window ledge. Jessica is scared. There is something about all these words, all this writing, that unnerves her.

'*All things wise and wonderful…*' Her voice is becoming a bit tremulous, but at least if she keeps singing…

There's a ship sails from China with a cargo of tea,
Laden with treasures for you and for me.
It brought me a brush, just imagine my bliss,
As I brush myself daily like this, like this, like this, like this.

There is a second knock at the door.

Jessica can't believe how childlike Ed looks. She lets him in and explains again about Morgan being asleep. She puts the kettle on, stands on a chair again to reach the cups and saucers she has just cleared away.

'Do you realise how worried everyone has been?' Ed tries to sound stern. 'Your mother is beside herself.'

'Beside herself with worry or with booze?' Jessica is tackling the bread knife. Ed can see she is no stranger to fending for herself. She pushes cheese around the slice of bread, making a meagre amount into a sandwich. She cuts it, passes him half and eats half herself.

There is silence as they eat. Each occasionally looks at the other, asking questions with their eyes, building a bridge over their wariness with each other.

'I left her a note.' Jessica picks up the empty plates, moves to the sink. 'I didn't think she'd be that worried. I was only in the way anyway, unless she wanted something to eat, or the dishes needed doing.

She washes their plates methodically, taking comfort in the familiar routine in these unfamiliar surroundings.

'Jessica, I'm sorry, I hadn't realised how bad things were for you.' Ed stands up and runs his fingers through his hair.

'Or maybe I had realised, if I'm honest. Just lately, though, it's as if everything has been happening like it's a dream.'

He sits down again, his hands over his eyes, his head bowed. Jessica stares out at the garden. It is abundant with late summer growth.

'I just couldn't take it anymore.' Her eyes are cold and sealed. She is keeping all the hurt inside. 'The other kids at school were teasing me, they knew how she was. I tried to keep her indoors away from people, but I couldn't. I couldn't ask anyone back to our house after school, and, apart from the farm, I couldn't go round to anyone else's. I didn't want anyone seeing her like that, I felt like tying her up, keeping her a prisoner.'

There is a catch in the child's voice. She starts to cry. 'I thought Morgan would understand, I thought I could talk to her and she'd tell me what to do. But when I got here…'

'How did you get here, Jessica?' Ed's voice is soft. He is looking at the girl as though it is the first time, he's really seen her.

'When I got up yesterday, mum was still in bed as usual. Her bag was there on the table from the night before and I took some money for the train fare.'

Jessica looks Ed in the eye. 'I stole from her to get the train. I know it's wrong, but I couldn't help it.' And she turns her head away, embarrassed.

'Jessica, it's alright, I'm not worried about the money. But how did you find your way. It's a long way for someone your age on their own.'

Jessica continues her story, her voice so quiet that Ed can hardly hear her. She keeps her head turned away from him.

'I walked to Bridlington station and then got the train to Sheffield. I asked the man in the station and he said that was the nearest. I told him I was going to see my mother who was ill. The station in Sheffield was so big and I was frightened that I would never find Morgan. That was the only time I was really scared.'

She pauses, remembering the noise and bustle of the station. How the people pushed and elbowed their way around, not caring if a small girl was looking lost. She remembers the boom of the tannoy's announcements, trains arriving, trains departing, the oily smell and the pigeons flying eerily in the station rafters.

'I got out of the station and got a bus. Buses are easier. I know my way with buses better than with trains. When I got to Barnsley I just asked. I knew the address from last year when Morgan brought me and William here for a holiday. I just walked and kept asking. People were really helpful. I just kept saying that my mother was ill, and I was here to help out.'

'But Morgan isn't your mother.' Jessica takes in a sharp breath, even though Ed's voice is gentle and kind.

'I know. But I wish she was. I've been wishing she was my mother for months. You don't know what it has been like at home.'

And Jessica hunches over, sobbing into her knees. Ed puts his arm around her shoulders, but she is inconsolable.

There's a ship sails from China with a cargo of tea,
All laden with treasure for you and for me.
It brought me some shoes, just imagine my bliss,
When I tap my feet lightly like this, like this, like this, like this.

The third knock is loud and officious. When Ed opens the door, the policeman comes into the kitchen, his eyes everywhere, hungry for information. He looks at Jessica, still sobbing and then at Ed.

'I'd like to know what's going on here, sir.' His words are polite, but his manner holds threat.

Ed explains how the girl has come to help Morgan. He feels as though the policeman is looking at him as though he's some kind of pervert. He stumbles over his words. Jessica is still sobbing with her back turned to the pair of them.

Morgan comes in looking like a wraith. She is paler than Ed has ever seen her and looks thin and sick.

'What's going on?' She is shocked to see so many people in the kitchen. She is used to her own company.

The policeman flashes his ID at her.

'One of the neighbours reported that there was a fracas last night, and that she's concerned for a child that has suddenly turned up here.' He tries to get a good look at Jessica, but she buries her head in her arms, crying still, but quieter.

Morgan is angry. Two pink spots appear on her otherwise white face. She looks around her, trying to understand why these people are suddenly in Grace's house.

Her gaze settles on Ed. Why hadn't he come before? She wants him to gather her up, to make everything alright the way he always said he would. But Ed stares back. There is an ocean of time between them, holding them apart.

'I think you should all leave.' Morgan is agitated. 'You have no right to be here. Just get out of here.' And she picks up a mug making as though to throw it.

And then suddenly there is Maggie. She doesn't need to knock. The door is open as it was for Jessica the night before. She simply walks in and moves towards Morgan, taking the mug out of her shaking hands. She encircles her in a hug, which Morgan feels she has been waiting for her whole life. Morgan begins to cry, burying her head in the older woman's chest.

The policeman is writing in his notebook. Ed moves towards Jessica. 'I'll sort this out now, officer.' He puts his arms around the girl, and she turns, sobbing towards him.

'That's as maybe, sir, but this seems to be a very strange situation, if you don't mind me saying. I mean, all this distress, there's obviously something been going on. And you, sir, well you could be anyone. I need to know that this child is in safe hands.'

'I'm her father.' Ed knows now that this is the truth. How could he ever have thought otherwise?

He had let Jessica down. He had let Leanne down. He knew now that he needed to start putting things right.

'I've only your word for that, sir.' The policeman still wasn't satisfied.

'And mine.' Maggie was still holding Morgan, gently,

331

soothing her. 'This is my son, and this child is his daughter. Jessica ran away from home, but she left a note, so we can sort this out now. There will be no more trouble, I can promise you.'

Like an actor in a play, the policeman moves out, leaving a space on the stage for Donald to move into. He says nothing, and no-one questions his appearance. There they stand in tableau. Morgan with Maggie, Jessica with Ed, and Donald, looking on, shocked at Morgan's pallor, saddened by her copious tears.

Miss Polly had a dolly who was sick, sick, sick,
So, she phoned for the doctor to be quick, quick, quick.
The doctor came with his bag and his hat,
And he rapped at the door with a rat-a-tat-tat.

He looked at the dolly and he shook his head,
And he said, 'Miss Polly, put her straight to bed!'
He wrote on a paper for a pill, pill, pill,
'I'll be back in the morning, yes, I will, will, will.

Maggie and Donald are staying with Morgan until the house is sold. They have promised Ed they will look after her and bring her home soon.

For two days, Morgan has stayed in bed. She is finding it hard to surface from the dreams that have suddenly possessed her.

There is Ed riding on a white horse, a white horse with red ribbons streaming from its tail. And Ed is riding towards her, but Leanne is barring his way. Then suddenly it's not Ed but William on the horse and he is screaming

332

and crying because he can't hold on any longer. Then she is in the sea, surrounded by mermaids, who look like Gwen or Grace or Aunty Molly and they are calling to her, Aunty Molly waving a hairbrush, Grace brandishing a rose.

Sometimes Maggie is there with a tray of food, but this isn't part of the dream. This is real and Maggie smooths her hair, helps her sit up and eat.

'You're exhausted, Morgan,' Maggie is saying. 'I knew you weren't well last time I saw you. You should have come home. I should have fetched you home.' And the woman frets and soothes and then goes away and Morgan is back with her dreams.

She dreams she is alone in a house, which she doesn't recognise. She moves from room to room, searching for something. The rooms are empty and unfamiliar, until she reaches the one at the top of the house, the one with a single round window.

She has been here before. There are someone's belongings all over the floor, spilling out of the wardrobes, spread over the settee. And suddenly there is Grace, moving through the room without touching the floor and she doesn't see Morgan at all, and Morgan is shouting to her, crying out her name but Grace passes by, without a word.

'Morgan wake-up. You are dreaming.' Maggie is there, wiping her tears, holding her.

George used to say that you'd know when a storm was coming because the birds would stop singing and everything would be unnaturally quiet and calm. And Morgan had seen the sea when a storm was at its height.

She had seen the way it spat and simmered like a stew on the stove. She had seen the way the waves threatened and sucked back, taunting the shore.

Now she dreams she is on the beach at Flamborough, and she is the only person there. The cliffs rear up behind her, cutting off the village. The seagulls and dippers plod around, land-bound, scouring the sands for decaying fish and crabs thrown up in the last tide.

She dreams that she is trying to get home, off the beach, up the Landing, but her feet won't move no matter how hard she tries. The waves are soft and lapping, but the birds have stopped singing and she knows there is a storm coming...

Morgan drags herself from sleep and Donald is there, sitting neatly on a chair beside her bed. He is watching her, his regrets etched on his grey face.

Morgan feels suddenly shy of this man, her father, the man she has loved to hate.

'I'll never let you down again, Morgan.' His eyes are bright with his own tears, but he does not brush them away.

'Please give me a chance to get to know you. A chance to make amends.'

Morgan holds out her hand in silence and Donald takes it with both of his.

*

Morgan and Donald are working side by side in the garden. Maggie is clearing the house and they are getting the garden sorted out ready for the first visitors who are coming round for a viewing.

'Maybe I should sell it to Pat's daughter, Tina. She asked me to sell it cheap as they were family, but I refused and threw a teapot at her.'

She prunes a rose bush viciously, hard back.

Donald laughs, 'Don't worry about Pat or Dot. They like nothing better than coming across a bargain. Comes from living just after there'd been a war on. Finding something on the cheap is something that stays with you.'

Morgan finds herself telling him about Pat and Dot's previous visit the year before and how William had called them the pantomime dames. Donald laughs, obviously recognising his daughters by the description, and as he laughs, his face colours up and the greyness begins to slip away.

'You should get to know them properly, you know, they're not so bad.'

'Don't tell me what I should do, you haven't earned the right.'

For the while, the silence is only broken by the click of shears, the dull thud of clods of weeds hitting the wheelbarrow.

'Morgan, you reminded me, not so long ago, of a story I used to tell you when you lived at home, before…' Donald leans against the shed, out of breath from his exertions.

'It was about a jealous father who killed his son and destroyed his bequest of healing herbs which the daughter, Airmid, kept set out in order on her cloak.'

Morgan sits back on her heels. 'I remember.'

'Well, I feel as though I have destroyed the pattern and order of our family, by the way I treated you as a child, by the way I was with Gwen.'

Morgan gets up, feels the rough bark of the tree, lets the

335

sharpness dig into her fingers, lets it hurt her.

'That can't be changed. It belongs to the past.'

'I know, I know.' Donald moves towards her, hesitating, not yet sure of how to be with her.

'But just as Airmid tried to get the herbs back in the right order, I want to set our family story straight. I would like you, Morgan, to discover the whole story, from your sisters, from your brother. And, more importantly, for them to hear your part of it too.'

The blood burns in Morgan's face as she turns away from Donald. She doesn't want this now. There is too much pain to be found in her own story, pain that has been squashed down for years.

'I know it will be painful.' Donald lays a gentle hand on her shoulder. 'But every story has many parts, and I don't think you will be able to settle until you know all of the parts to your own story.'

She turns to face him, the destroyer of the family, the father who disowned her. And Morgan feels a great surge of love for him, unbidden emotion, strong and honest.

As the years slide by, the little girl grows into a beautiful woman. One day she decides to hold a Grand Ball in the magnificent Golden Ballroom in the castle. She spends seven weeks writing out invitations, which are sent to everyone she has ever known. She takes the white sheets of paper, which had once held all the stories of the World and she folds them to white hearts, one for each guest.

On the evening of the Grand Ball, she asks the Truths and Lies to make two rows, the Truths to the right and the Lies to the left and the whole company watch as they dance elegantly across the Golden Ballroom, lit only by silver moonlight. Sometimes the Truths and Lies hold hands and other times they dance alone.

Nine

Maggie's story

You seemed to have everything I ever wanted, Morgan, and I suppose I was jealous. There you were, been to college, strong minded and independent. It wouldn't have been so bad if you'd got Ed to find himself another career. I always wanted him to move away from the farm, get a proper job. Maybe Peter would have sold up then and life would have been so different. But no, you carried on with your teaching job, you'd got what you wanted, and Ed just carried on with the farm.

It was as though you were floating around our livelihood like it was tainted. You never got involved in the work on the farm, never got your hands dirty. You said you didn't belong, well, whose fault was that then?

But then if I'm honest, you're not the only one to feel that you didn't belong. I was born and brought up on that farm, long before I knew Peter, and I never felt like I belonged, not even then. Even when I was a little girl, I wanted to move away, but you don't always get what you want in life, I know that now.

When my parents had South End Farm, it was a much smaller affair than it is now. Oh yes, it was our farm, not Peter's. Everyone presumes it was his family's farm, but he was the offcomer, not me. My earliest memories are of my parents working all hours to scrape a living from that damned land, year on year, no holidays and no respite. And my brother and me, we scratched around with the hens and got taken notice of pretty much the same as them.

Dad was worn out by the time he was fifty. He'd had it so hard in the war years that he had nothing left in him at the end of it. My brother was a fighter pilot. So proud of him Dad was, but he didn't survive the war, didn't come back to help out on the farm. It was as though I'd hardly known him. There he was on the farm one minute

337

and then it was just me with Mum and Dad. I didn't think they would ever get going again.

But then Peter came along. I was working as a barmaid in between helping out at home. It's a wonder he took a second look at me. I've never been a good-looking woman, and I've always had a sharp tongue. Mind you, he certainly took a second look at the farm and I've often wondered if that was really the attraction. He was a few years older than me, was Peter, and he had a bit of money put by. Once he saw the farm that was it. We were married and he was learning the ropes as quick as you like.

Things looked up for a bit then. Dad seemed to think he had his son back and him and Peter spent hours out on the land. It's different these days. There are more choices. As soon as we were married and Peter moved into the farmhouse, I knew that was that. I might have well had been fastened in with the hens. I knew I'd be on that farm forever.

Then Ed came along. He was the most beautiful thing that I'd ever seen. He was mine. He was precious and I never wanted to lose him. I was determined he wouldn't be a farmer and I did everything to discourage him. I wanted him to move away and take me with him. But then you came along, and I knew then that he'd stay and make the farm a home and a living for his own family.

In a way, I suppose I felt that you took away my chance of escaping the farm. But you didn't want to be on that farm any more than I did. You found your escape in teaching and all that blessed storytelling you did. And I was forced back to being who I've always been, farm wife and kitchen maid.

The only thing that made it bearable was that Peter said when things were more settled, we'd retire. I looked forward to that more than you can ever know. I planned out little trips away, little holidays. Nothing fancy. I looked forward to us just sitting together, talking, reading the papers, doing everyday things people take for granted, but doing them together. Thought I might even do a couple of evening classes, find myself a hobby. But I should have known better than to dream.

When Peter died, it wasn't just my dreams that went by the by. It suddenly hit me that I'd spent all those years with someone I really loved. I'd spent time telling him what I didn't want, laying into him with complaints and moaning. But I really loved that man, and I don't think he ever knew how much.

But now it's your turn to come and play farmer's wife, young lady. I've done my bit and I didn't like it anymore that you will. But I'm going to look for a few of those dreams that I've let slip by before it's too late.

As far as belonging is concerned, well you make your own belonging, you don't wait to be invited.

*

All the cleaning and polishing, the digging and delving, all the rubbing and scrubbing and the chitting and chatting, it has all paid off. And the little house with roses around the door has been sold to a young couple with rosy apple cheek.

Morgan has lost track of the number of people who have knocked at the door in the last few weeks. Maggie and Donald have helped her to clean up Grace's old house and to put it on the market. She knows it's time now for the next chapter in the house's story and she's happy to be handing it over to the couple who obviously think that it is the right place for their 'happily ever after' to begin.

And today Morgan is having a party. Maggie is helping her with the cooking and Donald is preparing a fire at the end of the garden.

'What have we got so far?'

She is covered in flour, her red hair streaked with white. 'Butterflies for Aunty Molly, Madeleines for Gwen and fairy cakes for Grace, of course.'

Maggie looks at her askance.

'It's OK, I'm not having a funny turn.' Morgan is beating eggs for all she's worth. 'The Celts used to set aside food for the Otherworld visitors who may turn up. I'm not expecting any of them to, I'm just making a gesture.'

Maggie sniffs. 'Well, I'm just making pies and plenty of them. People will be hungry after travelling over. I don't know where everyone is going to sleep.'

'Don't worry, we'll manage. Dot and Pat have offered to put Jessica and William up. It's about time that the children got to know their great aunts.'

'They're just aunts, aren't they?'

'I was referring to the size of them.' Morgan and Maggie laugh together, they are becoming used to each other, rubbing along quite well.

The two women move around each other in the small kitchen, like ribbons in a complicated maypole dance, they don't get in each other's way, just keep up the gentle weaving, each gently aware of the other.

'Dot told me what she remembers from when I was a little girl,' Morgan ventures, trying out the story, which is new to her.

'Oh, yes, and what did she have to say for the way they treated you?'

Maggie has never understood how anyone could have parted with a child, no matter how difficult to manage she was. As far as she can see, the whole of Morgan's family was little short of criminal. Oh, Donald was showing some feelings now, but…

'Well, I can sort of see how it was now, from what she said.'

'Oh, Morgan, don't be fooled. They should never have let you go.'

'Well, she was saying how strange and embarrassing it was when Gwen got pregnant again. I mean, her and Pat were grown up. All the neighbours thought their mum had been having an affair, or so Dot said.

It was really horrible in the house with Donald pretending it wasn't happening and Gwen going more and more inside herself.'

'She should have told him what's what.' Maggie thumps her rolling pin down hard, sends the flour flying into a dusty cloud.

'She wasn't like that. She was a real mouse. I can remember when she visited me at Aunty Molly's. I think she was more scared than I was when Aunty M shouted.

'I think she thought that if she kept quiet, she could have her baby back and everything would be alright again. And maybe it would have been if I'd been a quiet child.'

'Now don't go blaming yourself in all this.' Maggie crimps the edges of the pie. She can see now what Morgan has been through. She wishes she'd seen it earlier.

'No, but as far as they were concerned, I was running Gwen ragged. All they saw was their mum getting weaker and quieter. And there was this little red-haired monster who they couldn't accept as their sister at all. I suppose they were just protecting Gwen.'

'Taking the easy way out, more likely. Maybe they should have offered to look after you now and again, that might have helped. It's always easy to blame someone else.'

'Ah, well, they thought it was the right thing for Aunty

Molly to bring me up and who knows? Maybe they were right.'

'You don't mean that.'

Maggie leaves off cooking and catches Morgan up in a floury hug. Then she pulls away, a bit embarrassed. She isn't normally a demonstrative woman.

'Molly Flowerdew was a good woman,' she begins, holding Morgan by the shoulders, looking her directly in the eye, 'but I don't think she was ever meant to bring up children.' They hold each other's gaze for a moment.

'The only way Aunty Molly would have got on with children was if they could be baked and eaten.' Morgan bursts out laughing and the pair of them giggle and wipe tears with floury hands for the rest of the morning.

Later Grace's kitchen is full to overflowing with visitors and Morgan moves between them and the few that are standing around Donald's garden fire.

There is Ed, William and Jessica out by the fire with Donald. And there is Dot, Pat and Winnie in the kitchen with Maggie. In the house there are boxes packed with Grace's belongings and each marked for a different destination.

A lot of the big stuff is going to Dot and Pat's children who are starting up their own homes. Morgan is surprised how easy it has been to part with these things. They are just 'things' after all. She has kept the photographs and the blue and white tea set (sadly minus the teapot) to take home herself. There are memories wrapped up in them that she isn't prepared to part with just yet.

She carries a box out to the bonfire and hands it to Donald.

'Just letters, bills, bits of writing,' she says answering his inquisitive raising of the eyebrow.

Jessica comes around and slips her arm into Morgan's.

'Are the stories in there?' she whispers. 'I saw them, Morgan, all around the house, it was scary seeing them all written out and pinned to things, stuck under the kettle, under plant pots.'

Morgan bends down and holds Jessica's face between her hands.

'It's OK, Jessica, I wasn't feeling well and thought that if I didn't write them down, I would lose them. They're all in the box now.'

And they watch as Donald throws the box on the fire. Red sparks burst from the embers, coughing and spitting into the afternoon.

'Does that mean the stories are gone?' William comes up and reaches for Morgan's hand.

'How could they be?' She laughs. 'They're in my head and will always be there for when we need them.'

And as happens every now and again, it seems as though there is no room for the bug-eyed What-ifs who were only there in the first place to make up the numbers. And even though they are small and live with dust mites under the carpet and although there is an army of them, they are no stronger than ditch water and as they leave the great palace, no-one is any the wiser and no-one waves them on their way.

Most of the visitors have gone home. Jessica and William to stay with Dot and Pat, and Maggie's yawns are signalling for Donald and Winnie to go home to their beds. Morgan goes to answer a knock at the door, thinking one of her visitors has forgotten something.

David is on the doorstep and a taxi is winking its way down the road.

It's late, and Maggie and Ed have gone to bed. Morgan unpacks the blue and white tea set and makes David a cup of tea.

Somehow it is important that they should be drinking out of Grace's cups. She believes her grandmother could still be a fly on the wall, watching her family catching up with itself.

Morgan curls up in the old armchair. No-one wants it but she isn't throwing it away, it holds too many memories. It will fit in the Land Rover. Ed has assured her of that. Indulgently, he is happy to promise her the moon if it means she is coming home.

'Funny, isn't it, that most people seem to be trying to get away from their families, and yet we have gone through torment to get back to ours?' David walks around the kitchen, he can't settle, the flight had been long, and Ally is still in Australia.

'That's what comes of leaving our family too early, I suppose.'

Morgan is comfortable with him. She had expected a flood of all the old jealousy and resentment when she saw him standing in the doorway, but it hasn't happened. She looks at her brother, feels his restlessness, his weariness.

'What's happening with Ally, then?' She holds a cup out, motions for a refill.

David stops pacing the room, hangs his head, ignoring the proffered cup.

'She still thinks it's working out over there.' He runs his fingers through his hair, sighing. 'All the time she goes on

344

about her mother, her brother, worrying, fretting and then when I say let's go home then she gets all tough and huffy, you know how she can be?'

Morgan nods, silently. She knows Ally.

'She says we haven't given it long enough and we're bound to be homesick and then she goes off and buries herself in her work. She wants to come home, but she's too proud to admit we've made a mistake.'

David stops pacing, looks at Morgan. 'I love her so much, Morgan. I told her I had to come home to see you, put things right between us. But she said if I left, that would be the end of her and me. But she's wrong, I know she's wrong.'

Morgan feels as though she's seeing him for the first time. She wonders how she could have hated him so much. Why had she seen him as an intruder, the enemy?

She slouches into the armchair, curls her feet tightly under her. 'Why did you feel you had to come home to see me?'

The smell of the bonfire is still hanging in the air, she can smell it, taste it.

'I wanted to tell you what it was like, back then, when they... when they sent you to Aunty Molly's.'

David holds his hands out to her, but she can't take them. She folds her arms, clenches her fists.

'I tried to tell you once before, at the farm. Do you remember?'

She nods, wanting to smile encouragement at him, but aware that her face is set, closed.

'As soon as Mum told Dad she was expecting, things changed in our house and nothing was ever the same again. We all went through the motions and did the things we always did. It was as though we were pretending that it wasn't true. We seemed to think that if we didn't talk about it, nothing would happen, nothing would change. And when Mum brought you home from the hospital, you were so beautiful, that I thought it would all be alright. How could anyone not fall in love with this little red-haired bundle of a baby? Pat and Dot cooed, and Mum was beside herself with love for you.'

David sits on the floor, his legs crossed, and his hands limp as his side. It is as though he is there again, nearly thirty years ago.

'Even Dad seemed to mellow. He'd take you out for long walks and talk to you in his silly baby talk.'

Morgan feels herself smiling along with David at the reminiscence.

'So, what went wrong with the idyll?' She leans forward, almost allowing herself to touch his shoulder, hold his hands.

'It started with Mum I suppose. She'd just burst into tears at the least little thing. Sometimes when I got home from school, she'd be sitting there crying and you'd be upstairs yelling your head off. And then Dad would come in and there was no meal ready and the house a tip. It was as if she couldn't cope with any of it anymore.'

'She was depressed?'

'Yes, it sounds so straight forward, doesn't it? But it seemed much more than that at the time. It was as though everything was upside down, not working, broken.

That's how it felt to me at the time, anyway. I used to stay at my friend's house as late as I could, and then sneak in, hoping things had quietened down.

No-one seemed to notice if I was in or out. Everyone was running around after you and Mum.'

'But it must have got better as I got older. She can't have been depressed all the time. Couldn't she have had medication?'

'The pills knocked her out. Made her sick and then she'd be asleep for hours on end. But things did get better for a while, once you started walking, you know, toddling about. Oh, and then you started asking questions. We thought the questions would never stop.' David smiles as he remembers, and again he reaches out for Morgan's hands.

'I wasn't an evil little witch all the time then?' Morgan takes his hands, feels their honest roughness. David looks at her, a hurt look on his face.

'What makes you say that? You were never a little witch. Where does that idea come from?'

'Aunty Molly.'

They stay, each with their own thoughts, as the clock ticks its steady pace through the minutes. Briefly, Morgan wonders whether if Grace could hear the conversation, she would approve of the telling of this story.

David squeezes her hand. 'You should have seen yourself, toddling around after Dad. He always let you help him out in the garden. He was always the one to calm you down with a story.'

'So, what went wrong?'

'There was a big row. Dad was tired. He'd been working hard at school. And when he got home you were screaming up in your room and Mum was sitting reading a book. He just flipped I suppose. Came out with all sorts of things about her being lazy, weak, leaving all the work to him. And

Mum started to shout back. I had never seen her so angry with him. She never used to say boo to a goose.'

'What did she have to be angry about, it sounds as though everyone was bending over to help out.'

'Things she'd kept to herself for years. She'd always been the one to keep the peace between us all and all those things she'd kept quiet about, they all came out. She was screaming, crying, throwing things at him. It was awful.'

'I can't imagine her… she always seemed so - oh, I don't know, so meek.'

'It went on for ages. And at the end of it all, she went on about him not being the father after all. She was just trying to hurt him. She wasn't clever like he was with words and she just said the worst thing she could.'

'And he believed her?' Morgan sits back in the chair, tears prickling, her face white.

'It wasn't true, Morgan.' David gets up and starts to pace the room, round and round in his agitation. 'It wasn't true, she told me a few days later. She'd just wanted to hurt him.'

'But he believed her.'

'He didn't seem to be able to get it out of his head. He kept on being kind to you. He kept on reading you stories, letting you help him in the garden. But I saw him looking at you sometimes and the doubt was written all over his face.'

'So, they sent me away?'

'Not then. Mum took you to Aunty Molly's for a holiday. Just you two. I was so jealous. I used to love going there. But Dad told me it was a good idea if Mum got to know you. He was worried that she wasn't looking after you properly, you know, not bonding with you.'

'I vaguely remember her telling me lots of stories,'

Morgan wipes the tears, hangs her head to her chest.

'I'm sure she did. She was good at stories was Mum. She lived for books, they seemed to make more sense to her than people sometimes.'

'So, is that when I went to live with Aunty Molly? Did she just leave me there?'

'No, no. She brought you home, but she and Dad carried on arguing about you. She said you wanted her attention all the time, and she couldn't cope. She kept going on and on about how well Molly coped and maybe she should look after you for a while longer. She wore Dad down after a while and he just agreed so that things could go back to how they were, I think.'

'So that's when they sent me away.'

'Yes.' David sits on the arm of the chair. 'But it wasn't meant to be for ever, Morgan, it was only supposed to be for a while. But she just seemed to give in to the depression, then. It never seemed to go away. She still didn't cook or clean the house, and, in the end, Dad gave up work and stayed at home to look after her. When I asked them when they were going to bring you home, they just looked at me as though I was speaking a foreign language. They seemed to be in their own little world.'

'And I wasn't part of it.'

'None of us were part of it. By then Pat and Dot had left home anyway and I was old enough to look after myself. Except Dad had such expectations of me, wanted me to be him all over again. He never listened to me, to what I wanted. And to be honest, I got fed up after a while and that's when I decided to leave home. What was there to keep me there? You weren't there and Mum and Dad were like two shadows in some never-never land.'

'Where did you go? After Aunty Molly's'.

'I travelled all over, picking up bits of jobs, slept rough sometimes. I just wanted to get away from all that.'

'Did you ever think about me, want to come back and see me?'

'I thought about you a lot, but I thought you'd be OK with Aunty Molly. I'd always had a good time on the farm. I thought you'd be OK. Morgan, you have to see I was angry, confused. I was young and I was scared.'

And through the mists of time, we see a boy who wants to become a fish. But (as it is with boys in all times) he dallies on his journey, spends time in by-ways and valleys, in subways and alleys and he feeds himself on the glut of the orchards and the surfeit of detritus.

A boy who in another time might be called Hansel or Jack. A boy who has wriggled through holes in time until his clothes have become tattered as a scarecrow's. A boy who is becoming a man and who knows that after these seven or more years he must ignore the distraction of gingerbread houses and the lure of quick-fix fortunes. He knows he must make his way to the ocean.

Morgan gets up from the chair and goes to look out of the window. The embers of the fire are still glowing, and an occasional gust of wind stirs them into giving out an odd spark.

David stands shoulder to shoulder with her, staring out into the night.

'Then I fell in love, Morgan. Her father had given me a job on his fishing coble out of Hull and I was smitten from the moment I saw her. I called her my mermaid. She was beautiful and we shared the same hopes and dreams.'

350

The boy who wants to become a fish falls in love with a mermaid. She is so beautiful that shoals of fish swim alongside her, threading and weaving through the strands of her flaxen hair.

Little by little the boy sheds his mortal skin and becomes a merman. He woos the mermaid, flipping his body through waves, somersaulting like an acrobatic dolphin.

'We were wild. Oh, we were wild. We travelled where the fancy took us, but the places were always by the sea. We were drawn to the sea.'

And the wind blows them hither and thither as arm in arm they plumb the depths of rough seas, shelter under rocks with the ray and dogfish. And on fine days they bask on the calm of gentle waves, while kittiwakes pattern the sky.

'It was a glorious life. We just roamed, got jobs doing this and that. We were soul mates, Morgan. We saw the world the same way up. And one day we decided to get married. It was perfect - a quiet chapel on a cliff top. My mermaid crowned with apple blossom. There was hardly anyone there but that was how we wanted it. We were happy.'

Hand in hand on the edge of the sand they danced by the light of the moon, the moon, the moon.

And for seven years the merman and his mermaid spent their days riding the spume-topped waves or walked for dreamy hours on the beach, side-stepping crabs.

'Then Jake was born, and we loved him. But a child needs a fixed home, a port, an anchor. We both knew that a part of our lives had ended, and another had begun. For Jake we decided to settle down.'

And there comes a time when the merman and mermaid must hide their scales and plant roses in the garden to cover their fishy smell. For seven years he wears suits and becomes pale and the light in the mermaid's eyes begins to fade. She cuts her flaxen hair short, stands tall by the school gate and waits for her son to grow.

And as the mermaid and her son become rooted in God's good earth, the boy who wanted to be a fish, who became the man who shed his mortal skin, drifts away from them. He drifts like a rudderless skiff, can find no charts, no true course to steer by.

'When I got back in touch with the family at Mum's funeral, I realised that I had let you down. They kept going on about how 'this' was your fault and 'that' was your fault and I realised that everything that had gone wrong with Mum, her illness, was all being blamed on you. I didn't remember it being that way. I should have stayed. Maybe I could have persuaded them to bring you home. At least I should have come to visit you. I'm sorry, Morgan. I'm sorry.'

She turns to face him. 'All these years, I thought it was my fault. I thought that I was evil, cursed, and that I had made Mum ill and that was why I was sent away.'

'Oh, Morgan.' David hugs her tight.

'It's alright,' she says, pushing him back so that she can see his face. 'These last few weeks have made me see that what happened in our family is the result of several stories, not just mine. I wish I had realised that years ago.'

They wash and repack the blue striped cups and saucers

in silence. Morgan listens to the sounds of the house, the sounds she has become accustomed to over the past months. She remembers she hasn't cleared out the little room with the round window. She must remember to do it before they leave. Or maybe there isn't much in there after all. Maybe she'll leave it for the new owners to sort out.

*

And as times goes on one realises that there are palaces in every corner of the land and that princesses and princes are ten a penny. But the Prince we have got to know on our recent adventure truly loves his Princess, new as she is to princess-ship. And every day, every single day after the first cock crow of the morning, he turns to her and tells her 'you are beautiful, magical and you make me feel alive.'

From a certain rock on the beach at the Dyke you can see the whole bay. Morgan and Ed sit side by side watching as William searches the rock pools, concentration fierce on his young face. He stirs pool water with a stick, searching for crabs abandoned by the tide.

'I don't know how I could have left him, left you.' Morgan stares out to sea, unable to look Ed in the eye.

He catches her hand, his warm and strong. 'I can't say I understand it all, Morgan. But you came back. There were times when I didn't think you would, but like the tide you came back. You don't know how much that means.'

They sit staring out to sea. A picture postcard. A little boy finds wonder in rock pools and the waves roll and crash as waves do.

A fairy-tale ending. Well maybe it is and maybe it isn't. It's what we all want though, isn't it? However, although for now the Skeletons, the Truths and Lies and the What ifs are all locked up in Davy Jones's locker, they won't stay there for long.

But that's another story. It's late. You must pull the covers up to your chin, close your eyes and sleep. Let the dreams come. There is always an abundance of dreams.

The end.

Glossary

Hob: A type of small mythological household spirit who could live inside the house or outdoors. Folk lore Northern England.

Barmins: The grass between the cliff top path and the chalk cliff. (Colloquial).

Bugganes: Shapeshifters whose natural state is to be covered in a mane of coarse black hair. They have eyes like torches and glittering sharp tusks. Manx folk lore.

Fynoderee: Big shaggy creatures with fiery eyes. They are reputed to be stronger than a man. Manx folk lore.

Story references

Some of the references in this book are from well-known folk tales, myths and legends. You will probably have heard them when you were a child. And some are from stories my own mother told me although she would accuse me of telling 'stories' when she meant I was telling lies. In truth, many of the stories in this book are inventions of my own.

Acknowledgements

I owe a great deal of thanks to many people who have supported, helped and advised me during the making of this book.

Especially my thanks go to Charles Heathcote, Miriam Hirst, Margaret Pratt, Donald Rhodes, Annette Trowman, Philip Williams, and John Winkler. I appreciate the time you all took on my behalf. Huge thanks also to Anna and Jez de Silva for the cover design.

Printed in Great Britain
by Amazon